Dear Reader,

The night is a time for danger, for mystery—and romance. Silhouette Books is thrilled to offer you the second of three special volumes containing *Night Tales,* the award-winning series by bestselling author Nora Roberts. These stories feature characters who are creatures of the night, whether for work, play—or love.

Colt Nightshade made his living facing danger—alone. But he needed help searching for a runaway girl, whether he liked it or not. Tough lady cop Althea Grayson wanted answers from the rugged loner, but *Nightshade* had a few questions of his own to ask....

It was up to investigator Ryan Piasecki to catch an arsonist before more Fletcher buildings burned—and before his desire for Natalie Fletcher blazed out of control. For playing with fire was painless compared to the passion that might consume them both in *Night Smoke.*

Under cover of night, danger lurks in the shadows, but love triumphs over the dark....

Happy reading!

The Editors
Silhouette Books

NORA ROBERTS

NIGHT TALES

NIGHTSHADE
NIGHT SMOKE

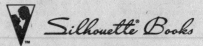
Silhouette Books

Published by Silhouette Books

America's Publisher of Contemporary Romance

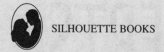 SILHOUETTE BOOKS

NIGHT TALES: NIGHTSHADE & NIGHT SMOKE

Copyright © 2005 by Harlequin Books S.A.

ISBN 0-373-28512-4

The publisher acknowledges the copyright holder of the individual works as follows:

NIGHTSHADE
Copyright © 1993 by Nora Roberts

NIGHT SMOKE
Copyright © 1994 by Nora Roberts

CONTENTS

NIGHTSHADE

For Dan

Prologue

It was a hell of a place to meet a snitch. A cold night, a dark street, with the smell of whiskey and sweat seeping through the pores of the bar door at his back. Colt drew easily on a slim cigar as he studied the spindly bag of bones who'd agreed to sell him information. Not much to look at, Colt mused—short, skinny, and ugly as homemade sin. In the garish light tossed fitfully by the neon sign behind them, his informant looked almost comical.

But there was nothing funny about the business at hand.

"You're a hard man to pin down, Billings."

"Yeah, yeah…" Billings nibbled on a grimy thumb, his gaze sweeping up and down the street. "A guy keeps healthy that way. Heard you were looking for me." He studied Colt, his eyes flying up, then away, soaring on nerves. "Man in my position has to be careful, you know? What you want to buy, it don't come cheap. And it's dangerous. I'd feel better with my cop. Generally I work through the cop, but I ain't been able to get through all day."

"I'd feel better without your cop. And I'm the one who's paying." To illustrate his point, Colt drew two fifties from his shirt pocket. He watched Billings's eyes dart toward the bills and linger greedily. Colt might be a man who'd take risks, but buying a pig in a poke wasn't his style. He held the money out of reach.

"Talk better if I had a drink." Billings jerked his head toward the doorway of the bar behind them. A woman's laugh, high and shrill, burst through the glass like a gunshot.

"You talk just fine to me." The man was a bundle of raw nerves, Colt observed. He could almost hear the thin bones rattle together as Billings shifted from foot to foot. If he didn't press his point now, the man was going to run like a rabbit. And he'd come too far and had too much at stake to lose him now. "Tell me what I need to know, then I'll buy you a drink."

"You're not from around here."

"No." Colt lifted a brow, waited. "Is that a problem?"

"Nope. Better you aren't. They get wind of you..." Billings swiped the back of his hand over his mouth. "Well, you look like you can handle yourself okay."

"I've been known to." He took one last drag before flicking the cigar away. Its single red eye gleamed in the gutter. "Information, Billings." To show good faith, Colt held out one of the bills. "Let's do business."

Even as Billings's eager fingers reached out, the frigid air was shattered by the shriek of tires on pavement.

Colt didn't have to read the terror in Billings's eyes. Adrenaline and instinct took over, with a kick as quick and hard as a mule's. He was diving for cover as the first shots rang out.

Chapter 1

Althea didn't mind being bored. After a rough day, a nice spot of tedium could be welcome, giving both mind and body a chance to recharge. She didn't really mind coming off a tough ten-hour shift after an even more grueling sixty-hour week and donning cocktail wear or slipping her tired feet into three-inch heels. She wouldn't even complain about being stuck at a banquet table in the ballroom of the Brown House while speech after droning speech muddled her head.

What she *did* mind was having her date's hand slide up her thigh under cover of the white linen tablecloth.

Men were so predictable.

She picked up her wineglass and, shifting in her seat, nuzzled her date's ear. "Jack?"

His fingers crept higher. "Mmm-hmm?"

"If you don't move your hand—say, within the next two

seconds—I'm going to stab it, really, really hard, with my dessert fork. It would hurt, Jack." She sat back and sipped her wine, smiling over the rim as he arched a brow. "You wouldn't play racquetball for a month."

Jack Holmsby, eligible bachelor, feared prosecutor, and guest of honor at the Denver Bar Association Banquet, knew how to handle women. And he'd been trying to get close enough to handle this particular woman for months.

"Thea…" He breathed her name, gifting her with his most charming, crooked smile. "We're nearly done here. Why don't we go back to my place? We can…" He whispered into her ear a suggestion that was descriptive, inventive and possibly anatomically impossible.

Althea was saved from answering—and Jack was spared minor surgery—by the sound of her beeper. Several of her tablemates began shifting, checking pockets and purses. Inclining her head, she rose.

"Pardon me. I believe it's mine." She walked away with a subtle switch of hips, a long flash of leg. The compact body in the backless purple dress glinting with silver beading caused more than one head to turn. Blood pressures were elevated. Fantasies were woven.

Not unaware, but certainly unconcerned, Althea strode out of the ballroom and into the lobby, toward a bank of phones. Opening her beaded evening bag, which contained a compact, lipstick, ID, emergency cash and her nine-millimeter, she fished out a quarter and made her call.

"Grayson." While she listened, she pushed back her fall of flame-colored hair. Her eyes, a tawny shade of brown, narrowed. "I'm on my way."

She hung up, turned and watched Jack Holmsby hurry toward her. An attractive man, she thought objectively. Nicely polished on the outside. A pity he was so ordinary on the inside.

"Sorry, Jack. I have to go."

Irritation scored a deep line between his brows. He had a bottle of Napoleon brandy, a stack of apple wood and a set of white satin sheets waiting at home. "Really, Thea, can't someone else take the call?"

"No." The job came first. It always came first. "It's handy I had to meet you here, Jack. You can stay and enjoy yourself."

But he wasn't giving up that easily. He dogged her through the lobby and out into the brisk fall night. "Why don't you come by after you've finished? We can pick up where we left off."

"We haven't left off, Jack." She handed her parking stub to an attendant. "You have to start to leave off, and I have no intention of starting anything with you."

She only sighed as he slipped his arms around her. "Come on, Thea, you didn't come here tonight to eat prime rib and listen to a bunch of lawyers make endless speeches." He lowered his head and murmured against her lips, "You didn't wear a dress like that to keep me at arm's length. You wore it to make me hot. And you did."

Mild irritation became brittle and keen. "I came here tonight because I respect you as a lawyer." The quick elbow to his ribs had his breath woofing out and allowed her to step back. "And because I thought we could spend a pleasant evening together. What I wear is my business, Holmsby, but I didn't choose it so that you'd grope me under the table or make ludicrous suggestions as to how I might spend the rest of my evening."

She wasn't shouting, but neither was she bothering to keep her voice down. Anger glinted in her voice, like ice under fog. Appalled, Jack tugged at the knot of his tie and darted glances right and left.

"For God's sake, Althea, keep it down."

"Exactly what I was going to suggest to you," she said sweetly.

Though the attendant was all eyes and ears, he politely cleared his throat. Althea turned to accept her keys. "Thank you." She offered him a smile and a generous tip. The smile had his heart skipping a beat, and he didn't glance at the bill before tucking it into his pocket. He was too busy dreaming.

"Ah…drive carefully, miss. And come back soon. Real soon."

"Thanks." She tossed her hair back, then slid gracefully behind the wheel of her reconditioned Mustang convertible. "See you in court, Counselor." Althea gunned the engine and peeled out.

Murder scenes, whether indoors or out, in an urban, suburban or pastoral setting, had one thing in common: the aura of death. As a cop with nearly ten years' experience, Althea had learned to recognize it, absorb it and file it away, while going about the precise and mechanical business of investigation.

When Althea arrived, a half block had been secured. The police photographer had finished recording the scene and was already packing up his gear. The body had been identified. That was why she was here.

Three black-and-whites sat, their lights flashing blue and their radios coughing static. Spectators—for death always drew them—were straining against the yellow police tape, greedy, Althea knew, for a glimpse of death to reaffirm that they were alive and untouched.

Because the night was cool, she grabbed the wrap she'd tossed into the back seat of her car. The emerald-green silk kept the chill off her arms and back. Flashing her badge to the rookie handling crowd control, she slipped under the barricade. She was grateful when she spotted Sweeney, a hard-bitten cop who had twice her years on the job and was in no hurry to give up his uniform.

"Lieutenant." He nodded to her, then took out a handkerchief and made a valiant attempt to clear his stuffy nose.

"What have we got here, Sweeney?"

"Drive-by." He stuffed the handkerchief back into his pocket. "Dead guy was standing in front of the bar, talking." He gestured to the shattered window of the Tick Tock. "Witnesses say a car came by, moving north, fast. Sprayed the area with bullets and kept going."

She could still smell the blood, though it was no longer fresh. "Any bystanders hit?"

"Nope. Couple of cuts from flying glass, that's all. They hit their mark." He glanced over his shoulder, and down. "He didn't have a chance, Lieutenant. Sorry."

"Yeah, me too." She stared down at the form sprawled on the stained concrete. There'd been nothing much to him to begin with, she thought. Now there was less. He'd been five-five, maybe a hundred and ten soaking wet, spindly bones and had had a face even a mother would have been hard-pressed to love.

Wild Bill Billings, part-time pimp, part-time grifter and full-time snitch.

And, damn it, he'd been hers.

"Forensics?"

"Been and gone," Sweeney confirmed. "We're ready to put him on ice."

"Then do it. Got a list of witnesses?"

"Yeah, mostly useless. It was a black car, it was a blue car. One drunk claims it was a chariot driven by flaming demons." He swore with inventive expertise, knowing Althea well enough not to worry about her taking offense.

"We'll take what we can get." She scanned the crowd— bar types, teenagers looking for action, a scattering of the homeless and—

Her antenna vibrated as she locked in on one man. Unlike the others, he wasn't goggle-eyed with either revulsion or excitement. He stood at his ease, his leather bomber jacket open to the wind, revealing a chambray shirt, a glint of silver on a chain. His rangy build made her think he'd be fast on his feet. Snug, worn jeans rode down long legs and ended at scuffed boots. Hair that might have been dark blond or brown ruffled in the breeze and curled well over his collar.

He smoked a thin cigar, his eyes scanning the scene as hers had. The light wasn't good, but she decided he looked tanned, which suited the sharply defined face. The eyes were deep-set, and the nose was long, and just shy of being narrow. The mouth was strong, the kind that looked as though it could thin into a sneer easily.

Some instinct had her dubbing him a pro before his eyes shifted and locked on hers with an impact like a bare-fisted punch.

"Who's the cowboy, Sweeney?"

"The— Oh." Sweeney's tired face creased in what might

have been a smile. Damned if she hadn't called it, he thought. The guy looked as though he should be wearing a Stetson and riding a mustang. "Witness," he told her. "Victim was talking to him when he got hit."

"Is that so?" She didn't look around when the coroner's team dealt with the body. There was no need to.

"He's the only one to give us a coherent account." Sweeney pulled out his pad, wet his thumb and flipped pages. "Says it was a black '91 Buick sedan, Colorado plates Able Charlie Frank. Says he missed the numbers 'cause the plate lights were out and he was a little busy diving for cover. Says the weapon sounded like an AK-47."

"Sounded like?" Interesting, she thought. She'd kept her eyes level with her witness's. "Maybe—" She broke off when she spotted her captain crossing the street. Captain Boyd Fletcher walked directly to the witness, shook his head, then grinned and enveloped the other man in the masculine equivalent of an embrace. There was a lot of back-thumping.

"Looks as though the captain's handling him for now." Althea pocketed her curiosity as she would a treat to be saved for later. "Let's finish up here, Sweeney."

Colt had watched her from the moment one long, smooth leg swung out of the door of the Mustang. A lady like that was worth watching—well worth it. He'd liked the way she moved—with an athletic and economical grace that wasted neither time nor energy. Certainly he'd liked the way she looked. Her neat, sexy little body had just enough curves to whet a man's appetite, and with all that green-and-purple silk rippling in the wind… The sunburst of hair, blowing away from a cool cameo face, brought much more interesting things to a man's mind than his grandmother's heirloom jewelry.

It was a cold night, and one look at that well-packed number had Colt thinking about heat.

It wasn't such a bad way to keep warm while he waited. He wasn't a man who waited well under the best of circumstances.

He hadn't been particularly surprised to see her flash ID to the baby-faced cop at the barricade. She carried authority beautifully on her luscious swimmer's shoulders. Idly lighting a cigar, he decided she was an assistant D.A., then realized his error when she went into conference with Sweeney.

The lady had *cop* written all over her.

Late twenties, he figured, maybe five-four without those ankle-wrecking heels, and a tidy one-ten.

They sure were making cops in interesting packages these days.

So he waited, sizing up the scene. He didn't have any feelings one way or the other about the remains of Wild Bill Billings. The man was no good to him now.

He'd dig up something, or someone, else. Colt Nightshade wasn't a man to let murder get in his way.

When he felt her watching him, he drew smoke in lazily, chuffed it out. Then he shifted his gaze until it met hers. The tightening in his gut was unexpected—it was raw and purely sexual. The one fleeting instant when his mind was wiped clean as glass was more than unexpected. It was unprecedented. Power slapped against power. She took a step toward him. He let out the breath he'd just realized he was holding.

His preoccupation made it easy for Boyd to come up behind him and catch him unawares.

"Colt! Son of a bitch!"

Colt turned, braced and ready for anything. But the flat intensity in his eyes faded into a grin that might have melted any woman within twenty paces.

"Fletch." With the easy warmth he reserved for friends, Colt returned the bear hug before stepping back to take stock. He hadn't seen Boyd in nearly ten years. It relieved him to see that so little had changed. "Still got that pretty face, don't you?"

"And you still sound like you've just ridden in off the range. God, it's good to see you. When'd you get into town?"

"Couple of days ago. I wanted to take care of some business before I got in touch."

Boyd looked past him to where the coroner's van was being loaded. "Was that your business?"

"Part of it. I appreciate you coming down like this."

"Yeah." Boyd spotted Althea, acknowledging her with an imperceptible nod. "Did you call a cop, Colt, or a friend?"

Colt looked down at the stub of his cigar, dropped it near the gutter and crushed it with his boot. "It's handy, you being both."

"Did you kill that guy?"

It was asked so matter-of-factly, that Colt grinned again. He knew Boyd wouldn't have turned a hair if he'd confessed then and there. "Nope."

Boyd nodded again. "Going to fill me in?"

"Yep."

"Why don't you wait in the car? I'll be with you in a minute."

"*Captain* Boyd Fletcher." Colt shook his head and chuckled. Though it was after midnight, he was as alert as he was relaxed, a cup of bad coffee in his hand and his scruffy boots propped on Boyd's desk. "Ain't that just something?"

"I thought you were raising horses and cattle in Wyoming."

"I do." His voice was a drawl, with the faintest whisper of a twang. "Now and again I do."

"What happened to the law degree?"

"Oh, it's around somewhere."

"And the air force?"

"I still fly. Just don't wear a uniform anymore. How long's it going to take for that pizza to get here?"

"Just long enough for it to be cold and inedible." Boyd leaned back in his chair. He was comfortable in his office. He was comfortable on the street. And, as he had been twenty years ago, in their prep school days, he was comfortable with Colt.

"You didn't get a look at the shooter?"

"Hell, Fletch, I was lucky to make the car before I was diving for cover and chewing asphalt. Not that that's going to help much. Odds are it was stolen."

"Lieutenant Grayson's tracking it. Now, why don't you tell me what you were doing with Wild Bill?"

"He contacted me. I've bee—" He broke off when Althea strolled in. She hadn't bothered to knock, and she was carrying a flat cardboard box.

"You two order pizza?" She dropped the box onto Boyd's desk, held out a hand. "Ten bucks, Fletcher."

"Althea Grayson, Colt Nightshade. Colt's an old friend." Boyd dug ten dollars out of his wallet. After folding the bill neatly and tucking it in a pocket of her purse, she set her beaded bag on a stack of files.

"Mr. Nightshade."

"Ms. Grayson."

"*Lieutenant* Grayson," she corrected. Popping up the lid on the box, she perused the contents, chose a slice. "I believe you were at my crime scene."

"Sure did look that way." He lowered his legs so that he could lean forward and take a piece himself. He caught her scent over the aroma of cooling sausage pizza. It was a whole lot more tantalizing.

"Thanks," she murmured when Boyd passed her a napkin. "I wondered what you were doing there, getting shot at with my snitch."

Colt's eyes narrowed. "Your snitch?"

"That's right." Like his hair, his eyes couldn't seem to decide what color they should be, Althea thought. They were caught somewhere between blue and green. And at the moment they were as cold as the wind whipping at the window.

"Bill told me he tried to reach his police contact off and on all day."

"I was in the field."

Colt's brow arched as he skimmed his gaze over the swirl of emerald silk. "Some field."

"Lieutenant Grayson spent all day putting the cap on a drug operation," Boyd interjected. "Now, kids, why don't we start over, and at the beginning?"

"Fine." Setting her half-eaten slice down, Althea wiped her fingers, then removed her wrap. Colt clenched his teeth to keep his tongue from falling out. Because she was turned away from him, Colt had the painful pleasure of gauging just how alluring a naked back could be when it was slim, straight and framed in purple silk.

After laying her coat over a file cabinet, Althea reclaimed her pizza and sat on the corner of Boyd's desk.

She knew just what she did to a man, Colt realized. He could see that smug, faintly amused female knowledge in her eyes. Colt had always figured every woman knew her own arsenal down to the last eyelash, but it was tough on a man when the woman was as heavily armed as this.

"Wild Bill, Mr. Nightshade…" Althea began. "What were you doing with him?"

"Talking." He knew his answer was obstinate, but at the moment he was trying to judge whether there was anything between the sexy lieutenant and his old friend. His old *married* friend, Colt mused. He was relieved, and more than a little surprised not to scent even a whiff of attraction between them.

"About?" Althea's voice was still patient, even pleasant. As if, Colt thought, she were questioning a small boy who was mentally deficient.

"The victim was Thea's snitch," Boyd reminded Colt. "If she wants the case—"

"And I do."

"Then it's hers."

To buy himself time, Colt reached for another slice of pizza. He was going to have to do something he hated, something that stuck in his craw like bad beef jerky. He was going to have to ask for help. And to get it he was going to have to share what he knew.

"It took me two days to track down Billings and get him to agree to talk to me." It had also cost him two hundred in bribes to clear the path, but he wasn't one to count the cost until the final tally. "He was nervous, didn't really want to talk unless he had his police contact with him. So I made it worth his while."

He glanced back at Althea. The lady was wiped out, he re-alized. The fatigue was hard to spot, but it was there—in the slight drooping of her eyelids, the faint shadows under them.

"I'm sorry you lost him, but I don't think your being there would have changed anything."

"We won't know that, will we?" She wouldn't let the re-gret color her voice, or her judgment. "Why did you go to so much trouble to contact Bill?"

"He used to have a girl working for him. Jade. Probably her street name."

Althea let her mind click back, nodded. "Yeah. Little blonde, baby face. She took a couple of busts for solicitation. I'll have to check, but I don't think she's worked the stroll for four or five weeks."

"That'd be about right." Colt rose to fill his cup with more of the sludge from the automatic brewer. "It would have been about that long ago that Billings got her a job. In the mov-ies." If he was going to drink poison, he'd take it like a man, without any cream or sugar to cut the bite. Sipping, he turned back. "I ain't talking Hollywood. This was the down-and-dirty stuff, for private viewers who have the taste and the money to buy thrills. Videotapes for hard-core connoisseurs." He shrugged and sat again. "Can't say it bothers me any, if we're talking about consenting adults. Though I prefer my sex in the flesh."

"But we're not talking about you, Mr. Nightshade."

"Oh, you don't have to call me *mister*, Lieutenant. Seems cold, when we're discussing such warm topics." Smiling, he leaned back. He had yet to ruffle her feathers, and for reasons he wasn't going to take the time to explore, he wanted to ruf-fle them good and proper. "Well, as it happens, something spooked Jade and she lit out. I'm not one to think a hooker's got a heart of gold, but this one at least had a conscience. She sent off a letter to a Mr. and Mrs. Frank Cook." He shifted his gaze to Boyd. "Frank and Marleen Cook."

"Marleen?" Boyd's brows shot up. "Marleen and Frank?"

"The same." Colt's smile was wry. "More old friends, Lieutenant. As it happens, I was what you might call intimate friends with Mrs. Cook about a million years ago. Being a woman of sound judgment, she married Frank, settled down in Albuquerque and had herself a couple of beautiful kids."

Althea shifted, crossed her legs with a rustle of silk. The silver dangling over his shirt was a Saint Christopher medal, she noted. The patron saint of travelers. She wondered if Mr. Nightshade felt the need for spiritual protection.

"I assume this is leading somewhere other than down memory lane?"

"Oh, it's leading right back to your professional front door, Lieutenant. I just prefer the circular route now and then." He took out a cigar, running it through his long fingers before reaching for his lighter. "About a month ago, Marleen's oldest girl—that's Elizabeth. You ever meet Liz, Boyd?"

Boyd shook his head. He didn't like where this was heading. Not one bit. "Not since she was in diapers. What is she, twelve?"

"Thirteen. Just." Colt flicked his lighter on, sucked his cigar to life. Thought he knew, all too well, that the tang of smoke wouldn't cloud the bitter taste in his throat. "Pretty as a picture, like her mama. Got Marleen's hair-trigger temper, too. There was some trouble at home, the kind I imagine most families have some time or other. But Liz got her back up and took off."

"She ran away?" Althea understood the runaway's mind well. Too well.

"Tossed a few things in her backpack and took off. Needless to say, Marleen and Frank have been living in hell the past few weeks. They contacted the police, but the official route wasn't getting them very far." He blew out smoke. "No offense. Ten days ago they called me."

"Why?" Althea asked.

"Told you. We're friends."

"Do you usually track down pimps and dodge bullets for friends?"

She had a way with sarcasm, all right, Colt mused. It was one more weapon in the arsenal. "I do favors for people."

"Are you a licensed investigator?"

Pursing his lips, Colt studied the tip of his cigar. "I'm not big on licenses. I put out some feelers, had a little luck tracing her north. Then the Cooks got Jade's letter." Clamping his cigar between his teeth, he drew a folded sheet of floral stationery from his inside jacket pocket. "Save time if you read it yourself," he said, and passed it to Boyd. Althea rose, going behind Boyd's back, laying a hand on his shoulder as she read with him.

It was a curiously intimate and yet asexual gesture. One, Colt decided, that spoke of friendship and trust.

The handwriting was as girlishly fussy as the paper. But the content, Althea noted, had nothing to do with flowers and ribbons and childhood fancies.

Dear Mr. and Mrs. Cook,

I met Liz in Denver. She is a nice kid. I know she is really sorry she ran away and would come back now if she could. I would help her out, but I got to get out of town. Liz is in trouble. I would go to the cops, but I'm scared and I don't think they listen to someone like me. She is not cut out for the life, but they won't let her go. She is young and so pretty, and they are making lots of money from the movies I think. I have been in the life for five years, but some of the stuff they want us to do for the camera gives me the creeps. I think they killed one of the girls, so I am getting out before they kill me. Liz gave me your address and asked me to write and say she was sorry. She's real scared and I hope you find her okay.

Jade

P.S. They have a place up in the mountains where they do the movies. And there is an apartment on Second Avenue.

Boyd didn't give the letter back, but laid it on his desk. He had a daughter of his own. He thought of Allison, sweet, feisty and six, and had to swallow a hot ball of sick rage.

"You could have come to me with this. You *should* have come to me."

"I'm used to working alone." Colt drew on his cigar again before tamping it out. "In any case, I intended to come to you after I put a few things together. I got the name of Jade's pimp, and I wanted to shake him down."

"And now he's dead." Althea's voice was flat as she turned to stare out of Boyd's window.

"Yeah." Colt studied her profile. It wasn't just anger he felt from her. There was a lot more mixed up with it. "Word must have gotten back that I was looking for him, and that he was willing to talk to me. Leads me to think that we're dealing with well-connected slime, and slime that doesn't blink at murder."

"This is a police matter, Colt," Boyd said quietly.

"No argument." Ready to deal, he spread his hands. "It's also a personal matter. I'm going to keep digging, Fletch. There's no law against it. I'm the Cooks' representative— their lawyer, if we need a handle."

"Is that what you are?" Her emotions under control again, Althea turned back to him. "A lawyer?"

"When it suits me. I don't want to interfere with your investigation," he said to Boyd. "I want the kid back—safely back—with Marleen and Frank. I'll cooperate completely. Anything I know, you'll know. But it has to be quid pro quo. Give me a cop to work with on this, Boyd." He smiled a little—just a quirk at the corner of his mouth, as if he were amused at himself. "And you of all people know how much I hate asking for an official partner on a job. But it's Liz that matters, all that matters. You know I'm good." He leaned forward. "You know I won't back off. Let me have your best man, and let's get these bastards."

Boyd pressed his fingers to his tired eyes. He could, of course, order Colt to back off. And he'd be wasting his breath. He could refuse to cooperate, could refuse to share any information the department unearthed. And Colt would work around him. Yes, he knew Colt was good, and he had some idea of the kind of work he'd done while in the military.

It would hardly be the first time Boyd Fletcher had bent the rules. His decision made, he gestured toward Althea.

"She's my best man."

Chapter 2

If a man had to have a partner, she might as well be easy on the eyes. In any case, Colt didn't intend to work *with* Althea so much as *through* her. She would be his conduit to the official end of the investigation. He'd keep his word—he always did, except when he didn't—and feed her whatever information he gleaned. Not that he expected her to do much with it.

There were only a handful of cops Colt respected, with Boyd topping the list. As far as Lieutenant Grayson was concerned, Colt figured she'd be decorative, marginally helpful and little else.

The badge, the bod and the sarcasm would probably be useful when it came to interviewing any possible connections.

At least he'd had a decent night's sleep—all six hours of it. He hadn't protested when Boyd insisted he check out of his hotel and check into the Fletcher household for the duration of his stay. Colt liked families—other people's, in any case—and he'd been curious about Boyd's wife.

He'd missed their wedding. Though he wasn't particularly fond of the spit and polish ceremonies called for, he would have gone. But it was a long way from Beirut to Denver, and he'd been busy with terrorists at the time.

He was delighted with Cilla. The woman hadn't turned a hair at having her husband bring home a strange man at 2:00 a.m. Bundled in a terry-cloth robe, she'd offered him the guest room, with the suggestion that if he wanted to sleep in he should put the pillow over his head. The kids apparently rose at seven to get ready for school.

He'd slept like a rock, and when he'd awakened to the sounds of shouts and clomping feet, he'd taken his hostess's advice and had caught another hour of sleep with his head buried.

Now, fortified by an excellent breakfast and three cups of first-class coffee prepared by the Fletchers' housekeeper, he was ready to roll.

His agreement with Boyd made the precinct house his first stop. He'd check in with Althea, grill her on any associates of Billings's, then go his own way.

It seemed to him that his old friend ran a tight ship. There was the usual din of ringing phones, clattering keyboards and raised voices inside the station. There were the usual scents of coffee, industrial-strength cleaners and sweaty bodies. But there was also an underlying sense of organization and purpose.

The desk sergeant had Colt's name, and he handed him a visitor's badge and directed him to Althea's office. Past the bull pen, and two doors down a narrow corridor he found her

door. It was shut, so he rapped once before pushing it open.
He knew she was there before he saw her. He scented her, as
a wolf scents his mate. Or his prey.

Gone were the bold silks, but she still looked more the fashion plate than the cop. The tailored slacks and jacket in smoke
gray did nothing to suggest masculinity. Nor did he think she
chose to deny her sex, for she'd accented the suit with a soft
pink blouse and a star-shaped jeweled lapel pin. Her mass of
hair had been trained back in some complicated braid that left
her face softly framed. Two heavy twists of gold glinted at her
ears.

The result was as neat as any maiden aunt could want, and
still had the knockout punch of frosted sex.

A lesser man might have licked his lips.

"Grayson."

"Nightshade." She gestured toward a chair. "Have a seat."

There was only one to spare, straight-backed and wood.
Colt turned it around and straddled it. As he did, he noted that
her office was less than half the size of Boyd's, and ruthlessly
organized. File drawers were neatly closed, papers properly
stacked, pencils sharpened to lethal points. There was a plant
on one of the rear corners of the desk that he was sure was
meticulously watered. There were no pictures of family or
friends. The only spot of color in the small, windowless room
was a painting, an abstract in vivid blues, greens and reds.
Slashes of colors that clashed and warred, rather than melded.

Some instinct told him it suited her down to the ground.

"So." He folded his arms over the back of the chair and
leaned forward. "You run the shooter's car through Motor Vehicles?"

"Didn't have to. It was on this morning's hot sheet." She

took her copy and offered it. "Reported stolen at eleven o'clock last night. Owners had been out for dinner, came out of the restaurant and found the car gone. Dr. and Dr. Wilmer, a couple of dentists celebrating their fifth anniversary. Looks like they're clean."

"Probably." He tossed the sheet back onto her desk. He hadn't really believed he'd find a connection through the car. "Don't guess it's turned up?"

"Not yet. I've got Jade's rap sheet, if you're interested." After replacing the hot sheet in its proper place, she picked up a file. "Janice Willowby. Age twenty-two. Couple of busts for solicitation—a few charges as a juvie for more of the same. One possession arrest, also as a juvenile, when she got rousted with a couple of joints in her purse. Went through the social services route, a halfway house, counseling, then turned twenty-one and went back on the streets."

It wasn't a new story. "Have we got any family? She might head home."

"A mother in Kansas City—or she was in Kansas City as of eighteen months ago. I'm trying to track her down."

"You've been busy."

"Not all of us start our day at—" she looked down at her watch "—ten."

"I do better at night, Lieutenant." He took out a cigar.

Althea eyed it, shook her head. "Not in here, pal."

Agreeably Colt tapped the cigar back into his pocket. "Who did Billings trust, other than you?"

"I don't know that he trusted anybody." But it hurt, because she knew he had trusted somebody. He'd trusted her, and somehow she'd missed a step. And now he was dead. "We had an arrangement. I gave him money, he gave me information."

"What kind?"

"With Wild Bill, it came in a variety pack. He had his fingers in a lot of pies. Little pies, mostly." She shifted some papers on her desk, tapping the edges neatly together. "He was strictly small-time, but he had big ears, knew how to fade into the background so you forgot he was around. People talked around him, because he looked like his brain would fit in a teacup. But he was smart." Her voice changed, tipping Colt off to something she had yet to admit even to herself. She was grieving. "Smart enough to keep from crossing the line that would send him up to hard time. Smart enough to keep from stepping on the wrong toes. Until last night."

"I didn't make any secret of the fact I was looking for him, and for information he could give me. But I sure as hell didn't want him dead."

"I'm not blaming you."

"No?"

"No." She pushed away from the desk far enough to allow her to swivel the chair around and face him. "People like Bill, no matter how smart, have short life expectancies. If he'd have been able to contact me, I might have met him at the same spot you did, with the same results." She'd thought that through, carefully, ruthlessly. "I might not like your style, Nightshade, but I'm not pinning this on you."

She sat very still, he noted, no gestures, no shrugs, no restless tapping. Like the painting on the wall behind her, she communicated vibrant passion without movement.

"And just what is my style, Lieutenant?"

"You're a renegade. The kind who doesn't just refuse to play by the rules, but rejoices in breaking them." Her eyes stayed level with his, and were cool as lake water. He wondered what it would take to warm them up. "You start things, but you don't always finish them. Maybe that means you bore easily, or you just run out of energy. Either way, it doesn't say much about your dependability."

Her rundown of his personality annoyed him, but when he spoke again, his slow southwestern drawl was amused. "You figured all that out since last night?"

"I ran a make on you. The prep school where you hung out with Boyd surprised me." Her lips curved, but the eyes had yet to warm. "You don't look like the preppie type."

"My parents thought it would tame me." He grinned. "Guess not."

"Neither did Harvard, where you got your law degree— which you haven't put to much use. Parts of your military career were classified, but all in all, I got the picture." There was a dish of sugared almonds on her desk. Althea leaned over and, after careful deliberation, chose the one she wanted. "I don't work with someone I don't know."

"Me either. So why don't you fill me in on Althea Grayson?"

"I'm the cop," she said simply. "And you're not. I assume you have a recent picture of Elizabeth Cook?"

"Yeah, I got one." But he didn't reach for it. He didn't have to take this kind of bull from some glamourpuss with a badge. "Tell me, Lieutenant, just who jammed a stick up your—"

The phone cut him off, which, considering the flash in Althea's eye, might have been for the best. At least he knew how to defrost those eyes now.

"Grayson." She waited a beat, then jotted something down on a pad. "Notify Forensics. I'm on my way." She rose, tucking the pad into a snakeskin purse. "We found the car." She was frowning when she slung the bag over her shoulder. "Since Boyd wants you in, you can come along for the ride— as an observer only. Got it?"

"Oh, yeah. I got it fine."

He followed her out, then quickly moved up so that they walked side by side. The woman had the best rear view this side of the Mississippi, and Colt didn't care to be distracted.

"I didn't have much time to play catch-up with Boyd last night," he began. "I wondered how it was that you're on such…easy terms with your captain."

She was walking down the stairs to the garage, and she stopped, turned, aimed one razor-sharp glance.

"What?" he demanded as she assessed him silently.

"I'm trying to decide if you're insulting me and Boyd— in which case I'd have to hurt you—or if you simply phrased your question badly."

He lifted a brow. "Try the second choice."

"All right." She continued down. "We were partners for over seven years." She reached the bottom of the steps and turned sharply to the right. The flat heels of her suede half boots clicked busily on the concrete. "When you trust someone with your life on a day-to-day basis, you'd better be on easy terms."

"Then he made captain."

"That's right." After taking out her keys, she unlocked her car. "Sorry, but the passenger seat's stuck all the way forward. I haven't had time to take it in and get it fixed."

Colt looked down at the spiffy sports car with some regret. A sexy car, sure, but with the seat in that position, he was going to have to fold himself up like an accordion and sit with his chin on his knees. "And you don't have a problem with that—Boyd's being captain?"

Althea slid in gracefully, smirking a bit as Colt grunted and arranged himself beside her. "No. Am I ambitious? Yes. Do I resent having the best cop I ever worked with as my superior? No. Do I expect to make captain myself within another five years? You bet your butt." She pushed mirrored aviator sunglasses over her eyes. "Fasten your seat belt, Nightshade." With that, she peeled out, shooting up the ramp of the garage and out onto the street.

He had to admire her driving. He had no choice, since she was behind the wheel and his life was in her hands. Easy terms? he wondered. Yeah, right. "So, you and Boyd are friends."

"That's right. Why?"

"I just wanted to establish that it wasn't all good-looking men of a certain age who put your back up." He grinned at her as she downshifted around a corner. "I like knowing it's just me. Makes me feel kind of special, you know?"

She smiled then and shot him what could have been a friendly look. It certainly was no more than friendly, and it really shouldn't have had his heart doing a slow roll in his chest. "I wouldn't say you put my back up, Nightshade. I just don't trust hotdoggers. But since we're both after the same thing here, and since Boyd's a pal on both sides, we can try to get along."

"Sounds reasonable. We've got the job and Boyd in common. Maybe we can find a couple of other things." Her radio was turned down low. Colt flicked the volume up and nodded approval at the slow, pulse-pumping blues. "There, that's one more thing. How do you feel about Mexican food?"

"I like my chili hot and my margaritas cold."

"Progress." He tried to shift in his seat, rapped his knee on the dash, and swore. "If we're going to do any more driving together, we take my four-wheel."

"We'll discuss it." She turned the music down again when she heard the police radio squawk to life.

"All units in the vicinity of Sheridan and Jewell, 511 in progress."

Althea swore as the dispatcher continued to call for assistance. "That's only a block down." She turned left and aimed a quick, dubious look at Colt. "Shots fired," she told him. "Police business, got it?"

"Sure."

"This is unit six responding," she said into the transmitter. "I'm on the scene." After squealing to a halt behind the black-and-white, she shoved open her door. "Stay in the car." With that terse order, she drew her weapon and headed for the entrance of a four-story apartment building.

She paused at the door, sucking in her breath. The minute she bolted through, she heard the blast of another gunshot.

One floor up, she thought. Maybe two. With her body braced and flattened against the wall, she scanned the cramped, deserted entryway, then started up. Screaming— No, she thought, crying. A child. Her mind cold, her hands steady, she swung her weapon toward the first landing, then followed it. A door opened to her left. Crouching, she aimed toward the movement and stared into the face of an elderly woman with terrified eyes.

"Police," Althea told her. "Stay inside."

The door shut. A bolt turned. Althea shifted toward the second staircase. She saw them then, the cop who was down, and the cop who was huddled over him.

"Officer." There was the snap of authority in her voice

when she dropped a hand on the uninjured cop's shoulder. "What's the status here?"

"He shot Jim. He came running out with the kid and opened up."

The uniformed cop was sheet-white, she noted, as pale as his partner, who was bleeding on the stairway. She couldn't tell which of them was shaking more violently. "What's your name?"

"Harrison. Don Harrison." He was pressing a soaked handkerchief to the gaping wound low on his partner's left shoulder.

"Officer Harrison, I'm Lieutenant Grayson. Give me the situation here, and make it fast."

"Sir." He took two short, quick breaths. "Domestic dispute. Shots fired. A white male assaulted the woman in apartment 2-D. He opened fire on us and headed upstairs with a small female child as a shield."

As he finished, a woman stumbled out of the apartment above. Where she clutched her side, blood trickled through her fingers. "He took my baby. Charlie took my baby. Please, God…" She fell weeping to her knees. "He's crazy. Please, God…"

"Officer Harrison." A sound on the stairs had Althea moving fast, then swearing. She should have known Colt wouldn't stay in the car. "Get on the horn, now," she continued. "Call for backup. Officer and civilian down. Hostage situation. Now tell me what he was carrying."

"Looked like a .45."

"Make the call, then get in here and back me up." She spared one look at Colt. "Make yourself useful. Do what you can for these two."

She raced up the stairs. She could hear the baby crying again, long terrified wails that echoed in the narrow corridors. By the time she reached the top floor, she heard the slam of a door. The roof, she decided. Braced on one side of the door, she turned the knob, kicked it open and went in low.

He fired once, wildly. The bullet sang more than a foot to her right. Althea took her stand, and faced him.

"Police!" she shouted. "Put down your weapon!"

He stood near the edge of the roof, a big man. Linebacker-size, she noted, his skin flushed with rage, his eyes glazed by chemicals. That she could handle. It was a .45 he was carrying. She could handle that, as well. But it was the child, the little girl of perhaps two that he was holding by one foot over the edge of the roof, that she wasn't sure she could deal with.

"I'll drop her!" He shouted it, like a chant against the brisk wind. "I'll do it! I'll do it! I swear to God, I'll drop her like a stone!" He shook the child, who continued to scream. One of her little pink tennis shoes flew off and fell five long stories.

"You don't want to make a mistake, do you, Charlie?" Althea inched away from the door, sidestepping slowly, her nine-millimeter aimed at the broad chest. "Bring her back from the edge."

"I'm going to drop the little bitch." He grinned when he said it, his teeth bared, his eyes glittering. "She's just like her mother. Whining and crying all the damn time. Thought they could get away from me. I found them, didn't I? Linda's real sorry now, isn't she? Real damn sorry now."

"Yes, she is." She had to get to the kid. There had to be a way to get to the child. Unbidden an old, obscene memory flashed through her head. The shouting, the threats, the fear.

Althea tramped on them as she would a roach. "You hurt the little girl and it's all over, Charlie."

"Don't tell me it's over!" Enraged, he swung the child like a sack of laundry. Althea's heart stopped, and so did the screaming. The little girl was merely sobbing now, quietly, helplessly, her arms dangling limply, her huge blue eyes fixed and glazed. "She tried to tell me it was over. It's over, Charlie," he mimicked in a singsong voice. "So I knocked her around some. God knows she deserved it, nagging me about getting work, nagging about every damn thing. And as soon as the kid came along, everything changed. I got no use for bitches in my life. But *I* say when it's over."

The wail of sirens rose up in the air. Althea sensed movement behind her, but didn't turn. Didn't dare. She needed the man focused on her, only on her. "Bring the kid in and you might get away. You want to get away, don't you, Charlie? Come on. Give her to me. You don't need her."

"You think I'm stupid?" His lips curled into a snarl. "You're just one more bitch."

"I don't think you're stupid." She caught a movement out of the corner of her eye, and would have sworn if she'd dared. It wasn't Harrison. It was Colt, slipping like a shadow toward the man's blind side. "I don't think you'd be stupid enough to hurt the kid." She was closer now, five feet away. Althea knew that it might as well be fifty.

"I'm going to kill her!" he shouted. "And I'm going to kill you, and I'm going to kill anybody who gets in my way! Nobody says it's over till I say it's over!"

It happened then, fast, like a blur at the corner of a dream. Colt lunged, wrapping one arm around the child's waist. Althea caught the flash of metal in his hand and recognized it as a .32. He might have used it, if saving the child hadn't been his priority. He pivoted back, swinging the child so that his body was her shield, and by the time he'd brought his weapon to bear, it was over.

Althea watched the .45 arch from her toward Colt and the girl. And she fired. The bullet drove him back. His knees hit the low curbing at the edge of the roof. He was the one who dropped like a stone.

Althea didn't permit herself even a sigh. She holstered her weapon and strode to where Colt was cuddling the weeping child. "She okay?"

"Looks like." In a move so natural she would have sworn he'd spent his life doing it, he settled the girl on his hip and kissed her damp temple. "You're okay now, baby. Nobody's going to hurt you."

"Mama." Choking on tears, she buried her face in Colt's shoulder. "Mama."

"We'll take you to your mama, honey, don't you worry." Colt still held his gun, but his other hand was busy stroking the girl's wispy blond hair. "Nice work, Lieutenant."

Althea glanced over her shoulder. Cops were already pounding up the stairs. "I've done better."

"You kept him talking so the kid had a shot, then you took him down. It doesn't get better than that." And there had been a look in her eyes, from the moment she'd started up the steps with a cop's blood on her hands. And it hadn't faded yet. A look he'd seen before, Colt mused. One he'd always termed a warrior's look.

Her eyes held his for another minute. "Let's get her out of here" was all she said.

"Fine." They started toward the door.

"Just one thing, Nightshade."

He smiled a little, certain this was the moment she'd thank him. "What's that?"

"Have you got a permit for that gun?"

He stopped, stared. Then his smile exploded into a deep, rich laugh. Charmed, the little girl looked up, sniffled, and managed a watery smile.

She didn't think about killing. Didn't permit herself. She'd killed before, and knew she would likely do so again. But she didn't think about it. She knew that if she reflected too deeply on that aspect of the job, she could freeze, or she could drink or she could grow callous. Or, worse—infinitely worse—she could grow to enjoy it.

So she filed her report and put it out of her mind. Or tried to.

She hand-carried a copy of the report to Boyd's office, laid it on his desk. His eyes flicked down to it, then back to hers. "The cop—Barkley—he's still in surgery. The woman's out of danger."

"Good. How's the kid?"

"She has an aunt in Colorado Springs. Social Services contacted her. The creep was her father. History of battering and drugs. His wife took the kid about a year ago and went to a women's shelter. Filed for divorce. She moved here about three months ago, got herself a job, started a life."

"And he found her."

"And he found her." .

"Well, he won't find her again." She turned toward the door, but Boyd was up and walking around the desk. "Thea." He shut the door, cutting off most of the din from the bull pen. "Are you okay?"

"Sure. I don't see IAD hassling me on this one."

"I'm not talking about Internal Affairs." He tilted his head. "A day or two off wouldn't hurt."

"It wouldn't help, either." She lifted her shoulders, let them fall. To Boyd she could say things she could never say to anyone else. "I didn't think I'd get to her in time. I didn't get to her," she added. "Colt did. And he shouldn't have been there."

"He was there." Gently Boyd laid his hands on her shoulders. "Oh-oh, it's the supercop complex. I can see it coming. Dodging bullets, filing reports, screaming down dark alleys, selling tickets to the Policemen's Ball, ridding the world of bad guys and saving cats from the tops of trees. She can do it all."

"Shut up, Fletcher." But she smiled. "I draw the line at saving cats."

"Want to come to dinner tonight?"

She rested a hand on the knob. "What's to eat?"

He shrugged, grinned. "Can't say. It's Maria's night off."

"Cilla's cooking?" She gave him a pained, sorrowful look. "I thought we were friends."

"We'll send out for tacos."

"Deal."

When she walked back into the bull pen, she spotted Colt. He had his boots up on a desk and a phone at his ear. She strolled over, sat on the corner and waited for him to finish the call.

"Paperwork done?" he asked her.

"Nightshade, I don't suppose I have to point out that this desk, this phone, this chair, are department property, and off-limits to civilians."

He grinned at her. "Nope. But go right ahead, if you want

to. You look good enough to eat when you're spouting proper procedure."

"Why, your compliments just take my breath away." She knocked his feet off the desk. "The stolen car's been impounded. The lab boys are going over it, so I don't see the point in rushing to take a look."

"Got a different plan?"

"Starting with the Tick Tock, I'm going to hit a few of Wild Bill's hangouts, talk to some people."

"I'm with you."

"Don't rub it in."

When she started toward the garage, he took her arm. "My car this time, remember?"

With a shrug, she went with him out to the street. His rugged black four-wheeler had a parking ticket on the windshield. Colt stuffed it in his pocket. "I don't suppose I can ask you to fix this."

"No." Althea climbed in.

"That's okay. Fletch'll do it."

She slanted him a look, and what might have been a smile, before turning to stare out of the windshield again. "You did good with that kid today." It galled her a bit to admit it, but it had to be done. "I don't think she'd have made it without you."

"Us," he said. "Some people might have called it teamwork."

She fastened her belt with a jerk of her wrist. "Some people."

"Don't take it so hard, Thea." Whistling through his teeth, he shoved the gearshift into First and cruised into traffic. "Now, where were we before we were interrupted? Oh, yeah, you were telling me about yourself."

"I don't think so."

"Okay, I'll tell me about you. You're a woman who likes structure, depends on it. No, no, it's more that you insist on it," he said. "That's why you're so good at your job, all that law and order."

She snorted. "You should be a psychiatrist, Nightshade. Who could have guessed a cop would prefer law and order?"

"Don't interrupt, I'm on a roll. You're what—twenty-seven, twenty-eight?"

"Thirty-two. You lost your roll."

"I'll pick it up again." He glanced down at her naked ring finger. "You're not married."

"Another brilliant deduction."

"You have a tendency toward sarcasm, and an affection for wearing silk and expensive perfume. Real nice perfume, Thea, the kind that seduces a man's mind before his body gets involved."

"Maybe you should be writing ad copy."

"There's nothing subtle about your sexuality. It's just there, in big capital letters. Now, some women would exploit it, some would disguise it. You don't do either, so I figure you've decided somewhere along the line that it's up to a man to deal with it. And that's not only smart, it's wise."

She didn't have an answer to that, he thought. Or didn't choose to give him one.

"You don't waste time, you don't waste energy. That way, when you need either one, you've got them. There's a cop's brain inside there, so you can size up a situation fast and act on it. And I figure you can handle a man every bit as coolly as you do your gun."

"An interesting analysis, Nightshade."

"You didn't flinch when you took that guy out today. It bothered you, but you didn't flinch." He pulled up in front of the Tick Tock and turned off the ignition. "If I've got to work with somebody, with the possibility of heading into a nasty situation, I like knowing she doesn't flinch."

"Well, gee, thanks. Now I can stop worrying that you don't approve of me." Her temper on the boil, she slammed out of the car.

"Finally…" Colt reached her in a few long-legged strides and swung his arm over her shoulder. "A little heat. It's a relief to see there's some temper in there, too."

She surprised them both by ramming an elbow into his gut. "You wouldn't be relieved if I cut it loose. Take my word for it."

They spent the next two hours going from bar to pool hall to grubby diner. It wasn't until they tried a hole-in-the-wall called Clancy's that they made some progress.

The lights were dim, a sop to the early drinkers, who liked to forget that the sun was still up. A radio behind the bar scratched out country music that told a sad tale of cheating and empty bottles. Several of those early customers were already scattered at the bar or at tables, most of them doing their drinking steadily and solo.

The liquor was watered, and the glasses were dingy, but the whiskey came cheap and the atmosphere was conducive to getting seriously drunk.

Althea walked to the end of the bar and ordered a club soda she had no intention of sampling. Colt opted for the beer on tap. She lifted a brow.

"Had a tetanus shot recently?" She took out a twenty, but kept her finger on the corner of the bill as their drinks were served. "Wild Bill used to come in here pretty regular."

The bartender glanced down at the bill, and back at Althea. Bloodshot eyes and the map of broken capillaries over his broad face attested to the fact that he swallowed as much as he served.

Althea prompted him. "Wild Bill Billings."

"So?"

"He was a friend of mine."

"Looks like you lost a friend."

"I was in here with him a couple of times." Althea drew the twenty back a fraction. "Maybe you remember."

"My memory's real selective, but it don't have no trouble making a cop."

"Good. Then you probably figured out that Bill and I had an arrangement."

"I probably figured out the arrangement got him splattered all over the sidewalk."

"You'd have figured that one wrong. He wasn't snitching for me when he got hit, and me, I'm just the sentimental type. I want who did him, and I'm willing to pay." She shoved the bill forward. "A lot more than this."

"I don't know nothing about it." But the twenty disappeared into his pocket.

"But you might know people who know people who know something." She leaned forward, a smile in her eyes. "If you put the word out, I'd appreciate it."

He shrugged, and would have moved away, but she put a hand on his arm. "I think that twenty's worth a minute or two more. Bill had a girl named Jade. She's skipped. He had a couple others, didn't he?"

"A couple. He wasn't much of a pimp."

"Got a name?"

He took out a dirty rag and began to wipe the dirty bar. "A black-haired girl named Meena. She worked out of here sometimes. Haven't seen her lately."

"If you do, you give me a call." She took out a card and dropped it onto the bar. "You know anything about movies? Private movies, with young girls?"

He looked blank and shrugged, but not before Althea saw the flash of knowledge in his eyes. "I ain't got time for movies, and that's all you get for twenty."

"Thanks." Althea strolled out. "Give him a minute," she said under her breath to Colt. Then she peered through the dirty window. "Look at that. Funny that he'd get an urge to make a call just now."

Colt watched the bartender hurry to the wall phone, drop in a quarter. "I like your style, Lieutenant."

"Let's see how much you like it after a few hours in a cold car. We've got a stakeout tonight, Nightshade."

"I'm looking forward to it."

Chapter 3

She was right about the cold. He didn't mind it so much, not with long johns and a sheepskin jacket to ward it off. But he did mind the dragging inactivity. He'd have sworn that Althea thrived on it.

She was settled comfortably in the passenger seat, working a crossword puzzle by the dim glow of the glove-compartment light. She worked methodically, patiently, endlessly, he thought, while he tried to stave off boredom with the B. B. King retrospective on the radio.

He thought of the evening they'd both missed at the Fletchers'. Hot food, blazing fire, warm brandy. It had even occurred to him that Althea might have defrosted a bit in unofficial surroundings. It might not have helped matters to think of her that way—the ice goddess melting—but it did something for his more casual fantasies.

In his current reality, she was all cop, and emotionally as distant from him as the moon. But in the daydream, assisted by the slow blues on the radio, she was all woman—seductive as the black silk he imagined her wearing, enticing as the crackling fire he pictured burning low in a stone hearth, soft as the white fur rug they lowered themselves to.

And her taste, once his mouth sampled hers, was honeyed whiskey. Drugging, sweet, potent. Her scent tangled up with her flavor in his senses until they were one and the same. An opiate a man could drown in.

The silk slipped away, inch by seductive inch, revealing the alabaster flesh beneath. Rose-petal smooth, flawless as glass, firm and soft as water. And when she reached for him, drew him in, her lips moved against his ear in whispered invitation.

"Want more coffee?"

"Huh?" He snapped back, swiveling his head around to stare at her in the shadowed car. She held a thermos out to him. "What?"

"Coffee?" Intrigued by the look on his face, she picked up his cup herself and filled it halfway. At first glance, she would have said there was temper in his eyes, ripe and ready to rip. But she knew that look, and knew it well. This was desire, equally ripe, equally ready. "Taking a side trip, Nightshade?"

"Yeah." He accepted the cup and drank deep, wishing it was whiskey. But his lips curved, his amusement with himself and the ridiculous situation easing the discomfort in his gut. "One hell of a trip."

"Well, try to keep up with our tour, will you?" She sipped from her own cup and offered him a share of her bag of candy. "There goes another one." Efficient, she set aside her cup and picked up her camera. She took two quick shots of the man entering the bar. He was only the second who had gone in during the past hour.

"They don't exactly do a thriving business down here, do they?"

"Most people like a little ambience with their liquor."

"Ferns and canned music?"

She set the camera aside again. "Clean glasses, for a start. I doubt we're going to see one of our moviemakers down here."

"Then why are we sitting in a cold car looking at a dive at eleven o'clock at night?"

"Because it's my job." She chose a single piece of candy, popped it into her mouth. "And because I'm waiting for something else."

It was the first he'd heard of it. "Want to clue me in?"

"No." She chose another piece and went back to her crossword puzzle.

"Okay, that tears it." He ripped the paper out of her hands. "You want to play games, Grayson? Let me tell you how I play. I get peeved when people hold out on me. I get especially peeved when I'm bored senseless while they're doing it. Then I get mean."

"Excuse me," she said, in a mild tone that was in direct contrast to the fire in her eyes. "I can hardly speak for the ball of terror in my throat."

"You want to be scared?" He moved fast, eerily so. She wouldn't have been able to evade him if she'd tried. So she submitted without any show of resistance when he grabbed her by the shoulders. "I figure I ought to be able to put the fear of God into you, Thea, and liven things up a bit for both of us."

"Back off. If you've finished your imitation of machismo, what I've been waiting for is about to walk into the bar."

"What?"

He turned his head, which presented Althea with the perfect opportunity to grab his thumb and twist it viciously. When he swore, she released him. "Meena. Wild Bill's other girl." Althea lifted her camera and took another shot. "I got her picture out of the files this afternoon. She's done time. Solicitation, running a confidence game, possession with intent to sell, disorderly behavior."

"A sweet girl, our Meena."

"*Your* Meena," Althea told him. "Since you play the big, bad type so well, you can go on in and charm Meena, get her out here so we can talk." Opening her purse, Althea took out an envelope with five crisp ten-dollar bills. "And if your charm fails, offer her fifty."

"You want me to go in and convince her I'm looking to party?"

"That's the ticket."

"Fine." He'd certainly done worse in his career than play the eager john in a seedy bar. But he shoved the envelope back into her lap. "I've got my own money."

Althea watched him cross the street, waiting until he'd disappeared inside. Then she leaned back and indulged herself for one moment by closing her eyes and letting out a long, long breath.

A dangerous man, Colt Nightshade, she thought. A deadly man. She hadn't felt simple anger when he lunged toward her and grabbed. She hadn't felt simple anything. What she'd experienced was complex, convoluted and confusing.

What she'd felt was arousal, gut-deep, red-hot, soul-searing arousal, mixed with a healthy dose of primal fear and teeth-baring fury.

It wasn't like her, she told herself as she took the time alone to gather her wits. Coming that close to losing control because a man pushed the wrong buttons—or the right ones—was uncharacteristic of her.

She pushed the buttons. That was Althea Grayson's number one hard-and-fast rule. And if Colt thought he could break that one, he was in for a big disappointment.

She'd worked too hard forming herself into what she was, laying out the stages of her life and following them. She'd come from chaos, and she'd beaten it back. Certainly it was necessary from time to time to change the pattern. She wasn't rigid. But nothing, absolutely nothing, jarred that pattern.

It was the case itself, she supposed. The child being held by strangers, almost certainly being abused.

Another pattern, she thought bitterly. All too familiar to her.

And the child that morning, she remembered. Helplessly trapped by the adults around her.

She shook that off, picked up the crumpled newspaper to fold it neatly and set it aside.

She was just tired, she told herself. The drug bust the week before had been vicious. And to tumble from that into this would have shaken anyone. What she needed was a vacation. She smiled to herself, imagining a warm white-sand beach, blue water, a tall spear of glistening hotel behind her. A big bed, room service, mud packs, and a private whirlpool.

And that was just what she was going to have when she capped this case and sent Colt Nightshade back to his cattle or his law practice or whatever the hell he called his profession.

Glancing toward the bar again, she was forced to nod in approval. Less than ten minutes had passed, and he was coming out, Meena in tow.

"Oh, a group thing?" Meena studied Althea through heavily kohled eyes. She pushed back her stiff black curls and smirked. "Well, now, honey, that's going to cost you extra."

"No problem." Gallantly Colt helped her into the back seat.

"I guess a guy like you can handle the two of us." She settled back, reeking of floral cologne.

"I don't think that'll be necessary." Althea took out her badge, flashed it.

Meena swore, shot Colt a look of intense dislike, then folded her arms. "Haven't you cops got anything better to do than roust us working girls?"

"We won't have to take you in, Meena, if you answer a few questions. Drive around a little, will you, Colt?" As he obliged, Althea turned in her seat. "Wild Bill was a friend of mine."

"Yeah, right."

"He did some favors for me. I did some for him."

"Yeah, I bet—" Meena broke off, narrowed her eyes. "You the cop he snitched for? The one he called classy?" Meena relaxed a little. There was a pretty good chance she wouldn't be spending the night in lockup after all. "He said you were okay. Said you always slipped him a few without whining about it."

Althea noted Meena's greedy little smile and lifted a brow. "I'm touched. Maybe he should've said I paid when he had something worth buying. Do you know Jade?"

"Sure. She hasn't been around for a few weeks. Bill said

she skipped town." Meena dug in her red vinyl purse and pulled out a cigarette. When Colt clicked on his lighter and offered the flame, she cupped her hand over his and slanted him a warm look under thickly blackened lashes. "Thanks, honey."

"How about this girl?" Colt took the snapshot of Elizabeth out of his pocket. After turning on the dome light, he offered it to Meena.

"No." She started to pass it back, then frowned. "I don't know. Maybe." While she considered, she blew out a stream of smoke, clouding the car. "Not on the stroll. Seems like maybe I saw her somewhere."

"With Bill?" Althea asked.

"Hell, no. Bill didn't deal in jailbait."

"Who does?"

Meena shifted her eyes to Colt. "Georgie Cool's got a few young ones in his stable. Nobody as fresh as this, though."

"Did Bill get you a gig, Meena? A movie gig?" Althea asked.

"Maybe he did."

"The answer's yes, or the answer's no." Althea took back the photo of Liz. "You waste my time, I don't waste my money."

"Well, hell, it don't bother me if some guy wants to take videos while I work. They paid extra for it."

"Have you got a name?"

Meena snorted in Althea's direction. "We didn't exchange business cards, sweetie."

"But you can give me a description. How many were involved. Where it went down."

"Probably." The sly look was back as Meena blew out smoke. "If I had some incentive."

"Your incentive's not to spend time in a cell with a two-hundred-pound Swede named Big Jane," Althea said mildly.

"You can't send me up. I'll scream entrapment."

"Scream all you want. With your record, the judge will just chuckle."

"Come on, Thea." Colt's drawl seemed to have thickened. "Give the lady a break. She's trying to cooperate. Aren't you, Meena?"

"Sure." Meena butted out her cigarette, licked her lips. "Sure I am."

"What she's trying to do is hose me." Althea realized she and Colt had picked up the good cop—bad cop routine without missing a beat. "And I want answers."

"She's giving them to us." He smiled at Meena in the rear-view mirror. "Just take your time."

"There were three of them," Meena said, and set her cherry-red lips in a pout. "The guy running the camera, another guy sitting back in a corner. I couldn't see him. And the guy who was, like, performing with me, you know? The guy with the camera was bald. A black guy, really big—like a wrestler or something. I was there about an hour, and he never opened his mouth once."

Althea flipped open her notebook. "Did they call each other by name?"

"No." Meena thought it through, shook her head. "No. That's funny, isn't it? They didn't talk to each other at all, as I remember. The one I was working with was a little guy—except for certain vital parts." She chuckled and reached for another cigarette. "Now, *he* did some talking. Trash talk, get it? Like for the camera. Some guys like that. He was, I don't know…in his forties, maybe, skinny, had his hair pulled back in a ponytail that hit his shoulder blades. He wore this Lone Ranger mask."

"I'm going to want you to work with a police artist," Althea told her.

"No way. No more cops."

"We don't have to do it at the station." Althea played her trump card. "If you give us a good enough description, one that helps us nail these film buffs, there's an extra hundred for you."

"Okay." Meena brightened. "Okay."

Althea tapped her pencil against her pad. "Where did you shoot?"

"Shoot? Oh, you mean the movie? Over on Second. Real nice place. It had one of them whirlpool tubs in the bathroom, and mirrors for walls." Meena leaned forward to brush her fingertips over Colt's shoulder. "It was…stimulating."

"The address?" Althea said.

"I don't know. One of those big condo buildings on Second. Top floor, too. Like the penthouse."

"I bet you'd recognize the building if we drove by it, wouldn't you, Meena?" Colt's tone was all friendly encouragement, as was the smile he shot her over his shoulder.

"Yeah, sure I would."

And she did. Minutes later she was pointing out the window. "That place, there. See the one up top, with the big windows and the balcony thing? It was in there. Real class joint. White carpet. This really sexy bedroom, with red curtains and a big round bed. There was gold faucets in the bathroom, shaped like swans. Jeez. I woulda loved to go back."

"You only went once?" Colt asked her.

"Yeah. They told Billy I wasn't the right type." With a

sound of disgust, she reached for yet another cigarette. "Get this. I was too old. I just had my twenty-second birthday, and those creeps tell Billy I'm too old. It really ticked me— Oh, yeah…" Suddenly inspired, she rapped Colt on the shoulder. "The kid. The one in the picture? That's where I saw her. I was leaving, but I went back 'cause I left my smokes. She was sitting in the kitchen. I didn't recognize her in the picture right off, 'cause she was all made-up when I saw her."

"Did she say anything to you?" Colt asked, struggling to keep his voice quiet and even. "Do anything?"

"No, just sat there. She looked stoned to me."

Because she sensed he needed something, Althea slid her hand across the seat and covered Colt's. His was rigid. She was surprised, but didn't protest, when he turned his hand over and gripped hers, palm to palm.

"I'm going to want to talk to you again." With her free hand, Althea reached into her purse for enough money to ensure Meena's continued cooperation. "I need a number where I can reach you."

"No sweat." Meena rattled it off while she counted her money. "I guess Billy had it right. You're square. Hey, maybe you could drop me at the Tick Tock. I think I'll go in and drink one for Wild Bill."

"We can't do anything without a warrant." Althea was repeating the statement for the third time as they stepped out of the elevator on the top floor of the building Meena had pointed out.

"You don't need a warrant to knock on a door."

"Right." With a sigh, Althea slipped a hand inside her jacket in an automatic check of her weapon. "And they're going to invite us in for coffee. If you give me a couple of hours—"

When he whirled, her jaw dropped. After the cool, matter-of-fact manner in which he'd handled everything up to this point, the raw fury on his face was staggering. "Get this Lieutenant—I'm not waiting another two *minutes* to see if Liz is in there. And if she is, if anybody is, I'm not going to need a damn warrant."

"Look, Colt, I understand—"

"You don't understand diddley."

She opened her mouth, then shut it again, shocked that she'd been about to shout that she did understand. Oh, yes, she understood very, very well. "We'll knock," she said tightly, and strode to the door of the penthouse and did so.

"Maybe they're hard of hearing." Colt used his fist to hammer. When the summons went unanswered, he moved so fast Althea didn't have time to swear. He'd already kicked the door in.

"Good, real good, Nightshade. Subtle as a brick."

"Guess I slipped." He pulled his gun out of his boot. "And look at this, the door's open."

"Don't—" But he was already inside. Cursing Boyd and all his boyhood friends, Althea drew her weapon and went in the door behind him, instinctively covering his back. She didn't need the light Colt turned on to see that the room was empty. It had a deserted feel. There was nothing left but the carpet, and the drapes at the windows.

"Split," Colt muttered to himself as he moved quickly from room to room. "The bastards split."

Satisfied she wouldn't need it, Althea replaced her gun. "I guess we know who our friendly bartender called this afternoon. We'll see what we can get from the rental contract, the neighbors…" Yet she thought if their quarry had been this slick so far, what they got would be close to useless.

She stepped into the bathroom. It was as Meena had described, the big black whirlpool tub, the swan-shaped faucets—brass, not gold—the all-around mirrors. "You've just jeopardized the integrity of a possible crime scene, Nightshade. I hope you're satisfied."

"She could have been here," he said from behind her.

She looked over, saw their reflections trapped in the mirrored tiles. It was the expression on his face, one she hadn't expected to see there, that softened her. "We're going to find her, Colt," she said quietly. "We're going to see that she gets back home."

"Sure." He wanted to break something, anything. It took every ounce of his will not to smash his fist through the mirrors. "Every day they've got her is a day she's going to have to live with, forever." Bending, he slipped his gun back in his boot. "God, Thea, she's just a child."

"Children are tougher than most people think. They close things off when they have to. And it's going to be easier because she has family who loves her."

"Easier than what?"

Than having no one but yourself, she thought. "Just easier." She couldn't help it. She reached out, laid a hand on his cheek. "Don't let it eat at you, Colt. You'll mess up if you do."

"Yeah." He drew it back, that dangerous emotion that led to dangerous mistakes. But when she started to drop her hand and move past him, Colt snagged her wrist. "You know something?" Maybe it was only because he needed contact, but he tugged her an inch closer. "For a minute there, you were almost human."

"Really?" Their bodies were almost brushing. A bad move, she thought. But it would be cowardly to pull back. "Wha am I usually?"

"Perfect." He lifted his free hand—because he'd wante to almost from the first moment he'd seen her—and tangle his fingers in her hair. "It's scary," he said. "It's the whol package—that face, the hair, the body, the mind. A mar doesn't know whether to bay at the moon or whimper at you feet."

She had to tilt her head back to keep her eyes level with his. If her heart was beating a bit faster, she could ignore it. It had happened before. If she felt the little pull of curiosity, even of lust, it wasn't the first time, and it could be controlled. But what was difficult, very difficult, to channel, was the unexpected clouding of her senses. That would have to be fought.

"You don't strike me as the type to do either," she said, and smiled, a cool, tight-lipped smirk that had most men backing off babbling.

Colt wasn't most men.

"I never have been. Why don't we try something else?" He said it slowly, then moved like lightning to close his mouth over hers.

If she had protested, if she had struggled—if there had been even a token pulling back—he would have released her and counted his losses. Maybe.

But she didn't. That surprised them both.

She could have, should have. She would think later. She could have stopped him cold with any number of defensive or offensive moves. She would think later. But there was such raw heat in his lips, such steely strength in his arms, such whirling pleasure in her own body.

Oh, yes, she would think later. Much later.

It was exactly as he'd imagined it. And he'd imagined it a lot. That tart, flamboyant flavor she carried on her lips was the twin of the one he'd sampled in his mind. It was as addicting as any opiate. When she opened for him, he dived deeper and took more.

She was as small, as slim, as supple, as any man could wish. And as strong. Her arms were locked hard around him, and her fingers were clutching at his hair. The low, deep sound of approval that vibrated in her throat had his blood racing like a fast-moving river.

Murmuring her name, he spun her around, ramming her against the mirrors, covering her body with his. His hands ran over her in a greedy sprint to take and touch and possess. Then his fingers were jerking at the buttons on her blouse in a desperate need to push aside the first barrier.

He wanted her now. No, no, he needed her now, he realized. The way a man needed sleep after a vicious day of hard labor, the way he needed to eat after a long, long fast.

He tore his mouth from hers to press it against her throat, reveling in the sumptuous taste of flesh.

Half-delirious, she arched back, moaning at the thrill of his hungry mouth on her heated skin. Without the wall for support, she knew, she would already have sunk to the floor. And it was there, just there, that he would take her, that they would take each other. On the cool, hard tile, with dozens of mirrors tossing back reflections of their desperate bodies.

Here and now.

And like a thief sneaking into a darkened house, an image of Meena, and what had gone on in that apartment, crept into her mind.

What was she doing? Good Lord, what was she *doing?* she raged at herself as she levered herself away.

She was a cop, and she had been about to indulge in some wild bout of mindless sex in the middle of a crime scene.

"Stop!" Her voice was harsh with arousal and self-disgust. "I mean it, Colt. Stop. Now."

"What?" Like a diver surfacing from fathoms-deep, he shook his head, nearly swayed. Good Lord, his knees were weak. To compensate, he braced a hand on the wall as he stared down at her. He'd loosened her hair, and it spilled rich and red over her shoulders. Her eyes were more gold than brown now, huge, and seductively misted. Her mouth was full, reddened by the pressure and demand of his, and her skin was flushed a pale, lovely rose.

"You're beautiful. Impossibly beautiful." Gently he skimmed a finger down her throat. "Like some exotic flower behind glass. A man just has to break that glass and take it."

"No." She grabbed his hand to keep from losing her mind again. "This is insane, completely insane."

"Yeah." He couldn't have agreed more. "And it felt great."

"This is an investigation, Nightshade. And we're standing in what is very possibly the scene of a major crime."

He smiled and lifted her hand to nip at her fingers. Just because this was a dead end for their investigation didn't mean all activity had to come to a halt. "So, let's go someplace else."

"We are going someplace else." She shoved him away, and quickly, competently redid her blouse. "Separately." She wasn't steady, she realized. Damn him, damn her, she wasn't steady.

He felt that the safest place for his hands at the moment, was his pockets so he shoved them in. She was right, one hundred percent right, and that was the worst of it.

"You want to pretend this didn't happen?"

"I don't pretend anything." Settling on dignity, she pushed her tumbled hair back, smoothed down her rumpled jacket. "It happened, now it's done."

"Not by a long shot, Lieutenant. We're both grown-ups, and though I can only speak for myself, that kind of connection just doesn't happen every day."

"You're right." She inclined her head. "You can only speak for yourself." She made it back to the living room before he grabbed her arm and spun her around to face him.

"You want me to press the point now?" His voice was quiet, deadly quiet. "Or do you want to be straight with me?"

"All right, fine." She could be honest, because lies wouldn't work. "If I were interested in a quick, hot affair, I'd certainly give you a call. As it happens, I have other priorities at the moment."

"You've got a list, right?"

She had to take a moment to get her temper back under wraps. "Do you think that insults me?" she asked sweetly. "I happen to prefer organizing my life."

"Compartmentalizing."

She arched a brow. "Whatever. For better or worse, we have a professional relationship. I want that girl found, Colt, every bit as much as you do. I want her back with her family, eating hamburgers and worrying over her latest math test. And I want to bring down the bastards who have her. More than you could possibly understand."

"Then why don't you help me understand?"

"I'm a cop," she told him. "That's enough."

"No, it's not." There had been passion in her face, the same kind of passion he'd felt when he had her in his arms.

Fierce and ragged and at the edge of control. "Not for you, or for me, either."

He let out a deep breath and rubbed the base of his neck, where most of his tension had lodged. They were both tired, he realized, tired and strung out. It wasn't the time and it wasn't the place to delve into personal reasons. He'd need to find some objectivity if he wanted to figure out Althea Grayson.

"Look, I'd apologize for back there if I was out of line. But we both know I wasn't. I'm here to get Liz back, and nothing's going to stop me. And after a taste of you, Thea, I'm going to be just as determined to have more."

"I'm not the soup du jour, Nightshade," she said wearily. "You'll only get what I give."

His grin flashed, quick and easy. "That's just the way I want it. Come on, I'll drive you home."

Saying nothing, Althea stared after him. She had the uncomfortable feeling that they hadn't resolved matters precisely as she'd wanted.

Chapter 4

Armed with a second cup of coffee, Colt stood at the edge of a whirlwind. It was obvious to him that getting three kids out of the house and onto a school bus was an event of major proportions. He could only wonder how a trio of adults could handle the orchestration on a daily basis and remain sane.

"I don't like this cereal," Bryant complained. He lifted a spoonful and, scowling, let the soggy mess plop back into his bowl. "It tastes like wet trees."

"You picked it out, because it had a whistle inside," Cilla reminded him as she slapped peanut-butter-and-jelly sandwiches together. "You eat it."

"Put a banana on it," Boyd suggested while he struggled to bundle Allison's pale, flyaway hair into something that might have passed for a braid.

"Ouch! Daddy, you're pulling!"

"Sorry. What's the capital of Nebraska?"

"Lincoln," his daughter said with a sigh. "I hate geography tests." While she pouted over it, she practiced her pliés for ballet class. "How come I have to know the stupid states and their stupid capitals, anyway?"

"Because knowledge is sacred." With his tongue caught in his teeth, Boyd fought to band the wispy braid. "And once you learn something, you never really forget it."

"Well, I can't remember the capital of Virginia."

"It's, ah..." As the sacred knowledge escaped him, Boyd swore under his breath. What the hell did he care? He lived in Colorado. One of the major problems with having kids, as he saw it, was that the parents were forced to go back to school. "It'll come to you."

"Mom, Bry's feeding Bongo his cereal." Allison sent her brother a smug, smarmy smile of the kind that only a sister can achieve.

Cilla turned in time to see her son thrusting his spoon toward their dog's eager mouth. "Bryant Fletcher, you're going to be wearing that cereal in a minute."

"But look, Mom, even Bongo won't eat it. It's crap."

"Don't say 'crap,'" Cilla told him wearily. But she noted that the big, scruffy dog, who regularly drank out of toilet bowls, had turned up his nose after one sample of soggy Rocket Crunchies. "Eat the banana, and get your coat."

"Mom!" Keenan, the youngest, scrambled into the room. He was shoeless and sockless, and was holding one grubby high-top sneaker in his hand. "I can't find my other shoe. It's not anywhere. Somebody musta stole it."

"Call a cop," Cilla muttered as she dumped the last peanut-butter-and-jelly sandwich into a lunch box.

"I'll find it, *señora.*" Maria wiped her hands on her apron. "Bless you."

"Bad guys took it, Maria," Keenan told her, his voice low and serious. "They came in the middle of the night and swiped it. Daddy'll go out and lock them up."

"Of course he will." Equally sober, Maria took his hand to lead him toward the stairs. "Now we go look for clues, *sí?*"

"Umbrellas." Cilla turned from the counter, running a hand through her short crop of brown hair. "It's raining. Do we have umbrellas?"

"We used to have umbrellas." His hairstyling duties completed, Boyd poured himself another cup of coffee. "Somebody stole them. Probably the same gang who stole Keenan's shoe and Bryant's spelling homework. I've already put a task force on it."

"Big help you are." Cilla went to the kitchen doorway. "Maria! Umbrellas!" She turned back, tripping over the dog, swore, then grabbed three lunch boxes. "Coats," she ordered. "You've got five minutes to make the bus."

There was a mad scramble, impeded by Bongo, who decided this was the perfect time to jump on everyone in sight.

"He hates goodbyes," Boyd told Colt as he deftly collared the mutt.

"The shoe was in the closet," Maria announced as she hustled Keenan into the kitchen.

"The thieves must have hidden it there. It's too diabolical." She offered him his lunch box. "Kiss."

Keenan grinned and planted a loud smack on her lips. "I get to be the milk monitor all week."

"It's a tough job, but I know you're up to it. Bry, the banana peel goes in the trash." As she handed him his lunch box, she hooked an arm around his throat, making him giggle as she kissed him goodbye. "Allison, the capital of Virginia's Richmond. I think."

"Okay."

After everyone exchanged kisses—including, Colt noted with some amusement, Bongo—Cilla held up one hand.

"Anyone leaving his or her umbrella at school will be immediately executed. Scram."

They all bolted. The door slammed. Cilla closed her eyes. "Ah, another quiet morning at the Fletchers'. Colt what can I offer you? Bacon, eggs? Whiskey?"

"I'll take the first two. Reserve the last." Grinning, he took the chair Bryant had vacated. "You put on this show every day?"

"With matinees on Saturdays." She ruffled her hair again, checked the clock on the stove. "I'd like to hang around with you guys, but I've got to get ready for work. I've got a meeting in an hour. If you find yourself at loose ends, Colt, stop by the radio station. I'll show you around."

"I might just do that."

"Maria, do you need me to pick up anything?"

"No, *señora.*" She already had the bacon sizzling. "*Gracias.*"

"I should be home by six." Cilla paused by the table to run a hand over her husband's shoulder. "I hear there's a big poker game here tonight."

"That's the rumor." Boyd tugged his wife down to him, and Colt saw their lips curve before they met. "You taste pretty good, O'Roarke."

"Strawberry jelly. Catch you later, Slick." She gave him one last, lingering kiss before she left him.

Colt listened to her race up the stairs. "You hit the bull's-eye, didn't you, Fletch?"

"Hmm?"

"Terrific wife, great kids. And the first time out."

"Looks that way. I guess I knew Cilla was it for me almost from the first." Remembering made him smile. "Took a little while to convince her she couldn't live without me, though."

It was tough not to envy that particular smile, Colt mused. "You and Althea, you were partners when you met Cilla, right?"

"Yeah. All three of us were working nights in those days. Thea was the first woman I'd ever partnered with. Turned out to be the best cop I'd ever partnered with, as well."

"I have to ask—you don't have to answer, but I have to ask." And how best to pose the question? Colt wondered as he picked up a fork and tapped it on the edge of the table. "You and Thea…before Cilla, there was nothing…personal?"

"There's plenty personal when you're partners, working together, sometimes around the clock." He picked up his coffee, his smile easy. "But there was nothing romantic, if that's what you're dancing around."

"It's none of my business." Colt shrugged, annoyed by just how much Boyd's answer relieved him. "I was curious."

"Curious why I didn't try to move in on a woman with her looks? Her brains? Her—what's the best word for it?" Amused by Colt's obvious discomfort, he chuckled as Maria silently served their breakfast. "Thanks, Maria. We'll call it style, for lack of something better. It's simple, Colt. I'm not going to say I didn't think about it. Could be Thea gave it a couple moments of her time, too. But we clicked as partners, we clicked as friends, and it just didn't take us down any of those other alleys." He scooped up some eggs, arched a brow. "You thinking about it?"

Colt moved his shoulders again, toyed with his bacon. "I can't say we've clicked as partners—or as friends, for that matter. But I figure we've already turned down one of those other alleys."

Boyd didn't pretend to be surprised. Anyone who said oil and water didn't mix just hadn't stirred them up enough. "There are some women who get under your skin, some that get into your head. And some who do both."

"Yeah. So what's the story on her?"

"She's a good cop, a person you can trust. Like anybody else, she's got some baggage, but she carries it well. If you want to know personal stuff, you'll have to ask her." He lifted his cup. "And she'd get the same answer from me about you."

"Has she asked?"

"Nope." Boyd sipped to hide his grin. "Now, why don't you tell me your progress in finding Liz?"

"We got a tip on the place on Second Avenue, but they'd already split." It still frustrated him. The whole bloody business frustrated him. "Figured I'd talk to the apartment manager, the neighbors. There's a witness who might be able to ID one or more of our movie moguls."

"That's a good start. Anything I can do to help?"

"I'll let you know. They've already had her a couple of weeks, Fletch. I'm going to get her back." He lifted his gaze, and the quiet rage in it left no room for doubt. "What worries me is what shape she'll be in when I do."

"Take it one step at a time."

"That sounds like the lieutenant." Colt preferred to take leaps, rather than steps. "I can't hook up with her until later this afternoon. She's in court or something."

"In court?" Boyd frowned, then nodded. "Right. The Marsten trial. Armed robbery, assault. She made a good collar on that one. Do you want me to send a uniform with you to Second Avenue?"

"No. I'd just as soon handle it myself."

It was good to be back on his own, Colt decided. Working alone meant you didn't have to worry about stepping on your partner's toes or debating strategy. And as far as Althea was concerned, it meant he didn't have to work overtime trying to keep himself from thinking of her as a woman.

First he rousted the apartment manager, Nieman, a short, balding man who obviously thought his position required him to wear a three-piece suit, a brutally knotted tie, and an ocean of pine-scented after-shave.

"I've already given my statement to the other officer," he informed Colt through the two-inch crack provided by the security chain on his door.

"Now you'll have to give it to me." Colt saw no need to disabuse Nieman of the notion that he was with the police. "Do you want me to shout my questions from out in the hall, Mr. Nieman?"

"No." Nieman shot the chain back, clearly annoyed. "Haven't I already had enough trouble? I was hardly out of my bed this morning before you people were banging on my door. Now the phone has been ringing off the hook with tenants calling, demanding to know what the police are doing sealing off the penthouse. The resulting publicity will take weeks for me to defuse."

"You got a real tough job, Mr. Nieman." Colt scanned the apartment as he entered. It wasn't as plush or as large as the empty penthouse, but it would do in a pinch. Nieman had furnished it in fussy French rococo. Colt knew his mother would have adored it.

"You can't imagine it." Resigned, Nieman gestured toward an ornately carved chair. "Tenants are such children, really. They need someone to guide them, someone to slap their hands when they break the rules. I've been a resident apartment manager for ten years, three in this building, and the stories I could tell…"

Because Colt was afraid he would do just that, he cut Nieman off. "Why don't you tell me about the penthouse tenants?"

"There's very little I can tell." Nieman plucked at the knees of his slacks before sitting. He crossed his legs at the ankles and revealed patterned argyle socks. "As I explained to the other detective, I never actually met them. They were only here four months."

"Don't you show the apartment to tenants, Mr. Nieman? Take their applications?"

"As a rule, certainly. In this particular case, the tenant sent references and a certified check for first and last month's rent via the mail."

"Is it usual for you to rent an apartment that way?"

"Not usual, no…" After clearing his throat, Nieman fiddled with the knot of his tie. "The letter was followed up with a phone call. Mr. Davis—the tenant—explained that he was a friend of Mr. and Mrs. Ellison. They had the penthouse before, for three years. Lovely couple, elegant taste. They moved to Boston. As he'd been acquainted with them, he had no need to view the apartment. He claimed to have attended several dinner parties and other affairs in the penthouse. He was quite anxious to have it, you see, and as his references were impeccable…"

"You checked them out?"

"Of course." Lips pursed, Nieman drew himself up. "I take my responsibilities seriously."

"What did this Davis do for a living?"

"He's an engineer with a local firm. When I contacted the firm, they had nothing but the highest regard for him."

"What firm?"

"I still have the file out." Nieman reached to the coffee table for a slim folder. "Foxx Engineering," he began, then recited the address and phone number. "Naturally, I contacted his landlord, as well. We apartment managers have a code of ethics. I was assured that Mr. Davis was an ideal tenant, quiet, responsible, tidy, and that his rent was always timely. This proved to be the case."

"But you never actually saw Mr. Davis?"

"This is a large building. There are several tenants I don't see. It's the troublemakers you meet regularly, and Mr. Davis was never any trouble."

Never any trouble, Colt thought grimly as he completed the slow process of door-to-door. He carried with him copies of the lease, the references, and Davis's letter. It was past noon, and he'd already interviewed most of the tenants who'd answered his knock. Only three of them claimed to have seen the mysterious Mr. Davis. Colt now had three markedly different descriptions to add to his file.

The police seal on the penthouse door had barred his entrance. He could have picked the lock and cut the tape, but he'd doubted he'd find anything worthwhile.

So he'd started at the top and was working his way down. He was currently canvassing the third floor, with a vicious case of frustration and the beginnings of a headache.

He knocked at 302 and felt himself being sized up through the peephole. The chain rattled, the bolt turned. Now he was being sized up, face-to-face, by an old woman with a wild mop of hair dyed an improbable orange. She had bright blue eyes that sprayed into dozens of wrinkles as she squinted to peer at him. Her Denver Broncos sweatshirt was the size of a tent, covering what Colt judged to be two hundred pounds of pure bulk. She had two chins and was working on a third.

"You're too good-looking to be selling something I don't want."

"No, ma'am." If Colt had had a hat, he'd have tipped it. "I'm not selling anything at all. The police are conducting an investigation. I'd like to ask you a few questions regarding some of your neighbors in the building."

"Are you a cop? You'd have a badge if you were."

It looked as though she were a great deal sharper than Nieman. "No, ma'am, I'm not a cop. I'm working privately."

"A detective?" The blue eyes brightened like light bulbs. "Like Sam Spade? I swear, that Humphrey Bogart was the sexiest man ever born. If I'd have been Mary Astor, I wouldn't have thought twice about some dumb bird when I could have had him."

"No, ma'am." It took Colt a moment, but he finally caught on to her reference to *The Maltese Falcon*. "I kind of went for Lauren Bacall, myself. They sure did set things humming in *The Big Sleep*."

Pleased, she let out a loud, lusty laugh. "Damned if they didn't. Well, come on in. No use standing here in the doorway."

Colt entered and immediately had to start dodging furniture and cats. The apartment was packed with both. Tables, chairs, lamps, some of them superior antiques, others yardsale rejects, were set helter-skelter throughout the wide living room. Half a dozen cats of all descriptions were curled, draped and stretched out with equal abandon.

"I collect," she told him, then plopped herself down on a Louis XV love seat. Her girth took up three-quarters of the cushions, so Colt wisely chose a ratty armchair with a faded pattern of colonial soldiers fighting redcoats. "I'm Esther Mavis."

"Colt Nightshade." Colt took it philosophically when a lean gray cat sprang into his lap and another leapt onto a wing of the chair to sniff at his hair.

"Well, just what are we investigating, Mr. Nightshade?"

"We're doing a check on the tenant who occupied the penthouse."

"The one who just moved out?" She scratched one of her chins. "Saw a bunch of burly men carrying stuff out to a van yesterday."

So had several other people, Colt thought. No one had bothered to note whether the van had carried the name of a moving company.

"Did you notice what kind of van, Mrs. Mavis?"

"Miss," she told him. "A big one. They didn't act like any movers I ever saw."

"Oh?"

"They worked fast. Not like people who get paid by the hour. You know. Moved out some good pieces, too." Her bright eyes scanned her living room. "I like furniture. There was this Belker table I'd have liked to get my hands on. Don't know where I'd put it, but I always find room."

"Could you describe any of the movers?"

"Don't notice men unless there's something special about them." She winked slyly.

"How about Mr. Davis? Did you ever see him?"

"Can't say for sure. I don't know most of the people in the building by name. Me and my cats keep to ourselves. What did he do?"

"We're looking into it."

"Playing it close to the vest, huh? Well, Bogey would've done the same. So, he's moved out?"

"It looks that way."

"I guess I won't be able to give him his package, then."

"Package?"

"Just came yesterday. Messenger brought it, dropped it here by mistake. Davis, Mavis…" She shook her head. "People don't pay enough attention to details these days."

"I know what you mean." Colt cautiously plucked a cat from his shoulder. "What sort of a package, Miss Mavis?"

"A package package." With a few grunts and whistles, she hauled herself to her feet. "Put it back in the bedroom. Meant to take it up to him today." She moved with a kind of tank-like grace through the narrow passages between the furniture and came back with a sealed, padded bag.

"Ma'am, I'd like to take that with me. If you have a problem with that, you can call Captain Boyd Fletcher, Denver PD."

"No skin off my nose." She handed Colt the package. "Maybe when you've cracked the case, you'll come let me know what's what."

"I'll just do that." On impulse, he took out the photo of Liz. "Have you seen this girl?"

Miss Mavis looked at it, frowned over it, then shook her head. "No, not that I recollect. Is she in trouble?"

"Yes, ma'am."

"Does it have something to do with upstairs?"

"I think so."

She handed the photo back. "She's a pretty little thing. I hope you find her real soon."

"So do I."

It wasn't his usual operating procedure. Colt couldn't have said why he made the exception, why he felt he had to. Instead of opening the package and dealing with its contents immediately, he left it sealed and drove to the courthouse.

He was just in time to hear the defense's cross of Althea. She was dressed in a rust-colored suit that should have been dull. Instead, the effect was subtly powerful, with her vibrant hair twisted up off her neck and a single strand of pearls at her throat.

Colt took a seat at the back of the courtroom and watched as she competently, patiently and devastatingly ripped the defense to shreds. She never raised her voice, never stumbled over words. Anyone looking or listening, including the jury, would have judged her a cool, detached professional.

And so she was, Colt mused as he stretched out his legs and waited. Certainly no one watching her now would imagine her flaming like a rocket in a man's arms. His arms.

No one would picture this tidy, controlled woman arching and straining as a man's hands—his hands—raced over her.

But he was damned if he could forget it.

And studying her now, when she was unaware of him and completely focused on the job at hand, he began to notice other things, little things.

She was tired. He could see it in her eyes. Now and again there was the faintest whisper of impatience in her voice as she was called on to repeat herself. She shifted, crossing her legs. It was a smooth movement, economical, as always. But he sensed something else beneath it. Not nerves, he realized. Restlessness. She wanted this over with.

When the cross was complete, the judge called for a fifteen-minute recess. She winced as the gavel struck. It was just a flicker of a movement across her face, but he caught it.

Jack Holmsby caught her arm before she could move by him. "Nice job, Thea."

"Thanks. You shouldn't have any trouble nailing him."

"I'm not worried about it." He shifted, just enough to block her path. "Listen, I'm sorry things didn't work out the other night. Why don't we give it another shot? Say, dinner tomorrow night, just you and me?"

She waited a beat, not so much amazed by his gall as fatigued by it. "Jack, do the words *no way in hell* have any meaning for you?"

He only laughed and gave her arm an intimate little squeeze. For one wild moment, she considered decking him and taking the rap for assault.

"Come on, Althea. I'd like a chance to make it up to you."

"Jack, we both know you'd like a chance to make me. And it isn't going to happen. Now let go of my arm while we're both on the same side of the law."

"There's no need to be—"

"Lieutenant?" Colt drawled out the word. He let his gaze sweep over Holmsby. "Got a minute?"

"Nightshade." It annoyed the hell out of her that he'd witnessed the little tussle. "Excuse me, Jack. I've got work to do."

She strode out of the courtroom, leaving Colt to follow. "If you've got something that's worth my time, spill it," she ordered. "I'm not real pleased with lawyers at the moment."

"Darling, I don't have any briefs with me—except the ones I'm wearing."

"You're a riot, Nightshade."

"You look like a lady who could use a laugh." He took her arm, and felt his own temper peak when she stiffened. Battling it down, he steered her toward the doors. "My car's out front. Why don't we take a ride while we catch up?"

"Fine. I walked over from the precinct. You can take me back."

"Right." He found another ticket on his windshield. Not surprising, since he'd parked in a restricted zone. He pocketed it, and climbed in. "Sorry I interrupted your mating ritual."

"Kiss my butt." She snapped her seat belt into place.

"Lieutenant, I've been dreaming of doing just that." Reaching over, he popped open the glove compartment. This time she didn't stiffen at the contact, only seemed to withdraw. "Here."

"What?" She glanced down at the bottle of aspirin.

"For your headache."

"I'm fine." It wasn't exactly a lie, she thought. What she had couldn't be termed a mere headache. It was more like a freight train highballing behind her eyes.

"I hate a martyr."

"Leave me alone." She closed her eyes and effectively cut him off.

She was far from fine. She hadn't slept. Over the years, she'd become accustomed to rolling on two or three hours a night. But last night she hadn't slept at all, and she was too proud to lay the blame where it belonged. Right at Colt's door.

She'd thought of him. And she'd berated herself. She'd run over the impossible scene in the penthouse, and she'd ached. Then she'd berated herself again. She'd tried a hot bath, a boring book, yoga, warm brandy. Nothing had done the trick.

So she'd tossed and turned, and eventually she'd crawled out of bed to roam restlessly through her apartment. And she'd watched the sun come up.

Since dawn, she'd worked. It was now slightly past one, and she'd been on the job for nearly eight hours without a break. And what made it worse, what made it next to intolerable, was that she could very well be stuck with Colt for another eight.

She opened her eyes again when he stopped with a jerk of brakes. They were parked in front of a convenience store.

"I need something," he muttered, and slammed out.

Fine, terrific, she thought, and shut her eyes again. Don't bother to ask if maybe *I* need something. Like a chain saw to slice off my head, for instance.

She heard him coming back. Odd, she mused, that she recognized the sound of his stride, the click of his boot heels, after so short a time. In defense, or simply out of obstinacy, she kept her eyes shut.

"Here." He pushed something against her hand. "Tea," he told her when she opened her eyes to stare down at the paper cup. "To wash down the aspirin." He popped the top on the bottle himself and shook out the medication. "Now take the damn pills, Althea. And eat this. You probably haven't eaten anything all day, unless it's chocolate bits or candied nuts. I've never seen a woman pick her way through a pound bag of candy the way you do."

"Sugar's loaded with energy." But she took the pills, and the tea. The package of cheese and crackers earned a frown. "Didn't they have any cupcakes?"

"You need protein."

"There's probably protein in cupcakes." The tea was too strong, and quite bitter, but it helped nonetheless. "Thanks." She sipped again, then broke down and opened the package of crackers. It was important to remember that she was responsible for her own actions, her own reactions and her own emotions. If she hadn't slept, it was her own problem. "The lab boys should have finished at the penthouse by now."

"They have. I've been there."

She muttered over a mouthful. "I'd rather you didn't go off on your own."

"I can't please everybody, so I please myself. I talked to the little weasel who manages the place. He never set eyes on the top-floor tenant."

While Althea chewed her way through the impromptu meal, he filled her in.

"I knew about Davis," she told him when he finished. "I got Nieman out of bed this morning. Already called the references. Phone disconnect on both. There is no Foxx Engineering at that address, or at any other address in Denver. Same for the apartment Davis used as a reference. Mr. and Mrs. Ellison, the former tenants, have never heard of him."

"You've been busy." Watching her, he tapped a finger on the steering wheel. "What was that you meant about not going off on your own?"

She smiled a little. The headache was backing off. "I carry a badge," she said, deadpan. "You don't."

"Your badge didn't get you into Miss Mavis's apartment."

"Should it have?"

"I think so." Darkly pleased to be one up on her, Colt reached into the back and showed Althea the package. "Messenger delivered it to the cat lady by mistake."

"Cat lady?"

"You had to be there. Uh-uh." He snatched it out of reach as she made a move toward it. "My take, darling. I'm willing to share."

Her temper spiked, then leveled off when she noticed that the package was still intact. "It's still sealed."

"Seemed fair," he said, meeting her eyes. "I figured we should open it together."

"Looks like you figured right this time. Let's have a look."

Colt reached down and drew a knife out of his boot. As he slit open the package, Althea narrowed her eyes.

"I don't think that toy's under the legal limit, champ."

"Nope," he said easily, and slid the knife back into his boot. Reaching into the package, he pulled out a videotape and a single sheet of paper.

Final edit. Okay for dupes? Heavy snows expected by weekend. Supplies good. Next drop send extra tapes and beer. Roads may be closed.

Althea held the sheet by a corner, then dug a plastic bag out of her purse. "We'll have it checked for prints. We could get lucky."

"It might tell us who. It won't tell us where." Colt slid the tape back into the bag. "Want to go to the movies?"

"Yeah." Althea set the bag on her lap, tapped it. "But I think this one calls for a private screening. I've got a VCR at home."

* * *

She also had a comfortable couch crowded with cushy pillows. Gleaming hardwood floors were accented by Navaho rugs. The art deco prints on the walls should have been at odds with the southwestern touches, but they weren't. Neither were the homey huddle of lush green plants on the curvy iron tea cart, the two goldfish swimming in a tube-shaped aquarium, or the footstool fashioned to resemble a squat, grinning gnome.

"Interesting place" was the best Colt could do.

"It does the job." She walked to a chrome-and-glass entertainment center, stepping out of her shoes on the way.

Colt decided that single gesture told him more about Althea Grayson than a dozen in-depth reports would have.

With her usual efficiency, she popped in the tape and flicked both the VCR and TV on.

There was no need to fast-forward past the FBI warning, because there wasn't one. After a five-second lag, the tape faded from gray.

And the show began.

Even for a man with Colt's experience, it was a surprise. He tucked his hands in his pockets and rocked back on his heels. It was foolish, he supposed, seeing as they were both adults, both professionals, but he felt an undeniable tug of embarrassment.

"I, ah, guess they don't believe in whetting the audience's appetite."

Althea tilted her head, studying the screen with a clinical detachment. It wasn't lovemaking. It wasn't even sex, according to her definition. It was straight porn, more pathetic than titillating.

"I've seen hotter stuff at bachelor parties."

Colt took his eyes from the screen long enough to arch a brow at her. "Oh, really?"

"Tape's surprisingly good quality. And the camera work, if you can call it that, seems pretty professional." She listened to the moans. "Sound, too." She nodded as the camera pulled back for a long shot. "Not the penthouse."

"Must be the place in the mountains. High-class rustic, from the paneling. Bed looks like a Chippendale."

"How do you know?"

"My mother's big on antiques. Look at the lamp by the bed. It's Tiffany, or a damn fine imitation. Ah, the plot thickens…."

They both watched as another woman walked into the frame. A few lines of dialogue indicated that she had come upon her lover and her best friend. The confrontation turned violent.

"I don't think that's fake blood." Althea hissed through her teeth as the first woman took a hard blow to the face. "And I don't think she was expecting that punch."

Colt swore softly as the rest of the scene unfolded. The mixture of sex and violence—violence that was focused on the women—made an ugly picture. He had to clench his fists to keep himself from slamming the television off.

It was no longer a matter of amused embarrassment. It was a matter of revulsion.

"You handling this, Nightshade?" Althea laid a hand on his arm. They both knew what he feared most—that Liz would come on-screen.

"I don't guess I'll be wanting any popcorn."

Instinctively Althea left her hand where it was and moved closer.

There was a plot of sorts, and she began to follow it. A weekend at a ski chalet, two couples who mixed and mingled in several ways. She moved beyond that, picking up the details. The furnishings. Colt had been right—they were first-class. Different camera angles showed that it was a two-story with an open loft and high beamed ceilings. Stone fireplace, hot tub.

In a few artistic shots, she saw that it was snowing lightly. She caught glimpses of screening trees and snow-capped peaks. In one outdoor scene that must have been more than uncomfortable for the actors, she noted that there was no other house or structure close by.

The tape ended without credits. And without Liz. Colt didn't know whether he was relieved or not.

"I don't think it's got much of a shot in the Oscar race." Althea kept her voice light as she rewound the tape. "You okay?"

He wasn't okay. There was a burning in his gut that needed some sort of release. "They were rough on the women," he said carefully. "Really vicious."

"Offhand, I'd say the main customers for this kind of thing would be guys who fantasize about dominance—physical and emotional."

"I don't think you can apply the word fantasy in conjunction with something like this."

"Not all fantasies are pretty," she murmured, thinking. "You know, the quality was good, but some of the acting— and I use the term loosely—was downright pitiful. Could be they let some of their clients live out those fantasies on film."

"Lovely." He took one careful, cleansing breath. "Jade's letter mentioned that she thought one of the girls had been killed. Looks like she might have been right."

"Sadism's a peculiar sexual tool—and one that can often get out of hand. We might be able to make the general area from the outside shots."

She started to eject the tape, but he whirled her around. "How can you be so damn clinical? Didn't that get to you? Doesn't anything?"

"Whatever does, I deal with it. Let's leave personalities out of this."

"No. It goes back to knowing who you're working with. We're talking about the fact that some girl might have been killed for the camera." There was a fury in him that he couldn't control, and a terrible need to vent it. "We've just seen two women slapped, shoved, punched, and threatened with worse. I want to know what watching that did to you."

"It made me sick," she snapped back, jerking away. "And it made me angry. And if I'd let myself, it would have made me sad. But all that matters, all that really matters, is that we have our first piece of hard evidence." She snatched out the tape and replaced it in its bag. "Now, if you want to do me a favor, you'll drop me back at the precinct so that I can turn this over. Then you can give me some space."

"Sure, Lieutenant." He strode to the door to yank it open. "I'll give you all the space you need."

Chapter 5

Colt was holding three ladies. And he thought it was really too bad that the lady he wanted was sitting across the table from him, upping his bet.

"There's your twenty-five, Nightshade, and twenty-five more." Althea tossed chips into the kitty. She held her cards close to her vest, like her thoughts.

"Ah, well…" Sweeney heaved a sigh and studied the trash in his hand as if wishing alone might turn it to gold. "Too rich for my blood."

From her seat between Sweeney and a forensic pathologist named Louie, Cilla considered her pair of fives. "What do you think, Deadeye?"

Keenan, dressed for bed in a Denver Nuggets jersey, bounced on her lap. "Throw the money in."

"Easy for you to say." But her chips clattered onto the pile.

After a personal debate that included a great deal of muttering, shifting and head shaking, Louie tossed in his chips, as well.

"I'll see your twenty-five," Colt drawled. He kept his cigar clamped between his teeth as he counted out chips. "And bump it again."

Boyd just grinned, pleased that he'd folded after the draw. The bet made the rounds again, with only Althea, Cilla and Colt remaining in.

"Three pretty queens," he announced, and laid down his cards.

Althea's eyes glinted when they met his. "Nice. But we don't have room for them in my full house." She spread her cards, revealing three eights and a pair of deuces.

"That puts my two fives to shame." Cilla sighed as Althea raked in the pot. "Okay, kid, you cost me seventy-five cents. Now you have to die." She hauled a giggling Keenan up as she rose.

"Daddy!" He spread his arms and grinned. "Help me! Don't let her do it!"

"Sorry, son." Boyd ruffled Keenan's hair and gave him a solemn kiss. "Looks like you're doomed. We're going to miss you around here."

Always ready to prolong the inevitable, Keenan hooked his arms around Colt's neck. "Save me!"

Colt kissed the waiting lips and shook his head. "Only one thing in this world scares me, partner, and that's a mama. You're on your own."

Levering in Cilla's arms, the boy made the rounds of the table. When he got to Althea, his eyes gleamed. "Okay? Can I?"

It was an old game, one she was willing to play. "For a nickel."

"I can owe you."

"You already owe me eight thousand dollars and fifteen cents."

"I get my allowance Friday."

"Okay, then." She took him onto her lap for a hug, and he sniffed her hair like a puppy. Colt saw her face soften, watched her hand slide up to stroke the tender nape of the boy's neck.

"It's good," Keenan announced, taking one last exaggerated sniff.

"Don't forget that eight thousand on Friday. Now beat it." After a kiss, she passed him back to Cilla.

"Deal me out," Cilla suggested, and, settling her son on her hip, she carried him upstairs to bed.

"A boy who can talk his way into a woman's lap's a boy to be proud of." Sweeney grinned as he gathered the cards. "My deal. Ante up."

During the next hour, Althea's pile of chips grew slowly, steadily. She enjoyed the monthly poker games that had become a routine shortly after Cilla and Boyd were married. The basic challenge of outwitting her opponents relaxed her almost as much as the domestic atmosphere that had seeped into every corner of the Fletcher home.

She was a cautious player, one who gambled only when satisfied with the odds, and who bet meticulously, thoughtfully, even then. She noted that Colt's pile multiplied, as well, but in fits and starts. He wasn't reckless, she decided. *Ruthless* was the word. Often he bumped the pot when he had nothing, or sat back and let others do the raising when he had a handful of gold.

No pattern, she mused, which she supposed was a pattern of its own.

After Sweeney won a piddling pot with a heart flush, she pushed back from the table. "Anybody want a beer?"

Everybody did. Althea strolled into the kitchen and began to pop tops. She was pouring herself a glass of wine when Colt walked in.

"Thought you could use some help."

"I can handle it."

"I don't figure there's much you can't handle." Damn, the woman was prickly, he thought. "I just thought I'd lend a hand."

Maria had prepared enough sandwiches to satisfy a hungry platoon on a long march. For lack of anything better to do Colt shifted some from platter to plate. He had to get it out, he decided. Now that they were alone and he had the opportunity, he wasn't sure how to start.

"I've got something to say about this afternoon."

"Oh?" Her tone frosty, Althea turned to the refrigerator and took out a bowl of Maria's incomparable guacamole dip.

"I'm sorry."

And nearly dropped it. "Excuse me?"

"Damn it, I'm sorry. Okay?" He hated to apologize—it meant he had made a mistake, one that mattered. "Watching that tape got to me. It made me want to smash something, someone. The closest I could come to it was ripping into you."

Because it was the last thing she would have expected, she was caught off guard. She stood with the bowl in her hand, unsure of her next move. "All right."

"I was afraid I'd see Liz," he continued, compelled to say

it all. "I was afraid I wouldn't." At a loss, he picked up one of the opened beers and took a long swallow. "I'm not used to being scared like this."

There was very little he could have said, and nothing he could have done, that would have gotten through her defenses more thoroughly. Touched, and shaken, she set the bowl on the counter and opened a bag of chips.

"I know. It got to me, too. It's not supposed to, but it did." She poured the chips into the bowl, wishing there was something else she could do. Anything else. "I'm sorry things aren't moving faster, Colt."

"They haven't been standing still, either. And I've got you to thank for most of that." He lifted a hand, then dropped it. "Thea, there was something else I wanted to do this afternoon besides punching somebody. I wanted to hold you." He saw the wariness flash into her eyes, quick as a heartbeat, and had to grind down his temper. "Not jump you, Thea. Hold you. There's a difference."

"Yes, there is." She let out a long, quiet breath. There was need in his eyes. Not desire, just need. The need for contact, for comfort, for compassion. That she understood. "I guess I could have used it, too."

"I still could." It cost him to make the first move, this sort of move. But he stepped toward her and held out his arms.

It cost her, as well, to respond, to move into his arms and encircle him with her own.

And when they were close, when her cheek was resting against his shoulder and his against her hair, they both sighed. The tension drained away like water through a broken dam.

He didn't understand it, wasn't sure he could accept it, but he realized it felt right. Very simply right. Unlike the first time he'd held her, there was no punch of lust, no molten fire in his blood. But there was a warmth, sweet and spreading and solid.

He could have held her like that, just like that, for hours.

She didn't often let herself relax so completely, not with a man, and certainly not with a man who attracted her. But this was so easy, so natural. The steady thudding of his heart lulled her. She nearly nuzzled. The urge was there—to rub her cheek against him, to close her eyes and purr. When she felt him sniffing her hair, she laughed.

"The kid's right," he murmured. "It's good."

"That's going to cost you a nickel, Nightshade."

"Put it on my tab," he told her as she lifted her head to smile at him.

Was it because she'd never looked at him quite that way that it hit him so hard? He couldn't be sure. All he knew was that she was outrageously beautiful, her hair loose and tumbling into his hands, glinting like flame in the hard kitchen light. Her eyes were smiling, deep and tawny and warm with humor. And her mouth—unpainted, curved, slightly parted. Irresistible.

He tilted his head, lowered it, waiting for her to stiffen or draw back. She did neither. Though the humor in her eyes had turned to awareness, the warmth remained. So he touched his lips to hers, gently testing, an experiment in emotions. With their eyes open, they watched each other, as if each were waiting for the other to move back, or leap forward.

When she remained pliant in his arms, he changed the angle, nipping lightly. He felt her tremble, only once, as her eyes darkened, clouded. But they remained open and on his.

She wanted to see him. Needed to. She was afraid that if

she closed her eyes she might fall into whatever pit it was that yawned before her. She had to see who he was, to try to understand what there was about this one man that made him capable of turning her system to mush.

No one had done so before. And she'd been proud of her ability to resist, or to control, and smugly amused by men and women who fell under the spell of another. In falling they had suffered the torments of love. She had never been certain the joys balanced those torments.

But as he deepened the kiss, slowly, persuasively deepened it so that not only her lips, but also her mind, her heart, her body, were involved in that contact, she wondered what she had missed by never allowing surrender to mix with power.

"Althea…" He whispered her name as he again, teasingly, changed the angle of the kiss. "Come with me…."

She understood what he was asking. He wanted her to let go, to tumble with him wherever the moment took them. To yield to him, even as he yielded to her.

To gamble, when she wasn't sure of the odds.

He closed his eyes first. The soft, drowsy warmth slid seamlessly into a numbing ache, an ache that was all pleasure. Her eyes fluttered closed on a sigh.

"Hey! How about those beers— Oops!" Boyd winced and struggled not to grin. He slipped his hands into his pockets, and had to prevent himself from whistling a tune as his old friend and his former partner jumped apart like thieves caught in a bust.

"Sorry, guys." He strolled over to gather up the beer bottles himself. It occurred to him that in all the years he'd known Althea, he'd never seen that bemused, punch-drunk look on her face. "Must be something about this kitchen," he added as he headed for the door. "Can't tell you how many times I've found myself occupied the same way in here."

The door swung shut behind him. Althea blew out a long breath.

"Oh, boy" was the best she could manage.

Colt laid a hand on her shoulder. Not for balance, he assured himself, though his legs were weak. Just to keep things nice and light. "He looked pretty damned pleased with himself didn't he?"

"He'll razz me about this," she muttered. "And he'll tell Cilla, so she can razz me, too."

"They've probably got better things to do."

"They're married," she shot back. "Married people love talking about other people's—"

"Other people's what?"

"Stuff."

The more unraveled she became, the more Colt liked it. He was positive that only a privileged few had ever seen the cool lieutenant flustered. He wanted to savor every moment of the experience. Grinning, he leaned back against the counter.

"So? If you really want to drive them crazy, you could let me come home with you tonight."

"In your dreams, Nightshade."

He lifted a brow. Her voice hadn't been quite steady. He liked that—a whole lot. "Well, there's truth in that, darling. Might as well be straight and tell you I'm not willing to wait much longer to turn that dream into reality."

She needed to calm down, needed to do something with her hands. Killing two birds with one stone, she picked up her wine and sipped. "Is that a threat?"

"Althea." There was a world of patience in his voice. That

amused him. He couldn't recall ever having been patient about anything before. "We both know what just went on here can't be turned into a threat. It was nice." He flicked a finger down her hair. "If we'd been alone somewhere, it would have turned out a lot nicer." The intent flickered in his eyes too quickly for her to avoid the result. His hand fisted in her hair, held her still. "I want you, Althea, and I want you bad. You can make out of that whatever you choose."

She felt a skip of something sprint down her spine. It wasn't fear. She'd been a cop long enough to recognize fear in all its forms. And she'd lived her life her own way long enough to remain cautious. "It seems to me that you want a great many things. You want Liz back, you want the men responsible for keeping her from her parents caught and punished. You want to do those things your way, with my cooperation. And—" she sipped her wine again, her eyes cool and level "—you want to go to bed with me."

She was amazing, Colt reflected. She had to be feeling some portion of the need and the desperation he was experiencing. Yet she might have been discussing a change in the weather. "That about sums it up. Why don't you tell me what you want?"

She was afraid she knew exactly what she wanted, and it was standing almost close enough to taste. "The difference between you and me, Nightshade, is that I know you don't always get what you want. Now I'm going to pack it in. I've had a long day. You can check with me tomorrow. We'll have the sketches from Meena. Something might turn up when we run them."

"All right." He'd let her go—for now, he thought. The trouble with a woman like Althea, he mused, was that a man would always be tempted to seduce her, and he would always crave her coming to him freely.

"Thea?"

She paused at the kitchen door, looked back. "Yes?"

"What are we going to do about this?"

She felt a sigh building—not one of weariness, one of longing—and choked it off. "I don't know," she said, as truthfully as she could. "I wish I did."

By nine-thirty the following morning, Colt was cooling his heels in Althea's office. There wasn't much room in her cubbyhole to cool anything. Out of sheer boredom, he flipped through some of the papers on her desk. Reports, he noted, in that peculiar language cops used, a language that was both concise and florid. Vehicles proceeded in a southwesterly direction, alleged perpetrators created disturbances, arresting officers apprehended suspects after responding to 312s and 515s.

She wrote a damn good report, if you were into such bureaucratic hogwash. Which, he decided, she obviously was. Rules-and-Regulations Grayson, he thought, and closed the file. Maybe his biggest problem was that he'd seen that there was a lot more to her than the straight-arrow cop.

He'd seen her hold a gun, steady as a rock, while her eyes were alive with fear and determination. He'd felt her respond like glory to an impulsive and urgent embrace. He'd watched her cuddle a child, soften with compassion and freeze like a hailstone.

He'd seen too much, and he knew he hadn't seen nearly enough.

Liz was his priority, had to be. Yet Althea remained lodged

inside him, like a bullet in the flesh. Hot, painful, and impossible to ignore.

It made him angry. It made him itchy. And when she swept into the room, it made him snarl.

"I've been waiting for the best part of a damn hour. I haven't got time for this."

"That's a shame." She dropped another file onto her desk, noting immediately that her papers had been disturbed. "Could be you're watching too much TV, Nightshade. That's the only place a cop gets to work on one case at a time."

"I'm not a cop."

"That's more than obvious. And next time you have to wait for me, keep your nose out of my papers."

"Listen, Lieutenant—" He broke off, swearing, when her phone rang.

"Grayson." She slipped into her chair as she spoke, her hand already reaching for a pencil. "Yeah. Yeah, I got it. That was quick work, Sergeant. I appreciate it. I'll be sure to do that if I get over your way. Thanks again." She broke the connection and immediately began to dial again. "Kansas City located Jade's mother," she told Colt. "She'd moved from the Kansas side to Missouri."

"Is Jade with her?"

"That's what I'm going to try to find out." As she completed the call, Althea checked her watch. "She waits tables at night. Odds are I'll catch her at home at this hour."

Before Colt could speak again, Althea shot up a hand for silence.

"Hello, I'd like to speak with Janice Willowby." A sleepy and obviously irritated voice informed her that Janice didn't live there. "Is this Mrs. Willowby? Mrs. Willowby, this is

Lieutenant Grayson, Denver Police— No, ma'am, she hasn't done anything. She isn't in any trouble. We believe she might be of some help to us on a case. Have you heard from your daughter in the last few weeks?" She listened patiently as the woman denied having been in contact with Janice and irritably demanded information. "Mrs. Willowby, Janice isn't a fugitive from justice, or under any sort of suspicion. However, we are anxious to contact her." Her eyes hardened, quickly, coldly. "Excuse me? Since I'm not asking you to turn your daughter in, I don't see a reward as being applicable. If—"

Colt thrust a hand over the receiver. "Five thousand," he stated. "If she gets us Jade, and Jade leads us to Liz." He saw the spitting denial in her eyes, but held firm. "It's not up to you. The reward's private."

Althea sucked in her disgust. "Mrs. Willowby, there is a private party authorizing the sum of five thousand for information on Janice, on the condition that this then results in the satisfactory close of the investigation. Yes, I'm quite sure you can have it in cash. Oh, yes, I'm sure you will see what you can do. You can reach me twenty-four hours a day, at this number." She repeated it twice. "Collect, of course. That's Lieutenant Althea Grayson, Denver. I hope you do."

After hanging up the phone, she sat simmering. "It's no wonder girls like Jade take off and end up on the streets. She didn't give a damn about her daughter, just wanted to be sure no backlash was going to come her way. If Jade had been in any trouble, she'd have been willing to trade her for cash in the blink of an eye."

"Not everybody has the maternal instincts of Donna Reed."

"You're telling me." Because emotions would interfere with the job at hand, Althea shelved them. "Meena's been working with the police artist, and she's come up with some pretty good likenesses. One of them matches one of the stars from the production we watched yesterday."

"Which one?"

"The guy in the red leather G-string. We're running a make through Vice to start. It'll take time."

"I don't have time."

She set aside the pencil, folded her hands. She wouldn't lose her temper, she promised herself. Not again. "Do you have a better way?"

"No." He turned away, then swung back. "Any prints on the car used to hit Billings?"

"Clean."

"The penthouse?"

"No prints. Some hair fibers. They won't help us catch them, but they'll be good for tying it up in court. The lab's working on the tape, and the note. We could get lucky."

"How about missing persons? A Jane Doe at the morgue? Jade said she thought one of the girls was killed."

"Nothing's turned up. If they did kill someone, and she'd been in the life for a while, a missing-persons report's unlikely. I've checked all the unidentified and suspicious deaths over the last three months. Nobody fits the profile."

"Any luck in the homeless shelters, runaway hostels, halfway houses?"

"Not yet." She hesitated, then decided it was best that they talk it through. "There's something I've been kicking around."

"Go ahead, kick it my way."

"We've got a couple of baby faces on the force. Good cops. We can put them undercover, out on the street. See if they get a movie offer."

Colt rolled it around in his head. That, too, would take time, he mused. But at least it was a chance. "It's a tricky spot. Do you have anyone good enough to handle it?"

"I said I did. I'd do it myself—"

"No." His abrupt denial was like the lash of a whip.

Althea inclined her head and continued without a flinch. "I said, I'd do it myself, but I can't pass for a teenager. Apparently our producer prefers kids. I'll set it in motion."

"Okay. Can you get me a dupe of the tape?"

She smiled. "Evenings too dull for you?"

"Very funny. Can you?"

She thought it through. It wasn't strictly procedure, but it couldn't do any harm. "I'll check with the lab. Meanwhile, I'm going to roust the bartender at Clancy's. I'm betting he's the one who tipped off the bunch on Second Avenue. We might sweat something out of him."

"I'll go with you."

She shook her head. "I'm taking Sweeney." She smiled, fully, easily. "A big Irish cop, a bar called Clancy's. It just seems to fit."

"He's a lousy poker player."

"Yeah, but a darlin' man," she said, surprising him by slipping into a perfect Irish brogue.

"How about I go along anyway?"

"How about you wait for me to call you?" She rose, pulled a navy blazer from the back of her chair. She wore pleated slacks of the same color and texture and a paler blue blouse in a silky material. Her shoulder harness and weapon looked so natural on her, they might have been fashion accessories.

"You will call me."

"I said I would."

Because it seemed right, he laid his hands on her shoulders, and briefly rested his brow on hers. "Marleen called me this morning. I don't like to think I was giving her false hope, but I told her we were getting closer. I had to tell her that."

"Whatever eases her mind is the right thing to say." She couldn't help it. She pressed a hand briefly to his cheek in comfort, then let it drop. "Hang tough, Nightshade. We've gathered a lot of information in a short amount of time."

"Yeah." He lifted his head and slid his hands down her arms until he could link fingers with her. "I'll let you go find your intimidating Irishman. But there's one more thing." He raised their linked hands, studying the contrast of texture, tone and size. "Sooner or later, we'll be going off the clock." His gaze shifted to meet hers. "Then we'll have to deal with other things."

"Then we'll deal with them. But you may not like the way it shakes down."

He caught her chin in one hand, kissed her hard, then released her before she could do more than hiss. "Same goes. You be careful out there, Lieutenant."

"I was born careful, Nightshade." She walked away, shrugging into the blazer as she went.

Ten hours later, she parked her car in her building's garage and headed for the elevator. She was ready for a hot bath pregnant with bubbles, a glass of icy white wine, and some slow blues, heavy on the bass.

As she rode to her floor, she leaned against the back wall and shut her eyes. They hadn't gotten very far with the bartender, Leo Dorsetti. Bribes hadn't worked, and veiled threats hadn't, either. Althea didn't doubt he had connections with the pornography ring. Nor did she doubt that he was worried that the same fate might befall him that had Wild Bill.

So she needed more than a threat. She needed to dig up something on Leo Dorsetti. Something solid enough that she could drag him downtown and into interrogation.

Once she had him, she could crack him. She was damn sure of that.

She jingled her keys as she walked through the open elevator doors and into the hall. Now it was time to put the cop on hold, at least for an hour or two. Obsessing over a case usually equalled making mistakes on a case. So she'd pack it away into a corner of her mind, let it sit, let it ripen, while the woman indulged in a purely selfish evening.

She'd already unlocked the door, pushed it open, when the alarm went off in her head. She didn't question what tripped it, just whipped out her weapon. Automatically she followed standard entry procedure, checking in corners and behind the door.

Her eyes scanned the room, noting that nothing was out of place—unless she counted the Bessie Smith record currently playing on the turntable. And the scent. She took a quick whiff, identifying cooking, something spicy. It made her mouth water in response, even as her mind stayed alert.

A sound from the kitchen had her whirling in that direction, ending in the spread-legged police stance, her weapon steady in both hands.

Colt stopped in the doorway, wiping his hands on a dishcloth. Smiling, he leaned back against the jamb. "Hi there, darling. And how was your day?"

Chapter 6

Althea lowered her gun. She didn't raise her voice. The words she chose, quiet and precise, made her feelings known with more clarity than a shout could have.

When she'd finished, Colt could only shake his head in admiration. "I don't believe I've ever been cussed out with more style. Now, I'd be obliged if you'd holster that gun. Not that I figure you'd use it and risk getting blood all over your floor."

"It might be worth it." She slapped her gun back in place, but her eyes never left his. "You have the right to remain silent…." she began.

Wisely, Colt stifled a chuckle. He held up a hand. "What're you doing?"

"I'm reading you your rights before I haul your butt in for nighttime breaking and entering."

He didn't doubt she'd do it. She'd have him booked, fingerprinted and photographed without breaking stride. "I'll waive them, providing you listen to an explanation."

"It better be good." Shrugging out of her blazer, she tossed it over the back of the chair. "How did you get in here?"

"I, ah... Through the door?"

Her eyes narrowed. "You have the right to an attorney."

Obviously humor wasn't going to do the trick. "Okay, I'm busted." He tossed up both hands in a gesture of surrender. "I picked the lock. It's a damn good one, too. Or maybe I'm getting rusty."

"You picked the lock." She nodded, as if it were no more than she'd expected. "You carry a concealed weapon—an ASP nine-millimeter..."

"Good eye, Lieutenant."

"And a knife that likely exceeds the legal limit," she continued. "Now it appears you also carry lock picks."

"They come in handy." And it was something he preferred not to dwell on when she was in this sort of mood. "Now, I figured you had a rough day, and you deserved coming home to a hot meal and some cold wine. I also figured you'd be a little testy coming in and finding me here. But I have to believe you'll come around after you've had a taste of my linguine."

Maybe, she thought, maybe if she closed her eyes for a minute, it would all go away. But when she tried it, he was still there, grinning at her. "Your linguine?"

"Linguine marinara. I'd claim it was my sainted mother's recipe, but she never boiled an egg in her life. How about that wine?"

"Sure. Why the hell not?"

"That's the way." He stepped back into the kitchen. De

ciding she could always kill him later, Althea followed. The aromas drifting through the air were heaven. "You like white," he said as he poured two glasses, using her best crystal. "This is a nice, full-bodied Italian that won't embarrass my sauce. Bold, but classy. See if it suits you."

She accepted the glass, allowed him to clink his against hers, then sipped. The wine tasted like liquid heaven. "Who the hell are you, Nightshade?"

"Why, I'm the answer to your prayers. Why don't we go in and sit down? You know you want to take your shoes off."

She did, but she obstinately kept them on as she walked back and lowered herself onto the couch. "Explain."

"I just did."

"If you cannot afford an attorney—"

"God, you're tough." He let out a long breath and stretched out beside her. "Okay, I have a couple of reasons. One, I know you've been putting in a lot of extra time on my business...."

"It's my—"

"Job?" he finished for her. "Maybe. But I know when someone's taking those extra steps, the kind that eat into personal time, and fixing you dinner's just a way of saying thanks."

It was a damn nice gesture, too, she thought, though she wasn't willing to say so. Yet. "You might have mentioned the idea to me earlier."

"It was an impulse. You ever have them?"

"Don't push your luck, Nightshade."

"Right. Well, to get back to the whys. There's also the fact that I haven't been able to snatch more than an hour at a time to clear this whole mess out of my head. Cooking helps me recharge. Maria wasn't likely to turn her stove over to me, so I thought of you." He reached out to curl a lock of her hair around his finger. "I think of you a lot. And finally, and simply, I wanted the evening with you."

He was getting to her. Althea wanted to believe that it was the glorious scents sneaking out of the kitchen that were weakening her. But she didn't believe it. "So you broke into my home and invaded my privacy."

"The only thing I poked into was your kitchen cupboards. It was tempting," he admitted, "but I didn't go any farther than that."

Frowning, Althea swirled the wine in her glass. "I don't like your methods, Nightshade. But I think I'm going to like your linguine."

She didn't like it. She adored it. It was difficult to harbor resentments when her palate was being so thoroughly seduced. She'd had men cook for her before, but she couldn't remember ever being so completely charmed.

Here was Colt Nightshade, very possibly armed to the teeth beneath his faded jeans and chambray shirt, serving her pasta by candlelight. Not that it was romantic, she thought. She was too smart to fall for any conventional trappings. But it was funny, and oddly sweet.

By the time she'd worked her way through one helping and was starting on a second, she'd filled him in on her progress. The lab reports were expected within twenty-four hours, the bartender at Clancy's was under surveillance, and an undercover officer was being prepped to hit the streets.

Colt filed her information away and traded it for some of his own. He'd talked to some of the local working girls that afternoon. Whether due to his charm or to the money that had changed hands, he'd learned that a girl who went by the street name Lacy hadn't been seen in any of her usual haunts for the past several weeks.

"She fits the profile," he continued, topping off Althea's wineglass. "Young, tiny. Girls said she was a brunette, but liked to wear a blond wig."

"Did she have a pimp?"

"Uh-uh. Free-lancer. I went by the rooms she'd been renting." Colt broke a piece of garlic bread in two and passed Althea half. "Talked to the landlord—a prince of a guy. Since she'd missed a couple of weekly rent payments, he'd packed up her stuff. Pawned what was worth anything, trashed the rest."

"I'll see if anybody at Vice knows about her."

"Good. I hit some of the shelters again," he went on. "The halfway houses, showing Liz's picture around, and the police sketches." He frowned, toying with the rest of his meal. "I couldn't get anyone to ID. Had a hard enough time convincing any of the kids that they should look at the pictures. Most of the kids want to act tough, invincible, and all you see is the confusion in their eyes."

"When you're dealing with that kind of confusion, you have to be tough. Most of them come from homes that are torn apart by drugs, drinking, physical and sexual abuse. Or they got into substance abuse all on their own and don't know how to get out again." She moved her shoulders. "Either way, running seems like the best way out."

"It wasn't like that for Liz."

"No," she agreed. It was time for him to turn it off, as well, she decided. If only for a few minutes. She scraped a last bite from her plate. "You know, Nightshade, you could give up playing the adventurer and go into catering. You'd make a fortune."

He understood what she was doing, and he put some effort into accommodating her. "I prefer small, private parties."

Her gaze flicked up to his, then back to her glass. "So, if it wasn't your sainted mother who taught you to make world-class linguine, who did?"

"We had this terrific Irish cook when I was growing up. Mrs. O'Malley."

"An Irish cook who taught you Italian cuisine."

"She could make anything—from lamb stew to coq au vin. 'Colt, me boy,' she used to tell me, 'the best thing a man can do for himself is to learn to feed himself well. Depending on a woman to fill your belly's a mistake.'" The memory made him grin. "When I'd gotten into trouble, which was most of the time, she'd sit me down in the kitchen. I'd get lectures on behavior, and the proper way to debone a chicken."

"Quite a combination."

"The stuff on behavior didn't stick." He toasted her. "But I make a hell of a chicken pot pie. And when Mrs. O'Malley retired—oh, almost ten years ago now—my mother went into a dark state of depression."

Althea's lips curved on the rim of her glass. "And hired another cook."

"A French guy with a bad attitude. She loves him."

"A French chef in Wyoming."

"I live in Wyoming," he said. "They live in Houston. We get along better that way. What about your family? Are they from around here?"

"I don't have one. What about your law degree? Why haven't you done anything with it?"

"I didn't say I hadn't." He studied her for a moment. She'd certainly dropped his question like a hot coal. It was something he'd have to come back to. "I found out I wasn't suited to spending hours hunched over law books, trying to outwit justice on technicalities."

"So you went into the air force."

"It was a good way to learn how to fly."

"But you're not a pilot."

"Sometimes I am." He smiled. "Sorry, Thea, I don't fit into a slot. I've got enough money that I can do what suits me when it suits me."

That wasn't good enough. "And the military didn't suit you?"

"For a while it did. Then I had enough." He shrugged and sat back. The candlelight flickered on his face and in his eyes. "I learned some things. Just like I learned from Mrs. O'Malley, and from prep school, from Harvard, and from this old Indian horse trainer I met in Tulsa some years back. You never know when you're going to use what you've learned."

"Who taught you to pick locks?"

"You're not going to hold that against me, are you?" He leaned forward to flick a finger over her hair, and to pour more wine. "I picked it up in the service. I was in what you might call a special detachment."

"Covert operations," she said, translating. It was no surprise. "That's why so much of your record's classified."

"It's old news, should be declassified by now. But that's the way of it, isn't it? Bureaucrats like secrets almost as much as they like red tape. What I did was gather information, or plant information, maybe defuse certain volatile situations, or stir them up, depending on the orders." He drank again. "I guess we could say I started doing favors for people—only these people ran the government." His lip curled. "Or tried to."

"You don't like the system, do you?"

"I like what works." For an instant only, his eyes darkened. "I saw plenty that didn't work. So..." He shrugged, and the mood was gone. "I got out, bought myself a few horses and cows, played rancher. Looks like old habits die hard, because now I do favors for people again. Only now I have to like them first."

"Some people might say that you've had a hard time deciding what you want to do when you grow up."

"Some people might. I figure I've been doing it. What about you? What's the back story on Althea Grayson?"

"It's nothing that would sell to the movies." Relaxed, she rested her elbows on the table, running a finger around the rim of her glass until the crystal sang. "I went straight into the academy when I was eighteen. No detours."

"Why?"

"Why a cop?" She mulled over her answer. "Because I do like the system. It's not perfect, but if you keep at it, you can make it work. And the law...there are people out there who want to make it work. Too many lives get lost in the cracks. It means something when you can pull one out."

"I can't argue with that." Without thinking about it, he laid a hand over hers. "I could always see that Boyd was meant to make law and order work. Until recently, he was about the only cop I respected enough to trust."

"I think you just gave me a compliment."

"You can be sure of it. The two of you have a lot in common. A clear-sightedness, a stubborn kind of valor, a steady compassion." He smiled, toying with her fingers. "The kid we got off the roof—I went to see her, too. She had a lot to say about the pretty lady with the red hair who brought her a baby doll."

"So I did a follow-up. It's my job to—"

"Bull." Delighted with her response, he picked up her hand, kissed it. "It had nothing to do with duty, and everything to do with you. Having a soft side doesn't make you less of a cop, Thea. It just makes you a kinder one."

She knew where this was leading, but she didn't pull her hand away. "Just because I have a soft spot for kids doesn't mean I've got one for you."

"But you do," he murmured. "I get to you." Watching her, he skimmed his lips down to her wrist. The pulse there beat steady, but it also beat fast. "I'm going to keep getting to you."

"Maybe you do." She was too smart to continue to deny the obvious. "That doesn't mean anything's going to come of it. I don't sleep with every man who attracts me."

"I'm glad to hear it. Then again, you're going to do a lot more than sleep with me." He chuckled and kissed her hand again. "God, I love it when you smirk, Thea. It drives me crazy. What I was going to say was, when we get each other to bed, sleeping's not going to be a priority. So maybe you should catch some shut-eye." He rose, pulling her to her feet. "Kiss me good-night, and I'll let you get some now."

The surprise in her eyes made him grin again. He'd wait until later to pat himself on the back for his strategy.

"You thought I cooked you dinner and kept you company so I could use it as a springboard to seduction." On a windy sigh, he shook his head. "Althea, I'm wounded. Close to crushed."

She laughed, keeping a friendly hand in his. "You know, Nightshade, sometimes I almost like you. Almost."

"See, that's just a couple of short steps away from you being nuts about me." He gathered her close, and the instant twisting in his gut mocked his light tone. "If I'd bothered to make dessert, you'd be begging for me."

Amused, she tucked her tongue in her cheek. "Your loss. Everybody knows cannoli turns me into a wild woman."

"I'll sure as hell remember that." He kissed her lightly, watched her smile. And felt his heart turn over. "There must be a bakery around here where I can pick up some Italian pastries."

"Nope. You missed your shot." She brought a hand to his chest, telling herself she was going to end the interlude now, while she could still feel her legs under her. "Thanks for the pasta."

"Sure." But he continued to stare down at her, his eyes sharpening, focusing, as if he were struggling to see past the ivory skin, the delicate bones. Something was happening here, he realized. Something internal that he couldn't quite get a grip on. "You have something in your eyes."

Her nerves were dancing. "What?"

"I don't know." He spoke slowly, as if measuring each word. "Sometimes I can almost see it. When I do, it makes me wonder where you've been. Where we're going."

Her lungs were backing up. She took a careful breath to clear them. "*You* were going home."

"Yeah. In a minute. Too easy to tell you you're beautiful," he murmured, as if speaking to himself. "You hear that too much, and it's too superficial to carry any weight with you. It should be enough for me, but there's something else in there. I keep coming back to it." Still seeking, he drew her closer. "What is it about you, Althea? What is it I can't shake loose?"

"There's nothing. You're too used to looking for shadows."

"No, you've got them." Slowly he slid a hand up to cup her cheek. "And what I have is a problem."

"What problem?"

"Try this."

He lowered his mouth to hers and had every muscle in her body going lax. It wasn't demanding, it wasn't urgent. It was devastating. The kiss tumbled her deeper, deeper, bombarding her with emotions she had no defense against. His feelings were free and ripe and poured over her, into her, so that she was covered and filled and surrounded by them.

No escape, she thought, and heard her own muffled sound of despair with a dull acceptance. He'd breached a defense she had taken for granted, one she might never fully shore up again.

She could tell herself again and again that she wouldn't fall in love, that she couldn't fall in love with a man she hardly knew. But her heart was already laughing at logic.

He felt her give—not all the way, not yet, but give yet another degree of self. There was more than heat here, though, sweet heaven, there was heat. But there was a kind of discovery, as well. For Colt, it was a revelation to discover that one woman—this woman—could tangle up his mind, rip open his heart, and leave him helpless.

"I'm losing ground here." He kept his hands firm on her shoulders as he pulled back. "I'm losing it fast."

"It's too much." It was a poor response, but the best she could summon.

"You're telling me." There was tension in her shoulders again, and in his. It compelled him to step away. "I've never felt like this before. And that's no line," he said when she turned away from him.

"I know. I wish it were." She gripped the back of the chair, where her shoulder holster hung. A symbol of duty, she thought. Of control, of what she had made of herself. "Colt, I think we're both getting in deeper than we might like."

"Maybe we've been treading water long enough."

She was very much afraid that she was ready, willing, even eager, to sink. "I don't let personal business interfere with my job. If we can't keep this under control, you should consider working with someone else."

"We've been working together just fine," he said between his teeth. "Don't pull out any lame excuses because you don't want to face up to what's going on between us."

"It's the best I've got." Her knuckles had turned white on the chair. "And it's not an excuse, only a reason. You want me to say you scare me. All right. You scare me. This scares me. And I don't think you want a partner who can't focus because you make her nervous."

"Maybe I'm happier with that than with one who's so focused it's hard to tell if she's human." She wasn't going to pull away from him now. He'd be damned if he'd let her. "Don't tell me you can't work on two levels, Thea, or that you can't function as a cop when you've got a problem in your personal life."

"Maybe I just don't want to work with you."

"That's tough. You're stuck. If you want to put this on

hold, I'll try to oblige you. But you're not backing off from Liz because you're afraid to let yourself feel something for me."

"I'm thinking about Liz, and what's best for her."

"How the hell would you know?" he exploded, and if it was unreasonable, he didn't give a damn. He was on the edge of falling in love with a woman who was calmly telling him she didn't want him in any area of her life. He was desperate to find a frightened girl, and the person who'd helped him make progress toward doing so was threatening to pull out. "How the hell would you know about her or anyone else? You've got yourself so wrapped up in regulations and procedure that you can't feel. No, not can't. Won't. You won't feel. You'll risk your life, but one brush with emotion and up goes the shield. Everything's so tidy for you, isn't it, Althea? There's some poor scared kid out there, but she's just another case for you, just another job."

"*Don't* you tell me how I feel." Her control snapped as she shoved the chair aside, clattering to the floor between them. "Don't tell me what I understand. You can't possibly know what's inside me. Do you think you know Liz, or any of those girls you talked with today? You've walked into shelters and halfway houses, and you think you understand?"

Her eyes glinted, not with tears, but with a rage so sharp he could only stand and let it slice at him. "I know there are plenty of kids who need help, and not always enough help to go around."

"Oh, that's so easy." She strode across the room and back in a rare show of useless motion. "Write a check, pass a bill, make a speech. It's so effortless. You haven't a clue what it's like to be alone, to be afraid or to be caught up in that grinding machine we toss displaced kids into. I spent most of my life in that machine, so don't tell me I don't feel. I know what it's like to want out so bad you run even when there's no place to go. And I know what it's like to be yanked back, to be helpless, to be abused and trapped and miserable. I understand plenty. And I know that Liz has a family who love her, and we'll get her back to them. No matter what, we'll get her back, and she won't be caught in that cycle. So don't you tell me she's just another case, because she matters. They all matter."

She broke off, running a shaky hand through her hair. At the moment, she wasn't sure which was bigger, her embarrassment or her anger. "I'd like you to go now," she said quietly. "I'd really like you to go."

"Sit down." When she didn't respond, he walked over and pressed her into a chair. She was trembling, and the fact that he'd played a part in causing that made him feel as if he'd punched a hole in something precious and fragile. "I'm sorry. That's a record for me, apologizing to the same person twice in one day." He started to brush a hand over her hair, but stopped himself. "Do you want some water?"

"No. I just want you to leave."

"I can't do it." He lowered himself to the footstool in front of her so that their eyes were level. "Althea…"

She sat back, her eyes shut. She felt as though she'd raced to the top of a mountain and leapt off. "Nightshade, I'm not in the mood to tell you my life story, so if that's what you're waiting for, you know where the door is."

"That'll keep." He took a chance and reached for her hand. It was steady now, he noted, but cold. "Let's try something else. What we've got here are two separate problems. Finding Liz is number one. She's an innocent, a victim, and she needs help. I could find her on my own, but that would take too long. Every day that goes by… Well, too many days have gone by already. I need you to work with me, because you can cut through channels it would take me twice as long to circumvent. And because I trust you to put everything you've got into getting her home."

"All right." She kept her eyes closed, willing the tension away. "We'll find her. If not tomorrow, the next day. But we'll find her."

"Second problem." He looked down at their hands, studying the way the second hand on her watch ticked off the time. "I think…ah, and since this is a new area for me, I want to qualify it by saying that it's only an opinion…"

"Nightshade." She opened her eyes again, and there was a ghost of a smile in them. "I swear you sound just like a lawyer."

He winced, shifted. "I don't think you should insult a man who's about to tell you he's pretty sure he's in love with you." She jolted. He'd have bet the farm that he could pull a gun and she wouldn't flinch. But mention love and she jumped six inches off the chair. "Don't panic," he continued while she searched for her voice. "I said 'I think.' That leaves us with a safe area to play with."

"Sounds more like a mine field to me." Because she was afraid it might start shaking again, she drew her hand away from his. "I think it would be wise, under the circumstances, to table that for the time being."

"Now who sounds like a lawyer?" He grinned, not at all sure why it seemed so appropriate to laugh at himself. "Darling, you think it puts the fear of God into you? Picture what it does to me. I only brought it up because I'm hoping that'll make it easier to deal with. For all I know, it's just a touch of the flu or something."

"That would be good." She choked back a laugh, terrified it would sound giddy. "Get plenty of rest, drink fluids."

"I'll give that a try." He leaned forward, not displeased to see the wariness in her eyes or the bracing of her shoulders. "But if it's not the flu, or some other bug, I'm going to do something about it. Whatever that might be can wait until we've settled the first problem. Until we do, I won't bring up love, or all the stuff that generally follows along after it—you know, like marriage and family and a two-car garage."

For the first time since he'd known her, he saw her totally at a loss. Her eyes were huge, and her mouth was slack. He would have sworn that if he tapped her, she'd keel over like a sapling in a storm.

"Guess it's just as well I don't, since talking about them in the abstract sense seems to have put you in a coma."

"I..." She managed to close her mouth, swallow, then speak. "I think you've lost your mind."

"Me, too." Lord knew why he felt so cheerful about it. "So for now let's concentrate on digging up those bad guys. Deal?"

"And if I agree, you're not going to sneak in any of that other stuff?"

His smile spread slowly. "Are you willing to take my word on it?"

"No." She steadied herself and smiled back. "But I'm willing to bet I can deflect anything you toss out."

"I'll take that bet." He held out a hand. "Partner." They shook, solemnly. "Now, why don't we—"

The phone interrupted what Althea was sure would have

been an unprofessional suggestion. She slipped by Colt and picked up the extension in the kitchen.

It gave him a moment to think about what he'd started. To smile. To think about how he'd like to finish it. Before he'd wound his fantasy up, she was striding back. She righted the chair, snagged her shoulder harness.

"Our friend Leo, the bartender? We just busted him for selling coke out of his back room." The warrior look was back on her face as she shrugged into the harness. "They're bringing him in for interrogation."

"I'm right behind you."

"Behind me is just where you'll stay, Nightshade," she said as she slipped into her blazer. "If Boyd clears it, you can observe through the glass, but that's the best deal you'll get."

He chafed at the restraint. "Let me sit in. I'll keep my mouth shut."

"Don't make me laugh." She grabbed her purse on the way to the door. "Take it or leave it—partner."

He swore at her, and slammed the door behind him. "I'll take it."

Chapter 7

Colt's initial frustration at being stuck behind the two-way glass faded as he watched Althea work. Her patient, detail by-detail interrogation had a style all its own. It surprised Colt to label that style not only meticulous, but relentless, as well.

She never allowed Leo to draw her off track, never betrayed any reaction to his sarcasm, and never—not even when Leo tried abusive language and veiled threats—raised her voice.

She played poker the same way, he remembered. Coolly, methodically, without a flicker of emotion until it was time to cash in her chips. But Colt was beginning to see through the aloof shell into the woman behind it.

Certainly he'd been able to surprise many varied emotion from the self-contained lieutenant. Passion, anger, sympathy, even speechless shock. He had a feeling he'd only scratched the surface. There was a wealth of emotions beneath that tidy, professional and undeniably stunning veneer. He intended to keep digging until he unearthed them all.

"Long night." Boyd came up behind him bearing two mugs of steaming coffee.

"I've had longer." Colt accepted the mug, sipped. "This stuff's strong enough to do the tango." He winced and drank again. "Does the captain usually come in for a routine interrogation?"

"The captain does when he has a personal interest." Fletcher watched Althea a moment, noting that she sat, serene and unruffled, as Leo jerkily lit one cigarette from the butt of another. "Is she getting anything?"

With some effort, Colt restrained an urge to beat against the glass just to prove he could do something. "He's still tap dancing."

"He'll wear out long before she does."

"I've already figured that out for myself." They both lapsed into silence as Leo snarled out a particularly foul insult and Althea responded by asking if he'd like to repeat that statement for the record. "She doesn't ruffle," Colt commented. "Fletch, have you ever seen the way a cat'll sit outside a mouse hole?" He flicked a glance at Boyd, then looked back through the glass. "That cat just sits there, hardly blinking, maybe for hours. Inside the hole, the mouse starts to go crazy. He can smell that cat, see those eyes staring in at him. After a while, I guess, the mouse circuits in his brain overload, and he makes a break for it. The cat just whips out one paw, and it's over."

Colt sipped more coffee, nodded at the glass. "That's one gorgeous cat."

"You've gotten to know her pretty well in a short amount of time."

"Oh, I've got a ways to go yet. All those layers," he murmured, almost to himself. "Can't say I've ever run into a woman who had me just as interested in peeling the layers of her psyche as peeling off her clothes."

The image had Boyd scowling into his coffee. Althea was a grown woman, he reminded himself, and more than able to take care of herself. Boyd remembered he'd been amused to find Colt and his former partner in a clinch in his kitchen. But the idea of it going further, of his friends leaping into the kind of quick, physical relationship that could leave them both battered at the finish, disturbed him.

Particularly when he thought of Colt's talent with women. It was a talent they both had, and both of them had enjoyed the benefits of that talent over the years. But they weren't discussing just any woman this time. This was Althea.

"You know," Boyd began, feeling his way with the care of a blind man in a maze, "Thea's special. She can handle pretty much anything that comes her way."

"And does," Colt added.

"Yeah, and does. But that's not to say that she doesn't have her vulnerabilities. I wouldn't want to see her hurt. I wouldn't like that at all."

Mildly surprised, Colt lifted a brow. "A warning? Sounds like the same kind you gave me about your sister Natalie about a million years ago."

"Comes to the same thing. Thea's family."

"And you think I could hurt her."

Boyd let out a weary breath. He wasn't enjoying this conversation. "I'm saying, if you did, I'd have to bruise several of your vital organs. I'd be sorry, but I'd have to do it."

Colt acknowledged that with a thoughtful nod. "Who won the last time we went at it?"

Despite his discomfort, Boyd grinned. "I think it was a draw."

"Yeah, that's how I remember it. It was over a woman then, too, wasn't it?"

"Cheryl Anne Madigan." This time Boyd's sigh was nostalgic.

"Little blonde?"

"Nope, tall brunette. Big...blue eyes."

"Right." Colt laughed, shook his head. "I wonder whatever happened to pretty Cheryl Anne."

They fell into a comfortable silence for a moment, reminiscing. Through the speakers they could hear Althea's calm, relentless questioning.

"Althea's a long way from Cheryl Anne Madigan," Colt murmured. "I wouldn't want to hurt her, but I can't promise it won't happen. The thing is, Fletch, for the first time I've run into a woman who matters enough to hurt me back." Colt took another bracing sip. "I think I'm in love with her."

Boyd choked and was forced to set down his mug before he dumped the contents all over his shirt. He waited a beat, tapped a hand against his ear as if to clear it. "You want to say that again? I don't think I caught it."

"You heard me," Colt muttered. Leave it to a friend, he thought, to humiliate you at an emotionally vulnerable moment. "I got almost the same reaction from her when I told her."

"You told her?" Boyd struggled to keep one ear on the interrogation while he absorbed this new and fascinating information. "What did she say?"

"Not much of anything."

The frustration in Colt's voice tickled Boyd so much, he had to bite the tip of his tongue to keep from grinning. "Well at least she didn't laugh in your face."

"She didn't seem to think it was very funny." Colt blew out a breath and wished Boyd had thought to lace the coffee with a good dose of brandy. "She just sat there, going pale, kind of gaping at me."

"That's a good sign." Boyd patted Colt's shoulder comfortingly. "It's real hard to throw her off that way."

"I figured it was best if it was out, you know? It would give us both time to decide what to do about it." He smiled through the glass at Althea, who continued to sit, cool and unruffled, while Leo gulped down water with a trembling hand. "Though I've pretty much figured out what I'm going to do about it."

"Which is?"

"Well, unless I wake up some morning real soon and realize I've had some sort of brain seizure, I'm going to marry her."

"Marry her?" Boyd rocked back on his heels and chuckled. "You and Thea? Lord, wait until I tell Cilla."

The murderous look Colt aimed at him only made Boyd's grin widen.

"I can't thank you enough for your support here, Fletch."

Boyd gamely swallowed another chuckle, but he couldn' defeat the grin. "Oh, you've got it, pal. All the way. It's just that I never thought I'd be using the word *marriage* in the same sentence with *Colt Nightshade.* Or *Althea Grayson,* for that matter. Believe me, I'm with you all the way."

* * *

Inside the interrogation room, Althea continued to wear down her quarry. She scented his fear, and used it ruthlessly.

"You know, Leo, a little cooperation would go a long way."

"Sure, a long way to seeing me greased like Wild Bill."

Althea inclined her head. "As much as it pains me to offer , you'd have protection."

"Right." Leo snorted out smoke. "You think I want cops n my butt twenty-four hours a day? You think it would work I did?"

"Maybe not." She used her disinterest as another tool, lowing down the pace of the interview until Leo was squirm- ng in his chair. "But, then again, no cooperation, no shield. ou go out of here naked, Leo."

"I'll take my chances."

"That's fine. You'll make bail on the drug charges—prob- bly deal them down so you won't do any time to speak of. ut it's funny how word spreads on the street, don't you aink?" She let that thought simmer in his brain. "Interested arties already know you've been tagged, Leo. And when you valk out, they won't be real sure about what you might have pilled while you were inside."

"I didn't tell you anything. I don't know anything."

"That's too bad. Because it might work against you, this gnorance. You see, we're closing in, and those same inter- sted parties might wonder if you helped out." Casually she pened a file and revealed the police sketches. "They might vonder if I got the descriptions of these suspects from you."

"I didn't give you anything." Sweat popped out on Leo's prehead as he stared at the sketches. "I never seen those uys before."

"Well, that may be. But I'd have to say—if the subject came up—that I talked with you. A long time. And that I have detailed sketches of suspects. You know, Leo," she added, leaning toward him, "some people add two and two and get five. Happens all the time."

"That ain't legal." He moistened his lips. "It's blackmail."

"Don't hurt my feelings. You want me to be your friend, Leo." She nudged the sketches toward him. "You see, it's all a matter of attitude, and whether or not I care if you walk out of here and end up a smear on the sidewalk. Can't say I do at the moment." She smiled, chilling him. "Now, if you were my friend, I'd do everything I could to make sure you lived a long and happy life. Maybe not in Denver, maybe someplace new. You know, Leo, a change of scene can work wonders. Change your name, change your life."

Something flickered in his eyes. She knew it was doubt. "You talking witness protection program?"

"I could be. But if I'm going to ask for something that big, I have to be able to prime the pump." When he hesitated, she sighed. "You'd better choose sides, pal. Remember Wild Bill? All he did was meet a guy. They might have been talking about the Broncos' chances for the Superbowl. Nobody gave him the benefit of the doubt. They just iced him."

The fear was back, running in the sweat down his temples. "I get immunity. And you drop the drug charges."

"Leo, Leo…" Althea shook her head. "A smart man like you knows how life works. You give me something, if it's good enough, I give you something back. It's the American way."

He licked his lips again, lit yet another cigarette. "Maybe I've seen these two before."

"These two?" Althea tapped the sketches, and then, like Colt's cat, she pounced. "Tell me."

It was 2:00 a.m. before she was finished. She'd questioned Leo, listened to his long, rambling story, made notes, made him backtrack, repeat, expand. Then she'd called in a police stenographer and had Leo go over the same ground again, making an official statement for the tape.

She was energized as she strode back to her office. She had names now, names to run through the computer. She had threads—thin threads, perhaps, but threads nonetheless, tying an organization together.

Much of what Leo had told her was speculation and gossip. But Althea knew that a viable investigation could be built on less.

Peeling off her jacket, she sat at her desk and booted up her computer. She was peering at the screen when Colt walked in and stuck a cup under her nose.

"Thanks." She sipped, winced and spared him a glance. "What is this? It tastes like a meadow."

"Herbal tea," he told her. "You've had enough coffee."

"Nightshade, you're not going to spoil our relationship by thinking you have to take care of me, are you?" She set the cup aside and went back to the screen.

"You're wired, Lieutenant."

"I know how much I can take before the system overloads. Aren't you the one who keeps saying time's what we don't have?"

"Yeah." From his position behind her chair, he lowered his hands to her shoulders and began to rub. "You did a hell of a job with Leo," he said before she could shrug his hands off.

"If I ever decide to go back to law, I'd hate to have you take on one of my clients."

"More compliments." His fingers were magic, easing without weakening, soothing without softening. "I didn't get as much as I wanted, but I think I got all he had."

"He's small-time," Colt agreed. "Passing a little business to the big boys, taking his commission."

"He doesn't know the main player. I'm sure he was telling the truth about that. But he ID'd the two Meena described. Remember the cameraman she'd told us about—the big African-American? Look." She gestured toward the screen. "Matthew Dean Scott, alias Dean Miller, alias Tidal Wave Dean."

"Catchy."

"He played some semipro football about ten years ago. Made a career out of unnecessary roughness. He broke an opposing quarterback's leg."

"These things happen."

"After the game."

"Ah, a poor sport. What else have we got on him?"

"I'll tell you what else *I've* got on him," she said, but she couldn't resist leaning back against his massaging hands. "He was fired for breaking training—having a woman in his room."

"Boys will be boys."

"This particular woman was tied up and screaming her lungs out. They dealt it down from rape to assault, but Scott's football days were over. After that, we've got him on a couple more assaults, indecent exposure, drunk and disorderly, petty larceny, lewd behavior." She punched another button on the key-board. "That was up to four years ago. After that, nothing."

"You figure he turned over a new leaf? Became a pillar of the community?"

"Sure, just like I believe men read girlie magazines because of the erudite articles."

"That's what motivates me." Grinning, he leaned down to kiss the top of her head.

"I bet. We've got a similar history on contestant number two," she continued. "Harry Kline, a small-time actor from New York whose rap sheet includes drunk and disorderly, possession, sexual assault, several DWIs. He drifted into porno films about eight years ago, and was, incredibly enough, fired from several jobs because of his violent and erratic behavior. He headed west, got a few similar gigs in California, then was arrested for raping one of his costars. The defense pleaded it down and, due to the victim's line of work, made it all go away. The victim's only justice came from the fact that Harry was finished in film—blue or otherwise. Nobody even partially legit would touch him. That was five years ago. There's been nothing on him since."

"Once again, one would think our friends either became solid citizens or died in their sleep."

"Or found a handy hole to hide in. Leo claimed that he was first approached—by Kline—two, maybe three years ago. He knows it was at least two. Kline wanted women, young women who were interested in making private films. Citing free enterprise, Leo obliged him and took his commission. The number he was given to contact Kline is out of service. I'll run it through the phone company to see if it was the penthouse or another location."

"He never saw the other man, the one Meena said sat off in the corner?"

"No. His only contacts were Scott and Kline. Apparently Scott would drop in for a few drinks and brag about how good he was with a camera, and how much money he was pulling in."

"And about the girls," Colt said under his breath. The fingers rubbing Althea's shoulders went rigid. "How he and his friends had— How did he put it? The pick of the litter?"

"Don't think about it." Instinctively she lifted a hand to cover his. "Don't, Colt. You'll mess up if you do. We're a big step closer to finding her. That's what you have to concentrate on."

"I am." He turned away and paced to the far wall. "I'm also concentrating on the fact that if I find out either of those slime touched Liz, I'm going to kill them." He turned back, his eyes blank. "You won't stop me, Thea."

"Yes, I will." She rose and went to him to take both of his fisted hands in hers. "Because I understand how much you'll want to. And that if you do, it won't change what happened. It won't help Liz. But we'll cross that bridge after we find her." She gave his hands a hard squeeze. "Don't go renegade on me now, Nightshade. I'm just starting to like working with you."

He pulled himself back, let himself look down at her. Though her eyes were shadowed and her cheeks were pale with fatigue, he could feel energy vibrating from her. She was offering him something. Compassion—with restrictions, of course. And hope, without any. The viciousness of his anger faded into the very human need for the comfort of contact.

"Althea..." His hands relaxed. "Let me hold you, will you?" She hesitated, her brow lifting in surprise. He could only smile. "You know, I'm beginning to read you pretty well.

You're worried about your professional image, snuggling up against a guy in your office." Sighing, he brushed a hand through her hair. "Lieutenant, it's almost three in the morning. There's nobody here to see. And I really need to hold you."

Once again she let instinct rule, and she moved into his arms. Every time, she mused as she settled her head in the curve of his neck, every time they stood like this, they fitted perfectly. And each time it was easier to admit it.

"Feel better?" she asked, and felt him move his head against her hair.

"Yeah. He didn't know anything about Lacy, the girl who's missing?"

"No." Without thinking, she stroked his back, soothing muscles there as he had soothed hers. "And when I mentioned the possibility of murder, he was genuinely shaken. He wasn't faking that. That's why I'm certain he gave us everything he had."

"The house in the mountains." Colt let his eyes close. "He couldn't give us much."

"West or maybe north of Boulder, near a lake." She moved her shoulders. "It's a little better than we had before. We'll narrow it down, Colt."

"I feel like I'm not putting the pieces together."

"We're putting the pieces we have together," she told him. "And you're feeling that way because you're tired. Go home." She eased back so that she could look up at him. "Get some sleep. We'll start fresh in the morning."

"I'd rather go home with you."

Amused, exasperated, she could only shake her head. "Don't you ever quit?"

"I didn't say I expected to, only that I'd rather." Lifting his hands, he framed her face, stroking his thumbs over her cheekbones, then back to her temples. "I want time with you, Althea. Time when there isn't so much on my mind, or on yours. Time to be with you, and time to figure out what it is about, just you, that makes me start thinking of long-term, permanent basis."

Instantly wary, she backed out of his arms. "Don't start that now, Nightshade."

Instantly relaxed, he grinned. "That sure does make you nervous. I never knew anyone so spooked by the thought of marriage—unless it was me. Makes me wonder why—and whether I should just sweep you right off your feet and find out the reasons after I've got a ring on your finger. Or—" he moved toward her, backing her against the desk "—if I should take things real slow, real easy, sliding you into the *I do*'s so slick that you wouldn't know you were hitched until it was over and done."

"Either way, you're being ridiculous." There was something lodged in her throat. Althea recognized it as nerves, and bitterly resented it. Feigning indifference, she picked up the tea and sipped. Now it tasted like cold flowers. "It's late," she said. "You go ahead. I can requisition a unit and drive myself home."

"I'll take you." He caught her chin in his hand and waited until her eyes were level with his. "And I mean that, Thea. Any way I can get you. But you're right—it's late. And I owe you."

"You don't—" Her denial ended on a moan when his mouth swooped down to cover hers.

She tasted frustration in the kiss, a jagged need that was

barely restrained. And most difficult of all to resist, she tasted the sweetness of affection, like a thin, soothing balm over the pulsing heat.

"Colt." Even as she murmured his name against his mouth, she knew she was losing. Her arms had already lifted to wrap around him, to bring him closer, to accept and to demand.

Her body betrayed her. Or was it her heart? She could no longer tell the two apart, as the needs of one so closely matched the needs of the other. Her fingers dug deep into his shoulders as she struggled to regain her balance. Then they went lax as she allowed herself one moment of madness.

It was Colt who drew back—for himself, and for her. She'd become more important than the satisfactions of the moment. "I owe you," he said again, carefully spacing the words as he stared down into her eyes. "If I didn't, I wouldn't let you go tonight. I don't think I could. I'll drive you home." He picked up her jacket, offered it to her. "Then I'm probably going to spend the rest of the night wondering what it would have been like if I'd just locked that door there and let nature take its course."

Shaken, she draped her jacket over her shoulders before walking to the door. But she'd be damned if she'd be outdone or outmaneuvered. She paused and sent one slow smile over her shoulder. "I'll tell you what it would have been like, Nightshade. It would have been like nothing you've ever experienced. And when I'm ready—if I'm ever ready—I'll prove it."

Stunned by the punch of that single cool smile, he watched her saunter off. Letting out a long breath, he pressed a hand to the knot in his gut. Sweet God, he thought, this was the woman for him. The only woman for him. And damned if *he* wasn't ready to prove it.

* * *

With four hours' sleep, two cups of black coffee and a cherry Danish under her belt, Althea was ready to roll. By 9:00 a.m., she was at her desk, putting through a call to the telephone company with an official request for a check on the number she'd gotten from Leo. By 9:15, she had a name and address, and the information that the customer had cancelled the service only forty-eight hours before.

Though she didn't expect to find anything, she was putting in a request for a search warrant when Colt walked in.

"You don't let moss grow under your feet, do you?"

Althea hung up the phone. "I don't let anything grow under my feet. I've got a line on the number from Leo. The customer canceled the service. I imagine we'll find the place cleaned out, but I can pick up a search warrant within the hour."

"That's what I love about you, Lieutenant—no wasted moves." He eased a hip down on her desk—and was delighted to discover she smelled as good as she looked. "How'd you sleep?"

She slanted a look up at him. Direct challenge. "Like a rock. You?"

"Never better. I woke up this morning with a whole new perspective. Can you be ready to roll by noon?"

"Roll where?"

"This idea I had. I ran it by Boyd, and he—" He scowled down at her shrilling phone. "How many times a day does that ring?"

"Often enough." She plucked up the receiver. "Grayson. Yes, this is Lieutenant Althea Grayson." Her head snapped up. "Jade." With a nod for Colt, Althea covered the receiver. "Line two," she whispered. "And keep your mouth shut." She continued to listen as Colt shot from the room to pick up an extension. "Yes, we have been looking for you. I appreciate you calling in. Can you tell me where you are?"

"I'd rather not." Jade's voice was thin, jumping with nerves. "I only called because I don't want any trouble. I'm getting a job and everything. A straight job. If there's trouble with the cops, I'll lose it."

"You're not in any trouble. I contacted your mother because you can be of some help on a case I'm investigating." Althea swiveled her chair to the right so that she could see Colt through the doorway. "Jade, you remember Liz, don't you? The girl whose parents you wrote?"

"I...I guess. Maybe."

"It took a lot of courage to write that letter, and to get out of the situation you'd found yourself in. Liz's parents are very grateful to you."

"She was a nice kid. Didn't really know the score, you know? She wanted out." Jade paused, and Althea heard the sound of a scraping match, a deep intake of breath. "Listen, there was nothing I could do for her. We only had a couple of minutes alone once or twice. She slipped me the address, asked me if I'd write her folks. Like I said, she was a nice kid in a bad spot."

"Then help me find her. Tell me where they've got her."

"I don't know. Man, I really don't. They took a couple of us up in the mountains a few times. Really out there, you know. Wilderness stuff. They had this really classy cabin, though. First-rate, with a Jacuzzi, and a big stone fireplace, and this big-screen TV."

"Which way did you go out of Denver? Can you remember that?"

"Well, yeah, sort of. It was like Route 36, toward Boulder, but we just kept going on it forever. Then we took this other little road for a while. Not a highway. One of those two-lane winding jobs."

"Do you remember going by any towns? Anything that sticks out in your mind?"

"Boulder. After that there wasn't much."

"Did you go up in the morning, afternoon, night?"

"The first time it was in the morning. We got a really early start."

"After Boulder, was the sun in front of you, or behind?"

"Oh, I get it. Ah…I guess it was kind of behind us."

Althea continued to press for details, about the location, the routine, descriptions of the people Jade had seen. As a witness, Jade proved vague but cooperative. Still, Althea had no problem recognizing Scott and Kline from Jade's descriptions. There was again a mention of a man who stayed in the background, keeping to the shadows, watching.

"He was creepy, you know?" Jade continued. "Like a spider, just hanging there. The job paid good, so I went back a couple of times. Three hundred for one day, and a fifty-dollar bonus if they needed you for two. I… You know you just can't make that kind of money on the street."

"I know. But you stopped going."

"Yeah, because sometimes they got really rough. I had bruises all over me, and one of the guys even split my lip while we were doing this scene. I got scared, because it didn't seem like they were acting. It seemed like they wanted to hurt you. I told Wild Bill, and he said how I shouldn't go back. And that he wasn't going to send any more girls. He said he was going to do some checking into it, and if it was bad, he was going to talk to his cop. I knew that was you, so that's why I called back when I got the message. Bill thinks you're okay."

Wearily Althea rubbed a hand over her brow. She didn't tell Jade that she should be using the past tense as far as Wild Bill was concerned. She didn't have the heart. "Jade, you said something in your letter about thinking they'd killed one of the girls."

"I guess I did." Her voice quavered, weakened. "Listen, I'm not going to testify or anything. I'm not going back there."

"I can't promise anything, only that I'll try to keep you out of it. Tell me why you think they killed one of the girls."

"I told you how they could get rough. And it wasn't no playacting, either. The last time I was up, they really hurt me. That's when I decided I wasn't going back. But Lacy, that's a girl I hung with some, she said how she could handle it, and how the money was too good to pass up. She went up again, but she never came back. I never saw her again."

She paused, another match scraped. "It's not like I can prove anything. It's just... She left all her stuff in her room, 'cause I checked. Lacy was real fond of her things. She had this collection of glass animals. Real pretty, crystal, like. She wouldn't have left them behind. She'd have come back for them, if she could. So I thought she was dead, or they were keeping her up there, like with Liz. And I figured I better split before they tried something with me."

"Can you give me Lacy's full name, Jade? Any other information about her?"

"She was just Lacy. That's all I knew. But she was okay."

"All right. You've been a lot of help. Why don't you give me a number where I can contact you?"

"I don't want to. Look, I've told you all I know. I want out of it. I told you, I'm starting over out here."

Althea didn't press. It was a simple matter to get the number from the phone company. "If you think of anything else, no matter how insignificant it seems, will you call me back?"

"I guess. Look, I really hope you get the kid out of there, and give those creeps what they deserve."

"We will. Thanks."

"Okay. Say hi to Wild Bill."

Before Althea could think of a reply, Jade broke the connection. When she looked up, Colt was standing in her doorway. His eyes held that blank, dangerous look again.

"You can get her back here. Material witness."

"Yeah, I could." Althea dialed the phone again. She'd get the number now. Keep it for backup. "But I won't." She held up a hand for silence before Colt could speak, and made the official request to the operator.

"A 212 area code," Colt noted as Althea scribbled on her pad. "You can get the NYPD to pick her up."

"No," she said simply, then slipped the pad into her purse and rose.

"Why the hell not?" Colt grabbed her arm as she reached for her coat. "If you can get that much out of her on the phone, you'd get that much more face-to-face."

"It's because I got that much out of her." Resentful of his interference, she jerked away. "She gave me everything she had, just for the asking. No threats, no promises, no maneuvering. I asked, she answered. I don't betray trusts, Nightshade. If I need her to drop the hammer on these bastards, then I'll use her. But not until then, and not if there's another way. And not," she added deliberately, "without her consent. Is that clear?"

"Yeah." He scrubbed his hands over his face. "Yeah, it's clear. And you're right. So, you want to pick up that warrant, check that other address?"

"Yes. Do you intend to tag along?"

"You bet. We should have just enough time to finish that before we take off."

She stopped in the doorway. "Take off?"

"That's right, Lieutenant. You and I are taking a little trip. I'll tell you all about it on the way."

Chapter 8

"I think we've all lost our minds." Althea gripped her seat as the nose of the Cessna rose into the soft autumn sky.

Comfortable at the controls, Colt spared her a glance. "Come on, tough stuff, don't you like planes?"

"Sure I like planes." A tricky patch of cross-currents sent the Cessna rocking. "But I like them with flight attendants."

"There's stuff in the galley. Once we level off, you can serve yourself."

That wasn't precisely what she'd meant, but Althea said nothing, just watched the land tilt away. She enjoyed flying, really. It was just that she had a routine. She would strap in, adjust her headset to the music of her choice, open a book and zone out for the length of the flight.

She didn't like to think of all the gauges over which she had no control.

"I still think this is a waste of time."

"Boyd didn't argue," Colt pointed out. "Look, Thea, we know the general location of the cabin. I studied that damn tape until my eyes bugged out. I'll recognize it when I see it, and plenty of the surrounding landmarks. This is worth a shot."

"Maybe" was all she'd give him.

"Think about it." Colt banked the plane and set his course. "They know the heat's on. That's why they pulled out of the penthouse. They're going to be wondering where that tape ended up, and if they try to contact Leo, they won't find him, since you've got him stashed in a safe house."

"So they'll stay out of Denver," she agreed. The engines were an irritating roar in her ears. "They might even pull up stakes and move on."

"That's just what I'm afraid of." Colt's mouth thinned as they left Denver behind. "What happens to Liz if they do? None of the options have a happy ending."

"No." That, and Boyd's approval, had convinced her to go with Colt. "No, they don't."

"I have to think they'd stick to the cabin for the time being. Even if they figure we know it exists, they wouldn't think we'd know its location. They don't know about Jade."

"I'll give you that, Nightshade. But it seems to me that you're relying on blind luck to guide you there."

"I've been lucky before. Better?" he asked when the plane leveled. "It's pretty up here, don't you think?"

There was snow on the peaks to the north, and there were broad, flat valleys between the ridges. They were cruising low enough that she could make out cars along the highway, communities that were little huddles of houses, and the deep, thick green of the forest to the west.

"It has its points." A thought erupted in her mind, making her swivel her head in his direction. "Do you have a pilot's license, Nightshade?"

He glanced over, stared, then nearly collapsed with laughter. "Lord, I'm crazy about you, Lieutenant. Do you want one of those big blowout weddings or the small, intimate kind?"

"You're crazy, period," she muttered, and shifted deliberately to stare out through the windscreen. She'd check on his license when they got back to Denver. "And you said you weren't going to bring up that kind of thing."

"I lied." He said it cheerfully. Despite the worry that never quite dissipated, he didn't think he'd ever felt better in his life. "I've got a problem with that. A woman like you could probably cure me of it."

"Try a psychiatrist."

"Thea, we're going to make a hell of a pair. Wait until my family gets a load of you."

"I'm not meeting your family." She attributed the sudden hollowness in her stomach to another spot of turbulence.

"Well, you're probably right about that—at least until we're ready to walk down the aisle. My mother tends to manage everything, but you can handle her. My father likes spit and polish, which means the two of you would get along like bacon and eggs. A regulation type, that's the admiral."

"Admiral?" she repeated, despite her vow to remain stubbornly silent.

"Navy man. Broke his heart when I joined the air force." Colt shrugged. "That's probably why I did it. Then I have this aunt… Well, better you should meet them for yourself."

"I'm not meeting your family," she said again, annoyed that the statement sounded more petulant than firm. She unstrapped herself and marched back into the tiny galley, rooting about until she found a can of nuts and a bottle of mineral water. Curiosity had her opening the small refrigerated compartment and studying a tin of caviar and a bottle of Beaujolais. "Whose plane is this?"

"Some friend of Boyd's. A weekend jockey who likes to take women up."

Her answer to that was a grunt as she came back to take her seat. "Must be Frank the lecher. He's been after me to fly the sexy skies for years." She chose a cashew.

"Oh, yeah? Not your type?"

"He's so obvious. But then, men tend to be."

"I'll have to remind myself to be subtle. You going to share those?"

She offered the can. "Is that Boulder?"

"Yep. I'm going to track northwest from here, circle around some. Boyd tells me he has a cabin up here."

"Yes. Lots of people do. They like to escape from the city on weekends and tramp through the snow."

"Not your speed?"

"I don't see any purpose for snow unless you're skiing. And the main purpose of skiing, as far as I'm concerned, is coming back to a lodge and having hot buttered rum in front of a fire."

"Ah, you're the adventurous type."

"I live for adventure. Actually, Boyd's place does have a nice view," she admitted. "And the kids get a big kick out of it."

"So you've been there."

"A few times. I like it better in late spring, early summer, when there isn't much chance of the roads being closed." She glanced down at the patchy snow in the foothills. "I hate the thought of being stuck."

"It might have its advantages."

"Not for me." She was silent for a time, watching hills and trees take over from city and suburbs. "It is pretty," she conceded. "Especially from up here. Like a segment on public television."

He grinned at that. "Nature at a distance? I thought city girls always yearned for a country retreat."

"Not this city girl. I'd rather—" There was a violent bump that sent nuts flying and had Althea grabbing for a handhold. "What the hell was that?"

Narrow-eyed, Colt studied his gauges while he fought to bring the nose of the plane back up. "I don't know."

"You don't know? What do you mean, you don't know? You're supposed to know!"

"Shh!" He tilted his head to listen hard to the engines. "We're losing pressure," he said, with the icy calm that had kept him alive in war-torn jungles, in deserts and in skies alive with flak.

Once she understood that the trouble was serious, Althea responded in kind. "What do we do?"

"I'm going to have to set her down."

Althea looked down, studying the thick trees and rocky hills fatalistically. "Where?"

"According to the map, there's a valley a few degrees east." Colt adjusted the course, fighting the wheel as he jiggled switches. "Watch for it," he ordered, then flipped on his radio. "Boulder tower, this is Baker Able John three."

"There." Althea pointed to what looked to be a very narrow spit of flat land between jagged peaks. Colt nodded, and continued to inform the tower of his situation.

"Hang on," he told her. "It's going to be a little rough."

She braced herself, refusing to look away as the land rushed up to meet them. "I heard you were good, Nightshade."

"You're about to find out." He cut speed, adjusting for the drag of currents as he finessed the plane toward the narrow valley.

Like threading a needle, Althea thought. Then she sucked in her breath at the first vicious thud of wheels on land. They bounced, teetered, shook, then rolled to a gentle halt.

"You okay?" Colt asked instantly.

"Yeah." She let out a breath. Her stomach was inside out, but apart from that she thought she was all in one piece. "Yeah, I'm fine. You?"

"Dandy." He reached out, grabbed her face in both of his hands and dragged her, straining against her seat belt, close enough to kiss. "By damn, Lieutenant," he said, and kissed her again, hard. "You never flinched. Let's elope."

"Can it." When a woman was used to level emotions, it was difficult to know what to do when she had the urge to laugh and scream simultaneously. She shoved him away. "You want to let me out of this thing? I could use some solid ground under my feet."

"Sure." He released the door, even helped her alight. "I'm going to radio in our position," he told her.

"Fine." Althea took a deep gulp of fresh, cold air and tried out her legs. Not too wobbly, she discovered, pleased. All in all, she'd handled her first—and hopefully last—forced landing rather well. She had to give Colt credit, she mused as she looked around. He'd chosen his spot, and he'd made it work.

She didn't get down on her knees and kiss the ground, but she was grateful to feel it under her. As an added bonus, the view was magnificent. They were cupped between mountain and forest, sheltered from the wind, low enough to look up at the snow cascading down from the rocky peaks without being inconvenienced by it.

There was a good clean scent to the air, a clear blue sky overhead, and a bracing chill that stirred the blood. With any luck, a rescue could be accomplished within the hour, so she could afford to enjoy the scenery without being overwhelmed by the solitude.

She was feeling in tune with the world when she heard Colt clamber out of the cockpit. She even smiled at him.

"So, when are they coming to get us?"

"Who?"

"Them. Rescue people. You know, those selfless heroes who get people out of tricky situations such as this."

"Oh, them. They're not." He dropped a tool chest on the ground, then went back inside for a short set of wooden steps.

"Excuse me?" Althea managed when she found her voice. She knew it was an illusion, but the mountains suddenly seemed to loom larger. "Did you say no one's coming to get us? Isn't the radio working?"

"Works fine." Colt climbed on the steps and uncovered the engine. He'd already stuck a rag in the back pocket of his jeans. "I told them I'd see if I could do the repairs on-site and keep in contact."

"You told them—" She moved fast, before either of them understood her intention. Her first swing caught him in the kidneys and had him tumbling off the steps. "You *idiot!* What do you mean, you'll do the repairs?" She swung again, but he dodged, more baffled than annoyed. "This isn't a Ford broken down on the highway, Nightshade. We haven't got a damn flat tire."

"No," he said carefully, braced and ready for her next move. "I think it's the carburetor."

"You think it's—" Her breath whistled out through her teeth, and her eyes narrowed. "That's it. I'm going to kill you with my bare hands."

She launched herself at him. Colt made a split-second decision, pivoted, and let her momentum carry them both to the ground. It only took him another second to realize the lady was no slouch at hand-to-hand. He took one on the chin that snapped his teeth together. It looked like it was time to get serious.

He scissored his legs around her and managed, after a short, grunting tussle, to roll her onto her back. "Hold on, will you? Somebody's going to get hurt!"

"You're damn right."

Since reason wouldn't work, he used his weight, levering himself over her as he cuffed her wrists with his hands. She bucked twice, then went still. They both knew she was only biding her time until she found an opening.

"Listen." He gave himself another moment to catch his breath, then spoke directly into her ear. "It was the most logical alternative."

"That's bull."

"Let me explain. If you still disagree afterward, we'll go for two falls out of three. Okay?" When she didn't respond, Colt set his teeth. "I want your word you won't take another punch at me until I finish."

It was a pity he couldn't see her expression at that moment. "Fine," Althea said tightly. Cautious, Colt eased back until he could watch her face. He was halfway into a sitting position when she brought her knee solidly into his crotch.

He didn't have the breath to curse her as he rolled into a ball.

"That wasn't a punch," she pointed out. She took the time to smooth back her hair, brush down her parka, before she rose. "Okay, Nightshade, let's hear it."

He only lifted a hand, made a couple of woofing noises, and waited for the stars to fade from behind his eyes. "You may have endangered our bloodline, Thea." He got creakily to his knees, breathing shallowly. "You fight dirty."

"It's the only way to fight. Spill it."

As his strength returned, he shot her a killing look. "I owe you. I owe you big. We're not injured," he ground out. "At least I wasn't until you started on me. The plane's undamaged. If you'll take a look around, you'll see that there isn't room to land another plane safely. They could send a copter, lift us out, but for what? Odds are, if I make a few minor adjustments I can fly us out."

Maybe it made sense, Althea thought. Maybe. But it didn't alter one simple fact. "You should have consulted me. I'm here, too, Nightshade. You had no right to make that decision on your own."

"My mistake." He turned to walk—limp—back to the steps. "I figured you were the logical type and, being a public servant, wouldn't want to see other public servants pulled out for an unnecessary rescue. And, damn it, Liz might be over that ridge." With a violent clatter, he pulled a wrench from the toolbox. "I'm not going back without her."

Oh, he would have to push that button, Althea thought as she turned away to stare into the deep green of the neighboring forest. He would have to let her hear that terrible worry in his voice, see the fire of it in his eyes.

He would have to be perfectly and completely right.

Pride was the hardest of all pills to swallow. Making the effort, she turned back and walked to stand beside the steps. "I'm sorry. I shouldn't have lost my temper."

His response was a grunt.

"Does it still hurt?"

He looked back down at her then, with a gleam in his eyes that would have made lesser women grovel. "Only when I breathe."

She smiled and patted his leg. "Try to think about something else. Do you want me to hand you tools or something?"

His eyes only narrowed further, until they were thin blue slits. "Do you know the difference between a ratchet and a torque wrench?"

"No." She tossed her hair back. "Why should I? I have a perfectly competent mechanic to look after my car."

"And if you break down on the highway?"

She sent him a pitying look. "What do you think?"

He ground his teeth and went back to the carburetor. "If I made a comment like that, you'd call it sexist."

She grinned behind his back, but when she spoke, her voice was sober. "Why is calling a tow truck sexist? I think there's some instant coffee in the galley," she continued. "I'll make some."

"It isn't smart to use the battery," he muttered. "We'll make do with soft drinks."

"No problem."

When she returned twenty minutes later, Colt was cursing the engine. "This friend of Boyd's should be shot for taking such haphazard care of his equipment."

"Are you going to fix it or not?"

"Yeah, I'm going to fix it." He found several interesting

names to call a bolt he was fighting to loosen. "It's just going to take a little longer than I expected." Prepared for some pithy comment, he glanced down. She merely stood there patiently, the breeze ruffling her hair. "What's that?" he asked, nodding down at her hands.

"I think it's called a sandwich." She held up the bread and cheese for his inspection. "Not much of one, but I thought you might be hungry."

"Yeah, I am." The gesture mollified him somewhat. He lifted his hands and showed her palms and fingers streaked with grease. "I'm a little handicapped."

"Okay. Bend over." When he obeyed, she brought the bread to his mouth. They watched each other over it as he took a bite.

"Thanks."

"You're welcome. I found a beer." She pulled the bottle out of her pocket and tipped it back. "We'll share." Then she held it to his lips.

"Now I know I love you."

"Just eat." She fed him more of the sandwich. "Do you have any idea how much longer it's going to take you to get us airborne?"

"Yeah." And because he did, he made sure he got his full share of the beer and the sandwich before he told her. "It'll be an hour, maybe two."

She blinked. "Two hours? We'll have run out of daylight by then. You don't plan to fly this out of here in the dark?"

"No, I don't." Though he remained braced for a sneak attack, he went back to the engine. "It'll be safer to wait until morning."

"Until morning," she repeated, staring at his back. "And just what are we supposed to do until morning?"

"Pitch a tent, for starters. There's one in the cabin, in the overhead. I guess old Frank likes to take his ladies camping."

"That's great. Just great. You're telling me we have to sleep out here?"

"We could sleep in the plane," he pointed out. "But it wouldn't be as comfortable, or as warm, as stretching out in a tent beside a fire." He began to whistle as he worked. He'd said he owed her one. He hadn't realized he'd be able to pay her back so soon, or so well. "I don't suppose you know how to start a campfire."

"No, I don't know how to start a damn campfire."

"Weren't you ever a Girl Scout?"

She made a sound like steam escaping a funnel. "No. Were you?"

"Can't say I was—but I was friendly with a few of them. Well, you go on and gather up some twigs, darling. I'll talk you through your first merit badge."

"I am not going to gather twigs."

"Okay, but it's going to get cold once that sun goes down. A fire keeps the chill—and other things—away."

"I'm not—" She broke off, looked uneasily around. "What other things?"

"Oh, you know. Deer, elk…wildcats…"

"Wildcats." Her hand went automatically to her shoulder rig. "There aren't any wildcats around here."

He lifted his head and glanced around as if considering. "Well, it might be too early in the year yet. But they do start coming down from the higher elevations near winter. Of course, if you want to wait until I've finished here, I'll get a fire going. May be dark by then, though."

He was doing it on purpose. She was sure of it. But then

again… She cast another look around, toward the forest, where the shadows were lengthening. "I'll get the damn wood," she muttered, and stomped off toward the trees. After she checked her weapon.

He watched her, smiling. "We're going to do just fine together," he said to himself. "Just fine."

Following Colt's instructions, Althea managed to start a respectable fire within a circle of stones. She didn't like it, but she did it. Then, because he claimed to be deeply involved in the final repairs to the plane, she was forced to rig the tent.

It was a lightweight bubble that Colt declared would nearly erect itself. After twenty minutes of struggle and swearing, she had it up. A narrow-eyed study showed her that it would shelter the two of them—as long as they slept hip to hip.

She was still staring at it, ignoring the chill of the dusk, when she heard the engine spring to life.

"Good as new," Colt shouted, then shut off the engines. "I have to clean up," he told her. He leapt out of the cabin, holding a jug of water. He used it sparingly, along with a can of degreaser from the toolbox. "Nice job," he said, nodding toward the tent.

"Thanks a bunch."

"There are blankets in the plane. We'll do well enough." Still crouched, he drew in a deep breath, tasting smoke and pine and good, crisp air. "Nothing quite like camping out in the hills."

She shoved her hands into her pockets. "I'll have to take your word for it."

He finished scrubbing his hands with a rag before he rose. "Don't tell me you've never done any camping."

"All right, I won't tell you."

"What do you do for a vacation?"

She arched a brow. "I go to a hotel," she said precisely. "Where they have room service, hot and cold running water and cable TV."

"You don't know what you're missing."

"I suppose I'm about to find out." She shivered once, sighed. "I could use a drink."

In addition to the Beaujolais, they feasted on rich, sharp cheese, caviar and thin crackers spread with a delicate pâté.

All in all, Althea decided, it could have been worse.

"Not like any camp meal I've ever had," Colt commented as he scooped more caviar onto a cracker. "I thought I'd have to go kill us a rabbit."

"Please, not while I'm eating." Althea sipped more wine and found herself oddly relaxed. The fire did indeed keep the chill away. And it was soothing to watch it flicker and hiss. Overhead, countless stars wheeled and winked, stabbing the cloudless black sky. A quarter-moon silvered the trees and lent a glow to the snow capping the peaks that circled them.

She'd stopped jerking every time an owl hooted.

"Pretty country." Colt lit an after-dinner cigar. "I never spent much time here before."

Neither had she, Althea realized, though she'd lived in Denver for a dozen years. "I like the city," she said, more to herself than Colt. She picked up a stick to stir the fire, not because it needed it, but because it was fun to watch the sparks fly.

"Why?"

"I guess because it's crowded. Because you can find anything you want. And because I feel useful there."

"And that's important to you, feeling useful."

"Yeah, it's important."

He watched the way the flames cast shadow and light over her face, highlighting her eyes, sharpening her cheekbones, softening her skin. "It was rough on you, growing up."

"It's over." When he took her hand, she neither resisted nor responded. "I don't talk about it," she said flatly. "Ever."

"All right." He could wait. "We'll talk about something else." He brought her hand to his lips, and felt a response, just a slight flexing, then relaxing, of her fingers. "I guess you never told stories around the campfire."

She smiled. "I guess not."

"I could probably think of one—just to pass the time. Lie or truth?"

She started to laugh, but then she shot to her feet, whipping out her weapon. Colt's reaction was lightning-fast. In an instant he was beside her, shoving her back, his own gun slapped from his boot into his palm.

"What?" he demanded, his eyes narrowed and searching every shadow.

"Did you hear that? There's something out there."

He cocked an ear, while she instinctively shifted to guard his back. After a moment of throbbing silence, he heard a faint rustling, then the far-off cry of a coyote. The plaintive call had Althea's blood drumming.

Colt swore, but at least he didn't laugh. "Animals," he told her, bending to replace his gun.

"What kind?" Her eyes were still scanning the perimeter, wary, watchful.

"Small ones," he assured her. "Badgers, rabbits." He laid

a hand over the ones that gripped her weapon. "Nothing you have to put a hole in, Deadeye."

She wasn't convinced. The coyote called again, and an owl hooted in counterpoint. "What about those wildcats?"

He started to respond, thought better of it, and tucked his tongue in his cheek. "Well, now, darling, they aren't likely to come too close to the fire."

Frowning, she replaced her weapon. "Maybe we should have a bigger fire."

"It's big enough." He turned her toward him, running his hands up and down her arms. "I don't think I've ever seen you so spooked."

"I don't like being this exposed. There's too much here, out here." And the sterling truth was that she would rather face a hopped-up junkie in a dark alley than one small, furry creature with fangs. "Don't grin at me, damn it!"

"Was I grinning?" He ran his tongue around his teeth and struggled to look sober. "It looks like you're going to have to trust me to get you through this."

"Oh, am I?"

He tightened his grip when she started to back away. The look in his eyes changed so quickly, from amusement to desire, that it took her breath away. "There's just you and me, Althea."

She let the clogged air slowly out of her lungs. "It looks like."

"I don't figure I have to tell you again how I feel about you. Or how much I want you."

"No." Tension flooded into her when he brushed his lips over her temple. And heat, a frightening spear of it, stabbed up her spine.

"I can make you forget where you are." He trailed his lips down to her jawline and nibbled up the other side. "If you'll let me."

"You'd have to be damn good for that."

He laughed, because there had been a challenge in the statement, even though her breath had caught on the words. "It's a long time until morning. I'm betting I can convince you before sunrise."

Why was she resisting something she wanted so terribly? Hadn't she told herself long ago never again to let fear cloud her desires? And hadn't she learned to sate those desires without penalty?

She could do so now, with him, and erase this grinding ache.

"All right, Nightshade." Fearlessly she linked her arms around his neck, met his eyes straight on. "I'll take that bet."

His hand fisted in her hair, dragged her head back. For one long, humming moment, they stared at each other. Then he plundered.

Her mouth was hot and honeyed under his, as demanding as hunger, as wild as the night. He plunged into the kiss, using tongue and teeth, knowing he could gorge himself on her and never be filled. So he took more, relentlessly savaging her mouth while she met demand with demand and power with power.

It was like the first time, she realized giddily. The first time he'd dragged her to him and made her taste what he had to offer. Like some fatal drug, the taste had her pulses pounding, her blood swimming fast and her mind spinning away from reason.

She wondered how she had expected to come away whole. And then she forgot to care.

She no longer wanted to be safe, to be in control. Now, here, with him, she wanted only to feel, to experience everything that had once seemed impossible, or at least unwise. And if she sacrificed survival, so be it.

Driven by greed, she tore at his coat, desperate to feel the hard, solid body beneath. He didn't have to be stronger than she, but if he was, she would accept the vulnerability that came with being a woman. And the power that raced alongside it.

She was like a volcano ready to erupt, and she wanted nothing more than to be joined with him when the tremors came.

She was stripping him of his sanity, layer by layer. Those wild lips, those frantic hands. On an oath that was almost a prayer, he half carried, half dragged her toward the tent, feeling like some primeval hunter flinging his chosen mate into his cave.

They tumbled into the small shelter together, a tangle of limbs, a tangle of needs. He yanked her coat down her shoulders, fighting for breath as he raced greedy kisses down her throat.

He felt the vibration of her groan against his lips as he fought her shoulder rig, tearing aside that symbol of control and violence, knowing he was losing control, overwhelmed by a violence of feelings that he couldn't suppress.

He wanted her naked and straining. And screaming.

Her breath caught in gasps as she tugged, pulled, ripped, at his clothes. The firelight glowed orange through the thin material of the tent, and she could see his eyes, the dark, dangerous purpose in them. She reveled in it, in the panicked excitement that racked her body where he groped and possessed.

He would ravage her tonight, she knew. And be ravaged in turn.

Levering himself back, he dragged her sweater up and over her head and tossed it aside. She wore lace beneath, a snow-white fancy that in a saner place, in a saner time, would have aroused him by its blatant femininity. He might have toyed with the straps, skimmed his fingers over her subtle peaks. Now he only ripped it apart in one jerky move to free her breasts for his greedy mouth.

The flavor of that warm, scented flesh hit his system like a blow. And her response, the lovely arching of her body against his, the long, throaty moan, the quick, helpless quiver, drove him toward a summit of pleasure he had never dreamed of.

He feasted.

A whimper caught in her throat. She dug her nails into the naked flesh of his shoulders, needing to drive him on, terrified of where he was taking her. She clutched at him for balance, moved under him in sinuous invitation, arching once more as he peeled her slacks away, skimming those impossibly clever fingers down her thighs.

The triangle of lace that shielded her tore jaggedly. Once again his mouth feasted.

Her cry of stunned release rippled through his blood. She shot up like a rocket, exploding, imploding, feeling herself scatter and burn. But where the release should have peaked and leveled, he gave her no respite. She clutched at the blanket while he battered her system with sensations that had no name, no form.

When he rose over her, every muscle trembling, he found her eyes open and on his. He watched her face, filled himself ith it even as he buried himself inside her in one desperate troke. Her eyes glazed, closed. His own vision grayed before he buried his face in her hair.

His body took over, matching the fast, furious rhythm of er hips. They rode each other like fury, greedy children gorging themselves on forbidden fruit. Her final cry of dark pleasure echoed through the air seconds before his own.

Strength sapped, he collapsed onto her, gulping in air as e felt her tremble beneath him from the aftershocks.

"Who won?" he managed after a moment.

She hadn't thought it possible to laugh at such a time, but chuckle rumbled into her throat. "Let's call it a draw."

"Good enough for me." He thought about lifting himself ff her, but was afraid he might shatter if he tried to move. Plenty good enough. I'm going to kiss you in a minute," he urmured, "but first I have to drum up the strength."

"I can wait." Althea let her eyes close again, and savored ie closeness. His body continued to radiate heat, and his eart was far from steady. She stroked her hand down his back r the simple pleasure of the contact, frowning a bit when er fingers ran over a raised scar. "What's this?"

"Hmm?" He stirred himself, surprised that he'd nearly allen asleep on top of her. "Iraq."

She hadn't realized he'd been there. It occurred to her that ere was quite a bit about him that lay in shadows. "I thought ou'd retired before that started."

"I had. I agreed to do a little job—sort of a side job."

"A favor."

"You could call it that. Caught a little flak—nothing to orry about." He tilted his head, nuzzling. "You have the most orgeous shoulders. Have I mentioned that?"

"No. Do you still do favors for the government?"

"Only if they ask nicely." He grunted and rolled so that he could shift her on top of him. "Better?"

"Mmm…." She rested her cheek on his chest. "But I think we might freeze to death."

"Not if we keep active." He grinned when she lifted her head to look down at him. "Survival methods, Lieutenant."

"Of course." Her lips curved into a smile. "I have to say, Nightshade, I like your methods."

"That so?" Gently he combed his fingers through her hair, tested its weight with his hand.

"That's very so. How soon do we have to add wood to that fire?"

"Oh, we've got a little while yet."

"Then we shouldn't waste time, should we?" Still smiling, she lowered her mouth to his.

"Nope." He felt himself hardening again inside her, and prepared to let her take the lead. As his lips curved against hers, he was struck by a stab of love so sharp it stole his breath. He clutched her close, held on. "I know it's a tired line, Thea, but it's never been like this for me before. Not with anyone."

That frightened her, and what frightened her more than the words was the flush of warmth they brought to her. "You talk too much."

"Thea…"

But she shook her head and rose up, taking him deep inside her, tantalizing his body so that the need for words slipped away.

Chapter 9

Colt awakened quickly. An old habit. He registered his surroundings—the pale light of dawn creeping into the tent, the rough blanket and hard ground beneath his back, and the soft, slender woman curled on top of him. It made him smile, remembering the way she'd rolled over him during the night, seeking a place more comfortable than the unyielding floor of the valley.

At the time, they'd both been too exhausted to do more than cuddle up and sleep. Now the sun had brought a reminder of the outside world, and their duties in it. Still, he took a moment to enjoy the lazy intimacy, and to imagine other times, other places, where it would once again be only the two of them.

Gently he tugged the blanket over her bare shoulder and let his fingers trail down over her hair where it lay pooled across her cheek and throat.

She shifted, her eyes opening and locking on his.

"Good reflexes, Lieutenant."

She ran her tongue over her teeth, letting her mind and body adjust to the situation. "I guess it's morning."

"Right the first time. Sleep okay?"

"I've slept better." Every muscle in her body ached, but she figured a couple of aspirin and some exercise would handle that. "You?"

"Like a baby," he said. "Some of us are used to roughing it."

She only lifted a brow, then rolled off him. "Some of us want coffee." The moment she left his warmth, the chill stung her skin. Shivering, she groped for her sweater.

"Hey." Before she could bundle up in the sweater, he grabbed her around the waist and hauled her to him. "You forgot something." His hand slid up her back to cup her head as his mouth met hers.

Her body went fluid, sweetly so, and her lips parted in invitation. She could feel herself melting into him, and wondered at it. All through the night they had come together, again and again, each time like lightning, with flashes of greed. But this was softer, steadier, stronger, like a candle that remained alight long after a raging fire had burned itself out.

"You sure are nice to wake up to, Althea."

She wanted to burrow into him, to grab hold and hang on as though her life depended on it. Instead, she flicked a finger down the stubble on his chin. "You're not so bad, Nightshade."

She moved away quickly, a little too quickly, to give herself the time and space to settle. Because he was beginning to read her very well, he smiled.

"You know, once we're married, we should get ourselves one of those king-size beds, so we'll have plenty of room to roll around and get tangled up."

She tugged the sweater on. When her head emerged, her eyes were cool. "Who's making the coffee?"

He nodded thoughtfully. "That is something we'll have to decide. Keeping those little routines straight helps a marriage run smooth."

She bit back a laugh and reached for her slacks. "You owe me some underwear."

He watched her pull the slacks up her long, smooth legs. "Buying it for you is going to be pure pleasure." He shrugged into his shirt while Althea hunted for her socks. Knowing the value of timing, he waited until she'd found them both. "Darling, I've been thinking…."

She answered with a grunt as she tugged on her shoes.

"How do you feel about getting hitched on New Year's Eve? Kind of romantic, starting out the next year as husband and wife."

This time she hissed out her breath. "I'll make the damn coffee," she muttered, and crawled out of the tent.

Colt gave her retreating bottom a friendly pat and chuckled to himself. She was coming around, he decided. She just didn't know it yet.

By the time Althea got the fire started again, she'd had more than enough of the great outdoors. Maybe it was beautiful, she thought as she rummaged through the small supply of pots they'd found on the plane. Maybe it was even magnificent, with its rugged, snow-capped peaks and densely forested slopes. But it was also cold, and hard and deserted.

They had a handful of nuts between them, and not a restaurant in sight.

Too impatient to wait until it boiled, she heated water until it was hot to the touch, then dumped in a generous amount of instant coffee. The scent was enough to make her drool.

"Now that's a pretty sight." Colt stood just outside the tent, watching her. "A beautiful woman bending over a campfire. And you do have a nice way of bending, Thea."

"Stuff it, Nightshade."

He strolled to her grinning. "Cranky before your coffee, darling?"

She knocked aside the hand he'd lifted to toy with her hair. He was charming her again, and it was just going to have to stop. "Here's breakfast." She shoved the can of nuts at him. "You can pour your own coffee."

Obligingly he crouched down and poured the mixture into two tin mugs. "Nice day," he said conversationally. "Low wind, good visibility."

"Yeah, great." She accepted the mug he offered. "God, I'd kill for a toothbrush."

"Can't help you there." He sampled the coffee, grimaced. It was mud, he decided, but at least it packed a punch. "Don't you worry, we'll be back in civilization before much longer. You can brush your teeth, have yourself a nice hot bubble bath, go to the hairdresser."

She started to smile—it was the bubble bath that did it— but then she whipped her head up and scowled. "Leave my hair out of this." Setting the mug down, she knelt and began to rummage through her purse. Once she found her brush, she sat cross-legged on the ground, her back to Colt, and began to drag it through her tangled hair.

"Here now." He sat behind her, snuggling her back into the vee of his legs. "Let me do that."

"I can do it myself."

"Yeah, but you're about to brush yourself bald." After a short tussle, he snatched the brush away. "You should take more care with this," he murmured, gently working out the tangles. "It's the most beautiful head of hair I've ever seen. Up close like this, I can see a hundred different shades of red and gold and russet."

"It's just hair." But if Althea had a point of vanity, Colt was stroking it now. And it felt wonderful. She couldn't resist a sigh as he brushed and lifted, caressed and smoothed. They might be in the middle of nowhere, but for that moment Althea felt as though she were in the lap of luxury.

"Look," Colt whispered against her ear. "At three o'clock."

Responding instinctively to the direction, Althea turned her head. There, just at the verge of the forest, stood a deer. No, not a deer, she realized. Surely no deer could be so huge. His shoulders were nearly as high as a man, and massive. His head was lifted, scenting the air, with his high crown of antlers spearing upward.

"It's, ah…"

"Wapiti," Colt murmured, wrapping his arms companionably around her waist. "American elk. That's one beautiful bull."

"Big. Big is what he is."

"Close to seven hundred pounds, by the look of him. There, he's caught our scent."

Althea felt her heart jolt when the elk turned his great head and looked at her. He seemed both arrogant and wise as he studied the humans who were trespassing on his territory.

And suddenly there was an aching in her throat, a response to beauty, a trembling deep inside, a kind of wonder. For a moment the three of them remained poised, measuring each other. A lark called, a searingly beautiful cascade of notes.

The elk turned, vanished into the shadowed trees.

"I guess he didn't want coffee and cashews," Althea said quietly. She couldn't say why she was moved. She only knew that she was, deeply. Relaxed against Colt, cradled in his arms, she was completely and inexplicably content.

"Can't say I blame him." Colt rubbed his cheek against her hair. "It's a hell of a way to start the day."

"Yeah." She turned, impulsively winding an arm around his neck, pressing her lips to his. "This is better."

"Much better," he agreed, sinking in when she deepened the kiss. He nuzzled, and was amused when she laughed and shoved his unshaven face away from the tender curve of her throat. "Once we're back in Denver, I want you to remind me where we left off."

"I might do that." With some regret, she drew away. "We'd better—what do you call it? Break camp? And, by the way," she added, shrugging into her shoulder rig, "you owe me more than new lingerie—you owe me breakfast."

"Put it on my tab."

Twenty minutes later, they were strapped into the cockpit. Colt checked his gauges while Althea applied blusher to her cheekbones.

"We ain't going to a party," he commented.

"I may not be able to brush my teeth," she said, and crunched down on a mint she'd found in her purse. "I may not be able to take a shower. But, by damn, I haven't lost all sense of propriety."

"I like your cheeks pale." He started the engines. "Kind of fragile."

After one narrow-eyed stare, she deliberately added more blusher. "Just fly, Nightshade."

"Yes, sir, Lieutenant."

He didn't see the point in telling her it would be a tricky takeoff. While she was occupied braiding her hair, he maneuvered the plane into the best position for taxiing. After touching a finger to the medal that rested under his shirt, he let her rip.

They jolted, bounced, shuddered and finally lifted, degree by degree. Colt fought the crosscurrents, dipping one wing, leveling off, nosing upward. Finally they cleared the ridge and shot over the tops of the trees.

"Not too shabby, Nightshade." Althea flipped her braid behind her back. When he glanced over, he saw the awareness in her eyes. The hands that were currently uncapping a tube of mascara were rock-steady, but she knew. He should have realized she would know.

"Boyd was right, Thea. You're a hell of a partner."

"Just try to hold this thing steady for a few minutes, will you?" Smiling to herself, she angled her purse mirror and began to do her lashes. "So, what's the plan?"

"Same as before. We circle this area. Look for cabins. The one we want has a sloped drive."

"That certainly narrows things down."

"Shut up. It's also a two-story with a covered wraparound deck and a trio of windows on the front, facing west. The sun was going down in one scene in the video," he explained. "According to the other information we have, there's a lake some-where in the general area. I also saw fir and spruce, which gives us the elevation. The cabin was whitewashed logs. It shouldn't be that hard to spot."

He might be right about that, but Althea knew there was something else that needed to be said. "She might not be there, Colt."

"We're going to find out." He banked the plane and headed west.

Because she could see the worry come into his eyes, Althea changed tack. "Tell me, what rank were you in the air force?"

"Major." He drummed up a smile. "Looks like I outrank you."

"You're retired," she reminded him. "I bet you looked swell in uniform."

"I wouldn't mind seeing you in dress blues. Look."

Following his direction, she spotted a cabin below. It was a three-level structure fashioned from redwood. She noted two others, separated from each other by lines of trees.

"None of them fit."

"No," he agreed. "But we'll find the one that does."

They continued to search, with Althea peering through binoculars. Hideaways were snuggled here and there, most of them seemingly unoccupied. A few had smoke puffing out of a chimney and trucks or four-wheel-drive vehicles parked outside.

Once she saw a man in a bright red shirt splitting wood. She spotted a herd of elk grazing in a frosty meadow, and the flash of white-tail deer.

"There's nothing," she said at length. "Unless we want to do a documentary on— Wait." A glint of white caught her attention, then was lost. "Circle around. Four o'clock." She continued to scan, searching the snow-dusted ridges.

And there it was, two stories of whitewashed logs, a trio of windows facing west, the deck. At the end of the sloping gravel drive sat a muscular-looking truck. As further proof of habitation, smoke was spiraling out of the chimney.

"That could be it."

"I'm betting it is." Colt circled once, then veered off.

"I might take that bet." She unhooked the radio mike. "Give me the position. I'll call it in, get a surveillance team up here so we can go back and talk a judge into issuing a warrant."

Colt gave her the coordinates. "Go ahead and call it in. But I'm not waiting for a piece of paper."

"What the hell do you think you can do?"

His eyes flashed to hers, then away. "I'm setting the plane down, and I'm going in."

"No," she said, "you're not."

"You do what you have to." He angled for the meadow where Althea had spotted the grazing elk. "There's a good chance she's in there. I'm not leaving her."

"What are you going to do?" she demanded, too incensed to noticed the perilous descent. "Break in, guns blazing? That's movie stuff, Nightshade. Not only is it illegal, but it puts the hostage in jeopardy."

"You've got a better idea?" He braced himself. They were going to slide once the wheels hit. He hoped to God they didn't roll.

"We'll get a team up here with surveillance equipment. We figure out who owns the cabin, get the paperwork pushed through."

"Then we break in? No thanks. You said you'd been skiing, right?"

"What?"

"You're about to do it in a plane. Hold on."

She jerked her head around, gaped through the windscreen as the glittering meadow hurled toward them. She had time for an oath—a vicious one—but then she lost her breath at the impact.

They hit, and went sliding. Snow spewed up the side of the plane, splattering the windows. Althea watched almost philosophically as they hurtled toward a wall of trees. Then the plane spun in two wicked circles before coming to a grinding stop.

"You maniac!" She took deep breaths, fighting back the worst of her temper. She would have let it loose, but there wasn't enough room to maneuver in the cabin. And when she murdered him she wanted to do it right.

"I landed a plane in the Aleutians once, when the radar was down. It was a lot worse than this."

"What does that prove?" she demanded.

"That I'm still a hell of a pilot?"

"Grow up!" she shouted. "This isn't fantasyland. We're closing in on suspected kidnappers, suspected murderers, and there's very possibly an innocent kid caught in the middle. We're going to do this right, Nightshade."

With one jerk, he unstrapped himself, then grabbed both her hands at the wrists. "You listen to me." She would have winced at the way his fingers dug into her flesh, but the fury in his eyes stopped her. "I know what's real, Althea. I've seen enough reality in my life—the waste of it, and the cruelty of it. I know that girl. I held her when she was a baby, and I'm not leaving her welfare up to paperwork and procedure."

"Colt—"

"Forget it." He shoved her hands aside, jerked back. "I'm not asking for your help, because I'm trying to respect your ideas of rules and regulations. But I'm going after her, Thea, and I'm going now."

"Wait." She held up a hand, then dragged it through her hair. "Let me think a minute."

"You think too damn much." But when he started to rise, she shoved a fist into his chest.

"I said wait." Then she tipped her head back, closed her eyes and thought it through.

"How far is it to the cabin?" she asked after a moment. "Half a mile?"

"More like three-quarters."

"The roads leading in were all plowed."

"Yeah." Impatience shimmered around him. "So?"

"It would have been handier if I could have been stuck in a snowdrift. But a breakdown's good enough."

"What are you talking about?"

"I'm talking about working together." She opened her eyes, pinned him with them. "You don't like the way I work, I don't like the way you work. So we're going to have to find a middle ground. I'm calling this in, arranging to have the local police back us up, and I'm going to have them get word to Boyd. See if he can get some paperwork started."

"I told you—"

"I don't care what you told me," she said calmly. "This is how it's going down. We can't go bursting in there. Number one, we might be wrong about the cabin. Number two," she said, cutting him off again, "it puts Liz in increased jeopardy if they're holding her there. And number three, without probable cause, without proper procedure, these bastards might wiggle out, and I want them put away. Now, you listen…"

He didn't like it. It didn't matter how much sense it made or how good a plan she'd devised. But during the long trek to the cabin she defused whatever arguments he voiced with calm, simple logic.

She was going in.

"What makes you think they'll let you inside just because you ask?"

She tilted her head, slanted a look up from under her lashes. "I haven't wasted any on you, Nightshade, but I have a tremendous amount of charm at my disposal." She lengthened her stride to match his. "What do you think most men will do when a helpless woman comes knocking, begging for help because she's lost, her car's broken down and—" she gave a delicate shiver and turned her voice into a purr "—and it's so awfully cold outside."

He swore and watched his breath puff away in smoke. "What if they offer to drive you back to your car and fix it?"

"Well, I'll be terribly grateful. And I'll stall them long enough to do what needs to be done."

"And if they get rough?"

"Then you and I will have to kick butt, won't we?"

He couldn't help but look forward to that. And yet… "I still think I should go in with you."

"They're not going to be sympathetic if the little woman has a big strong man with her." Sarcasm dripped in the chilly air. "With any luck, the local boys will be here before things get nasty." She paused, judging the distance. "We're close enough. One of them might be out for a morning stroll. We don't want to be spotted together."

Colt shoved his fists into his pockets, then made them relax. She was right—more, she was good. He pulled his hands out, grabbed her shoulders and hauled her close. "Watch your step, Lieutenant."

She kissed him, hard. "Same goes."

She turned, walked away with long, ground-eating strides. He wanted to tell her to stop, to tell her he loved her. Instead, he headed over the rough ground toward the rear of the cabin. This wasn't the time to throw her any emotional curves. He'd save them for later.

Blocking everything from his mind, he sprinted through the hard-crusted snow, keeping low.

Althea moved fast. She wanted to be out of breath and a little teary-eyed when she reached the cabin. Once she came into view of the windows, she switched to a stumbling run, pantomiming relief. She all but fell against the door, calling and banging.

She recognized Kline when he opened it. He wore baggy gray sweats, and his bleary eyes were squinting against the smoke from the cigarette tucked into the corner of his mouth. He smelled of tobacco and stale whiskey.

"Oh, thank God!" Althea slumped against the doorjamb. "Thank God! I was afraid I'd never find anyone. I feel like I've been walking forever."

Kline sized her up. She was one sweet-looking babe, he decided, but he wasn't big on surprises. "What do you want?"

"My car…" She pressed a fluttering hand to her heart. "It broke down—it must be a mile from here, at least. I was coming to visit some friends. I don't know, maybe I made a wrong turn." She shuddered, wrapped her parka closer around her. "Is it all right if I come in? I'm so cold."

"There ain't nobody up around here. No other cabins near here."

She closed her eyes. "I knew I must have turned wrong somewhere. Everything starts to look the same. I left Englewood before sunup—wanted to start my vacation first thing." Staring up at him, wide-eyed, she managed a weak smile. "Some vacation so far. Look, can I just use the phone, call my friends so they can come get me?"

"I guess." The broad was harmless, Kline decided. And a pleasure to look at.

"Oh, a fire…" With a moan of relief, Althea dashed toward it. "I didn't know I could be so cold." While she rubbed her hands together, she beamed over her shoulder at Kline. "I can't thank you enough for helping me out."

"No problem." He pulled the dangling cigarette from his mouth. "We don't get much traffic up here."

"I can see why." She shifted her gaze to the windows. "Still, it is lovely. And this place!" She circled, looking dazzled. "It's just fabulous. I guess if you were all cozied up by the fire with a bottle of wine, you wouldn't mind sitting out a blizzard or two."

His lips curled. "I like to cozy up with something other than a bottle."

Althea fluttered her lashes, lowered them modestly. "It certainly is romantic, Mr—?"

"Kline. You can call me Harry."

"All right, Harry. I'm Rose," she said, giving him her middle name in case he'd recognized the name of Wild Bill's cop. She offered her hand. "It's a real pleasure. I think you've saved my life."

"What the hell's going on down there?"

Althea glanced up to the loft and saw a tall, wiry man with an untended shock of blond hair. She tagged him as the second male actor in the video.

"Got us an unexpected guest, Donner," Kline called up. "Car broke down."

"Well, hell…" Donner blinked his eyes clear and took a good look. "You're out early, sweetie."

"I'm on vacation," she said, and flashed him a smile.

"Isn't that nice?" Donner started downstairs, preening, Althea noticed, like a rooster in a henhouse. "Why don't you fix the lady a cup of coffee, Kline?"

"Tidal Wave's already in the kitchen. It's his turn."

"Fine." Donner sent what was meant to be an intimate smile toward Althea. "Tell him to pour another cup for the lady."

"Why don't you—"

"Oh, I would *love* a cup of coffee," Althea said, turning her big brown eyes on Kline. "I'm just frozen."

"Sure." He shrugged, shot Donner a look that made Althea think of one male dog warning off a competitor, then strode off.

How many more of the organization were in the cabin? she wondered. Or was it just the three of them?

"I was just telling Harry how beautiful your house is." She wandered the living room, dropping her purse onto a table. "Do you live here year-round?"

"No, we just use it now and again."

"It's so much bigger than it looks from outside."

"It does the job." He moved closer as Althea sat on the arm of a chair. "Maybe you'd like to hang out here for your vacation."

She laughed, making no objection when he brushed a finger through her hair. "Oh, but my friends are expecting me. Still, I do have two weeks…" She laughed again, low and throaty. "Tell me, what do you guys do around here for fun?"

"You'd be surprised." Donner laid a hand on her thigh.

"I don't surprise easily."

"Back off." Kline came back in with a mug of black coffee. "Here you are, Rose."

"Thanks." She sniffed deeply, curling her shoulders in for effect. "I feel warm and toasty already."

"Why don't you take off your coat?" Donner put a hand to her collar, but she shifted, smiling.

"As soon as my insides defrost a little more." She'd taken the precaution of removing her shoulder rig, but she preferred more camouflage, as her weapon was snug at the small of her back. "Are the two of you brothers?" she asked conversationally.

Kline snorted. "Not hardly. You could say we're partners."

"Oh, really? What kind of business are you in?"

"Communications," Donner stated, flashing white teeth.

"That's fascinating. You sure have a lot of equipment." She glanced toward the big-screen TV, the state-of-the-art VCR/DVD and stereo. "I love watching movies on long winter nights. Maybe we can get together sometime and…" She let her words trail off, alerted by a movement at the back of the loft. Glancing up, she saw the girl.

Her hair was tousled, and her eyes were unbearably tired. She'd lost weight, Althea thought, but she recognized Liz from the snapshot Colt had shown her.

"Why, hello there," she said, and smiled.

"Get back in your room," Kline snapped. "Now."

Liz moistened her lips. She was wearing tattered jeans and a bright blue sweater that was tattered at the cuffs. "I wanted some breakfast." Her voice was quiet, Althea noted, but not cowed.

"You'll get it." He glanced back at Althea, satisfied that she was smiling with friendly disinterest. "Now get on back to your room until I call you."

Liz hesitated, long enough to aim one cold glare at him. That warmed Althea's heart. The kid wasn't beaten yet, Althea noted as Liz turned and walked to the door behind her. It shut with a slam.

"Kids," Kline muttered, and lit another cigarette.

"Yeah." Althea smiled sympathetically. "Is she your sister?"

Kline choked on the smoke, but then he grinned. "Right. Yeah, she's my sister. So, you wanted to use the phone?"

"Oh, yes." Setting the mug of coffee aside, Althea rose. "I appreciate it. My friends'll be getting worried about me soon."

"There it is." He gestured. "Help yourself."

"Thanks." But when she picked up the receiver, there was no dial tone. "Gee, I think it's dead."

Kline swore and strode over, pulling a thin L-shaped tool from his pocket. "Forgot. I, ah, lock it up at night, so the kid can't use it. She was making all these long-distance calls and running up the bill. You know how girls are."

"Yes." Althea smiled. "I do." When she heard the dial tone, she punched in the number for the local police. "Fran," she said merrily, addressing the dispatcher as they had arranged. "You won't believe what happened. I got lost, my car broke down. If it hadn't been for these terrific guys, I don't know what I'd have done." She laughed, hoping Colt was making his move. "I do *not* always get lost. I hope Bob's up to coming for me."

While Althea chatted with the police dispatcher, Colt shimmied up a pole to the second floor. With his binoculars, he'd seen everything he needed to see through the expansive glass of the cabin. Althea was holding her own, and Liz was on the second floor.

They'd agreed that if the opportunity presented itself, he would get her out of the house. Out of harm's way. He might have preferred a direct route—straight through Kline and the other jerk in the living room, and on into the big guy doing kitchen duty.

But Liz's safety came first. Once he got her out, he'd be coming back.

With a grunt, he swung himself onto the narrow overhang and clutched at the window ledge. He saw Liz lying on a rumpled bed, her body turned away and curled up protectively. His first urge was to throw up the window and leap inside. Afraid he might frighten her into crying out, he tapped gently on the glass.

She shifted. When he tapped again, she turned wearily over, unfocused eyes gazing into the sunlight. Then she blinked and cautiously pushed herself up from the bed. Hurriedly Colt put a finger to his lips, signaling silence. But it didn't stop the tears. They poured out of her eyes as she rushed to the window.

"Colt!" She shook the window, then laid her cheek against the glass and wept. "I want to go home! Please, please, I want to go home!"

He could barely hear her through the glass. Afraid their

voices would carry, he tapped again, waiting until she turned her head to look at him.

"Open the window, baby." He mouthed it carefully, but she only shook her head.

"Nailed shut." Her breath hitched, and she rubbed her fists against her eyes. "They nailed it shut."

"Okay, okay. Look at me. Look." He used hand signals to focus her attention. "A pillow. Get a pillow."

A dim spark glowed in her eyes. He'd seen it before, that cautious return of hope. She moved fast, doing as he instructed.

"Hold it against the glass. Hold it steady, and turn your head. Turn your head away, baby."

He used his elbow to smash the glass, satisfied that the pillow muffled most of the noise. When he'd broken enough to ease his body through, he nudged the pillow aside and swung inside.

She was immediately in his arms, clinging, sobbing. He picked her up, cradled her like a baby. "Shh…Liz. It's going to be all right now. I'm going to take you home."

"I'm sorry. I'm so sorry."

"Don't worry about it. Don't worry about anything." He drew back to look into her eyes. She looked so thin, he thought, so pale. And he had a lot more to ask of her. "Honey, you're going to have to be tough for a little while longer. We're going to get you out, and we have to move fast. Do you have a coat? Shoes?"

She shook her head. "They took them. They took everything so I couldn't run away. I tried, Colt, I swear I did, but—"

"It's all right." He pressed her face to his shoulder again, recognizing bubbling hysteria. "You're not going to think about it now. You're just going to do exactly what I tell you. Okay?"

"Okay. Can we go now? Right now?"

"Right now. Let's wrap you in this blanket." He dragged it off the bed with one hand and did his best to bundle it around her. "Now we're going to have to take a little fall. But if you hang on to me, and stay real loose, real relaxed, it's going to be fine." He carried her to the window, careful to cover her face against the cold and the jagged teeth of broken glass. "If you want to scream, you scream in your head, but not out loud. That's important."

"I won't scream." With her heart hammering, she pressed hard against his chest. "Please, just take me home. I want Mom."

"She wants you, too. So does your old man." He kept talking in the same low, soothing tone as he inched toward the edge. "We're going to call them as soon as we get out of here." He said a quick prayer and jumped.

He knew how to fall, off a building, down stairs, out of a plane. Without the child, he would simply have tucked and rolled. With her, he swiveled his body to take the brunt of the impact, so that he would land on his back and cushion her.

The impact stole his breath, wrenched his shoulder, but he was up almost as soon as he landed, with Liz still cradled against his chest. He sprinted toward the road and was halfway there when he heard the first shot.

Chapter 10

Althea drew out her conversation with the police dispatcher, pausing in her own chatter to take in the information that her backup's E.T.A. was ten minutes. She sincerely hoped Colt had managed to get Liz away from the cabin, but either way, it looked like it was going to go down as smooth as silk.

"Thanks, Fran. I'm looking forward to seeing you and Bob, too. Just let me get some idea of where I am from Harry. I don't have a clue." Beaming a new smile in Harry's direction, Althea cupped a hand over the phone. "Do you have, like, an address or something? Bob's going to come pick me up and take a look at my car."

"No problem." He glanced over as Tidal Wave came in from the kitchen. "Hope you made enough breakfast for our guest," Harry told him. "She's had a rough morning."

"Yeah, there's enough." Tidal Wave turned his hard brown eyes on Althea, narrowed them. "Hey! What the hell is this?"

"Try for some manners," Donner suggested. "There's a lady present."

"Lady, hell! That's a cop. That's Wild Bill's cop."

He made his lunge, but Althea was ready. She'd seen the recognition in his eyes and had already reached for her weapon. There wasn't time to think or to worry about the other two men, as two hundred and sixty pounds of muscle and bulk rammed her.

Her first shot veered wide as she went flying, slamming against an antique table. A collection of snuff bottles crashed, spewing shards of amethyst and aquamarine. She saw stars. Through them, she saw her opponent bearing down on her like a freight train.

Pure instinct had her rolling to the left to avoid a blow. Tidal Wave was big, but she was quick. Althea scrambled to her knees and gripped her weapon in both hands.

This time her shot was true. She had only an instant to note the spread of blood on his white T-shirt before she leapt to her feet.

Donner was heading for the door, and Kline was swearing as he dragged open a drawer. She saw the glint of chrome.

"Freeze!"

Her order had Donner throwing up his hands and turning into a statue, but Kline whipped out the gun.

"Do it and die," she told him, stepping back so that she could keep both Kline and Donner in sight. "Drop it, Harry, or you're going to be staining the carpet like your friend there."

"Son of a bitch." Teeth set, he tossed the weapon down.

"Good choice. Now, on the floor, facedown, hands behind your head. You, too, Romeo," she told Donner. While they obeyed, she picked up Kline's gun. "You two should know better than to invite a stranger into the house."

Lord, she hurt, Althea realized now that her adrenaline was leveling off. From the top of her head to the soles of her feet, she was one huge ache. She hoped Tidal Wave's flying tackle hadn't dislodged anything vital.

She caught the thin wail of a siren in the distance. "Looks like old Fran told the troops to come in. Now, in case you don't get the picture, I'm the law, and you're under arrest."

Althea was calmly reading her prisoners their rights when Colt burst in, a gun in one hand, a knife in the other. By her calculations, it had been roughly three minutes since she'd fired the first shot. The man moved fast.

She spared him a glance, then finished the procedure. "Cover these idiots, will you, Nightshade?" she asked as she picked up the dangling receiver. "Officer Mooney? Yes, this is Lieutenant Grayson. We'll need an ambulance out here. I have a suspect down with a chest wound. No, the situation's under control. Thank you. You were a big help."

She hung up and looked back at Colt. "Liz?"

"She's okay. I told her to wait by the road for the cops. I heard the shots." His hands were steady. He could be grateful for that. But his insides were jelly. "I figured they'd made you."

"You figured right. That one." She jerked her head toward Tidal Wave. "He must have seen me with Wild Bill. Why don't you go find us a towel? We'd better try to stop that bleeding."

"The hell with that!" The fury came so suddenly, and so violently, that the two men on the floor quaked. "Your head's cut."

"Yeah?" She touched her fingers to the throbbing ache at her right temple, then studied her blood-smeared fingers in disgust. "Hell. That better not need stitches. I really hate stitches."

"Which one of them hit you?" Colt scanned the three men with icy eyes. "Which one?"

"The one I shot. The one who's currently bleeding to death. Now get me a towel, and we'll see if we can have him live long enough to go to trial." When he didn't respond, she stepped between him and the wounded man. Colt's intentions were clear as crystal. "Don't pull this crap on me, Nightshade. I'm not a damsel in distress, and white knights annoy the hell out of me. Got it?"

"Yeah." He sucked in his breath. There were too many emotions ripping through him. None of them could change the situation. "Yeah, I got it, Lieutenant."

He turned away to do as she'd asked. After all, he thought, she could handle the situation. She could handle anything.

It wasn't until they were in the plane again that he began to calm. He had to at least pretend to be calm for Liz's sake. She'd clung to him, begging him not to send her back with the police, to stay with her. So he'd agreed to fly back with Liz in the copilot's seat and Althea in the jump seat behind.

Looking lost in his coat, Liz stared through the windscreen. No matter how Colt had tried to bundle her up, she continued to shiver. When they leveled off, heading east, the tears began to flow. They fell fast, hot, down her cheeks. Her shoulders shook violently, but she made no sound. No sound at all.

"Come on, baby." Helpless, Colt reached out to take her hand. "Everything's all right now. Nobody's going to hurt you now."

But the silent tears continued.

Saying nothing, Althea rose. She came forward, calmly untrapped Liz. Communicating by touch, Althea urged Liz to shift, then took her place in the chair. Then she gathered the girl on her lap, cradled her head on her shoulder. Enfolded her grief.

"Don't hold back," she murmured.

Almost at once, Liz's sobs echoed through the cabin. The pain in them cut at Althea's heart as she rocked the girl and held her close. Devastated by the weeping, Colt lifted a hand to brush it down Liz's tangled hair. But she only curled closer to Althea at the touch.

He dropped his hand and concentrated on the sky.

It was Althea's gentle insistence that convinced Liz it would be wise to go to the hospital first. She wanted to go home, she said over and over again. And over and over again, Althea patiently reminded Liz that her parents were already on their way to Denver.

"I know it's hard." Althea kept her arm tight around Liz's shoulders. "And I know it's scary, but the doctor needs to check you out."

"I don't want him to touch me."

"I know." How well she knew. "But he's a she." Althea smiled, rubbing her hand down Liz's arm. "She won't hurt you."

"It'll be over real quick," Colt assured her. He fought to keep his easy smile in place. What he wanted to do was scream. Kick something. Kill someone.

"Okay." Liz glanced warily toward the examining room again. "Please…" She pressed her lips together and looked pleadingly at Althea.

"Would you like me to go in with you? Stay with you?" At Liz's nod, she drew the girl closer. "Sure, no problem. Colt, why don't you go find a soft-drink machine, maybe a candy bar?" She smiled down at Liz. "I could sure use some chocolate. How about you?"

"Yeah." Liz drew in a shaky breath. "I guess."

"We'll be back in a few minutes," Althea told Colt. He could read nothing in her eyes. Feeling useless, he strode down the corridor.

Inside the examining room, Althea helped Liz exchange her tattered clothes for a hospital gown. She noted the bruises on the girl's flesh, but made no comment. They would need an official statement from Liz, but it could wait a little longer.

"This is Dr. Mailer," she explained as the young doctor with the soft eyes approached the table.

"Hello, Liz." Dr. Mailer didn't offer her hand, or touch her patient in any way. She specialized in trauma patients, and she understood the terrors of rape victims. "I'm going to need to ask you some questions, and to run some tests. If there's anything you want to ask me, you go ahead. And if you want me to stop, to wait a while, you just say so. Okay?"

"All right." Liz lay back and focused on the ceiling. But her hand remained tight around Althea's.

Althea had requested Dr. Mailer because she knew the woman's reputation. As the examination progressed, she was more than satisfied that it was well deserved. The doctor was gentle, kind and efficient. It seemed she instinctively knew when to stop, to give Liz a chance to regroup, and when to continue.

"We're all done." Dr. Mailer stripped off her gloves and smiled. "I just want you to rest in here for a little while, and I'm going to have a prescription for you before you leave."

"I don't have to stay here, do I?"

"No." Dr. Mailer closed a hand over Liz's. "You did fine. When your parents get here, we'll talk again. Why don't I see about getting you something to eat?"

As she left, Dr. Mailer sent Althea a look that clearly stated that they, too, would talk later.

"You did do fine," Althea said, helping Liz to sit up. "Do you want me to go see if Colt found that candy bar? I don't imagine that's the sort of food Dr. Mailer had in mind, so we'll have to sneak it while we can."

"I don't want to be alone here."

"Okay." Althea took her brush from her purse and began to untangle Liz's hair. "Let me know if I'm pulling."

"When I saw you downstairs—at the cabin—I thought you were another of the women they brought up. That it was going to happen again." Liz squeezed her eyes shut. Tears spilled through her lashes. "That they were going to make me do those things again."

"I'm sorry. There wasn't any way to let you know I was there to help you."

"And when I saw Colt at the window, I thought it was a dream. I kept dreaming somebody would come, but no one did. I was afraid Mom and Dad just didn't care."

"Honey, your parents have been trying to find you all along." She tipped Liz's chin upward. "They've been so worried. That's why they sent Colt. And I can tell you he loves you, too. You can't imagine the stuff he's bullied me into doing so he could find you."

Liz tried to smile, but it quivered and fell. "But they don't know about— Maybe they won't love me after they find out…everything."

"No." Althea's fingers firmed on Liz's chin. "It'll upset them, and it will hurt them, and it'll be hard, really hard, for them. That's because they do love you. Nothing that happened is going to change that."

"I—I can't do anything but cry."

"Then that's all you have to do, for now."

Liz swiped a shaky hand across her cheeks. "It was my fault I ran away."

"It was your fault you ran away," Althea agreed. "That's all that was your fault."

Liz jerked her head away. The tears gushed out again as she stared at the tiles on the floor. "You don't understand how it feels. You don't know what it's like. How awful it is. How humiliating."

"You're wrong." Gently, firmly, Althea cupped Liz's face again, lifting it until their eyes met. "I do understand. I understand exactly."

"You?" Air shuddered out between Liz's lips. "It happened to you?"

"When I was just about your age. And I felt as though someone had carved something out of me that I'd never get back again. I thought I'd never get clean again, be whole again. Be me again. And I cried for a long, long time, because there didn't seem to be anything else I could do."

Liz accepted the tissue Althea pressed into her hand. "I kept telling myself it wasn't me. It wasn't really me. But I was so scared. It's over. Colt keeps saying it's over now, but it hurts."

"I know." Althea cradled Liz in her arms again. "It hurts more than anything else can, and it's going to hurt for a while. But you're not alone. You have to keep remembering you're not alone. You have your family, your friends. You have Colt. And you can talk to me whenever you need to."

Liz sniffled, rested her cheek against Althea's heart. "What did you do? After. What did you do?"

"I survived," Althea murmured, staring blankly over Liz's head. "And so will you."

Colt stood in the doorway of the examining room, his arms piled high with cans of soda and candy bars. If he'd felt useless before, he now felt unbearably helpless.

There was no place for him here, no way for him to intrude on this woman pain. His first and only reaction was rage. But where to channel it? He turned away to dump the cans and candy onto a table in the waiting room. If he couldn't comfort either of them, couldn't stop what had already happened, then what could he do?

He scrubbed his hands over his face and tried to clear his mind. Even as he dropped them, he saw Liz's parents dashing from the elevator.

This, at least, he could do. He strode to meet them.

Inside the examining room, Althea finished tidying Liz's hair. "Do you want to get dressed?"

Liz managed what passed for a smile. "I don't ever want to put those clothes on again."

"Good point. Well, maybe I can scrounge up—" She turned at a flurry of movement in the doorway. She saw a pale woman and a haggard man, both with red-rimmed eyes.

"Oh, baby! Oh, Liz!" The woman raced forward first, with the man right on her heels.

"Mom!" Liz was sobbing again even as she threw open her arms. "Mom!"

Althea stepped aside as parents and child were reunited, with tears and desperate embraces. When she spotted Colt in the doorway, she moved to him. "You'd better stay with them. I'll tell Dr. Mailer they're here before I go."

"Where are you going?"

She slid her purse back on her shoulder. "To file my report."

She did just that before she went home to indulge in that long, steamy bath. She soaked until her body was numb. Giving in to exhaustion, both physical and emotional, she fell into bed naked and slept dreamlessly until the battering on her door awoke her.

Groggy, she fumbled for her robe, belting it as she walked to the door. She scowled at Colt through the peephole, then yanked the door open.

"Give me one good reason why I shouldn't book you for disturbing the peace. My peace."

He held out a flat, square box. "I brought you pizza."

She blew out a breath, then drew one in—as well as the rich scent of cheese and spice. "That might get you off. I guess you want to come in with it."

"That was the idea."

"Well, come on, then." With that dubious invitation, she walked away to fetch plates and napkins. "How's Liz holding up?"

"Surprisingly well. Marleen and Frank are as solid as they come."

"They'll have to be." She came back to set the plates on the table. "I hope they understand they're all going to need counseling."

"They've already talked to Dr. Mailer about it. She's going to help them find a good therapist back home." Trying to choose his words properly, he took his time sliding pizza onto the plates. "The first thing I want to do is thank you. And don't brush me off, Thea. I'd really like to get this out."

"All right, then." She sat, picked up a slice. "Get it out."

"I'm not just talking about the official cooperation, the way you helped me find her and get her out. I owe you big for that, but that's professional. You got anything to drink with this?"

"There's some burgundy in the kitchen."

"I'll get it," he said as she started to rise.

Althea shrugged and went back to eating. "Suit yourself." She was working on her second slice when Colt came back with a bottle and two glasses. "I guess I was too tired to realize I was starving."

"Then I don't have to apologize for waking you up." He filled both glasses, but didn't drink. "The other thing I have to thank you for is the way you were with Liz. I figured getting her out was enough—playing that white knight you said irritates you so much." He looked up, met her eyes. There was a new understanding in them, and a weariness she hadn't seen before. "It wasn't. Telling her it was all right, that it was over—that wasn't enough, either. She needed you."

"She needed a woman."

"You are that. I know it's a lot to expect—over and above, so to speak—but she asked about you a couple of times after you left." He toyed with the stem of his glass. "They're going to be staying in town at least for another day, until Dr. Mailer has some of the results in. I was hoping you could talk to Liz again."

"You don't have to ask me that, Colt." She reached out for his hand. "I got involved, too."

"So did I, Thea." He turned their joined hands over, brought them to his lips. "I'm in love with you. Big-time. No, don't pull away from me." He tightened his grip before she could. "I've never said that to another woman. I used alternate terms." He smiled a little. "I'm crazy about you, you're special to me, that kind of thing. But I never used *love,* not until you."

She believed him. What was more frightening, she wanted to believe him. Tread carefully, she reminded herself. One step at a time. "Listen, Colt, the two of us have been on a roller coaster since we met—and that's only been a short while. Things, emotions, get blown out of proportion on roller coasters. Why don't we slow this down some?"

He could feel her nerves jittering, but he couldn't be amused by them this time. "I had to accept that I couldn't change what had happened to Liz. That was hard. I can't change what I feel for you. Accepting that's easy."

"I'm not sure what you want from me, Colt, and I don't think I can give it to you."

"Because of what happened to you before. Because of what I heard you telling Liz in the examining room."

She withdrew instantly and completely. "That was between Liz and me," she said coldly. "And it's none of your business."

It was exactly the reaction he'd expected, the one he'd prepared for. "We both know that's not true. But we'll talk about it when you're ready." Knowing the value of keeping an opponent off balance, he picked up his wine. "You know they're giving Scott a fifty-fifty chance of making it."

"I know." She watched him warily. "I called the hospital before I went to bed. Boyd's handling the interrogation of Kline and Donner for now."

"Can't wait to get at them, can you?"

"No." She smiled again. "I can't."

"You know, I heard those shots, and it stopped my heart." Feeling more relaxed, he bit into his pizza. "I come tearing back, ready to kick butt, crash through the door like the cavalry, and what do I see?" He shook his head and tapped her glass with his. "There you are, blood running down your face…" He paused to touch a gentle finger to the bandage at her temple. "A gun in each hand. There's a three-hundred-pound hulk bleeding at your feet, and two others facedown with their hands behind their heads. You're just standing there, looking like Diana after the hunt, and reciting Miranda. I have to say, I felt pretty superfluous."

"You did okay, Nightshade." She let out a small, defeated breath. "And I guess you deserve to know that I was awfully glad to see you. You looked like Jim Bowie at the Alamo."

"He lost."

She gave in and leaned forward to kiss him. "You didn't."

"We didn't," he corrected, pleased that her mouth had been soft, relaxed and friendly. "I brought you a present."

"Oh, yeah?" Because the dangerous moment seemed to have passed, her lips curved and she kissed him again. "Gimme."

He reached behind himself for his coat, dug into the pocket. Taking out a small paper bag, he tossed it into her lap.

"Aw, and you wrapped it so nice." Chuckling, she dipped

into the bag. And pulled out a lacy bra and panties, in sheer midnight blue. Her chuckle turned into a rich appreciative laugh.

"I pay my debts," he informed her. "Since I figured you probably had a supply of the white kind, I picked out something a little different." He reached over to feel the silk and lace. "Maybe you'll try them on."

"Eventually." But she knew what she wanted now. What she needed now. And she rose to take it. She combed her fingers through his hair, tugging so that his face lifted and his mouth met hers. "Maybe you'll come to bed with me."

"Absolutely." He skimmed his hands up her hips, keeping his mouth joined to hers as he stood to gather her close. "I thought you'd never ask."

"I didn't want the pizza to get cold."

He slipped a finger down the center of her body to toy with the belt of her robe. "Still hungry?"

She tugged his shirt out of his jeans. "Now that you mention it." Then she laughed as he swung her up into his arms. "What's this for?"

"I decided to sweep you off your feet. For now." He started toward the bedroom, deciding she was in for another surprise.

The spread was turned back, but the plain white sheets were barely disturbed from her nap. Colt laid her down, following her onto the bed as he skimmed light, teasing kisses over her face.

Her fingers were busy undoing his buttons. She knew what it would be like, and was prepared—eager—for the storm and the fire and the fast flood of sensations. When her hands pushed away cotton and encountered warm, firm flesh, she gave a low, satisfied moan.

He continued to kiss her, nibbling, nuzzling, as she hastily stripped off his clothes. There was a frantic energy burning in her that promised the wild, the frenzied. Each time desire stabbed through him, he absorbed the shock and kept his pace easy.

Eager, edgy, Althea turned her mouth to his and arched against him. "I want you."

He hadn't realized that three breathy words could make the blood swim in his head. But it would be too easy to take what she offered, too easy to lose what she held back. "I know. I can taste it."

He dipped his mouth to hers again, drawing out the kiss with such trembling tenderness that she groaned again. The hand that had been fisted tight against his bare shoulder went lax.

"And I want you," he murmured, levering back to stare down at her. "All of you." Fascinated, he drew his fingers through her hair, spreading it out until it lay flaming against the white sheet. Then he lowered his head again, gently, so gently, to kiss the bandage at her temple.

Emotion curled inside her like a spiked fist. "Colt—"

"Shh…I just want to look."

And look he did, while he traced her face with a fingertip, rubbed her lower lip with his thumb, then trailed it down to her jawline, skimmed over the pulse that fluttered in her throat.

"The sun's going down," he said quietly. "The light does incredible things to your face, your eyes. Just now they're gold, with darker, brandy-colored specks sprinkled through them. I've never seen eyes like yours. You look like a painting." He brushed his thumb over her collarbone. "But I can touch you, feel you tremble, know you're real."

She lifted a hand, wanting to drag him back to her, to make the ache go away. "I don't need words."

"Sure you do." He smiled a little, turning his face into her palm. "Maybe I haven't found the right ones, but you need them." He started to press his lips to her wrist, and then he noticed the faint smudge of bruises. And remembered.

His brows drew together when he straddled her and took both of her hands. He examined her wrists carefully before looking down at her again. "I did this."

Sweet God, she thought, there had to be a way to stop this terrible trembling. "It doesn't matter. You were upset. Make love with me."

"I don't like knowing I hurt you in anger, or that I'm liable to do it again eventually." Very carefully, he touched his lips to each of her wrists, and felt her pulse scramble. "You make it too easy to forget how soft you are, Althea." The sleeves of her robe slithered down her arms as he skimmed his lips to her elbow. "How small. How incredibly perfect you are. I'll have to show you."

He cupped a hand under her head, lifting her so that her hair tumbled back, her face tilted up. Then his mouth was on hers again, savoring a deep, dreamy kiss that left her weak. He felt her give, felt yet another layer dissolve. Her arms linked around his neck; her muscles quivered.

What was he doing to her? She only knew she couldn't think, couldn't resist. She'd been prepared for need, and he'd given her tenderness. What defense could there be against passion wrapped so softly in sweetness? His mouth was gentle, enchanting her even as it seduced.

She wanted to tell him that seduction was unnecessary, but, oh, it felt glorious to surrender to the secrets he unearthed with that quietly devastating mouth and those slow, easy hands.

The last rays of the sun slanted across her eyes as he eased her back so that he could trail his lips down her throat. She heard the whisper of her robe as he slipped it down to bare her shoulder, to free it for lazy, openmouthed kisses and the moist trail of his tongue.

He could feel it the instant she let herself go. The warmth of triumph surged through him as her hands, as gentle as his, began to caress. He resisted the urge to quicken his pace, and let his hands explore her, over the robe, under it, then over again, as her body melted like warm wax.

All the while, he watched her face, aroused by each flicker of emotion, lured by the way her breath would catch, then rush through her lips at his touch. He could have sworn he felt her float as he slipped the robe away.

Then her eyes opened, dark and heavy. He understood that, though she had surrendered, she would not be passive. Her hands were as thorough as his, seeking, touching, possessing, with that unbearable tenderness.

Until he was as seduced as she.

Soft, breathy moans. Quiet secrets told in murmurs. Long, lingering caresses. The sunlight faded to dusk, and dusk to that deepening of night. There was need, but no frantic rush to sate it. There was pleasure, and the dreamy desire to prolong it.

Indulgence. Tonight there was only indulgence.

He touched, she trembled. She tasted, he shuddered.

When at last he slipped into her, she smiled and gathered him close. The rhythm they set was patient, loving, and as true as music. They climbed together, steadily, beautifully, until his gasp echoed hers. And then they floated back to earth.

* * *

She lay a long time in silence, dazed by what had happened. He had given her something, and she had given freely in return. It couldn't be taken back. She wondered what steps could be taken to protect herself now that she had fallen in love.

For the first time. For the only time.

Perhaps it would pass. A part of her cringed at the thought of losing what she'd just found. No matter how firmly she reminded herself that her life was precisely the way she wanted it, she couldn't bring herself to think too deeply about what it would be like without him.

And yet she had no choice. He would leave. And she would survive.

"You're thinking again." He rolled onto his back, hooking an arm around her to gather her close. "I can almost hear your brain humming." Outrageously content, he kissed her hair, closed his eyes. "Tell me the first thing that pops into your mind."

"What? I don't—"

"No, no, don't analyze. This is a test. The first thing, Thea. Now."

"I was wondering when you were going back," she heard herself say. "To Wyoming."

"Ah." He smiled—smugly. "I like knowing I'm the first thing on your mind."

"Don't get cocky, Nightshade."

"Okay. I haven't made any firm plans. I have some loose ends to tie up first."

"Such as?"

"You, for starters. We haven't set the date."

"Colt…"

He grinned again. Maybe it was wishful thinking, but he thought he'd heard exasperation in her tone instead of annoyance. "I'm still shooting for New Year's Eve—I guess I've gotten sentimental—but we've got time to hash that out. Then there's the fact that I haven't finished what I came here to do."

That brought her head up. "What do you mean? You found Liz."

"It's not enough." His eyes glowed in the shadows. "We don't have the head man. It's not finished until we do."

"That's for me and the department to worry about. Personal vendettas have no place here."

"I didn't say it was a vendetta." Though it was. "I intend to finish this, Althea. I'd like to keep working with you on this."

"And if I say no?"

He twirled her hair around his finger. "I'll do my best to change your mind. Maybe you haven't noticed, but I can be tenacious."

"I've noticed," she muttered. But there was a part of her that glowed at the idea that their partnership wasn't at an end. "I suppose I can give you a few more days."

"Good." He shifted her so that he could run a hand down her side to her hips. "Does the deal include a few more nights?"

"I suppose it could." Her smile flashed wickedly. "If you make it worth my while."

"Oh, I will." He lowered his head. "That's a promise."

Chapter 11

With the scream still tearing at her throat, Althea shot up in bed. Blind with terror and rage, she fought the arms that wound around her, struggling wildly against the hold while she sucked in the air to scream again. She could feel his hands on her, feel them groping at her, hot, hurtful. But this time...God, please, this time...

"Althea." Colt shook her, hard, forcing his voice to remain calm and firm, though his heart was hammering against his ribs in fast, hard blows. "Althea, wake up. You're dreaming. Pull out of it."

She clawed her way through the slippery edges of the dream, still fighting him, still dragging in air. Reality was a dim light through the murky depths of the nightmare. With a final burst of effort, she grasped at it, and at Colt.

"Okay, okay..." Still shaken by the sound of the scream

that had awakened him, he rocked her, holding her close to warm her body, which was chill with clammy sweat. "Okay, baby. Just hold on to me."

"Oh, God…" Her breath came out in a long, shaky sob as she buried her face against his shoulder. Her hands fisted impotently at his back. "Oh, God… Oh, God…"

"It's okay now." He continued to stroke and soothe, growing concerned when her hold on him increased. "I'm right here. You were dreaming, that's all. You were only dreaming."

She'd fought her way out of the dream, but the fear had come back with her, and it was too huge to allow for shame. So she clung, shivering, trying to absorb some portion of the strength she felt in him.

"Just give me a minute. I'll be all right in a minute." The shaking would stop, she told herself. The tears would dry. The fear would ebb. "I'm sorry." But it wasn't stopping. Instinctively she turned her face into his throat for comfort. "God, I'm sorry."

"Just relax." She was quivering like a bird, he thought, and she felt as frail as one. "Do you want me to turn on the light?"

"No." She pressed her lips together, hoping to stop the trembling in her voice. She didn't want the light. Didn't want him to see her until she'd managed to compose herself. "No. Let me get some water. I'll be fine."

"I'll get it." He brushed the hair from her face, and was shaken all over again to find it wet with tears. "I'll be right back."

She brought her knees up close to her chest when he left her. Control, she ordered herself, but dropped her head onto her knees. While she listened to water striking glass, watched the splinter of light spill through the crack around the bathroom door, she took long, even breaths.

"Sorry, Nightshade," she said when he came back with the water. "I guess I woke you up."

"I guess you did." Her voice was steadier, he noted. But her hands weren't. He cupped his around hers and lifted the glass to her lips. "Must have been a bad one."

The water eased her dry throat. "Must have been. Thanks." She pushed the glass back into his hands, embarrassed that she couldn't hold it herself.

Colt set the glass on the night table before easing down on the bed beside her. "Tell me."

She moved her shoulders dismissively. "Chalk it up to a rough day and pizza."

Very firmly, very gently, he took her face in his hands. The light he'd left on in the bathroom sent out a dim glow. In it he could see how pale she was.

"No. I'm not going to brush this off, Thea. You're not going to brush me off. You were screaming." She tried to turn her head away, but he wouldn't permit it. "You're still shaking. I can be every bit as stubborn as you, and right now I think I have the advantage."

"I had a nightmare." She wanted to snap at him, but couldn't find the strength. "People have nightmares."

"How often do you have this one?"

"Never." She lifted a weary hand and dragged it through her hair. "Not in years. I don't know what brought it on."

He thought he did. And unless he was very much mistaken, he thought she did, as well. "Do you have a shirt, a nightgown or something? You're cold."

"I'll get one."

"Just tell me where." Her quick, annoyed sigh did quite a bit toward easing his mind.

"Top drawer of the dresser. Left-hand side."

He rose, and opening the drawer grabbed the first thing that came to hand. Before he tugged it over her head, he examined the oversize man's undershirt. "Nice lingerie you have, Lieutenant."

"It does the job."

He smoothed it down over her, tucked pillows behind her, as fussy as a mother with a colicky infant.

She scowled at him. "I don't like being pampered."

"You'll live through it."

When he was satisfied he'd made her as comfortable as possible, he tugged on his jeans. They were going to talk, he decided, and sat beside her again. Whether she wanted to or not. He took her hand, waited until they were eye-to-eye.

"The nightmare. It was about when you were raped, wasn't it?" Her fingers went rigid in his. "I told you I heard you talking to Liz."

She ordered her fingers to relax, willed them to, but they remained stiff and cold. "It was a long time ago. It doesn't apply now."

"It does when it wakes you up screaming. It brought it all back," he continued quietly. "What happened to Liz, seeing her through it."

"All right. So what?"

"Trust me, Althea." He said it quietly, his eyes on hers. "Let me help."

"It hurts," she heard herself say. Then she shut her eyes. It was the first time she had admitted that to anyone. "Not all the time. Not even most of the time. It just sneaks up now and then and slices at you."

"I want to understand." He brought her hand to his lips. When she didn't pull away, he left it there. "Talk, talk to me."

She didn't know where to begin. It seemed safest to start at the beginning. Letting her head rest against the pillows, she closed her eyes again.

"My father drank, and when he drank, he got drunk, and when he got drunk, he got mean. He had big hands." She curled hers into fists, then relaxed them. "He used them on my mother, on me. My earliest memory is of those hands, the anger in them that I couldn't understand, and couldn't fight. I don't remember him very well. He tangled with somebody meaner one night and ended up dead. I was six."

She opened her eyes again, realizing that keeping them closed was just another way of hiding. "Once he was gone, my mother decided to take up where he'd left off—in the bottle. She didn't hit it as hard as he did, but she was more consistent."

He could only wonder how the people she'd described could have created anything as beautiful or as true as the woman beside him. "Did you have anyone else?"

"I had grandparents, on my mother's side. I don't know where they lived. I never met them. They hadn't had anything to do with her since she'd run off with my father."

"But did they know about you?"

"If they did, they didn't care."

He said nothing, trying to comprehend it. But he couldn't, simply couldn't understand family not caring. "Okay. What did you do?"

"When you're a child, you do nothing," she said flatly.

"You're at the mercy of adults, and the reality is, a great many adults have no mercy." She paused a moment to pick up the threads of the story. "When I was about eight, she went out— she went out a lot—but this time she didn't come home. A couple of days later, a neighbor called Social Services. They scooped me up into the system."

She reached for the water again. This time her hands didn't shake. "It's a long, typical story."

"I want to hear it."

"They placed me in a foster home." She sipped her water. There wasn't any point in telling him how frightened, how lost, she'd been. The facts were enough. "It was okay. Decent. Then they found her, slapped her wrists a couple of times, told her to clean up her act, and gave me back."

"Why in the hell did they do that?"

"Things were different back then. The court believed the best place for a kid was with her mother. Anyway, she didn't stay dry for long, and the cycle started all over again. I ran away a few times, they dragged me back. More foster homes. They don't leave you in any one too long, especially when you're recalcitrant. And I'd developed my own mean streak by that time."

"Small wonder."

"I bounced around in the system. Social workers, court hearings, school counselors. All overburdened. My mother hooked up with another guy and finally took off for good. Mexico, I think. In any case, she didn't come back. I was twelve, thirteen. I hated not being able to say where I wanted to go, where I wanted to be. I took off every chance I got. So they labeled me a j.d.—juvenile delinquent—and they put me in a girls' home, which was one step up from reform school."

Her lips twisted into a dry smile. "That put the fear of God into me. It was rough, as close to prison as I ever want to be. So I straightened up, put on my best behavior. Eventually they placed me in foster care again."

She drained the glass and set it aside. She knew her hands wouldn't be steady for long. "I was scared that if I didn't make it work this time, they'd put me back until I was eighteen. So I took a real shot at it. They were a nice couple, naive, maybe, but nice, good intentions. They wanted to do something to right society's ills. She was PTA president, and they went to protest rallies against nuclear power plants. They talked about adopting a Vietnamese orphan. I guess I smirked at them behind their backs sometimes, but I really liked them. They were kind to me."

She took a moment, and he said nothing, waiting for her to build to the next stage. "They gave me boundaries, good ones, and they treated me fairly. There was one drawback. They had a son. He was seventeen, captain of the football team, homecoming king, A student. The apple of their eye. A real company man."

"Company man?"

"You know, the kind who's all slick and polished on the outside, he's got a terrific rap, lots of charm, lots of angles. And underneath, he's slime. You can't get to the slime because you keep slipping on all that polish, but it's there." Her eyes glinted at the memory. "I could see it. I hated the way he looked at me when they weren't watching." Her breath was coming quicker now, but her voice was still controlled. "Like I was a piece of meat he was sizing up, getting ready to grill. They couldn't see it. All they saw was this perfect child who never gave them a moment's grief. And one night, when they were out, he came home from a date. God."

When she covered her face with her hands, Colt gathered her close. "It's all right, Thea. That's enough."

"No." She shook her head violently, pushed back. She'd gone this far. She'd finish it. "He was angry. I suppose his girl hadn't surrendered to his many charms. He came into my room. When I told him to get out, he just laughed and reminded me it was his house, and that I was only there because his parents felt sorry for me. Of course, he was right."

"No. No, he wasn't."

"He was right about that," Althea insisted. "Not about the rest, but about that. And he unzipped his pants. I ran for the door, but he threw me back on the bed. I hit my head pretty hard on the wall. I remember being dizzy for a minute, and hearing him telling me that he knew girls like me usually charged for it, but that I should be flattered that he was going to give me a thrill. He got on the bed. I slapped him, I swore at him. He backhanded me, and pinned me. And I started to scream. I kept screaming and screaming while he raped me. When he was finished, I wasn't screaming anymore. I was just crying. He got off the bed, and zipped up his pants. He warned me that if I told anyone he'd deny it. And who were they going to believe, someone like him, or someone like me? He was blood, so there was no contest. And he could always get five of his buddies to say that I'd been willing with all of them. Then they'd just put me back in the home.

"So I didn't say anything, because there was nothing to say and no one to say it to. He raped me twice more over the next month, before I got the nerve to run away again. Of course, they caught me. Maybe I'd wanted them to that time. I stayed in the home until I was eighteen. And when I got out, I knew no one was ever going to have that kind of control over me again. No one was ever going to make me feel like I was nothing ever again."

Unsure what to do, Colt reached up tentatively to brush a tear from her cheek. "You made your life into something, Althea."

"I made it into mine." She let out a breath, then briskly rubbed the tears from her cheeks. "I don't like to dwell on before, Colt."

"But it's there."

"It's there," she agreed. "Trying to make it go away only brings it closer to the surface. I learned that, too. Once you accept it's simply a part of what makes you what you are, it doesn't become as vital. It didn't make me hate men, it didn't make me hate myself. It did make me understand what it is to be a victim."

He wanted to gather her close, but was afraid she might not want to be touched. "I wish I could make the hurt go away."

"Old scars," she murmured. "They only ache at odd moments." She sensed his withdrawal, and felt the ache spread. "I'm the same person I was before I told you. The trouble is, after people hear a story like that, they change."

"I haven't changed." He started to touch her, drew back. "Damn it, Thea, I don't know what to say to you. What to do for you." Rising, he paced away from the bed. "I could make you some tea."

She nearly laughed. "Nightshade's cure-all? No thanks."

"What do you want?" he demanded. "Just tell me."

"Why don't you tell me what you want?"

"What I want." He strode to the window, whirled back. "I want to go back to when you were fifteen and kick that bastard's face in. I want to hurt him a hundred times worse than he hurt you. Then I want to go back further and break your father's legs, and I want to kick your mother's butt while I'm at it."

"Well, you can't," she said coolly. "Pick something else."

"I want to hold you!" he shouted, jamming his fists into his pockets. "And I'm afraid to touch you!"

"I don't want your tea, and I don't want your sympathy. So if that's all you have to offer, you might as well leave."

"Is that what you want?"

"What I want is to be accepted for who and what I am. Not to be tiptoed around like an invalid because I survived rape and abuse."

He started to snap back at her, then stopped himself. He wasn't thinking of her, he realized, but of his own rage, his own impotence, his own pain. Slowly he walked back to the bed and sat beside her. Her eyes were still wet; he could see them gleaming against the shadows. He slipped his arms around her, gently drew her close until her head rested on his shoulder.

"I'm not going anywhere," he murmured. "Okay?"

She sighed, settled. "Okay."

Althea awakened at sunrise with a dull headache. She knew instantly that Colt was no longer beside her. Wearily she rolled onto her back and rubbed her swollen eyes.

What had she expected? she asked herself. No man would be comfortable around a woman after hearing a story like the one she'd told him. And why in God's name had she dumped out her past that way? How could she have trusted him with pieces of herself that she'd never given anyone before?

Even Boyd, the person she considered her closest friend, knew only about the foster homes. As for the rest, she'd buried it—until last night.

She didn't doubt that her tie to Liz had unlocked the door and let the nightmare back in. But she should have been able to handle it, to hold back, to safeguard her privacy. The fact that she hadn't could mean only one thing.

Indulging in a sigh, Althea pushed herself up and rested her brow on her knees.

She was in love with Colt. Ridiculous as it was, she had to face the truth. And, just as she'd always suspected, love made you stupid, vulnerable and unhappy.

There ought to be a pill, she mused. A serum she could take. Like an antidote for snakebite.

The sound of footsteps had her whipping her head up. Her eyes widened when Colt came to the doorway carrying a tray.

He had a split second to read her reaction before she closed it off. She'd thought he'd taken a hike, he realized grimly. He was going to have to show the lady that he was sticking, no matter how hard she tried to shake him off.

"Morning, Lieutenant. I figured you'd planned on a full day."

"You figured right." Cautious, she watched as he crossed to the bed, waited until he'd set the tray at her feet. "What's the occasion?" she asked, gesturing toward the plates of French toast.

"I owe you a breakfast. Remember?"

"Yeah." Her gaze shifted from the plates to his face. Love still made her feel stupid, it still made her feel vulnerable, but it no longer made her unhappy. "You're a regular whiz in the kitchen."

"We all have our talents." He sat cross-legged on the other

side of the tray and dug in. "I figure—" he chewed, swallowed "—after we're married, I can handle the meals, you can handle the laundry."

She ignored the quick sprint of panic and sampled her first bite. "You ought to see someone about this obsessive fantasy life of yours, Nightshade."

"My mother's dying to meet you." He grinned when Althea's fork clattered against her plate. "She and Dad send their best."

"You—" Words failed her.

"She and my father know Liz. I called to relieve their minds, and I told them about you." Smiling, he brushed her hair back from her shoulders. He hadn't known a woman could look so sexy in a man's undershirt. "She's for a spring wedding—you know, all that June-bride stuff. But I told her I wasn't waiting that long."

"You're out of your mind."

"Maybe." His grin faded. "But I'm in yours, Thea. I'm in there real good, and I'm not getting out."

He was right about that, but it didn't change the bottom line. She was not walking down the aisle and saying 'I do.' That was that.

"Listen, Colt." Try reason, she thought. "I'm very fond of you, but—"

"You're what?" His mouth quirked again. "You're what of me?"

"Fond," she spit out, infuriated by the gleam of good humor in his eyes.

"Euphemisms." Affectionately he patted her hand, shook his head. "You disappoint me, I had you pegged as a straight shooter."

Forget reason. "Just shut up and let me eat."

He obliged her, because it gave him time to think, and to study her. She was still a bit pale, he mused. And her eyes were swollen from the bout of tears during the night. But she wouldn't let herself be fragile. He had to admire her unceasing supply of strength. She didn't want sympathy, he remembered, she wanted understanding. She would just have to learn to accept both from him.

She'd accepted his comfort the night before. Whether she knew it or not, she'd already come to rely on him. He wasn't about to let her down.

"How's the coffee?"

"Good." And because it was, because the meal he'd prepared had already conquered her headache, she relented. "Thanks."

"My pleasure." He leaned forward, touched his mouth to hers. "I don't suppose I could interest you in an after-breakfast tussle."

She smiled now, fully, easily. "I'll have to take a rain check." But she spread a hand over his chest and kissed him again. Her fingers closed over his medal. "Why do you wear this?"

"My grandmother gave it to me. She said that when a man was determined not to settle down in one place, he should have someone looking out for him. It's worked pretty well so far." He set the tray on the floor, then scooped Althea into his arms.

"Nightshade, I said—"

"I know, I know." He hitched her up more comfortably. "But I had this idea that if we had that tussle in the shower, we could stay pretty much on schedule."

She laughed, nipped at his shoulder. "I'm a firm believer in time management."

She had more than a full day to fit into twenty-four hours. There was a mountain of paperwork waiting for her, and she needed to talk to Boyd about his interrogation of Donner and Kline before she met with them herself. She wanted, for personal, as well as professional, reasons, to interview Liz again.

She sat down and began efficiently chipping away at the mountain.

Cilla knocked on the open door. "Excuse me, Lieutenant. Got a minute?"

"For the captain's wife," she said, smiling and gesturing Cilla inside, "I've got a minute and a half. What are you doing down here?"

"Boyd filled me in." Cilla leaned down, peered close and, as a woman would, saw through the meticulously applied cosmetics to the signs of a difficult night. "Are you all right?"

"I'm fine. I have decided that anyone who camps out on purpose needs immediate psychiatric help, but it was an experience."

"You should try it with three kids."

"No," Althea said definitely. "No, I shouldn't."

With a laugh, Cilla rested a hip against the edge of the desk. "I'm so glad you and Colt found the girl. How's she doing?"

"It'll be rough for a while, but she'll come through."

"Those creeps should be—" Cilla's eyes flashed, but she cut herself off. "I didn't come here to talk cop, I came to talk turkey."

"Oh?"

"As in Thanksgiving. Don't give me that look." Cilla an
gled her chin, readying for battle. "Every year you've go
some excuse for not coming to Thanksgiving dinner, and thi
time I'm not buying it."

"Cilla, you know I appreciate the offer."

"The hell with that. You're family. We want you." Even a
Althea was shaking her head, Cilla was plowing on. "Deb and
Gage are coming. You haven't seen them in a year."

Althea thought of Cilla's younger sister, Deborah, and he
husband. She would like to see Deb again. They'd gotten
close while Deborah was in Denver finishing up college. And
Gage Guthrie. Althea pursed her lips as she thought of him
She genuinely liked Deborah's husband, and a blind man
could have seen that he adored his wife. But there was some
thing about him—something Althea couldn't put her finge
on. Not a bad thing, she thought now, not a worrying thing
But something.

"Taking a side trip?" Cilla asked.

"Sorry." Althea snapped back and fiddled with the paper
on her desk. "You know I'd love to see them again, Cilla
but—"

"They're bringing Adrianna." Cilla's secret weapon wa
her sister's baby girl, whom Althea had seen only in snapshot
and videotapes. "You and I both know what a sucker you are
for babies."

"You want to keep that down?" Althea stated with an un
easy glance toward the bull pen. "I've got a reputation to up
hold around here." She sighed and leaned back in her chair
"You know I want to see them, all of them. And since I'm sure
they'll be here through the holiday weekend, I will. We'l
shoot for Saturday."

"Thanksgiving dinner." Cilla dusted her hands together as she straightened. "You're coming this year, if I have to tell Boyd to make it an order. I'm having my family. My whole family."

"Cilla—"

"That's it." Cilla folded her arms. "I'm taking this to the captain."

"You're in luck," Boyd said as he came to the door. "The captain happens to be available. And he's brought you a present." He stepped aside.

"Natalie!" With a whoop of pleasure, Cilla threw her arms around her sister-in-law and squeezed. "I thought you were in New York."

"I was." Natalie's dark green eyes sparkled with laughter as she drew Cilla back to kiss her. "I had to fly in for a few days, and I figured I'd make this my first stop. I didn't know I'd hit the jackpot. You look great."

"You look phenomenal, as always." It was perfectly true. The tall, willow-slim woman with the sleek blond hair and the conservatively cut suit would always turn heads. "The kids are going to be thrilled."

"I can't wait to get my hands on them." She turned, held out both hands. "Thea. I can't believe I'm lucky enough to get all three of you at once."

"It's really good to see you." With their hands still linked, Althea pressed her cheek to Natalie's. In the years Althea had been Boyd's partner, she and his younger sister had become fast friends. "How are your parents?"

"Terrific. They send love to everyone." In an old habit, she glanced around Althea's office, let out a sigh. "Thea, can't you at least get a space with a window?"

"I like this one. Fewer distractions."

"I'm calling Maria as soon as I get to the station," Cilla announced. "She'll whip up something special for tonight. You're coming, Thea."

"Wouldn't miss it."

"What is this?" Colt demanded as he tried to squeeze into the room. "A conference? Thea, you're going to have to get a bigger—" He broke off, stared. "Nat?"

Her stunned expression mirrored his. "Colt?"

His grin split his face. "Son of a gun." He elbowed past Boyd to grab Natalie in a hug that lifted her feet from the floor. "I'll be damned. Pretty Natalie. What's it been? Six years?"

"Seven." She kissed him full on the mouth. "We ran into each other in San Francisco."

"At the Giants game, right. You look better than ever."

"I am better than ever. Why don't we have a drink later, and catch up?"

"Now, that's…" He fumbled to a halt when he glanced at Althea. She was sitting on the edge of her desk, watching their reunion with an expression of mild curiosity and polite interest. When he realized his arm was still around Natalie's waist, he dropped it quickly to his side. "Actually, I, ah…"

How was a man supposed to talk to an old female friend when the woman he loved was studying him as if he were something smeared on a glass slide?

Natalie caught the look that passed between Althea and Colt. Surprise came first, then a chuckle she disguised by clearing her throat. Well, well, she thought, what an interesting stew she'd dropped into. She couldn't resist stirring the pot.

"Colt and I go way back," she said to Althea. "I had a terrible crush on him when I was a teenager." She smiled wickedly up at Colt. "I've been waiting for years for him to take advantage of it."

"Really?" Althea tapped a finger to her lips. "He doesn't strike me as being slow off the mark. A little dense, maybe, but not slow."

"You're right about that. Cute, too, isn't he?" She winked at Althea.

"In an overt sort of way," Althea agreed, enjoying Colt's discomfort. "Why don't you and I have that drink later, Natalie? It sounds as though you and I have quite a bit to chat about."

"It certainly does."

"I don't think this is the place to set up social engagements." Well aware that he was outnumbered and outgunned, Colt stuck his hands into his pockets. "Althea looks busy."

"Oh, I've got a minute or two. What are you doing in town, Natalie?"

"Business. Always nice when you can mix it with pleasure. I have an emergency meeting in an hour with the board of directors on one of Boyd's and my downtown units. Owning real estate is a full-time job. Without proper management, it can be a huge headache," she explained.

"You don't happen to own one on Second Avenue, do you?" Althea asked.

"Mmm, no. Is one up for sale?" A gleam came into her eyes, and then she laughed. "It's a weakness," she explained. "There's something about owning property, even with all the problems that come with it."

"What's the trouble now?" Boyd asked, trying to work up some interest.

"The manager decided to up all the rents and keep the dif ference." Natalie said, her eyes hardening in startling contras to her soft, lovely face. "I hate being duped."

"Pride," Boyd said, and tapped a finger on her nose. "Yo hate making a mistake."

"I didn't make a mistake." Her chin angled upward. "Th man's résumé was outstanding." When Boyd continued t grin, she wrinkled her nose at him. "The problem is, yo have to give a manager autonomy. You can't be everywher at once. I remember one manager we had who was runnin a floating crap game in an empty apartment. He kept it rente under a fake name," she continued, nearly amused now. "He' even filled out an application, complete with faked referen ces. He made enough profit off the games to afford the over head, so the rent came in like clockwork. I'd never have foun out if someone hadn't tipped the cops and they raided th place. It turned out he'd done the same thing twice before."

"Good Lord," Althea said, looking stunned.

"Oh, it wasn't that bad," Natalie went on. "Actually, it wa pretty exciting stuff. I just— What is it?" she demanded whe Althea sprang to her feet.

"Let's move." Colt was already headed out the door.

Althea grabbed her coat and sprinted after him. "Boyd, ru a make on—"

"Nieman," he called out. "I got it. You want backup?"

"I'll let you know."

When the room emptied, Natalie threw up her hands an stared at Cilla. "What brought that on?"

"Cops." Cilla shrugged. That said it all.

Chapter 12

"I can't believe we let that slip by us." Colt slammed the door to the Jeep and peeled away from the curb. This time he didn't bother to remove the parking ticket under the windshield wiper.

"We're going on a hunch," Althea reminded him. "We could very well get slapped down."

"You don't think so."

She shut her eyes a moment, letting the pieces fall into place. "It fits," she said grimly. "Not one single tenant could swear they'd ever seen this Mr. Davis. He was the man who wasn't there—maybe because he never was."

"And who would have had access to the penthouse? Who could have faked references—references that didn't have to exist? Who could have slipped through the building virtually unnoticed, because he was always there?"

"Nieman."

"I told you he was a weasel," Colt said between his teeth.

She was forced to agree, but cautiously. "Don't get ahead of yourself, Nightshade. We're doing some follow-up questioning. That's all."

"I'm getting answers," he shot back. "That's all."

"Don't make me pull rank on you, Colt." She said it quietly, calming him. "We're going in there to ask questions. We may be able to shake him into slipping up. We may very well have to walk out without him. But now we have a place to start digging."

They'd dig, all right, Colt thought. Deep enough to bury Nieman. "I'll follow your lead," he said. For now. He pulled up at a red light, drumming his fingers impatiently on the wheel. "I'd like to, ah…explain about Nat."

"Explain what?"

"That we aren't—weren't. Ever," he said savagely. "Got it?"

"Really?" She'd laugh about this later, she was sure. Once there weren't so many other things on her mind. Still, she wasn't so preoccupied that she'd blow a chance to bait him. "Why not? She's beautiful, she's fun, she's smart. Looks like you fell down on that one, Nightshade."

"It wasn't that I didn't… I mean, I thought about it. Started to—" He swore, revved the engine when the light turned. "She was Boyd's sister, all right? Before I knew it, she was like my sister, too, so I couldn't…think about her that way."

She sent him a long, curious look. "Why are you apologizing?"

"I'm not." His voice took on a vicious edge, because he realized he was doing just that. "I'm explaining. Though God knows why I'd bother. You think what you want."

"All right. I think you're overreacting to a situation in typical, and predictable, male fashion." The look he speared at her should have sliced to the bone. She merely smiled. "I don't hold it against you. Any more than I would hold it against you if you and Natalie *had* been involved. The past is just that. I know that better than anyone."

"I guess you do." He jammed the gearshift into fourth, then reached out to cover her hand with his. "But we weren't involved."

"I'd have to say that was your loss, pal. She's terrific."

"So are you."

She smiled at him. "Yeah, I am."

Colt steered to the curb, parking carelessly in a loading zone. He waited while Althea called in their location. "Ready?"

"I'm always ready." She stepped out of the car. "I want to play this light," she told Colt. "Just follow-up questions. We've got nothing on him. Nothing. If we push too hard, we'll lose our chance. If we're right about this—"

"We are right. I can feel it."

So could she. She nodded. "Then I want him. For Liz. For Wild Bill." And for herself, she realized. To help her close the door this ordeal had opened again.

They walked in together and approached Nieman's apartment. Althea sent Colt one last warning look, then knocked.

"Yes, yes…" Nieman's voice came through the door. "What is it?"

"Lieutenant Grayson, Mr. Nieman." She held her shield up to the peephole. "Denver PD. We need a few minutes of your time."

He pulled open the door to the width of the security chain.

His eyes darted from Althea's face to Colt's and back again. "Can't this wait? I'm busy."

"I'm afraid not. It shouldn't take long, Mr. Nieman. Just routine."

"Oh, very well." With a definite lack of grace, he yanked off the chain. "Come in, then."

When she did, Althea noted the packing boxes set on the carpet. Many were filled with shredded paper. For Althea, they were as damning as a smoking gun.

"As you can see, you've caught me at a bad time."

"Yes, I can see that. Are you moving, Mr. Nieman?"

"Do you think I would stay here, work here, after this—this scandal?" Obviously insulted, he tugged on his tightly knotted tie. "I think not. Police, reporters, badgering tenants. I haven't had a moment's peace since this began."

"I'm sure it's been a trial for you," Colt stated. He wanted to get his hands on that tie. Nieman would hang nicely from it.

"It certainly has. Well, I suppose you must sit." Nieman waved a hand toward chairs. "But I really can't spare much time. I've a great deal of packing left to do. I don't trust the movers to do it," he added. "Clumsy, always breaking things."

"You've had a lot of experience with moving?" This from Althea as she sat and took out her pad and pencil.

"Naturally. As I've explained before, I travel. I enjoy my work." He smiled by tightening his lips over his teeth. "But I find it tedious to remain in one place for too long. Landlords are always looking for a responsible, experienced manager."

"I'm sure they are." She tapped her pencil against the pad. "The owners of this building…" She began to flip pages.

"Johnston and Croy, Inc."

"Yes." She nodded when she found the notation. "They were quite upset when they were told about the activities in the penthouse."

"I should say." Nieman hitched up the knees of his trousers and sat. "They're a respectable company. Quite successful in the West and Southwest. Of course, they blame me. That's to be expected."

"Because you didn't do a personal interview with the tenant?" Althea prompted.

"The bottom line in real estate, Lieutenant, is regular monthly rentals and low turnover. I provided that."

"You also provided the scene of the crime."

"I can hardly be held responsible for the conduct of my tenants."

It was time, Althea decided, to take a risk. A calculated one. "And you never entered the premises? Never checked on it?"

"Why would I? I had no reason to bother Mr. Davis or go into the penthouse."

"You never went in while Mr. Davis was in residence?" Althea asked.

"I've just said I didn't."

She frowned, flipped more pages. "How would you explain your fingerprints?"

Something flickered in Nieman's eyes, then was gone. "I don't know what you mean."

She was reaching, but she pressed a bit further. "I wondered how you would explain it if I told you that your fingerprints were found inside the penthouse—since you claim never to have entered the premises."

"I don't see…" He was scrambling now. "Oh, yes, I remember now. A few days before…before the incident…the smoke alarm in the penthouse went off. Naturally, I used my passkey to investigate when no one answered my knock."

"You had a fire?" Colt asked.

"No, no, simply a defective smoke detector. It was so minor an incident, I quite forgot it."

"Perhaps you've forgotten something else," Althea said politely. "Perhaps you forgot to tell us about a cabin, west of Boulder. Do you manage that property, as well?"

"I don't know what you're talking about. I don't manage any property but this."

"Then you just use it for recreation," Althea continued. "With Mr. Donner, Mr. Kline and Mr. Scott."

"I have no knowledge of a cabin," Nieman said stiffly, but a line of sweat had popped out above his top lip. "Nor do I know any people by those names. Now you'll have to excuse me."

"Mr. Scott isn't quite up to visitors," Althea told him, and remained seated. "But we can go downtown and see Kline and Donner. That might refresh your memory."

"I'm not going anywhere with you." Nieman rose then. "I've answered all your questions in a reasonable and patient manner. If you persist in this harassment, I'll have to call my attorney."

"Feel free." Althea gestured toward the phone. "He can meet us at the station. In the meantime, I'd like you to think back to where you were on the night of October 25. You could use an alibi."

"Whatever for?"

"Murder."

"That's preposterous." He drew a handkerchief out of his breast pocket to wipe his face. "You can't come in here and accuse me this way."

"I'm not accusing you, Mr. Nieman. I'm asking for your whereabouts on October 25, between the hours of 9:00 and 11:00 p.m. You might also tell your lawyer that we'll be questioning you about a missing woman known as Lacy, and about the abduction of Elizabeth Cook, who is currently in protective custody. Liz is a very bright and observant girl, isn't she, Nightshade?"

"Yeah." She was amazing, Colt thought. Absolutely amazing. She was cracking Nieman into pieces with nothing but innuendo. "Between Liz and the sketches, the D.A. has plenty to work with."

"I don't believe we mentioned the sketches to Mr. Nieman." Althea closed her notebook. "Or the fact that both Kline and Donner were thoroughly interrogated yesterday. Of course, Scott is still critical, so we'll have to wait for his corroboration."

Nieman's face went pasty. "They're lying. I'm a respectable man. I have credentials." His voice cracked. "You can't prove anything on the word of some two-bit actors."

"I don't believe we mentioned Kline and Donner were actors, did we, Nightshade?"

"No." He could have kissed her. "No, we didn't."

"You must be psychic, Nieman," Althea stated. "Why don't we go to the station and see what else you can come up with?"

"I know my rights." Nieman's eyes glittered with rage as he felt the trap creaking shut. "I'm not going anywhere with you."

"I'll have to insist." Althea rose. "Go ahead and call your lawyer, Nieman, but you're coming in for questioning. Now."

"No woman's going to tell me what to do." Nieman lunged, and though Althea was braced, even eager, Colt stepped between them and merely used one hand to shove Nieman back onto the couch.

"Assaulting an officer," he said mildly. "I guess we'll take him in on that. It should give you enough time to get a search warrant."

"More than enough," she agreed. She took out her cuffs.

"Ah, Lieutenant…" Colt watched as she competently secured Nieman's skinny wrists. "They didn't find prints upstairs, did they?"

"I never said they did." She tossed her hair back. "I simply asked what he'd say *if* I said they were found."

"I was wrong," he decided. "I do like your style."

"Thanks." Satisfied, she smiled. "I wonder what we might find in all these neatly packed boxes."

They found more than enough. Tapes, snapshots, even a detailed journal in Nieman's own hand. It painstakingly recorded all his activities, all his thoughts, all his hatred for women. It described how the woman named Lacy had been murdered, and how her body had been buried behind the cabin.

By that afternoon, he had been booked on enough charges to keep him away from society for a lifetime.

"A little anticlimactic," Colt commented as he followed Althea into her office, where she would type up her report. "He was so revolting, I couldn't even drum up the energy to kill him."

"Lucky for you." She sat, booted up her machine. "Listen, if it's any consolation, I believe he was telling the truth about not touching Liz himself. I'm betting the psychiatric profile bears it out. Impotence, accompanied by rage against women and voyeuristic tendencies."

"Yeah, he just likes to watch." His fury came and went. Althea had been right about not being able to change what had been.

"And to make piles of money from his hobby," she added. "Once he rounded up his cameraman and a couple of sleazy actors, he went into the business of pandering to others with his peculiar tastes. Got to give him credit. He kept a very precise set of books on his porn business. Kept him in antiques and silk ties."

"He won't need either one in a cell." He rested his hands on her shoulders. "You did good, Thea. Real good."

"I usually do." She glanced over her shoulder to study him. Now all she had to do was figure out what to do about Colt. "Listen, Nightshade, I really want to get this paperwork moving, and then I need some downtime. Okay?"

"Sure. I hear there's going to be some spread at the Fletchers' tonight. Are you up for it?"

"You bet. Why don't I meet you there?"

"All right." He leaned down to press his lips to her hair. "I love you, Thea."

She waited until he left, shutting her door behind him. *I know,* she thought, *I love you, too.*

She went to see Liz. It helped to be able to give the girl and her family some sort of resolution. Colt had beaten her to it, had already come and gone. But Althea sensed that Liz needed to hear it from her, as well.

"We'll never be able to repay you." Marleen stood with her arm around Liz as if she couldn't bear not to touch her daughter. "I don't have the words to tell you how grateful we are."

"I—" She'd almost said she'd just been doing her job. It

was the truth, but it wasn't all of it. "Just take care of each other," she said instead.

"We're going to spend a lot more time doing just that." Marleen pressed her cheek against Liz's. "We're going home tomorrow."

"We're going into family counseling," Liz told Althea. "And I—I'm going to join a rape victims' support group. I'm a little scared."

"It's all right to be scared."

Nodding, Liz looked at her mother. "Mom, can I—I just want to talk to Lieutenant Grayson for a minute."

"Sure." Marleen clung for a final moment. "I'll just go down to the lobby, help your father when he gets back with that ice cream."

"Thanks." Liz waited until her mother left the room. "Dad doesn't know how to talk about what happened to me yet. It's awful hard on him."

"He loves you. Give him time."

"He cried." Liz's own eyes filled with tears. "I never saw him cry before. I thought he was too busy with work and stuff to care. I was stupid to run away." Once she'd blurted it out, she exhaled deeply. "I didn't think they understood me, or what I wanted. Now I see how bad I hurt them. It won't ever be exactly the same again, will it?"

"No, Liz, it won't. But if you help each other through it, it can be better."

"I hope so. I still feel so empty inside. Like a part of me's not there anymore."

"You'll fill it with something else. You can't let this block off your feelings for other people. It can make you strong, Liz, but you don't want it to make you hard."

"Colt said—" She sniffled and reached for the box of tissues her mother had left on the coffee table. "He said whenever I felt like I couldn't make it, I should think of you."

Althea stared. "Of me?"

"Because you'd had something horrible happen to you, and you'd used it to make yourself beautiful. Inside and out. That you hadn't just survived, you'd triumphed." She gave a watery smile. "And I could, too. It was funny to hear him talk that way. I guess he must like you a lot."

"I like him, too." And she did, Althea realized. It wasn't a weakness to love someone, not when you could admire and respect him at the same time. Not when he saw exactly what you were, and loved you back.

"Colt's the best," Liz stated. "He never lets you down, you know? No matter what."

"I think I do."

"I was wondering... I know the counseling's important, and everything, but I wonder if I could just call you sometimes. When I—when I don't think I can get through it."

"I hope you will." Althea rose to go over and sit beside Liz. She opened her arms. "You call when you're feeling bad. And when you're feeling good. We all need somebody who understands us."

Fifteen minutes later, Althea left the Cooks to their ice cream and their privacy. She decided she had a lot of thinking to do. She'd always known where her life was going. Now that it had taken this sudden and dramatic detour, she needed to get her bearings again.

But Colt was waiting for her in the lobby.

"Hey, Lieutenant." He tipped her head back and kissed her lightly.

"What are you doing here? Marleen said you'd been by already."

"I went with Frank. He needed to talk."

She touched a hand to his cheek. "You're a good friend, Nightshade."

"It's the only kind of friend there is." She smiled, because she knew he meant it. "Want a lift?"

"I've got my car." But when they walked outside together she discovered she didn't want that downtime alone after all. "Look, do you want to take a walk or something? I'm wired."

"Sure." He draped an arm casually over her shoulder. "You can help me scope out some of the shop windows. My mother has a birthday next week."

Resistance surged instantly—a knee-jerk response. "I'm no good at picking out presents for people I don't know."

"You'll get to know her." He strolled to the corner and turned left, heading toward a row of downtown shops. He glanced in one window at an elegant display of fine china and crystal. "Hey, you're not the type who, like, registers a pattern and that stuff, are you? You know, for wedding presents?"

"Get a grip." She moved past him so that he had to lengthen his stride to catch up.

"What about a trousseau? Do women still do that?"

"I haven't any idea, or any interest."

"It's not that I mind the T-shirt you wore in bed last night. I was just thinking that something a little more...no, a little less, would be nice for the honeymoon. Where do you want to go?"

"Are you going to cut this out?"

"No."

With an impatient breath, she turned and stared at the next window. "That's a nice sweater." She pointed to a rich blue cowl-neck on a mannequin. "Maybe she'd go for cashmere."

"Maybe." He nodded. "Fine. Let's go get it."

"See, that's your problem." Althea whirled around, hands on hips. "You don't give anything enough thought. You look at one thing, and boom—that's it."

"When it's the right thing, why look around?" He smiled and tugged on her hair. "I know what works for me when I see it. Come on." He took her hand and pulled her into the shop. "The blue sweater in the window?" he said to the clerk. "Have you got it in a size…" He measured in the air with his hands.

"Ten?" the clerk guessed. "Certainly, sir. Just one moment."

"You didn't ask how much it cost," Althea pointed out.

"When something's right, cost is irrelevant." He turned to smile at her. "You're going to keep me in line. I appreciate that. I tend to let details slip."

"There's news." She stepped away to poke through a rack of silk blouses.

He was careless, Althea reminded herself. He was impulsive and rash and quick on the draw. All the things she was not. She preferred order, routine, meticulous calculation. She had to be crazy to think they could mesh.

She turned her head, watching him as he waited for the clerk to ring up the sweater and gift-wrap it.

But they did mesh, she realized. Everything about him fitted her like a glove. The hair wasn't really blond or brown and was never quite disciplined. The eyes, caught somewhere between blue and green, that could stop her heart with one look. His recklessness. His dependability.

His total and unconditional understanding.

"Problem?" he asked when he caught her staring.

"No."

"Would you like a pink bow, sir, or blue?"

"Pink," he said, without glancing back. "Do you have any wedding dresses in here?"

"Not formal ones, no, sir." But the clerk's eyes lit up at the prospect of another sale. "We do have some very elegant tea gowns and cocktail suits that would be perfect for a wedding."

"It should be something festive," he decided, and the humor was back in his eyes. "For New Year's Eve."

Althea straightened her shoulders, turned on her heel to face him. "Get this, Nightshade. I am not marrying you on New Year's Eve."

"Okay, okay. Pick another date."

"Thanksgiving," she told him, and had the pleasure of watching his mouth fall open as he dropped the box the clerk had handed him.

"What?"

"I said Thanksgiving. Take it or leave it." She tossed her hair back and strode out the door.

"Wait! Damn!" He started after her, kicked the gift box halfway across the room. The clerk called after him as he scooped it up on the run.

"Sir, the dresses?"

"Later." He swung through the door and caught up with Althea halfway down the block. "Did you say you'd marry me on Thanksgiving?"

"I hate repeating myself, Nightshade. If you can't keep up, that's your problem. Now, if you've finished your shopping, I'm going back to work."

"Just one damn minute." Exasperated, he stuffed the box under his arm, crushing the bow. It freed his hands to snag her by the shoulders. "What made you change your mind?"

"It must have been your smooth, subtle approach," she said dryly. Lord, she was enjoying this, she realized. Deep-down enjoying it. "Keep manhandling me, pal, and I'll haul you in."

He shook his head, as if to realign his thoughts. "You're going to marry me?"

She arched a brow. "Ain't no flies on you."

"On Thanksgiving. *This* Thanksgiving. The one that's coming up in a few weeks?"

"Getting cold feet already?" she began, then found her mouth much too occupied for words. It was a heady kiss, filled with promises and joy. "Do you know the penalty for kissing a police officer on a public street?" she asked when she could speak again.

"I'll risk it."

"Good." She dragged his mouth back to hers. Pedestrians wound around them as they clung. "You're going to get life for this, Nightshade."

"I'm counting on it." Carefully he drew her back so that he could see her face. "Why Thanksgiving?"

"Because I'd like to have a family to celebrate it with. Cilla's always bugging me to join them, but I…I couldn't."

"Why?"

"Is this an interrogation or an engagement?" she demanded.

"Both, but this is the last one. Why are you going to marry me?"

"Because you nagged me until I broke down. And I felt sorry for you, because you seemed so set on it. Besides, I love you, and I've kind of gotten used to you, so—"

"Hold on. Say that again."

"I said I've kind of gotten used to you."

Grinning, he kissed the tip of her nose. "Not that part. The part right before that."

"Where I felt sorry for you?"

"Uh-uh. After that."

"Oh, the I-love-you part."

"That's the one. Say it again."

"Okay." She took a deep breath. "I love you." And let it out. "It's tougher to say it all by itself that way."

"You'll get used to it."

"I think you're right."

He laughed and crushed her against him. "I'm betting on it."

Epilogue

"I think I need to consider this again."

Althea stood in front of the full-length mirror in Cilla's bedroom, staring at her own reflection. There was a woman inside the mirror, she noted dispassionately. A pale woman with a tumble of red hair. She looked elegant in a slim ivory suit trimmed with lace and accented with tiny pearl buttons that ran the length of the snugly fitted jacket.

But her eyes were too big, too wide, and too fearful.

"I really don't think this is going to work."

"You look fabulous," Deborah assured her. "Perfect."

"I wasn't talking about the dress." She pressed a hand to her queasy stomach. "I meant the wedding."

"Don't start." Cilla tugged at the line of Althea's ivory silk jacket. "You're fidgeting again."

"Of course I'm fidgeting." For lack of anything better to

do, Althea reached up to make sure the pearl drops at her ears were secure. Colt's mother had given them to her, she remembered, and felt a trickle of warmth at the memory. Something to be handed down, his mother had said, as they had been from Colt's grandmother to her.

Then she'd cried a little, and kissed Althea's cheek and welcomed her to the family.

Family, Althea thought on a fresh wave of panic. What did she know about family?

"I'm about to commit myself for life to a man I've known a matter of weeks," she muttered to the woman in the mirror. "I should *be* committed."

"You love him, don't you?" Deborah asked.

"What does that have to do with it?"

Laughing, Deborah took Althea's restless hand in hers. "Only everything. I didn't know Gage very long, either." And had known the depths of his secrets for an even shorter time. "But I loved him, and I knew. I've seen the way you look at Colt, Thea. You know, too."

"Lawyers," Althea complained to Cilla. "They always turn things around on you."

"She's great, isn't she?" Pride burst through as Cilla gave her sister a hard squeeze. "The best prosecutor east of the Mississippi."

"When you're right, you're right," Deborah returned with a grin. "Now, let's take a look at the matron of honor." She tilted her head to examine her sister. "You look wonderful, Cilla."

"So do you." Cilla brushed a hand through her sister's dark hair. "Marriage and motherhood agree with you."

"If you two will finish up your admiration hour, I'm having a nervous breakdown over here." Althea sat down on the bed, squeezed her eyes shut. "I could make a run for it out the back."

"He'd catch you," Cilla decided.

"Not if I had a really good head start. Maybe if I—" A knock on the door interrupted her. "If that's Nightshade, I am not going to talk to him."

"Of course not," Deborah agreed. "Bad luck." She opened the door to her husband and daughter. That was good luck, she thought as she smiled at Gage. The very best luck of all.

"Sorry to break in on the prep work, but we've got some restless people downstairs."

"If those kids have touched that wedding cake…" Cilla began.

"Boyd saved it," Gage assured her. Barely. With the baby tucked in one arm, he slipped the other around his wife. "Colt's wearing a path in the den carpet."

"So he's nervous," Althea shot back. "He should be. Look what he's gotten us into. Boy, would I like to be a fly on the wall down there."

Gage grinned, winked at Deborah. "It has its advantages." He nuzzled his infant daughter when she began to fuss.

"I'll take her, Gage." Deborah gathered Adrianna into her arms. "You go help Boyd calm down the groom. We're nearly ready."

"Who said?" Althea twisted her hands together.

Cilla brushed Gage out of the room, closed the door. It was time for the big guns. "Coward," she said softly.

"Now, just a minute…"

"You're afraid to walk downstairs and make a public commitment to the man you love. That's pathetic."

Catching on, Deborah soothed the baby, and played the game. "Now, Cilla, don't be so harsh. If she's changed her mind—"

"She hasn't. She just can't make it up. And Colt's doing everything to make her happy. He's selling his ranch, buying land out here."

Althea got to her feet. "That's unfair."

"It certainly is." Deborah ranged herself beside Althea, and bit the inside of her lip to keep from grinning. "I'd think you'd be a little more understanding, Cilla. This is an important decision."

"Then she should make it instead of hiding up here like some vestal virgin about to be sacrificed."

Althea's chin jutted out. "I'm not hiding. Deb, go out and tell them to start the damn music. I'm coming down."

"All right, Thea. If you're sure." Deborah patted her arm, winked at her sister, and hurried out.

"Well, come on." Althea stormed to the door. "Let's get going."

"Fine." Cilla sauntered past her, then started down the steps.

Althea was nearly to the bottom before she realized she'd been conned. The two sisters had pulled off the good cop–bad cop routine like pros.

Now her stomach jumped. There were flowers everywhere, banks of color and scent. There was music, soft, romantic. She saw Colt's mother leaning heavily against his father and smiling bravely through a mist of tears. She saw Natalie beaming and dabbing at her eyes. Deborah, her lashes wet, cradling Adrianna.

There was Boyd, reaching out to take Cilla's hand, kissing her damp cheek before looking back at Althea to give her an encouraging wink.

Althea came to a dead stop. If people cried at weddings, she deduced, there had to be a good reason.

Then she looked toward the fireplace, and saw nothing but Colt.

And he saw nothing but her.

Her legs stopped wobbling. She crossed to him, carrying a single white rose, and her heart.

"Good to see you, Lieutenant," he murmured as he took her hand.

"Good to see you, too, Nightshade." She felt the warmth from the fire that glowed beside them, the warmth from him. She smiled as he brought her hand to his lips, and her fingers were steady.

"Happy Thanksgiving."

"Same goes." She brought their joined hands to her lips in turn. Maybe she didn't know about family, but she'd learn. They'd learn. "I love you, very much."

"Same goes. Ready for this?"

"I am now."

As the fire crackled, they faced each other and the life they'd make together.

* * * * *

NIGHT SMOKE

For opposites who attract.

Prologue

Fire. It cleansed. It destroyed. With its heat, lives could be saved. Or lives could be taken. It was one of the greatest discoveries of man, and one of his chief fears.

And one of his fascinations.

Mothers warned their children not to play with matches, not to touch the red glow of the stove. For no matter how pretty the flame, how seductive the warmth, fire against flesh burned.

In the hearth, it was romantic, cozy, cheerful, dancing and crackling, wafting scented smoke and flickering soft golden light. Old men dreamed by it. Lovers wooed by it.

In the campfire, it shot its sparks toward a starry sky, tempting wide-eyed children to roast their marshmallows into black goo while shivering over ghost stories.

There were dark, hopeless corners of the city where the

homeless cupped their frozen hands over trash-can fires, their faces drawn and weary in the shadowy light, their minds too numb for dreams.

In the city of Urbana, there were many fires.

A carelessly dropped cigarette smoldering in a mattress. Faulty wiring, overlooked, or ignored by a corrupt inspector. A kerosene heater set too close to the drapes, oily rags tossed in a stuffy closet. A flash of lightning. An unattended candle.

All could cause destruction of property, loss of life. Ignorance, an accident, an act of God.

But there were other ways, more devious ways.

Once inside the building he took several short, shallow breaths. It was so simple, really. And so exciting. The power was in his hands now. He knew exactly what to do, and there was a thrill in doing it. Alone. In the dark.

It wouldn't be dark for long. The thought made him giggle as he climbed to the second floor. He would soon make the light.

Two cans of gasoline would be enough. With the first he splashed the old wooden floor, soaking it, leaving a trail as he moved from wall to wall, from room to room. Now and again he stopped, pulling stock from the racks, scattering matchbooks over the stream of flammables, adding fuel that would feed the flames and spread them.

The smell of the accelerant was sweet, an exotic perfume that heightened his senses. He wasn't panicked, he wasn't hurried as he climbed the winding metal stairs to the next floor. He was quiet, of course, for he wasn't a stupid man. But he knew the night watchman was bent over his magazines in another part of the building.

As he worked, he glanced up at the spider-like sprinklers in the ceiling. He'd already seen to those. There would be no hiss of water from the pipes as the flames rose, no warning buzz from smoke alarms.

This fire would burn, and burn, and burn, until the window glass exploded from the angry fists of heat. Paint would blister, metal would melt, rafters would fall, charred and flaming.

He wished…for a moment he wished he could stay, stand in the center of it all and watch the sleeping fire awaken, grumbling. He wanted to be there, to admire and absorb as it stirred, snapped, then stretched its hot, bright body. He wanted to hear its triumphant roar as it hungrily devoured everything in its path.

But he would be far away by then. Too far to see, to hear, to smell. He would have to imagine it.

With a sigh, he lit the first match, held the flame at eye level, admiring the infant spark, mesmerized by it. He was smiling, as proud as any expectant father, as he tossed the tiny fire into a dark pool of gas. He watched for a moment, only a moment, as the animal erupted into life, streaking along the trail he'd left for it.

He left quietly, hurrying now, into the frigid night. Soon his feet had picked up the rhythm of his racing heart.

Chapter 1

Annoyed, exhausted, Natalie stepped into her penthouse apartment. The dinner meeting with her marketing executives had run beyond midnight. She could have come home then, she reminded herself as she stepped out of her shoes. But no. Her office was en route from the restaurant to her apartment. She simply hadn't been able to resist stopping in for one more look at the new designs, one last check on the ads heralding the grand opening.

Both had needed work. And really, she'd only intended to make a few notes. Draft one or two memos.

So why was she stumbling toward the bedroom at 2:00 a.m.? she asked herself. The answer was easy. She was compulsive, obsessive. She was, Natalie thought, an idiot. Particularly since she had an eight-o'clock breakfast meeting with several of her East Coast sales reps.

No problem, she assured herself. No problem at all. Who needed sleep? Certainly not Natalie Fletcher, the thirty-two-year-old dynamo who was currently expanding Fletcher Industries into one more avenue of profit.

And there *would* be profit. She'd put all her skill and experience and creativity into building Lady's Choice from the ground up. Before profit, there would be the excitement of conception, birth, growth, those first pangs and pleasures of an infant company finding its own way.

Her infant company, she thought with tired satisfaction. Her baby. She would tend and teach and nurture—and, yes, when necessary, walk the floor at 2:00 a.m.

A glance in the mirror over the bureau told her that even a dynamo needed rest. Her cheeks had lost both their natural color as well as their cosmetic blush and her face looked entirely too fragile and pale. The simple twist that scooped her hair back and had started the evening looking sophisticated and chic now only seemed to emphasize the shadows that smudged her dark green eyes.

Because she was a woman who prided herself on her energy and stamina, she turned away from the reflection, blowing her honey-toned bangs out of her eyes and rotating her shoulders to ease the stiffness. In any case, sharks didn't sleep, she reminded herself. Even business sharks. But this one was very tempted to fall on the bed fully dressed.

That wouldn't do, she thought, and shrugged out of her coat. Organization and control were every bit as important in business as a good head for figures. Ingrained habit had her walking to the closet, and she was draping the velvet wrap on a padded hanger when the phone rang.

Let the machine get it, she ordered herself, but by the second ring she was snatching up the receiver.

"Hello?"

"Ms. Fletcher?"

"Yes?" The receiver clanged against the emeralds at her ear. She was reaching up to remove the earring when the panic in the voice stopped her.

"It's Jim Banks, Ms. Fletcher. The night watchman over at the south side warehouse. We've got trouble here."

"Trouble? Did someone break in?"

"It's fire. Holy God, Ms. Fletcher, the whole place is going up."

"Fire?" She brought her other hand to the receiver, as if it might leap from her ear. "At the warehouse? Was anyone in the building? Is anyone in there?"

"No, ma'am, there was just me." His voice shook, cracked. "I was downstairs in the coffee room when I heard an explosion. Must've been a bomb or something, I don't know. I called the fire department."

She could hear other sounds now, sirens, shouts. "Are you hurt?"

"No, I got out. I got out. Mother of God, Ms. Fletcher, it's terrible. It's just terrible."

"I'm on my way."

It took Natalie fifteen minutes to make the trip from her plush west-side neighborhood to the dingy south side, with its warehouses and factories. But she saw the fire, heard it before she pulled up behind the string of engines. Men with their faces smeared with soot manned hoses, wielded axes. Smoke and flame belched from shattered windows and spewed through gaps in the ruined roof. The heat was enormous. Even at this distance it shot out, slapping her face while the icy February wind swirled at her back.

Everything. She knew everything inside the building was lost.

"Ms. Fletcher?"

Struggling against horror and fascination, she turned and looked at a round middle-aged man in a gray uniform.

"I'm Jim Banks."

"Oh, yes." She reached out automatically to take his hand. It was freezing, and as shaky as his voice. "You're all right? Are you sure?"

"Yes, ma'am. It's an awful thing."

They watched the fire and those who fought it for a moment, in silence. "The smoke alarms?"

"I didn't hear anything. Not until the explosion. I started to head upstairs, and I saw the fire. It was everywhere." He rubbed a hand over his mouth. Never in his life had he seen anything like it. Never in his life did he want to see its like again. "Just everywhere. I got out and called the fire department from my truck."

"You did the right thing. Do you know who's in charge here?"

"No, Ms. Fletcher, I don't. These guys work fast, and they don't spend a lot of time talking."

"All right. Why don't you go home now, Jim? I'll deal with this. If they need to talk to you, I have your beeper number, and they can call."

"Nothing much to do." He looked down at the ground and shook his head. "I'm mighty sorry, Ms. Fletcher."

"So am I. I appreciate you calling me."

"Thought I should." He gave one last glance at the building, seemed to shudder, then trudged off to his truck.

Natalie stood where she was, and waited.

A crowd had gathered by the time Ry got to the scene. A fire drew crowds, he knew, like a good fistfight or a flashy juggler. People even took sides—and a great many of them rooted for the fire.

He stepped out of his car, a lean, broad-shouldered man with tired eyes the color of the smoke stinging the winter sky. His narrow, bony face was set, impassive. The lights flashing around him shadowed, then highlighted, the hollows and planes, the shallow cleft in his chin that women loved and he found a small nuisance.

He set his boots on the sodden ground and stepped into them with a grace and economy of motion that came from years of training. Though flames still licked and sparked, his experienced eye told him that the men had contained and nearly suppressed it.

Soon it would be time for him to go to work.

Automatically he put on the black protective jacket, covering his flannel shirt and his jeans down past the hips. He combed one hand through his unruly hair, hair that was a deep, dark brown and showed hints of fire in sunlight. He set his dented, smoke-stained hat on his head, lit a cigarette, then tugged on protective gloves.

And while he performed these habitual acts, he scanned the scene. A man in his position needed to keep an open mind about fire. He would take an overview of the scene, the weather, note the wind direction, talk to the fire fighters. There would be all manner of routine and scientific tests to run.

But first, he would trust his eyes, and his nose.

The warehouse was most probably a loss, but it was no longer his job to save it. His job was to find the whys and the hows.

He exhaled smoke and studied the crowd.

He knew the night watchman had called in the alarm. The man would have to be interviewed. Ry looked over the faces, one by one. Excitement was normal. He saw it in the eyes of the young man who watched the destruction, dazzled. And shock, in the slack-jawed woman who huddled against him. Horror, admiration, relief that the fire hadn't touched them or theirs. He saw that, as well.

Then his gaze fell on the blonde.

She stood apart from the rest, staring straight ahead while the light wind teased her honey blond hair out of its fancy twist. Expensive shoes, Ry noted, of supple midnight leather, as out of place in this part of town as her velvet coat and her fancy face.

A hell of a face, he thought idly, lifting the cigarette to his lips again. A pale oval that belonged on a cameo. Eyes... He couldn't make out their color, but they were dark. No excitement there, he mused. No horror, no shock. Anger, maybe. Just a touch of it. She was either a woman of little emotion, or one who knew how to control it.

A hothouse rose, he decided. And just what was she doing so far out of her milieu at nearly four o'clock in the morning?

"Hey, Inspector." Grimy and wet, Lieutenant Holden trudged over to bum a cigarette. "Chalk up another one for the Fighting Twenty-second."

Ry knew Holden, and was already holding the pack out. "Looks like you killed another one."

"This was a bitch." Cupping his hands against the wind, Holden lit up. "Fully involved by the time we got here. Call came in from the night watchman at 1:40. Second and third floors took most of it, but the equipment on one's pretty well gone, too. You'll probably find your point of origin on the second."

"Yeah?" Though the fire was winding down, Ry knew Holden wasn't just shooting the breeze.

"Found some streamers going up the steps at the east end. Probably started the fire with them, but not all the material went up. Ladies' lingerie."

"Hmmm?"

"Ladies' lingerie," Holden said with a grin. "That's what they were warehousing. Lots of nighties and undies. You've got a nice stream of underwear and matchbooks that didn't go up." He slapped Ry on the shoulder. "Have fun. Hey, probie!" he shouted to one of the probationary firefighters. "You going to hold that hose or play with it? Got to watch 'em every minute, Ry."

"Don't I know it…"

Out of the corner of his eye, Ry watched his hothouse flower pick her way toward a fire engine. He and Holden separated.

"Isn't there anything you can tell me?" Natalie asked an exhausted firefighter. "How did it start?"

"Lady, I just put them out." He sat on a running board, no longer interested in the smoldering wreck of the warehouse. "You want answers?" He jerked his thumb in Ry's direction. "Ask the inspector."

"Civilians don't belong at fire scenes," Ry said from behind her. When she turned to look at him, he saw that her eyes were green, a deep jade green.

"It's my fire scene." Her voice was cool, like the wind that teased her hair, with a faint drawl that made him think of cowboys and schoolmarms. "My warehouse," she continued. "My problem."

"Is that so?" Ry took another survey. She was cold. He knew from experience that there was no place colder than a fire scene in winter. But her spine was straight, and that delicate chin lifted. "And that would make you…?"

"Natalie Fletcher. I own the building, and everything in it. And I'd like some answers." She cocked one elegantly arched brow. "And that would make you—?"

"Piasecki. Arson investigator."

"Arson?" Shock had her gaping before she snapped back into control. "You think this was arson."

"It's my job to find out." He glanced down, nearly sneered. "You're going to ruin those shoes, Miz Fletcher."

"My shoes are the least of my—" She broke off when he took her arm and started to steer her away. "What are you doing?"

"You're in the way. That would be your car, wouldn't it?" He nodded toward a shiny new Mercedes convertible.

"Yes, but—"

"Get in it."

"I will not get in it." She tried to shake him off and discovered she would have needed a crowbar. "Will you let go of me?"

She smelled a hell of a lot better than smoke and sodden debris. Ry took a deep gulp of her, then tried for diplomacy. It was something, he was proud to admit, that had never been his strong suit.

"Look, you're cold. What's the point in standing out in the wind?"

She stiffened, against both him and the wind. "The point is, that's my building. What's left of it."

"Fine." They'd do it her way, since it suited him. But he placed her between the car and his body to shelter her from the worst of the cold. "It's kind of late at night to be checking your inventory, isn't it?"

"It is." She stuck her hands in her pockets, trying fruitlessly to warm them. "I drove out after the night watchman called me."

"And that would have been…"

"I don't know. Around two."

"Around two," he repeated, and let his gaze skim over her again. There was a snazzy dinner suit under the velvet, he noted. The material looked soft, expensive, and it was the same color as her eyes. "Pretty fancy outfit for a fire."

"I had a late meeting and didn't think to change into more appropriate clothes before I came." Idiot, she thought, and looked back grimly at what was left of her property. "Is there a point to this?"

"Your meeting ran until two?"

"No, it broke up about midnight."

"How come you're still dressed?"

"What?"

"How come you're still dressed?" He took out another cigarette, lit it. "Late date?"

"No, I went by my office to do some paperwork. I'd barely gotten home when Jim Banks, the night watchman, called me."

"Then you were alone from midnight until two?"

"Yes, I—" Her eyes cut back to his, narrowed. "Do you think I'm responsible for this? Is that what you're getting at here—? What the hell was your name?"

"Piasecki," he said, and smiled. "Ryan Piasecki. And I don't think anything yet, Miz Fletcher. I'm just separating the details."

Her eyes were no longer cool, controlled. They had flared to flash point. "Then I'll give you some more. The building and its contents are fully insured. I'm with United Security."

"What kind of business are you in?"

"I'm Fletcher Industries, Inspector Piasecki. You may have heard of it."

He had, most certainly. Real estate, mining, shipping. The conglomerate owned considerable property, including several holdings in Urbana. But there were reasons that big companies, as well as small ones, resorted to arson.

"You run Fletcher Industries?"

"I oversee several of its interests. Including this one." Most particularly this one, she thought. This one was her baby. "We're opening several speciality boutiques countrywide in the spring, in addition to a catalog service. A large portion of my inventory was in that building."

"What sort of inventory?"

Now she smiled. "Lingerie, inspector. Bras, panties, negligees. Silks, satins, lace. You might be familiar with the concept."

"Enough to appreciate it." She was shivering now, obviously struggling to keep her teeth from chattering. He imagined her feet would be blocks of ice in those thin, pricey shoes. "Look, you're freezing out here. Get in the car. Go home. We'll be in touch."

"I want to know what happened to my building. What's left of my stock."

"Your building burned down, Miz Fletcher. And it's unlikely there's anything left of your stock that would raise a man's blood pressure." He opened the car door. "I've got a job to do. And I'd advise you to call your insurance agent."

"You've got a real knack for soothing the victims, don't you, Piasecki?"

"No, can't say that I do." He took a notebook and pencil stub from his shirt pocket. "Give me your address and phone number. Home and office."

Natalie took a deep breath, then let it out slowly, before she gave him the information he wanted. "You know," she added. "I've always had a soft spot for public servants. My brother's a cop in Denver."

"That so?"

"Yes, that's so." She slid into the car. "You've managed, in one short meeting, to change my mind." She slammed the door, sorry she didn't do it quickly enough to catch his fingers. With one last glance at the ruined building, she drove away.

Ry watched her taillights disappear and added another note to his book. Great legs. Not that he'd forget, he mused as he turned away. But a good inspector wrote everything down.

Natalie forced herself to sleep for two hours, then rose and took a stinging-cold shower. Wrapped in her robe, she called her assistant and arranged to have her morning appointments canceled or shifted. With her first cup of coffee, she phoned her parents in Colorado. She was on cup number two by the time she had given them all the details she knew, soothed their concern and listened to their advice.

With cup number three, she contacted her insurance agent

and arranged to meet him at the site. After downing aspirin with the remains of that cup, she dressed for what promised to be a very long day.

She was nearly out of the door when the phone stopped her.

"You have a machine," she reminded herself, even as she darted back to answer it. "Hello?"

"Nat, it's Deborah. I just heard."

"Oh." Rubbing the back of her neck, Natalie sat on the arm of a chair. Deborah O'Roarke Guthrie was a double pleasure, both friend and family. "I guess it's hit the news already."

There was a slight hesitation. "I'm sorry, Natalie, really sorry. How bad is it?"

"I'm not sure. Last night it looked about as bad as it gets. But I'm going out now, meeting my insurance agent. Who knows, we may salvage something."

"Would you like me to come with you? I can reschedule my morning."

Natalie smiled. Deborah would do just that. As if she didn't have enough on her plate with her husband, her baby, her job as assistant district attorney.

"No, but thanks for asking. I'll let you know something when I know something."

"Come to dinner tonight. You can relax, soak up some sympathy."

"I'd like that."

"If there's anything else I can do, just tell me."

"Actually, you could call Denver. Keep your sister and my brother from riding east to the rescue."

"I'll do that."

"Oh, one more thing." Natalie rose, checked the contents

of her briefcase as she spoke. "What do you know about an Inspector Piasecki? Ryan Piasecki?"

"Piasecki?" There was a slight pause as Deborah flipped through her mental files. Natalie could all but see the process. "Arson squad. He's the best in the city."

"He would be," Natalie muttered.

"Is arson suspected?" Deborah said carefully.

"I don't know. I just know he was there, he was rude, and he wouldn't tell me anything."

"It takes time to determine the cause of a fire, Natalie. I can put some pressure on, if you want me to."

It was tempting, just for the imagined pleasure of seeing Piasecki scramble. "No thanks. Not yet, anyway. I'll see you later."

"Seven o'clock," Deborah insisted.

"I'll be there. Thanks." Natalie hung up and grabbed her coat. With luck, she'd beat the insurance agent to the site by a good thirty minutes.

Luck was with her—in that area, anyway. When Natalie pulled up behind the fire-department barricade, she discovered she was going to need a great deal more than luck to win this battle.

It looked worse, incredibly worse, than it had the night before.

It was a small building, only three floors. The cinder-block outer walls had held, and now stood blackened and streaked with soot, still dripping with water from the hoses. The ground was littered with charred and sodden wood, broken glass, twisted metal. The air stank of smoke.

Miserable, she ducked under the yellow tape for a closer look.

"What the hell do you think you're doing?"

She jolted, then shaded her eyes from the sun to see more clearly. She should have known, Natalie thought, when she saw Ry making his way toward her through the wreckage.

"Didn't you see the sign?" he demanded.

"Of course I saw it. This is my property, Inspector. The insurance adjuster is meeting me here shortly. I believe I'm within my rights in inspecting the damage."

He gave her one disgusted look. "Don't you have any other kind of shoes?"

"I beg your pardon?"

"Stay here." Muttering to himself, he stalked to his car, came back with a pair of oversize fireman's boots. "Put these on."

"But—"

He took her arm, throwing her off balance. "Put those ridiculous shoes into the boots. Otherwise you're going to hurt yourself."

"Fine." She stepped into them, feeling absurd.

The tops of the boots covered her legs almost to the knee. The navy suit and matching wool coat she wore were runway-model smart. A trio of gold chains draped around her neck added flash.

"Nice look," he commented. "Now, let's get something straight. I need to preserve this scene, and that means you don't touch anything." He said it even though his authority to keep her out was debatable, and he'd already found a great deal of what he'd been looking for.

"I have no intention of—"

"That's what they all say."

She drew herself up. "Tell me, Inspector, do you work

alone because you prefer it, or because no one can stand to be around you for longer than five minutes?"

"Both." He smiled then. The change of expression was dazzling, charming—and suspicious. She wasn't sure, but she thought the faintest of dimples winked beside his mouth. "What are you doing clunking around a fire scene in a five-hundred-dollar suit?"

"I…" Wary of the smile, she tugged her coat closed. "I have meetings all afternoon. I won't have time to change."

"Executives." He kept his hand on her arm as he turned. "Come on, then. Be careful where you go—the site's not totally safe, but you can take a look at what she left you. I've still got work to do."

He led her in through the mangled doorway. The ceiling was a yawning pit between floors. What had fallen, or had been knocked through, lay in filthy layers of sodden ash and alligatored wood. She shivered once at the sight of the twisted mass of burned mannequins that lay sprawled and broken.

"They didn't suffer," Ry assured her, and her eyes flashed back to his.

"I'm sure you can view this as a joke, but—"

"Fire's never a joke. Watch your step."

She saw where he'd been working, near the base of a broken inner wall. There was a small wire screen in a wooden frame, a shovel that looked like a child's toy, a few mason jars, a crowbar, a yardstick. While she watched, Ry pried off a scored section of baseboard.

"What are you doing?"

"My job."

She set her teeth. "Are we on the same side here?"

He glanced up. "Maybe." With a putty knife, he began to

scrape at residue. He sniffed, he grunted and, when he was satisfied, placed it in a jar. "Do you know what oxidation is, Ms. Fletcher?"

She frowned, shifted. "More or less."

"The chemical union of a substance with oxygen. It can be slow, like paint drying, or fast. Heat and light. A fire's fast. And some things help it move faster." He continued to scrape, then looked up again, held out the knife. "Take a whiff."

Dubious, she stepped forward and sniffed.

"What do you smell?"

"Smoke, wet…I don't know."

He placed the residue in the jar. "Gasoline," he said, watching her face. "See, a liquid seeks its level, goes into cracks in the floor, into dead-air corners, flows under baseboard. If it gets caught under there, it doesn't burn. You see the place I cleared out here?"

She moistened her lips, studied the floor he had shoveled or swept clear of debris. There was a black stain, like a shadow burned into the wood. "Yes?"

"The charred-blob pattern. It's like a map. I keep at this, layer by layer, and I'll be able to tell what happened, before, during."

"You're telling me someone poured gas in here and lit a match?"

He said nothing, only scooted forward a bit to pick up a scrap of burned cloth. "Silk," he said with a rub of his fingertips. "Too bad." He placed the scrap in what looked like a flour tin. "Sometimes a torch will lay out streamers, give the fire more of an appetite. They don't always burn." He picked up an almost perfectly preserved cup from a lacy bra. Amused, his eyes met Natalie's over it. "Funny what resists, isn't it?"

She was cold again, but not from the wind. It was from within, and it was rage. "If this fire was deliberately set, I want to know."

Interested in the change in her eyes, he sat back on his haunches. His black fireman's coat was unhooked, revealing jeans, worn white at the knees, and a flannel shirt. He hadn't left the scene since his arrival.

"You'll get my report." He rose then. "Draw me a picture. What did this place look like twenty-four hours ago?"

She closed her eyes for a moment, but it didn't help. She could still smell the destruction.

"It was three stories, about two thousand square feet. Iron balconies and interior steps. Seamstresses worked on the third floor. All of our merchandise is handmade."

"Classy."

"Yes, that's the idea. We have another plant in this district where most of the sewing is done. The twelve machines upstairs were just for finish work. There was a small coffee room to the left, rest rooms… On the second, the floor was made of linoleum, rather than wood. We stored the stock there. I kept a small office up there, as well, though I do most of my work uptown. The area down here was for inspecting, packaging and shipping. We were to begin fulfilling our spring orders in three weeks."

She turned, not quite sure where she intended to go, and stumbled over debris. Ry's quick grab saved her from a nasty spill.

"Hold on," he murmured.

Shaken, she leaned back against him for a moment. There was strength there, if not sympathy. At the moment, she preferred it that way. "We employed over seventy people in this plant alone. People who are out of work until I can sort this out." She whirled back. He gripped her arms to keep her steady. "And it was deliberate."

Control, he thought. Well, she didn't have it now. She was as volatile as a lit match. "I haven't finished my investigation."

"It was deliberate," she repeated. "And you're thinking I could have done it. That I came in here in the middle of the night with a can of gasoline."

Her face was close to his. Funny, he thought, he hadn't noticed how tall she was in those fancy ankle-breaking shoes. "It's a little hard to picture."

"Hired someone, then?" she tossed out. "Hired someone to burn down the building, even though there was a man in it? But what's one security guard against a nice fat insurance check?"

He was silent for a moment, his eyes locked on hers. "You tell me."

Infuriated, she wrenched away from him. "No, Inspector, you're going to have to tell me. And whether you like it or not, I'm going to be on you like a shadow through every step of the investigation. Every step," she repeated. "Until I have all the answers."

She strode out of the building, dignified despite the awkward boots. Her temper was barely under control when she saw the car pull up beside hers. Recognizing it, she sighed, made her way to the tape barrier and under it.

"Donald." She held out her hands. "Oh, Donald, what a mess…"

Gripping her hands, he looked beyond her to the building. For a moment he just stood there, holding her hands, shaking his head. "How could this have happened? The wiring? We had the wiring checked two months ago."

"I know. I'm so sorry. All your work." Two years of his life, she thought, and hers. Up in smoke.

"Everything?" There was a faint tremor in his voice, in his hand as it gripped hers. "Is it all gone?"

"I'm afraid it is. We have other inventory, Donald. This isn't going to whip us."

"You're tougher than me, Nat." After a last quick squeeze he released her hands. "This was my biggest shot. You're the CEO, but I feel like I was captain. And my ship just sank."

Natalie's heart went out to him. It wasn't simply business with Donald Hawthorne, she thought, any more than it was simply business with her. This new company was a dream, a fresh excitement, and a chance for both of them to try something completely different.

No, not just to try, she reminded herself. To succeed.

"We're going to have to work our butts off for the next three weeks."

He turned back, a small smile curving his lips. "Do you really think we can pull it off, after this, on schedule?"

"Yes, I do." Determination hardened her lips. "It's a delay, that's all. So we shuffle things around. We'll certainly have to postpone the audit."

"I can't even think of that now." He stopped, blinked. "Jesus, Nat, the files, the records."

"I don't think we're going to salvage any of the paperwork that was in the warehouse." She looked back toward her building. "It's going to make things more complicated, add some work hours, but we'll put it back together."

"But how can we manage the audit when—"

"It goes on the back burner until we're up and running. We'll talk about it back at the office. As soon as I meet the insurance agent, get the ball rolling, I'm heading back in." Already her mind was working out the details, the steps and stages. "We'll put on some double shifts, order new material, pull in some inventory from Chicago and Atlanta. We'll make it work, Donald. Lady's Choice is going to open in April, come hell or high water."

His smile flashed into a grin. "If anybody can make it work, you can."

"*We* can," she told him. "Now I need you to get back uptown, start making calls." PR, she knew, was his strong suit. He was overly impulsive perhaps, but she needed the action-oriented with her now. "You get Melvin and Deirdre hopping, Donald. Bribe or threaten distributors, plead with the union, soothe the clients. That's what you do best."

"I'm on it. You can count on me."

"I know I can. I'll be in the office soon to crack the whip."

Boyfriend? Ry wondered as he watched the two embrace. The tall, polished executive with the pretty face and shiny shoes looked to be her type.

As a matter of course, he noted down the license number of the Lincoln beside Natalie's car, then went back to work.

Chapter 2

"She's going to be here any minute." Assistant District Attorney Deborah O'Roarke Guthrie put fisted hands on her hips. "I want the whole story, Gage, before Natalie gets here."

Gage added another log to the fire before he turned to his wife. She'd changed out of her business suit into soft wool slacks and a cashmere sweater of midnight blue. Her ebony hair fell loose, nearly to her shoulders.

"You're beautiful, Deborah. I don't tell you that often enough."

She lifted a brow. Oh, he was a smooth operator, and charming. And clever. But so was she. "No evasions, Gage. You've managed to avoid telling me everything you know so far, but—"

"You were in court all day," he reminded her. "I was in meetings."

"That's beside the point. I'm here now."

"You certainly are." He walked to her, slipped his arms through hers and circled her waist. His lips curved as they lowered to hers. "Hello."

More than two years of marriage hadn't diluted her response to him. Her mouth softened, parted, but then she remembered herself and stepped back. "No, you don't. Consider yourself under oath and in the witness chair, Guthrie. Spill it. I know you were there."

"I was there." Annoyance flickered in his eyes before he crossed over to pour mineral water for Deborah. Yes, he'd been there, he thought. Too late.

He had his own way of combating the dark side of Urbana. The gift—or the curse—he'd been left with after surviving what should have been a fatal shooting gave him an edge. He'd been a cop too long to close his eyes to injustice. Now, with the odd twist fate had dealt him, he fought crime his own way, with his own special talent.

Deborah watched him stare down at his hand, flex it. It was an old habit, one that told her he was thinking of how he could make it, make himself fade to nothing.

And when he did, he was Nemesis, a shadow that haunted the streets of Urbana, a shadow that had slipped into her life, and her heart as real and as dear to her as the man who stood before her.

"I was there," he repeated, and poured a glass of wine for himself. "But too late to do anything. I didn't beat the first engine company by more than five minutes."

"You can't always be first on the scene, Gage," Deborah murmured. "Even Nemesis isn't omnipotent."

"No." He handed her the glass. "The point is, I didn't see who started the fire. If indeed it was arson."

"Which you believe it was."

He smiled again. "I have a suspicious mind."

"So do I." She tapped her glass against his. "I wish there was something I could do for Natalie. She's worked so hard to get this new company off the ground."

"You're doing something," Gage told her. "You're here. And she'll fight back."

"That's one thing you can count on." She tilted her head. "I don't suppose anyone saw you around the warehouse last night."

Now he grinned. "What do you think?"

She blew out a breath. "I think I'll never quite get used to it." When the doorbell sounded, Deborah set her glass aside. "I'll get it." She hurried to the door, then opened her arms to Natalie. "I'm so glad you could come."

"I wouldn't miss one of Frank's meals for anything." Determined to be cheerful, Natalie kissed Deborah, then linked arms with her as they walked back into the sitting room. She offered her host a brilliant smile. "Hello, gorgeous."

She kissed Gage, as well, accepted the drink he offered and a seat by the fire. She sighed once. A beautiful house, a beautiful couple, so incredibly in love. Natalie told herself if she were inclined toward domesticity, she might be envious.

"How are you coping?" Deborah asked her.

"Well, I love a challenge, and this is a big one. The bottom line is, Lady's Choice will have its grand opening, nationwide, in three weeks."

"I was under the impression that you lost quite a bit of merchandise," Gage commented. Cloaked by the shadow of his gift, he'd watched her arrive at the scene the night before. "As well as the building."

"There are other buildings."

In fact, she had already arranged to purchase another warehouse. It would, even after the insurance payoff, put a dent in the estimated profits for the year. But they would make it up, Natalie thought. She would see to that.

"We're going to be working overtime for a while to make up some of the losses. And I can pull some stock in from other locations. Urbana's our flagship store. I intend for it to go off with a bang."

She sipped her wine, running the stages through her mind. "I've got Donald with a phone glued to his ear. With his background in public relations, he's the best qualified to beg and borrow. Melvin's already flown out on a four-city jaunt to swing through the other plants and stores. He'll work some of his wizardry in figuring who can spare what merchandise. And Deirdre's working on the figures. I've talked to the union leaders, and some of the laborers. I intend to be back in full production within forty-eight hours."

Gage toasted her. "If anyone can do it…" He was a businessman himself. Among other things. And knew exactly how much work, how much risk and how much sweat Natalie would face. "Is there anything new on the fire itself?"

"Not specifically." Frowning, Natalie glanced into the cheerful flames in the hearth. So harmless, she thought, so attractive. "I've talked with the investigator a couple of times. He implies, he interrogates, and, by God, he irritates. But he doesn't commit."

"Ryan Piasecki," Deborah stated, and it was her turn to

smile. "I stole a few minutes today to do some checking on him. I thought you'd be interested."

"Bless you." Natalie leaned forward. "So, what's the story?"

"He's been with the department for fifteen years. Fought fires for ten, and worked his way up to lieutenant. A couple of smears in his file."

Natalie's lips curved smugly. "Oh, really?"

"Apparently he belted a city councilman at a fire scene. Broke his jaw."

"Violent tendencies," Natalie muttered. "I knew it."

"It was what they call a class C fire," Deborah continued. "In a chemical plant. Piasecki was with engine company 18, and they were the first to respond. There was no backup. Economic cutbacks," she added as Natalie's brows knit. "Number 18 lost three men in that fire, and two more were critically injured. The councilman showed up with the press in tow and began to pontificate on our system at work. He'd spearheaded the cutbacks."

Damn it. Natalie blew out a breath. "I guess I'd have belted him, too."

"There was another disciplinary action when he stormed into the mayor's office with a bagful of fire-site salvage and dumped it on the desk. It was from a low-rent apartment building on the east side, that had just passed inspection— even though the wiring was bad, the furnace faulty. No smoke alarms. Broken fire escapes. Twenty people died."

"I wanted you to tell me that my instincts were on target," Natalie muttered. "That I had a good reason for detesting him."

"Sorry." Deborah had developed a soft spot for men who

fought crime and corruption in untraditional manners. She shot Gage a look that warmed them both.

"Well." Natalie sighed. "What else do you have on him?"

"He moved to the arson squad about five years ago. He has a reputation for being abrasive, aggressive and annoying."

"That's better."

"And for having the nose of a bloodhound, the eyes of a hawk, and the tenacity of a pit bull. He keeps digging and digging until he finds the answers. I've never had to use him in court, but I asked around. You can't shake him on the stand. He's smart. He writes everything down. Everything. And he remembers it. He's thirty-six, divorced. He's a team player who prefers to work alone."

"I suppose it should make me feel better, knowing I'm in competent hands." Natalie moved her shoulders restlessly. "But it doesn't. I appreciate the profile."

"No problem," Deborah began, then broke off when the sound of crying came through the baby monitor beside her. "Sounds like the boss is awake. No, I'll go," she said when Gage got to his feet. "She just wants company."

"Am I going to get a peek?" Natalie asked.

"Sure, come on."

"I'll tell Frank to hold dinner until you're done." With a frown in his eyes, Gage watched Natalie head upstairs with his wife.

"You know," Natalie said as they started up to the nursery, "you look fabulous. I don't see how you manage it all. A demanding career, a dynamic husband and all the social obligations that go with him, and the adorable Adrianna."

"I could tell you it's all a matter of time management and prioritizing." With a grin, Deborah opened the door of the nursery. "But what it really comes down to is passion. For the job, for Gage, for our Addy. There's nothing you can't have, if you're passionate about it."

The nursery was a symphony of color. Murals on the ceiling told stories of princesses and magic horses. Primary tones brightened the walls and bled into rainbows. With her hands gripped on the rail of her Jenny Lind crib, legs wobbling, ten-month-old Addy pouted, oblivious of the ambiance.

"Oh, sweetie." Deborah reached down, picked her up to nuzzle. "Here you are, all wet and lonely."

The pout transformed into a beaming, satisfied smile. "Mama."

Natalie watched while Deborah laid Addy on the changing table.

"She's prettier every time I see her." Gently she brushed at the dark thatch of hair on the baby's head. Pleased with the attention, Addy kicked her feet and began to babble.

"We're thinking about having another."

"Another?" Natalie blinked into Deborah's glowing face. "Already?"

"Well, it's still in the what-if stage. But we'd really like to have three." She pressed a kiss to the soft curve of Addy's neck, chuckling when she tugged on her hair. "I just love being a mother."

"It shows. Can I?" Once the fresh diaper was in place, Natalie lifted the baby.

There was envy, she discovered, for this small miracle who curved so perfectly into her arms.

Two days later, Natalie was at her desk, a headache drumming behind her eyes. She didn't mind it. The incessant throbbing pushed her forward.

"If the mechanic can't repair the machines, get new ones. I want every seamstress on-line. No, tomorrow afternoon won't do." She tapped a pen on the edge of her desk, shifted the phone from ear to ear. "Today. I'll be in myself by one to check on the new stock. I know it's a madhouse. Let's keep it that way."

She hung up and looked at her three associates. "Donald?"

He skimmed a hand over his burnished hair. "The first ad runs in the *Times* on Saturday. Full-page, three-color. The ad, with necessary variations, will be running in the other cities simultaneously."

"The changes I wanted?"

"Implemented. Catalogs shipped today. They look fabulous."

"Yes, they do." Pleased, Natalie glanced down at the glossy catalog on her desk. "Melvin?"

As was his habit, Melvin Glasky slipped off his rimless glasses, polishing them as he spoke. He was in his mid-fifties, addicted to bow ties and golf. He was thin of frame and pink of cheek, and sported a salt-and-pepper toupee that he naively believed was his little secret.

"Atlanta looks the best, though Chicago and L.A. are gearing up." He gestured to the report on her desk. "I worked out deals with each location for inventory transfers. Not everybody was happy about it." His lenses glinted like diamonds when he set them back on his nose. "The store manager in Chicago defended her stock like a mama bear. She didn't want to give up one brassiere."

Natalie's lips twitched at his drawling pronunciation. "So?"

"So I blamed it on you."

Natalie leaned back in her chair and chuckled. "Of course you did."

"I told her that you wanted twice what you'd told me you needed. Which gave me negotiating room. She figured you should filch from catalog. I agreed." His eyes twinkled. "Then I told her how you considered catalog sacred. Wouldn't touch one pair of panties, because you wanted all catalog orders fulfilled within ten days of order. You're inflexible."

Her lips twitched again. In the eighteen months they'd worked together on this project, she'd come to adore Melvin. "I certainly am."

"So I told her how I'd take the heat, and half of what you ordered."

"You'd have made a hell of a politician, Melvin."

"What do you think I am? In any case, you've got about fifty percent of your inventory back for the flagship store."

"I owe you. Deirdre?"

"I've run the projected increases in payroll and material expenses." Deirdre Marks tossed her flyaway ginger braid behind her shoulder. Her slightly flattened tones were pure Midwest, and her mind was as quick and controlled as a high-tech computer. "Also the outlay for the new site and equipment. With the incentive bonuses you authorized, we'll be in the red. I've done graphs—"

"I've seen them." Mulling over her options, Natalie rubbed the back of her neck. "The insurance money, when it comes through, will offset that somewhat. I'm willing to risk my investment, and add to it, to see that this works."

"From a straight financial standpoint," Deirdre continued, "any return looks dim. At least in the foreseeable future. First-year sales alone would have to be in excess of…" She shrugged her narrow shoulders at Natalie's stubborn expression. "You have the figures."

"Yes, and I appreciate the extra work. The files at the south side warehouse were destroyed. Fortunately, I'd had Maureen make copies of the bulk of them." She rubbed her eyes, caught herself and folded her hands. "I'm very aware that the majority of new business ventures fold within the first year. This isn't going to be one of them. I'm not looking for short-term profits, but for long-term success. I intend for Lady's Choice to be at the top on retail and direct sales within ten years. So I'm certainly not going to take a step back at the first real obstacle."

She flicked a finger over a button when her buzzer sounded. "Yes, Maureen?"

"Inspector Piasecki would like to see you, Ms. Fletcher. He doesn't have an appointment."

Automatically Natalie scanned her desk calendar. She could spare Piasecki fifteen minutes and still make it to the new warehouse. "We'll have to finish this later," she said with a glance at her associates. "Show him in, Maureen."

Ry preferred meeting friends or foes on their own turf. He hadn't yet decided which category Natalie Fletcher fell into. He had, however, decided to swing by her office to get a first-hand look at that part of her operation.

He couldn't say he was disappointed. Fancy digs for a fancy lady, he thought. Thick carpet, lots of glass, soft-colored, cushy chairs in the waiting area. Original paintings on the walls, live, thriving plants.

And her secretary, or assistant, or whatever title the pretty little thing at the lobby desk carried, worked with top-grade equipment.

The boss's office was no surprise, either. Ry's quick scan showed him more thick carpet, in slate blue, rosy walls decorated with the splashy modern art he'd never cared for. Antique furniture—probably the real thing.

Her desk was some old European piece, he supposed. They went in for all that gingerbread work and curves. Natalie sat behind it, in one of her tidy suits, a wide, tinted window at her back.

Three other people stood like soldiers ready to snap to attention at her command. He recognized the younger man as the one she'd embraced at the fire site. Tailored suit, shiny leather shoes, ruthlessly knotted tie. Pretty face, blow-dried hair, soft hands.

The second man was older, and looked to be on the edge of a smile. He wore a polka-dot bow tie and a mediocre toupee.

The woman made a fine foil for her boss. Boxy jacket—slightly wrinkled—flat-heeled shoes, messy hair that couldn't decide if it wanted to be red or brown. Closing in on forty, Ry judged, and not much interested in fighting it.

"Inspector," Natalie waited a full ten seconds before rising and holding out a hand.

"Ms. Fletcher." He gave her long, narrow fingers a perfunctory squeeze.

"Inspector Piasecki is investigating the warehouse fire." And in his usual uniform of jeans and a flannel shirt, she noted. Didn't the city issue official attire? "Inspector, these are three of my top-level executives—Donald Hawthorne, Melvin Glasky and Deirdre Marks."

Ry nodded at the introductions, then turned his attention to Natalie again. "I'd have thought a smart woman like you would know better than to put her office on the forty-second floor."

"I beg your pardon?"

"It makes rescue hell—not only for you, but for the department. No way to get a ladder up here. That window's for looks, not for ventilation or escape. You've got forty-two floors to get down, in a stairway that's liable to be filled with smoke."

Natalie sat again, without asking him to join her. "This building is equipped with all necessary safety devices. Sprinklers, smoke detectors, extinguishers."

He only smiled. "So was your warehouse, Ms. Fletcher."

Her headache was coming back, double-time. "Inspector, did you come here to update me on your investigation, or to criticize my work space?"

"I can do both."

"If you'll excuse us." Natalie glanced toward her three associates. Once the door had closed behind them, Natalie gestured to a chair. "Let's clear the air here. You don't like me, I don't like you. But we both have a common goal. Very often I have to work with people I don't care for on a personal level. It doesn't stop me from doing my job." She tilted her head, aimed what he considered a very cool, very regal stare at him. "Does it stop you?"

He crossed his scuffed hightops at the ankles. "Nope."

"Good. Now what do you have to tell me?"

"I've just filed my report. You no longer have a suspicious fire. You've got arson."

Despite the fact that she'd been expecting it, her stomach clutched once. "There's no question?" She shook her head before he could speak. "No, there wouldn't be. I've been told you're very thorough."

"Have you? You ought to try aspirin, before you rub a hole in your head."

Annoyed, Natalie dropped the hand she'd been using to massage her temple. "What's the next step?"

"I've got cause, method, point of origin. I want motive."

"Aren't there people who set fires simply because they enjoy it? Because they're compelled to?"

"Sure." He started to reach for a cigarette, then noticed there wasn't an ashtray in sight. "Maybe you've got a garden-variety spark. Or maybe you've got a hired torch. You were carrying a lot of insurance, Ms. Fletcher."

"That's right. I had a reason for it. I lost over a million and a half in merchandise and equipment alone."

"You were covered for a hell of a lot more."

"If you know anything at all about real estate, Inspector, you're aware that the building was quite valuable. If you're looking for insurance fraud, you're wasting your time."

"I've got time." He rose. "I'm going to need a statement, Ms. Fletcher. Official. Tomorrow, my office, two o'clock."

She rose, as well. "I can give you a statement here and now."

"My office, Ms. Fletcher." He took a card out of his pocket, set it on her desk. "Look at it this way. If you're in the clear, the sooner we get this done, the sooner you collect your insurance."

"Very well." She picked up the card and slipped it into the pocket of her suit. "The sooner the better. Is that all for the moment, Inspector?"

"Yeah." His eyes skimmed down to the cover of the catalog lying on the desk. An ivory-skinned model was curled over a velvet settee, showing off a backless red gown with a froth of tantalizing lace at the bodice.

"Nice." His gaze shot back to Natalie's. "A classy way to sell sex."

"Romance, Inspector. Some people still enjoy it."

"Do you?"

"I don't think that applies."

"I just wondered if you believe in what you're selling, or if you just go for the bucks." Just as he'd wondered if she wore her own products under those neatly tailored suits.

"Then I'll satisfy your curiosity. I always believe in what I'm selling. And I enjoy making money. I'm very good at it." She picked up the catalog and held it out to him. "Why don't you take this along? All our merchandise is unconditionally guaranteed. The toll-free number will be in full operation on Monday."

If she'd expected him to refuse or fumble, she was disappointed. Ry rolled the catalog into a tube and tucked it into his hip pocket. "Thanks."

"Now, if you'll excuse me, I have an outside appointment."

She stepped out from behind the desk. He'd been hoping for that. Whatever he thought about her, he enjoyed her legs. "Need a lift?"

Surprised, she turned away from the small closet at the end of the room. "No. I have a car." It more than surprised her when he came up behind her to help her on with her coat. His hands lingered lightly, briefly, on her shoulders.

"You're stressed out, Ms. Fletcher."

"I'm busy, Inspector." She turned, off balance, and was annoyed when she had to jerk back or bump up against him.

"And jumpy," he added, with a quick, satisfied curve of his lips. He'd wondered if she was as elementally aware of him as he was of her. "A suspicious man might say those were signs of guilt. It so happens I'm a suspicious man. But you know what I think?"

"I'm fascinated by what you think."

Sarcasm apparently had no effect on him. He just continued to smile at her. "I think you're just made up that way. Tense and jumpy. You've got plenty of control, and you know just how to keep the fires banked. But now and again it slips. It's interesting when it does."

It was slipping now. She could feel it sliding greasily out of her hands. "Do you know what I think, Inspector?"

The dimple that should have been out of place on his strong face winked. "I'm fascinated by what you think, Ms. Fletcher."

"I think you're an arrogant, narrow-minded, irritating man who thinks entirely too much of himself."

"I'd say we're both right."

"And you're in my way."

"You're right about that, too." But he didn't move, wasn't quite ready to. "Damned if you don't have the fanciest face."

She blinked. "I beg your pardon?"

"An observation. You're one classy number." His fingers itched to touch, so he dipped them into his pockets. He'd thrown her off. That was obvious from the way she was staring at him, half horrified, half intrigued. Ry saw no reason not to take advantage of it. "A man's hard-pressed not to do a little fantasizing, once he's had a good look at you. I've had a couple of good looks now."

"I don't think..." Only sheer pride prevented her stepping back. Or forward. "I don't think this is appropriate."

"If we ever get to know each other better, you'll find out that propriety isn't at the top of my list. Tell me, do you and Hawthorne have a personal thing going?"

His eyes, dark, intense, close, dazzled her for a moment. "Donald? Of course not." Appalled, she caught herself. "That's none of your business."

Her answer pleased him, on professional and personal levels. "Everything about you is my business."

She tossed up her chin, eyes smoldering. "So, this pitiful excuse for a flirtation is just a way to get me to incriminate myself?"

"I didn't think it was that pitiful. Obvious," he admitted, "but not pitiful. On a professional level, it worked."

"I could have lied."

"You have to think before you lie. And you weren't thinking." He liked the idea of being able to frazzle her, and pushed a little farther. "It so happens that, on a strictly personal level, I like the way you look. But don't worry, it won't get in the way of the job."

"I don't like you, Inspector Piasecki."

"You said that already." For his own pleasure, he reached out, tugged her coat closed. "Button up. It's cold out there. My office," he added as he turned for the door. "Tomorrow, two o'clock."

He strolled out, thinking of her.

Natalie Fletcher, he mused, punching the elevator button for the lobby. High-class brains in a first-class package. Maybe she'd torched her own building for a quick profit. She wouldn't be the first or the last.

But his instincts told him no.

She didn't strike him as a woman who looked for short-cuts.

He stepped into the elevator car, which tossed his own image back to him in smoked glass.

Everything about her was top-of-the-line. And her background just didn't equal fraud. Fletcher Industries generated enough profit annually to buy a couple of small Third World countries. This new arm of it was Natalie's baby, and even if it folded in the first year, it wouldn't shake the corporate foundations.

Of course, there was emotional attachment to be considered. Those same instincts told him she had a great deal of emotional attachment to this new endeavor. That was enough for some to try to eke out a quick profit to save a shaky investment.

But it didn't jibe. Not with her.

Someone else in the company, maybe. A competitor, hoping to sabotage her business before it got off the ground. Or a classic pyro, looking for a thrill.

Whatever it was, he'd find it.

And, he thought, he was going to enjoy rattling Natalie Fletcher's cage while he was going about it.

One classy lady, he mused. He imagined she'd look good—damn good—modeling her own merchandise.

The beeper hooked to his belt sounded as he stepped from the elevator. Another fire, he thought, and moved quickly to the nearest phone.

There was always another fire.

Chapter 3

Ry kept her cooling her heels for fifteen minutes. It was a standard ploy, one she'd often used herself to psych out an opponent. She was determined not to fall for it.

There wasn't even enough room in the damn closet he called an office to pace.

He worked in one of the oldest fire stations in the city, two floors above the engines and trucks, in a small glassed-in box that offered an uninspiring view of a cracked parking lot and sagging tenements.

In the adjoining room, Natalie could see a woman pecking listlessly at a computer keyboard that sat on a desk overflowing with files and forms. The walls throughout were a dingy yellow that might, decades ago, have been white. They were checkerboarded with photos of fire scenes—some of which were grim enough to have had her turning away—bulletins, flyers, and a number of Polish jokes in dubious taste.

Obviously Ry had no problem shrugging off the clichéd humor about his heritage.

Metal shelves were piled with books, binders, pamphlets, and a couple of trophies, each topped with a statuette of a basketball player. And, she noted with a sniff, dust. His desk, slightly larger than a card table and badly scarred, was propped up under one shortened leg by a tattered paperback copy of *The Red Pony*.

The man didn't even have respect for Steinbeck.

When her curiosity got the better of her, Natalie rose from the folding chair, with its torn plastic seat, and poked around his desk.

No photographs, she noted. No personal mementos. Bent paper clips, broken pencils, a claw hammer, a ridiculous mess of disorganized paperwork. She pushed at some of that, then jumped back in horror when she revealed the decapitated head of a doll.

She might have laughed at herself, if it wasn't so hideous. The remnant of a child's toy, the frizzy blond hair nearly burned away, the once rosy face melted into mush on one side. One bright blue eye remained staring.

"Souvenirs," Ry said from the doorway. He'd been watching her for a couple of minutes. "From a class A fire up in the east sixties. The kid made it." He glanced down at the head on his desk. "She was in a little better shape than her doll."

Her shudder was quick and uncontrollable. "That's horrible."

"Yeah, it was. The kid's father started it with a can of kerosene in the living room. The wife wanted a divorce. When he was finished, she didn't need one."

He was so cold about it, she thought. Maybe he had to be. "You have a miserable job, Inspector."

"That's why I love it." He glanced around as the outer door opened. "Have a seat. I'll be right with you." Ry pulled the office door closed before he turned to the uniformed fire-fighter who'd come in behind him.

Through the glass, Natalie could hear the mutter of voices. She didn't need to hear Ry raise his voice—as he soon did—to know that the young fireman was receiving a first-class dressing-down.

"Who told you to ventilate that wall, probie?"

"Sir, I thought—"

"Probies don't think. You're not smart enough to think. If you were, you'd know what fresh air does for a fire. You'd know what happens when you let it in and there's a damn puddle of fuel oil sloshing under your boots."

"Yes, sir. I know, sir. I didn't see it. The smoke—"

"You'd better learn to see through smoke. You'd better learn to see through everything. And when the fire goes into the frigging wall, you don't take it on yourself to give it a way out while you're standing in accelerant. You're lucky to be alive, probie, and so's the team who were unlucky enough to be with you."

"Yes, sir. I know, sir."

"You don't know diddly. That's the first thing you remember the next time you go in to eat smoke. Now get out of here."

Natalie crossed her legs when Ry came into the room. "You're a real diplomat. That kid couldn't have been more than twenty."

"Be nice if he lived to a ripe old age, wouldn't it?" With a flick of his wrist, Ry tugged down the blinds, closing them in.

"Your technique makes me regret I didn't bring a lawyer with me."

"Relax." He moved to his desk, pushed some files out of his way. "I don't have the authority to arrest, just to investigate."

"Well, I'll sleep easy now." Deliberately she took a long look at her watch. "How long do you think this is going to take? I've already wasted twenty minutes."

"I got held up." He sat, opened the bag he'd brought in with him. "Have you had lunch?"

"No." Her eyes narrowed as he took out a wrapped package that smelled tantalizingly of deli. "Are you telling me that you've kept me waiting in here while you picked up a sandwich?"

"It was on my way." He offered her half of a corned beef on rye. "I've got a couple of coffees, too."

"I'll take the coffee. Keep the sandwich."

"Suit yourself." He handed her a small insulated cup. "Mind if we record this?"

"I'd prefer it."

Eating with one hand, he opened a desk drawer, took out a tape recorder. "You must have a closet full of those suits." This one was the color of crushed raspberries, and fastened at the left hip with gold buttons. "Do you ever wear anything else?"

"I beg your pardon?"

"Small talk, Ms. Fletcher."

"I'm not here for small talk," she snapped back. "And stop calling me *Ms.* Fletcher in that irritating way."

"No problem, Natalie. Just call me Ry." He switched on the recorder and began by reciting the time, date and location of the interview. Despite the tape, he took out a notebook and pencil. "This interview is being conducted by Inspector Ryan Piasecki with Natalie Fletcher, re the fire at the Fletcher Industries warehouse, 21 South Harbor Avenue, on February 12 of this year."

He took a sip of his coffee. "Ms. Fletcher, you are the owner of the aforesaid building, and its contents."

"The building and its contents are—were—the property of Fletcher Industries, of which I am an executive officer."

"How long has the building belonged to your company?"

"For eight years. It was previously used to warehouse inventory for Fletcher Shipping."

The heater beside him began to whine and gurgle. Ry kicked it carelessly. It went back to a subdued hum.

"And now?"

"Fletcher Shipping moved to a new location." She relaxed a little. It was going to be routine now. Business. "The warehouse was converted nearly two years ago to accommodate a new company. We used the building for manufacturing and warehousing merchandise for Lady's Choice. We make ladies' lingerie."

"And what were the hours of operation?"

"Normally eight to six, Monday through Friday. In the last six months, we expanded that to include Saturdays from eight to noon."

He continued to eat, asking standard questions about business practices, security, vandalism. Her answers were quick, cool and concise.

"You have a number of suppliers."

"Yes. We use American companies only. That's a firm policy."

"Ups the overhead."

"In the short term. I believe, in the long term, the company will generate profits to merit it."

"You've put a lot of personal time into this company. Incurred a lot of expenses, invested your own money."

"That's right."

"What happens if the business doesn't live up to your expectations?"

"It will."

He leaned back now, enjoying what was left of his cooling coffee. "If it doesn't."

"Then I would lose my time, and my money."

"When was the last time you were in the building, before the fire?"

The sudden change of topic surprised but didn't throw her. "I went by for a routine check three days before the fire. That would have been the ninth of February."

He noted it down. "Did you notice any inventory missing?"

"No."

"Damaged equipment?"

"No."

"Any holes in security?"

"No. I would have dealt with any of those things immediately." Did he think she was an idiot? "Work was progressing on schedule, and the inventory I looked over was fine."

His eyes cut back to hers, lingered. "You didn't look over everything?"

"I did a spot check, Inspector." The stare was designed to make her uncomfortable, she knew. She refused to allow it. "It isn't a productive use of time for me or my staff to examine every negligee or garter belt."

"The building was inspected in November. You were up to code on all fire regulations."

"That's right."

"Can you explain how it was that, on the night of the fire, the sprinkler and smoke alarm systems were inoperative?"

"Inoperative?" Her heart picked up a beat. "I'm not sure what you mean."

"They were tampered with, Ms. Fletcher. So was your security system."

She kept her eyes level with his. "No, I can't explain it. Can you?"

He took out a cigarette, flicked a wooden match into flame with his thumbnail. "Do you have any enemies?"

Her face went blank. "Enemies?"

"Anyone who'd like to see you fail, personally or professionally?"

"I— No, I can't think of anyone, personally." The idea left her shaken. She pulled a hand through her hair, from the crown to the tips that swung at chin level. "Naturally, I have competitors...."

"Anyone who's given you trouble?"

"No."

"Disgruntled employees? Fire anyone lately?"

"No. I can't speak for every level of the organization. I have managers who have autonomy in their own departments, but nothing's come back to me."

He continued to smoke as he asked questions, took notes. He wound the interview down, closing it by logging the time.

"I spoke to your insurance adjuster this morning," he told her. "And your security guard. I have interviews set up with the foremen at the warehouse." When she didn't respond, he crushed out his cigarette. "Want some water?"

"No." She let out a breath. "Thank you. Do you think I'm responsible?"

"What I know goes into the report, not what I think."

"I want to know." She stood then. "I'm asking you to tell me what you think."

She didn't belong here. That was the first thought that crossed his mind. Not here, in the cramped little room that smelled of whatever the men were cooking downstairs. Boardrooms and bedrooms. He was certain she'd be equally adept in both venues.

"I don't know, Natalie, maybe it's your pretty face affecting my judgment, but no—I don't think you're responsible. Feel better?"

"Not much. I suppose my only choice now is to depend on you to find out the who and why." She let out a little sigh. "As much as it galls me, I have a feeling you're just the man for the job."

"A compliment, and so early in our relationship."

"With any luck, it'll be the first and the last." She shifted, reached down for her briefcase. He moved quickly and quietly. Before she could lift it, his hand closed over hers on the strap.

"Take a break."

She flexed her hand under his once, felt the hard, callused palm, then went still. "Excuse me?"

"You're revved, Natalie, but you're running on empty. You need to relax."

It was unlikely she would, or could, with him holding on to her. "What I need to do is get back to work. So, if that's all, Inspector…"

"I thought we were on a first-name basis now. Come on, I want to show you something."

"I don't have time," she began as he pulled her out of the room. "I have an appointment."

"You always seem to. Aren't you ever late?"

"No."

"Every man's fantasy woman. Beautiful, smart, and prompt." He led her down a staircase. "How tall are you without the stilts?"

She lifted a brow at his description of her elegant Italian pumps. "Tall enough."

He stopped, one step below her, and turned. They were lined up, eye to eye, mouth to mouth. "Yeah, I'd say you are, just tall enough."

He tugged her, as he might have a disinterested mule, until they reached the ground floor.

There were scents wafting out from the kitchen. Chili was on the menu for tonight. A couple of men were checking equipment on one of the engines. Another was rolling a hose on the chilly concrete floor.

Ry was greeted with salutes and quick grins, Natalie with pursed lips and groans.

"They can't help it," Ry told her. "We don't get legs like yours walking through here every day. I'll give you a boost."

"What?"

"I'll give you a boost," he repeated as he opened the door on an engine. "Not that the guys wouldn't appreciate the way that skirt would ride up if you climbed in on your own. But—" Before she could protest, Ry had gripped her by the waist and lifted her.

She had a moment to think the strength in his arms was uncannily effortless before he joined her.

"Move over," he ordered. "Unless you'd rather sit on my lap."

She scooted across the seat. "Why am I sitting in a fire engine?"

"Everybody wants to at least once." Very much at home, he stretched his arm over the seat. "So, what do you think?"

She scanned the gauges and dials, the oversize gearshift, the photo of Miss January taped to the dash. "It's interesting."

"That's it?"

She caught her bottom lip between her teeth. She wondered which control operated the siren, which the lights. "Okay, it's fun." She leaned forward for a better view through the windshield. "We're really up here, aren't we? Is this the—"

He caught her hand just before she could yank the cord over her head. "Horn," he finished. "The men are used to it, but believe me, with the acoustics in here and the outside doors shut, you'd be sorry if you sounded it."

"Too bad." She skimmed back her hair as she turned her face toward him. "Are you showing me your toy to relax me, or just to show off?"

"Both. How'm I doing?"

"Maybe you're not quite the jerk you appear to be."

"You keep being so nice to me, I'm going to fall in love."

She laughed and realized she was almost relaxed. "I think we're both safe on that count. What made you decide to sit in a fire engine for ten years?"

"You've been checking up on me." Idly he lifted his fingers, just enough to reach the tips of her hair. Soft, he thought, like sunny silk.

"That's right." She shot him a look. "So?"

"So, I guess we're even. I'm a third-generation smoke eater. It's in the blood."

"Mmm…" That she understood. "But you gave it up."

"No, I shifted gears. That's different."

She supposed it was, but it wasn't a real answer. "Why do you keep that souvenir on your desk?" She watched his eyes closely as she asked. "The doll's head."

"It's from my last fire. The last one I fought." He could still remember it—the heat, the smoke, the screaming. "I carried the kid out. The bedroom door was locked. My guess is he'd herded his wife and kid in—you know, you can't live with me, you won't live without me. He had a gun. It wasn't loaded, but she wouldn't have known that."

"That's horrible." She wondered if she would have risked the gun, and thought she would have. Better a bullet, fast and final, than the terrors of smoke and flame. "His own family."

"Some guys don't take kindly to divorce." He shrugged. His own had been painless enough, almost anticlimactic. "The way it came out, he made them sit there while the fire got bigger, and the smoke snuck under the door. It was a frame house, old. Went up like a matchstick. The woman had tried to protect the kid, had curled over her in a corner. I couldn't get them both at once, so I took the kid."

His eyes changed now, darkened, focused on something only he could see. "The woman was gone, anyway. I knew she was gone, but there's always a chance. I was headed down the steps with the kid when the floor gave way."

"You saved the child," Natalie said gently.

"The mother saved the child." He could never forget that,

294   *Night Smoke*

could never forget that selfless and hopeless devotion. "The son of a bitch who torched the house jumped out the second-story window. Oh, he was burned, smoke inhalation, broken leg. But he lived through it."

He cared, she realized. She hadn't seen that before. Or hadn't wanted to. It changed him. Changed her perception of him. "And you decided to go after the men who start them, instead of the fires themselves."

"More or less." He snapped his head up, like a wolf scenting prey, when the alarm shrilled. The station sprang to life with running feet, shouted orders. Ry pitched his voice over the din. "Let's get out of the way."

He pushed open the door, caught Natalie in one arm and swung out.

"Chemical plant," someone said as they hurried by, pulling on protective gear.

In seconds, it seemed, the engines were manned and screaming out the arched double doors.

"It's so fast," Natalie said, ears still ringing, pulse still jumping. "They move so fast."

"Yeah."

"It's exciting." She pressed a hand to her speeding heart. "I didn't realize. Do you miss it?" She looked up at him then, and her hand went limp.

He was still holding her against him, and his eyes were dark and focused on hers. "Now and again."

"Well, it's— I should go."

"Yeah. You should go." But he shifted her until she was wrapped in both his arms. Maybe it was a knee-jerk reaction to the sirens, maybe it was the exotic and irresistible scent of her, but his blood was pumping.

And he wanted to see, just once, if she tasted as good as she looked.

"This is insane," she managed to say. She knew what he intended to do. What she wanted him to do. "This has got to be wrong."

His lips curved, just a little. "What's your point?" Then his mouth closed over hers.

She didn't push back. For nearly one heartbeat, she didn't respond. In that instant she thought she'd been paralyzed, struck deaf, dumb and blind. Then, in a tidal wave, every sense flooded back, every nerve snapped, every pulse jolted.

His mouth was hard, as his hands were, as his body was. She felt terrifyingly, gloriously, feminine pressed against him. A need she hadn't been aware of exploded into bloom. Her briefcase hit the floor with a thud as she wrapped herself around him.

He was no longer thinking "just once." A man would starve to death after only one taste. A man would certainly beg for more. She was soft and strong and sinfully sweet, with a flavor that both tempted and tormented.

Heat radiated between them as the wind whipped in through the open doors at their back. The clatter of street noises, horns and tires, sounded around them, along with her dazed, throaty moan.

He pulled back once to look at her face, saw himself in the cloudy green of her eyes, and then his mouth crushed hers again.

No, this wasn't going to happen just once.

She couldn't breathe. No longer wanted to. His lips were moving against hers, forming words she could neither hear nor understand. For the first time in her memory, she could do nothing but feel. And the feelings came so fast, so sharp and strong, they left her in tatters.

He pulled back again, staggered by what had ripped through him in so short a time. He was winded, weak, and the sensation infuriated as much as it baffled him. She only stood there, staring at him with a mixture of shock and hunger in her eyes.

"Sorry," he muttered, and hooked his thumbs in his pockets.

"Sorry?" she repeated. She sucked in a deep breath, wondered if her head would ever stop spinning. *"Sorry?"*

"That's right." He couldn't decide whether to curse her or himself. Damn it, his knees were weak. "That was out of line."

"Out of line."

She brushed her hair back from her face, furious to find her skin heated. He'd torn aside every defense, every line of control, and now he dared to apologize? Her chin snapped up, her shoulders straightened.

"You've certainly got a way with words. Tell me, Inspector, do you paw all your suspects?"

His eyes narrowed, kindled. "It was mutual pawing, and no, you're the first."

"Lucky me." Amazed, appalled, that she was very near tears, Natalie snatched up her briefcase. "I believe this concludes our meeting."

"Hold it." Ryan played fair and cursed them both when she continued striding toward the doors. "I said, hold it." He headed after her, and with one hand on her arm he spun her around.

Her breath hissed out between clenched teeth. "I refuse to

give in to the typical cliché of slapping you, but it's costing me."

"I apologized."

"Stuff it."

Be reasonable, he cautioned himself. It was either that or kiss her again. "Look, Ms. Fletcher, you didn't exactly fight me off."

"A mistake, I assure you, that will not be repeated." She made it to the sidewalk this time before he caught her.

"I don't want you," he said definitely.

Insulted, provoked beyond her control, she jabbed a finger into his chest. "Oh, really? Then perhaps you'd care to explain that ham-handed maneuver in there?"

"There was nothing ham-handed about it. I hardly touched you, and you went off like a rocket. It's not my fault if you were ripe."

Her eyes went huge, ballistic. "Ripe? *Ripe?* Why you— you overbearing, arrogant self-absorbed idiot!"

"Tell him, honey" was the advice of a toothy bag lady who shoved past with her teetering cart. "Don't let him get away with it."

"That was a bad choice of words," Ry responded, goaded into adding more fuel to the fire. "I should have said *repressed.*"

"I am going to hit you."

"And," he continued, ignoring her, "I should have said I don't like wanting you."

Natalie concentrated for one moment on simply breathing. She would not, absolutely would not, lower herself to having a public brawl on the sidewalk. "That, Inspector Piasecki, may be the first and last time we ever have the same sentiment about anything. I don't like it, either."

"Don't like me wanting you, or don't like you wanting me?"

"Either."

He nodded, and they eyed each other like boxers between rounds. "So, we'll talk it out tonight."

"We will not."

He would, he promised himself, be patient if it killed him. Or her. "Natalie, just how complicated do you want to make this?"

"I don't want to make it complicated, *Ry.* I want to make it impossible."

"Why?"

She speared him with a look, skimming her gaze from the toes of his shoes to the top of his head. "I should think that would be obvious, even to you."

He rocked back on his heels. "I don't know what it is about that snotty attitude of yours—it just does something for me. You want to play this traditional, with me asking you out to dinner, that routine?"

She closed her eyes and prayed for patience. "I don't seem to be getting through." She opened them again. "No, I don't want you asking me out to dinner, or any routine. What happened inside there was—"

"Wild. Incredible."

"An aberration," she said between her teeth.

"It wouldn't be a hardship to prove you wrong. But if we started that again out here, we'd probably be arrested before we were finished." Ryan was enjoying himself now, immersed in the simple challenge of her. And he intended to win. "But I see what it is. I've spooked you. Now you're afraid to be alone with me, afraid you'll lose control."

Heat stung her cheeks. "That's very lame."

He shrugged. "Works for me."

She studied him. He wanted to prove something? He was about to be disappointed. "All right. Eight o'clock. Chez Robert, on Third. I'll meet you there."

"Fine."

"Fine." She turned away. "Oh, Piasecki," she called over her shoulder. "They frown on eating with your fingers."

"I'll keep it in mind."

Natalie was sure she had lost her mind. She dashed into her apartment at 7:15. Facts, figures, projections, graphs, were all running through her head. And her phone was ringing.

She caught the cordless on the fly and dashed into the bedroom to change. "Yes? What?"

"Is that how Mom taught you to answer the phone?"

"Boyd." Some of the tension of the day drained away at the sound of her brother's voice. "I'm sorry. I've just come in from the last of several mind-numbing meetings."

"Don't look for sympathy here. You're the one who opted to carry on the family tradition."

"Right you are." She stepped out of her shoes. "So how's the fight against crime and corruption in Denver, Captain Fletcher?"

"We're holding our own. Cilla and the kids send love, kisses and so forth."

"And send mine back at them. Aren't they going to talk to me?"

"I'm at the station. I'm a little concerned about crime out there in Urbana."

She searched through her closet, the phone caught in the curve of her shoulder. "How did you find out the fire was arson already? I barely found out myself."

"We have ways. Actually, I just got off the phone with the investigator in charge."

"Piasecki?" Natalie tossed a black dinner dress on her bed. "You talked to him?"

"Ten minutes ago. It sounds like you're in good hands, Nat."

"Not if I can help it," she muttered.

"What?"

"He appears to know his job," she said calmly. "Though his methods lack a certain style."

"Arson's a dirty business. And a dangerous one. I'm worried about you, pal."

"Don't be. You're the cop, remember." She struggled out of her jacket, promising herself she'd hang it up before she left. "I'm the CEO in the ivory tower."

"I've never known you to stay there. I want you to keep me up-to-date on the investigation."

"I can do that." She wiggled out of her skirt, and guiltily left it pooled on the floor. "And tell Mom and Dad, if you talk to them before I do, that things are under control. I won't bore you with all the business data—"

"I appreciate that."

She grinned. Boyd had no patience with ledgers or bar graphs. "But I'm about to put another very colorful feather in the Fletcher Industries cap."

"With underwear."

"Lingerie, darling." A little breathless, she fastened on a strapless black bra. "You can buy underwear at a drugstore."

"Right. Well, I can tell you on a personal level, Cilla and I have both thoroughly enjoyed the samples you sent out. I particularly liked the little red thing with the tiny hearts."

"I thought you would." She stepped into the dress, tugged it up to her hips. "With Valentine's Day coming up, you should think about ordering her the matching peignoir."

"Put it on my tab. Take care of yourself, Nat."

"I intend to. With any luck, I'll be seeing you next month. I'm going to scout out locations in Denver."

"Your room's ready for you anytime. And so are we. I love you."

"I love you, too. Bye."

She hung up by dropping the phone on the bed, freeing herself to zip the dress into place. Not exactly a sedate number, she mused, turning toward the mirror. Not with the way it draped off the shoulders and veed down over the curve of the breasts.

Repressed? She shook back her hair. This ought to show him.

The phone rang again, making her swear in disgust. She ignored the first ring and picked up her brush. By the third, she'd given up and pounced on the phone.

"Hello?"

Just breathing, quick, and a faint chuckle.

"Hello? Is someone there?"

"Midnight."

"What?" Distracted, she carried the phone to the dresser to select the right jewelry. "I'm sorry, I didn't catch that."

"Midnight. Witching hour. Wait and see."

When the phone clicked, she disconnected, set it down with a shake of her head. Cranks.

"Use the answering machine, Natalie," she ordered herself. "That's what it's there for."

A glance at her watch had her swearing again. She forgot the call as she went into grooming overdrive. She absolutely refused to be late.

Chapter 4

Natalie arrived at Chez Robert precisely at eight. The four-star French restaurant, with its floral walls and candlelit corners, had been a favorite of hers since she relocated to Urbana. Just stepping inside put her at ease. She had no more than checked her coat when she was greeted enthusiastically by the maître d'.

He kissed her hand with a flourish and beamed. "Ah, Mademoiselle Fletcher...a pleasure, as always. I didn't know you were dining with us this evening."

"I'm meeting a companion, André. A Mr. Piasecki."

"Pi..." Brows knit, André scanned his reservation book while he mentally sounded out the name. "Ah, yes, two for eight o'clock. Pizekee."

"Close enough," Natalie murmured.

"Your companion has not yet arrived, *mademoiselle*. Let

me escort you to your table." With a few quick and ruthless adjustments, André shifted Ryan's reservation to suit his favorite customer, moving the seating from a small central table in the main traffic pattern to Natalie's favorite quiet corner booth.

"Thank you, André." Already at home, Natalie settled into the booth with a little sigh. Beneath the table, her feet slipped out of her shoes.

"My pleasure, as always. Would you care for a drink while you wait?"

"A glass of champagne, thank you. My usual."

"Of course. Right away. And, *mademoiselle,* if I may be so presumptuous, the lobster Robert, tonight it is…" He kissed his fingers.

"I'll keep that in mind."

While she waited, Natalie took out her date book and began to make notations on her schedule for the next day. She had nearly finished her champagne when Ry walked up to the table.

She didn't bother to glance up. "It's a good thing I'm not a fire."

"I'm never late for a fire." He took his seat, and they spent a moment measuring each other.

So, he owned a suit, Natalie thought. And he looked good in it. Dark jacket, crisp white shirt, subtle gray tie. Even though his hair wasn't quite tamed, it was definitely a more classic look than she'd expected from him.

"I use it for funerals," Ry said, reading her perfectly.

She only lifted a brow. "Well, that certainly sets the tone for the evening, doesn't it?"

"You picked the spot," he reminded her. He glanced around

the restaurant. Quiet class, he mused. Just a tad ornate and stuffy—exactly what he'd expected. "So, how's the food here?"

"It's excellent."

"Mademoiselle Fletcher." Robert himself, small, plump, and tuxedoed, stopped by the table to kiss Natalie's hand. *"Bienvenue…"* he began.

Ry sat back, took out a cigarette and watched as they rattled away in French. She spoke it like a native. That, too, he'd expected.

"Du champagne pour mademoiselle," Robert told the waiter. *"Et pour vous, monsieur?"*

"Beer," Ry said. "American, if you've got it."

"Bien sûr." Robert strutted back to the kitchen to harass his chef.

"Well, Legs, that should have made your point," Ry commented.

"Excuse me?"

"Just how out of place will he be in a fancy French restaurant where the owner kisses your knuckles and asks after your family?"

"I don't know what you're—" Natalie frowned as she picked up her glass. "How do you know he asked after my family?"

"I have a French-Canadian grandmother. I probably speak the lingo nearly as well as you do, even if the accent isn't as classy." He blew out a stream of smoke and smiled at her through it. "I didn't peg you as a snob, Natalie."

"I certainly am not a snob." Insulted, she set her glass down again, her shoulders stiffening. But when he only continued to smile, a little frisson of guilt worked its way through her conscience. "Maybe I wanted to make you a little uncomfortable." She sighed, gave up. "A lot uncomfortable. You annoyed me."

"I did better than that." Angling his head, he gave her a long, slow study. She looked like something a man might beg for. Creamy skin flowing out of a black dress, just a few sparkles here and there, sleek golden hair curving around her face. Big, sulky green eyes, red mouth.

Oh, yes, he decided. A man would surely beg.

Her nerves began to jangle as he continued to stare. "Is there a problem?"

"No, no problem. Did you wear that dress to make me uncomfortable?"

"Yes."

He picked up his menu. "It's working. How's the steak here?"

Relax, she ordered herself. Obviously he was trying to make her crazy. "You won't get better in the city. Though I generally prefer the seafood."

She pouted a bit as she studied her menu. The evening was not going as she'd planned. Not only had he seen through her, but he'd already turned the tables so that she looked and felt foolish. Try again, she told herself, and make the best of a bad deal.

After they'd given their orders, Natalie took a deep breath. "I suppose, since we're here, we might as well have a truce."

"Were we fighting?"

"Let's just try for a pleasant evening." She picked up her champagne flute again, sipped. She was, after all, an expert in negotiations and diplomacy. "Let's start with the obvious. Your name. Irish first, Eastern European last."

"Irish mother, Polish father."

"And a French-Canadian grandmother."

"On my mother's side. My other grandmother's a Scot."

"Which makes you—"

"An all-American boy. You've got high-tea hands." He picked up her hand, startling her by running his fingers down hers. "They go with your name. Upper-crust. Classy."

"Well." After she'd tugged her hand free, she cleared her throat, giving undue attention to buttering a roll. "You said you were third-generation in the department."

"Do I make you nervous when I touch you?"

"Yes. Let's try to keep this simple."

"Why?"

Since she had no ready answer for that, she let out a little huff of relief when their appetizers were served. "You must have always wanted to be a firefighter."

All right, he decided, they could cruise along at her speed for now. "Sure I did. I practically grew up at engine company 19, where my pop worked."

"I imagine there was some family pressure."

"No. How about you?"

"Me?"

"The Fletcher tradition. Big business, corporate towers." He lifted a brow. "Family pressure?"

"Plenty of it," she said, and smiled. "Ruthless, unbending, determined. And all from my corner." Her eyes glinted with amusement. "It had always been assumed that my brother Boyd would take over the reins. Both he and I had different ideas about that. So he strapped on a badge and a gun, and I harassed my parents into accepting me as heir apparent."

"They objected?"

"No, not really. It didn't take them long to realize I was serious. And capable." She took a last bite of her coquilles Saint-Jacques and offered Ry the rest. "I love business. The wheeling, the dealing, the paperwork, the meetings. And this new company. It's all mine."

"Your catalog's a big hit down at the station."

The amusement settled in, and felt comfortable. "Oh, really?"

"A lot of the men have wives, or ladies. I'm just helping you pick up a few orders."

"That's generous of you." She studied him over the rim of her glass. "What about you? Are you going to make any orders?"

"I don't have a wife, or a lady." Those smoky eyes flicked over her face again. "At the moment."

"But you did have. A wife."

"Briefly."

"Sorry. I'm prying."

"No problem." He shrugged and finished off his beer. "It's old news. Nearly ten years old. I guess you could say she fell for the uniform, then decided she didn't like the hours I had to be in it."

"Children?"

"No." He regretted that, sometimes wondered if he always would. "We were only together a couple of years. She hooked up with a plumber and moved to the suburbs." He reached out, skimmed a fingertip down the side of her neck, along the curve of her shoulder. "I'm beginning to think I like your shoulders as much as your legs." His eyes locked on hers. "Maybe it's the whole package."

"That's a fascinating compliment." She didn't give in to

the urge to shift away, but she did switch from champagne to water. Suddenly her mouth was dry as dust. "But don't you think the current circumstances require a certain professional detachment?"

"No. If I thought you had anything to do with setting that fire, maybe." He liked the way her eyes lit and narrowed when he pushed the right button. "But, as it stands, I can do my job just fine, and still wonder what it would be like to make love with you."

Her pulse jolted, scrambled. She used the time while their entrées were served to steady it. "I'd prefer if you'd concentrate on the first. In fact, if you could bring me up-to-date—"

"Seems a waste to talk shop in a joint like this." But he shrugged his shoulders. "The bottom line is arson, an incendiary fire. The motive could be revenge, money, straight vandalism or malicious destruction. Or kicks."

"A pyromaniac." She preferred that one, only because it was less personal. "How do you handle that?"

"First, you don't go in biased. A lot of times people, and the media, start shouting 'pyro' whenever there's a series of fires. Even if they seem related, it's not always the case."

"But it often is."

"And it's often simple. Somebody burns a dozen cars because he's ticked he bought a lemon."

"So don't jump to conclusions."

"Exactly."

"But if it *is* someone who's disturbed?"

"Head doctors are always working on the whys. Are you going to let me taste that?"

"Hmmm? Oh, all right." She nudged her plate closer to

his so that he could sample her lobster. "Do you work with psychiatrists?"

"Mostly the shrinks don't come into it until you've got the firebug in custody. That's good stuff," he added, nodding toward her plate. "Anyway, that could be after any number of fires, months of investigation. Maybe they blame his mother. She paid too much attention to him. Or his father, because he didn't pay enough. You know how it goes."

Amused, interested, she cut off a piece of lobster and slipped it onto his plate. "You don't think much of psychiatry?"

"I didn't say that. I just don't go in for blaming somebody else when you did the crime."

"Now you sound like my brother."

"He's probably a good cop. Want some of this steak?"

"No, thanks." Like a bulldog, she kept her teeth in the topic. "Wouldn't you, as an investigator, have to know something about the psychology of the fire starter?"

Ry chewed his steak, signaled for another beer. "You really want to get into this?"

"It's interesting. Particularly now."

"Okay. Short lesson. You can divide pathological fire starters into four groups. The mentally ill, the psychotic, the neurotic, and the sociopath. You're going to have some overlap most of the time, but that sorts them. The neurotic, or psychoneurotic, is the pyromaniac."

"Aren't they all?"

"No. The true pyro's a lot rarer than most people think. It's an uncontrollable compulsion. He *has* to set the fire. When the urge hits him, he goes with it, wherever, whenever. He's not really thinking about covering up or getting away, so he's usually easy to catch."

"I thought *pyro* was more of a general term." She started to tuck her hair behind her ear. Ry beat her to it, letting his fingers linger for a moment.

"I like to see your face when I talk to you." He kept his hand on hers, bringing them both back to the table. "I like to touch you when I talk to you."

Silence hung for a full ten seconds.

"You're not talking," Natalie pointed out.

"Sometimes I just like to look. Come here a minute."

She recognized the light in his eyes, recognized her own helpless response to it. And to him. Deliberately she eased away. "I don't think so. You're a dangerous man, Inspector."

"Thanks. Why don't you come home with me, Natalie?"

She let out a long, quiet breath. "You're also a very blunt one."

"A woman like you could get poetry and fancy moves any time she wanted." Ry neither had them nor believed in them. "You might want to try something more basic."

"This is certainly basic," she agreed. "I think we could use some coffee."

He signaled the waiter. "You didn't answer my question."

"No, I didn't. And no." She waited until the table was cleared, the coffee order given. "Despite a certain elemental attraction, I think it would be unwise to pursue this any further. We're both committed to our careers, diametrically opposed in personality and lifestyle. Even though our relationship has been brief and abrasive, I think it's clear we have nothing in common. We are, as we might say in my business, a bad risk."

He said nothing for a minute, only studied her, as if considering. "That makes sense."

Her stomach muscles relaxed. She even smiled at him as she picked up her coffee. "Good, then we're agreed—"

"I didn't say I agreed," he pointed out. "I said it made sense." He lit a cigarette, his eyes on hers over the flame. "I've been thinking about you, Natalie. And I've got to tell you, I don't much like the way you make me feel. It's distracting, annoying and inconvenient."

Her chin angled. "I'm so glad we cleared this up," she said coolly.

"God knows it gets me right in the gut when you talk to me like that. Duchess to serf." He shook his head, drew in smoke. "I must be perverse. Anyway, I don't like it. I'm not altogether sure I like you." His eyes narrowed, the light in them stopping the pithy comment before it could slip through her lips. "But I've never wanted anyone so damn much in my whole life. That's a problem."

"*Your* problem," she managed.

"Our problem. I've got a rep for being tenacious."

She set her cup down, carefully, before it could slip from her limp fingers. "I'd think a simple no would do, Ry."

"So would I." He shrugged. "Go figure. I haven't been able to clear you out of my head since I saw you standing there freezing at the fire scene. I made a mistake when I kissed you this afternoon. I figured once I had, that would be it. Case closed."

He moved quickly, and so smoothly she barely had time to blink before his mouth was hot and hard on hers. Dazed, she lifted a hand to his shoulder, but her fingers only dug in, held on, as she was buffeted with fresh excitement.

"I was wrong." He drew back. "Case isn't closed, and that's *our* problem."

"Yeah." She let out a shaky breath. No amount of common sense could outweigh her instant and primitive response to him. He touched, she wanted. It was as simple and as terrifying as that. But common sense was her only defense. "This isn't going to work. It's ridiculous to think that it could. I'm not prepared to jump into an affair simply because of some basic animal lust."

"See? We do have something in common." Despite the fact that the kiss had stirred him to aching, he smiled at her. "The lust part."

Laughing, she dragged her hair back from her face. "Oh, I need to get away from you for a while and consider the options."

"This isn't a business deal, Ms. Fletcher."

She looked at him again and wished she could have some distance, just a little distance, so that she could think clearly. "I never make a decision without considering the bottom line."

"Profit and loss?"

Wary, she inclined her head. "In a manner of speaking. You could call it risk and reward. Intimate relationships haven't been my strong suit. That's been my choice. If I'm going to have one with you, however brief, that will be my choice, as well."

"That's fair. Do you want me to work up a prospectus?"

"Don't be snide, Ry." Then, because it soothed some of the tension to realize she'd annoyed him, she smiled. "But I'd certainly give it my full attention." Playing it up, she cupped her chin on her hands, leaning closer, skimming her gaze over his face. "You are very attractive, in a rough-edged, not-quite-tamed sort of way."

He shifted, drew hard on his cigarette. "Thanks a lot."

"No, really." So, she thought, he could be embarrassed. "The faint cleft in the chin, the sharp cheekbones, the lean face, the dark, sexy eyes." Her lips curved as he narrowed those eyes. "And all that hair, just a little unruly. The tough body, the tough attitude."

Impatient, he crushed out his cigarette. "What are you pulling here, Natalie?"

"Just giving you back a little of your own. Yes, you're a very attractive package. Wasn't that your word? Dangerous, dynamic. Like Nemesis."

Now he winced. "Give me a break."

Her chuckle was warm and deep. "No, really. There's a lot of similarity between you and Urbana's mysterious upholder of justice. You both appear to have your own agenda, and your own rough-edged style. He fights crime, appearing and disappearing like smoke. An interesting connection between the two of you.

"I might even wonder if you could be him—except that he's a very romantic figure. And there, Inspector, you part company."

She tossed back her hair and laughed. "I believe you're speechless. Who would have thought it would be that easy to score a point off you?"

She might have scored one, but the game wasn't over. He caught her chin in his hand, held it steady and close, even as her eyes continued to dance. "I guess I could handle it if you wanted to treat me like an object. Just promise to respect me in the morning."

"Nope."

"You're a hard woman, Ms. Fletcher. Okay, scratch respect. How about awe?"

"I'll consider it. If and when it becomes applicable. Now, why don't we get the check? It's late."

When the check was served, as it always was in such establishments, with a faint air of apology, Natalie reached for it automatically. Ry pushed her hand aside and picked it up himself.

"Ry, I didn't mean for you to pay the tab." Flustered, she watched him pull out a credit card. She knew exactly what a meal cost at Chez Robert, and had a good idea what salary a city employee pulled down. "Really. It was my idea to come here."

"Shut up, Natalie." He figured the tip, signed the stub.

"Now I feel guilty. Damn it, we both know I picked this place to rub your nose in it. At least let me split it."

He pocketed his wallet. "No." He slid out of the booth, offered his hand. "Don't worry," he said dryly. "I can still make the rent this month. Probably."

"You're just being stubborn," she muttered.

"Where's the ticket for your coat?"

Male ego, she thought on a disgusted sigh as she took the ticket from her purse. She exchanged good-nights with André and Robert before Ry helped her into her coat.

"Do you need a lift?" Ry asked her.

"No, I have my car."

"Good. I don't have mine. You can give me a ride home."

She shot a suspicious look over her shoulder as they stepped outside. "If this is some sort of maneuver, I'll tell you right now, I'm not faliing for it."

"Fine. I can take a cab." He scanned the street. "If I can find one. It's a cold night," he added. "Feels like snow on the way."

Her breath streamed out. "My car's in the lot around the corner. Where am I taking you?"

"Twenty-second, between Seventh and Eighth."

"Terrific." It was about as far out of her way as possible. "I have to make a stop first, at the store."

"What store?" He slipped an arm around her waist, as much for pleasure as to protect her from the cold.

"My store. We had the carpets laid today, and I didn't have time to check it before dinner. Since it's halfway between your place and mine, I might as well do it now."

"I didn't think business execs checked on carpet at nearly midnight."

"This one does." She smiled sweetly. "But if it's inconvenient for you, I'd be happy to drop you off at the bus stop."

"Thanks anyway." He waited while she unlocked her car. "Do you have any stock in that place yet?"

"About twenty percent of what we want for the grand opening. You're welcome to browse."

He slid into the car. "I was hoping you'd say that."

She drove well. That was no surprise. From what Ry had observed, Natalie Fletcher did everything with seamless competence. The fact that she could be shaken, the fact that the right word, the right look, at the right time, could bring a faint bloom to her cheeks, made her human. And outrageously appealing.

"Have you always lived in Urbana?" As she asked, she automatically turned down the radio.

"Yeah. I like it."

"So do I." She liked the movement of the city, the noise, the crowds. "We've had holdings here for years, of course, but I never lived in Urbana."

"Where?"

"Colorado Springs, mostly. That's where we're based, home and business. I like the East." The streets were dark now, and the wind was whipping through the canyons formed by the spearing buildings. "I like eastern cities, the way people live on top of each other and rush to get everywhere."

"No western comments about overcrowding and crime rates?"

"Fletcher Industries was founded on real estate, remember? The more people, the more housing required. And, as to crime…." She shrugged. "We have a hardworking police force. And Nemesis."

"You're interested in him."

"Who wouldn't be? Of course, as the sister of a police captain, I should add that I don't approve of private citizens doing police work."

"Why not? He seems to get the job done. I wouldn't mind having him on my side." He frowned as she stopped at a light. The streets were nearly empty here, with dark pockets and narrow alleys. "Do you do many runs like this alone?"

"When necessary."

"Why don't you have a driver?"

"Because I like to drive myself." She shot him a look just as the light turned green. "You're *not* going to be typical and give me a lecture about the dangers facing a woman alone in the city…."

"It's not all museums and French restaurants."

"Ry, I'm a big girl. I've spent time alone in Paris, Bangkok, London and Bonn, among other cities. I think I can handle Urbana."

"The cops, and your pal Nemesis, can't be everywhere," he pointed out.

"Any woman who has a big brother knows just how to drop a man to his knees," she said blithely. "And I've taken a self-defense course."

"That should make every mugger in the city tremble."

Ignoring the sarcasm, she pulled up to the curb and turned off the engine. "This is it."

The quick surge of pride rose the moment she was out of the car and facing the building. Her building. "So, what do you think?"

It was sleek and feminine, like its owner. All marble and glass, and its wide display window was scrolled with the Lady's Choice logo in gold leaf. The entrance door was beveled glass etched with rosettes that glinted in the backwash from the streetlights.

Pretty, he thought. Impractical. Expensive.

"Nice look."

"As our flagship store, I wanted it to be impressive, classic, and…" She ran her fingertip over the etching. "Subtly erotic."

She dealt with the locks. Sturdy, Ry noted with some approval. Solid. Just inside the door, she paused to enter her code on the computerized security system. Natalie turned on the lights, relocked the front door.

"Perfect." She nodded with approval at the mauve carpet. The walls were teal, freshly painted. A curvy love seat and gleaming tea table were set in a corner to invite customers to relax and decide over merchandise.

Racks were recessed. Natalie could already envision them full, dripping with silks and laces in pastels, bold, vibrant colors and creamy whites.

"Most of the stock hasn't been put out yet. My manager and her staff will see to that this week. And the window treatment. We have the most incredible brocade peignoir. That'll be the focus."

Ry moved over to a faceless mannequin, fingered the lace at the leg of a jade teddy. The same color as Natalie's eyes, he thought. "So, what do you charge for something like this?"

"Mmm…" She examined the piece herself. Silk, seed pearls at the bodice. "Probably about one-fifty."

"One hundred and fifty? Dollars?" He shook his head in disgust. "One good tug and it's a rag."

Instantly she bristled. "Our merchandise is top-quality. It will certainly hold up to normal wear."

"Honey, a little number like this isn't designed for normal." He cocked a brow. "Looks about your size."

"You keep dreaming, Piasecki." She tossed her coat over the love seat. "The point of good lingerie is style, texture. The sheen of silk, the foam of lace. Ours is designed to make a woman feel attractive and good about herself—pampered."

"I thought the idea was to make a man beg."

"That couldn't hurt," she tossed back. "Look around, if you like. I'm going to run upstairs and check a couple of invoices while I'm here. It won't take me more than five minutes."

"I'll come with you. Offices upstairs?" he asked as they started toward a white floating staircase.

"Just the manager's. We'll have more merchandise up there, and changing rooms. We've also set up a separate area for brides. Specialized wedding-dress undergarments, honeymoon lingerie. Once we're fully operational—"

She broke off when he grabbed her arm. "Quiet."

"What—?"

"Quiet," he said again. He didn't hear it. Not yet. But he could smell it. Just the faintest sting in the air. "Do you have extinguishers in here?"

"Of course. In the storeroom, up in the office." She tugged at his hand. "What is this? Are you going to try to cite me for fire-code violations?"

"Get outside."

With her gaping after him, he darted toward the back of the store.

She was organized, he had to admit. He found the fire extinguisher, up to code, in full view in the crowded storeroom.

"What are you doing with that?" she demanded when he came back.

"I said get outside. You've got a fire."

"A—" He was halfway up the steps before she unfroze and raced after him. "That's impossible. How do you know? There's nothing—"

"Gas," he snapped out. "Smoke."

She started to tell him he was imagining things. But she smelled it now. "Ry…"

He cursed and kicked aside a streamer of papers and matches. It hadn't caught yet, but he saw where they were leading. The glossy white door was closed, and smoke was creeping sulkily under it.

He felt the door, and the heat pushing against it. His head whipped toward hers, the eyes cold. "Get out," he said again. "Call it in."

A scream strangled in her throat as he kicked the door open. Fire leapt out. Ry walked into it.

Chapter 5

It was like a dream. A nightmare. Standing there, frozen, while flame licked at the door frame and Ry stepped in to meet it. In the instant he disappeared into smoke and fire, her heart seemed to stop, its beat simply ceasing. Then the panic that had halted it whipped it to racing. Her head buzzed with the echo of a hundred pulses as she dashed to the door after him.

She could see him, smothering the fire that sprinted across the floor and ate merrily at the base of the walls. Smoke billowed around him, seared her eyes, burned her lungs. Like some warrior, he challenged it, fought it down. In horror, she saw it strike back and lick slyly at his arm.

Now she did scream, leaping in to pound at the smoke that puffed from his back. He whirled to face her, furious to find her there.

"You're on fire." She barely choked the words out. "For God's sake, Ry! Let it go."

"Stay back."

With an arching movement, he smothered the flames that had begun to lap at the central desk. The paperwork left on its top, he knew, would feed the fire. Focused, he turned to attack the smoldering baseboard, the intricately carved trim that was flaming.

"Take this." He shoved the extinguisher into her hands. The main fire was out, and the smaller ones were all but smothered. He nearly had it. From the terror in her eyes, he could see that she didn't realize the beast was nearly beaten. "Use it," he ordered, and in one stride he had reached the flaming curtains and torn them down. There would be pain later—he knew that, as well. But now he fought the fire hand to hand.

Once the smoldering, smoke-stained lace was nothing more than harmless rags, he snatched the extinguisher out of her numbed hands and killed what was left.

"It didn't have much of a start." But his jacket was still smoking. He yanked it off, tossed it aside. "Wouldn't have gotten this far this fast, if there weren't so many flammables in here." He set the nearly empty extinguisher aside. "It's out."

Still he checked the room, kicking through the ruined drapes, searching for any cagey spark that waited to burn clean again.

"It's out," he repeated, and shoved her toward the door. "Get downstairs."

She stumbled, almost falling to her knees. A violent fit of coughing nearly paralyzed her. Her stomach heaved, her head spun. Near fainting, she braced a hand against the wall and fought to breathe.

"Damn it, Natalie." In one sweep, he had her up in his arms. He carried her through the blinding smoke, down the elegant staircase. "I told you to get out. Don't you ever listen?"

She tried to speak, and only coughed weakly. It felt as though she were floating. Even when he laid her against the cool cushions of the love seat, her head continued to reel.

He was cursing her. But his voice seemed far away, and harmless. If she could just get one breath, she thought, one full breath to soothe her burning throat.

He watched her eyes roll back. Jerking her ruthlessly, he pushed her head between her knees.

"Don't you faint on me." His voice was curt, his hand on the back of her head firm. "Stay here, breathe slow. You hear me?"

She nodded weakly. He left her, and when cold, fresh air slapped her cheeks, she shivered. After propping the outside door open, Ry came back, rubbing his hands up and down her spine.

She'd scared him, badly. So he did what came naturally to combat the fear—he yelled at her.

"That was stupid and thoughtless! You're lucky to get out of there with a sick stomach and some smoke inhalation. I *told* you to get out."

"You went in." She winced as the words tormented her abused throat. "You went right in."

"I'm trained. You're not." He hauled her back into a sitting position to check her over.

Her face was dead white under sooty smears, but her eyes were clear again. "Nausea?" he asked in clipped tones.

"No." She pressed the heels of her hands to her stinging eyes. "Not now."

"Dizzy?"

"No."

Her voice was hoarse, strained. He imagined her throat felt as though it had been scored with a hot poker. "Is there any water around here? I'll get you some."

"I'm all right." She dropped her hands, let her head fall back against the cushion. Now that the sickness was passing, fear was creeping in. "It seemed so fast, so horribly fast. Are you sure it's out?"

"It's my job to be sure." Frowning, he caught her chin, his eyes narrowing as he studied her face. "I'm taking you to the hospital."

"I don't need a damn hospital." In a bad-tempered movement, she shoved at him. Then gasped when she saw his hands. "Ry, your hands!" She grabbed his wrists. "You're burned!"

He glanced down. There were a few welts, some reddening. "Nothing major."

Reaction set in with shudders. "You were on fire, I saw your jacket catch fire."

"It was an old jacket. Stop," he ordered when tears swam in her eyes, overflowed. "Don't." If he hated one thing more than fire, it was a woman's tears. He swore and crushed his mouth to hers, hoping that would stop the flood.

Her arms came hard around him, surprising him with their strength and urgency. But her mouth trembled beneath his, moving him to gentle the kiss. To soothe.

"Better?" he murmured, and stroked her hair.

"I'm all right," she said again, willing herself to believe it. "There should be a first-aid kit in the storeroom. You need to put something on your hands."

"It's no big deal…." he began, but she shoved away from him and rose.

"I have to do something. Damn it, I have to do something."

She dashed off. Baffled by her, Ry stood and moved to re-lock the door. He needed to go up again and ventilate the office, but he wanted her out of the way before he made a preliminary investigation. He tugged off his tie, loosened his collar.

"There's some salve in here." Steadier now, Natalie came back in with a small first-aid kit.

"Fine." Deciding tending to him would do her some good, he sat back and let her play nurse. He had to admit the cool balm and her gentle fingers didn't do him any harm, either.

"You're lucky it isn't worse. It was insane, just walking into that room."

He cocked a brow. "You're welcome."

She looked up at him then. His face was smeared from the smoke, his eyes were reddened from it. "I am grateful," she said quietly. "Very grateful. But it was just things, Ry. Just things." She looked away again, busying herself replacing the tube of salve. "I guess I owe you a new suit."

"I hate suits." He shifted uncomfortably when he heard her quick, unsteady sob. "Don't cry again. If you really want to thank me, don't cry."

"All right." She sniffed inelegantly and rubbed her hands over her face. "I was so scared."

"It's over." He gave her hand an awkward pat. "Will you be all right for a minute? I want to go up and open the window. The smoke needs a way to escape."

"I'll come—"

"No, you won't. Sit here." He rose again, put a firm hand on her shoulder. "Please stay here."

He turned and left her. Natalie used the time he was gone to compose herself. And to think. When he came back down, she was sitting with her hands folded in her lap.

"It was the same as the warehouse, wasn't it?" She lifted her gaze to his. "The way it was set. We can't pretend it was a coincidence."

"Yes," he said. "It was the same. And no, we can't. We'll talk about this later. I'll drive you home."

"I'm—"

The words slid back down her throat when he dragged her roughly to her feet. "If you tell me one more time that you're all right, I'm going to punch you. You're sick, you're scared, and you sucked in smoke. Now this is the way we're going to work this. I'm driving you home. We'll report this on the phone in that snazzy car of yours. You're going to go to bed, and tomorrow you're going to see a doctor. Once you check out, we'll go from there."

"Stop yelling at me."

"I wouldn't have to yell if you'd listen." He grabbed her coat. "Put this on."

"This is my property. I have a right to be here."

"Well, I'm taking you out." He shoved her arm into the sleeve of her coat. "If you don't like it, call your fancy lawyers and sue me."

"There's no reason for you to take this attitude."

He started to swear, stopped himself. As a precaution, he took one slow breath. "Natalie, I'm tired." His voice was quiet now, nearly reasonable. "I've got a job to do here, and I can't do it if you're in my way. So cooperate. Please."

He was right, she knew he was right. She turned away, picked up her purse. "Keep my car. I'll arrange to have it picked up tomorrow."

"I appreciate it."

She gave him the car keys and the keys to the shop. "I'll be here tomorrow, Ry."

"I figured you would." He lifted a hand and rubbed his knuckles along her jawline. "Hey—try not to worry. I'm the best."

She nearly smiled. "So I've been told."

It was nearly eight the following morning when the cab dropped Natalie off in front of Lady's Choice. She noted, without surprise, that her car was out front, a fire-department sign visible through the windshield.

Instead of bothering with the buzzer, she used the spare set of keys she'd picked up that morning at the office and let herself in.

She couldn't smell the smoke. That was a relief. She'd spent a great deal of time during the night worrying and calculating the possible losses if the stock already in place had been damaged by smoke.

The first floor looked as pristine and elegant as it had the night before. If Ry gave her the go-ahead, she'd contact her manager and reestablish business as usual.

She took off her coat and gloves and started upstairs.

For Ry, it had been a long and productive night. He'd stopped in at the station after he dropped Natalie off, to change and to pick up his tools. He'd worked alone through the night—the way he preferred it. He was just sealing an evidence jar when she walked in.

"Good morning, Legs." Crouched on the floor amid the rubble, he didn't bother to look past them.

She scanned the room, sighed. The carpet was a blackened mess. Charred pieces of wood trim had been pried from the sooty walls and lay scattered. The elegant Queen Anne desk was blackened and scored, and the Irish-lace drapes were a heap of useless rags.

Despite the open window where the light wind shook in thin snow, the air stank with stale smoke.

"Why does it always look worse the next day?"

"It's not so bad. A little paint, new trim."

She ran a fingertip over the wallpaper, the violet-and-rosebud pattern she'd chosen personally. Ruined now, she thought.

"Easy for you to say."

"Yeah," he agreed, labeling the evidence jar. "I guess it is."

He glanced up then. Today she'd scooped her hair up. The style appealed to him, the way it showed off the line of her neck and jaw. This morning's suit was royal purple, military in style. It looked, he thought, as though the lady were ready for a fight.

"How'd you sleep?"

"Surprisingly well, all in all." Except for one bone-chilling nightmare she didn't want to mention. "You?"

He hadn't been to bed at all, and merely shrugged. "Have you called your adjuster?"

"I will, as soon as his office opens." Her voice cooled automatically. "Are you going to interview me again, Inspector?"

Annoyance flared briefly in his eyes. "I don't think that's necessary, do you?" He began to replace his tools in their box. "I'll have a report by tomorrow."

She closed her eyes a moment. "I'm sorry. I'm not angry with you, Ry. I'm just angry."

"Fair enough."

"Can you—?" She broke off, turning quickly at the sound of footsteps on the stairs. "Gage." She forced a smile, held out her hands when he walked in.

"I heard." With one quick glance, he took in the damage. "I thought I'd come by and see if there was anything I could do."

"Thanks." She kissed him lightly on the cheek before she turned back to Ry. He was still crouched—very much, she thought, intrigued, like an animal about to spring. "Gage Guthrie, Inspector Ryan Piasecki."

"I've heard you do good work."

After a moment, Ry straightened and accepted the hand Gage offered. "I've heard the same about you." Feeling territorial, Ry measured the man as he spoke to Natalie. "Are you two pals?"

"That's right. And a bit more." She watched, fascinated, as Ry's eyes kindled. "If you can follow the connections, Gage is married to my brother's wife's sister."

The fire banked; Ry's shoulders relaxed. "Extended family."

"In a manner of speaking." Judging the situation quickly and accurately, Gage decided to do a little checking on the inspector himself. "Are you looking at the same fire starter here?"

"We're not ready to release that information."

"He's got his official hat on," Natalie said dryly. "Unofficially," she continued, ignoring Ry's scowl, "it looks the same. When we came in last night—"

"You were here?" Gage interrupted her, gripping Natalie's arm. "You?"

"I had a few things I wanted to check on. Fortunately." Blowing out a breath, she took another scan of the room. "It could have been a lot worse. I happened to have a veteran fire-fighter along."

Gage relaxed fractionally. "You've got no business going around the city alone, at night."

"Yeah." Ry took out a cigarette. "You try to tell her."

Natalie merely lifted a brow. "Do you go around the city, Gage, alone? At night?"

He tucked his tongue in his cheek. If she only knew. "It's entirely different. And don't give me a lecture on equality," he went on, before she could speak. "I'm all for it. In the home, in the workplace. But on the street it comes down to basic common sense. A woman's more of a target."

"Mmm, hmm…" Natalie smiled pleasantly. "And does Deborah buy that line from you?"

Now his lips did curve. "No. She's every bit as hardheaded as you." Frustrated that he'd been on the other side of town when Nat needed him, Gage tucked his hands in his pockets. "If I can't do anything else, I can offer you any of the facili-ties or staff of Guthrie International."

"I'll take you up on that if it becomes necessary." She sent him a quick, hopeful look. "I don't suppose you could use your influence to keep your wife from calling my brother and Cilla and relating all of this?"

He patted her cheek. "Not a chance. Maybe I should men-tion that she talked to Althea last week and filled her in on what happened at the warehouse."

Giving in to fatigue, Natalie rubbed her temples. Althea

Grayson, her brother's former partner on the force, was very pregnant. "I'm surrounded by cops," she muttered. "There's no reason to get Althea upset in her condition. She and Colt should be concentrating on each other."

"It's a problem when you have so many people who care about you. Stay out of empty buildings," Gage added, and kissed her. "Nice to meet you, Inspector."

"Yeah. See you."

"Give Deborah and Addy my love," Natalie said as she walked Gage to the doorway. "And stop worrying about me."

"I'll do the first, but not the second."

"Who's Addy?" Ry asked before he heard the downstairs door close behind Gage.

"Hmmm? Oh, their baby." Distracted, she circled around a charred hole in the carpet to examine her antique filing cabinets. It was some consolation to see that they were undamaged. "I really need to clear this up, Ry. Too many people are losing sleep."

"You've got a lot of close ties." He walked to the open window and put out his cigarette. "I can't make this work any faster to please them. Just take your friend's advice. Stay off the streets at night and out of empty buildings."

"I don't want advice. I want answers. Someone broke in here last night and tried to burn me out. How and why?"

"Okay, Ms. Fletcher, I can give you the how." Ry leaned a hip against the partially burned desk. "On the night of February twenty-sixth, a fire was discovered by Inspector Piasecki, and Natalie Fletcher, owner of the building."

"Ry..."

He held up a hand to stop her. "After entering the building, Piasecki and Fletcher started up to the second floor when

Piasecki detected the odor of an accelerant, and smoke. Piasecki then ordered Fletcher to flee the building. An order, I might add, that she stupidly ignored. Finding an extinguisher in the storeroom, Piasecki proceeded to the fire, which had involved an office on the second floor. Streamers of paper, clothing and matchbooks were observed. The fire was extinguished without extensive damage."

"I'm very aware of that particular sequence of events."

"You wanted a report, you're getting one. An examination of the debris led the investigator to believe that the fire had been started approximately two feet inside the door, with the use of gasoline as an accelerant. No forced entry into the building could be determined by the inspector, or the police department. Arson is indicated."

She took a careful breath. "You're angry with me."

"Yeah, I'm angry with you. You're pushing me, Natalie, and yourself. You want this all tidied up, because people are worried about you, and you're concerned with selling your pantyhose on time. And you're missing one small, very important detail."

"No, I'm not." She was pale again, and rigid. "I'm trying not to be frightened by it. It isn't difficult to add the elements and come up with the fact that someone is doing this to me deliberately. Two of my buildings within two weeks. I'm not a fool, Ry."

"You're a fool if you're not frightened by it. You've got an enemy. Who?"

"I don't know," she shot back. "If I did, don't you think I'd tell you? You've just told me there was no forced entry. That means someone I know, someone who works for me, could have gotten in here and started the fire."

"It's a torch."

"Excuse me?"

"A pro," Ry explained. "Not a very good one, but a pro. Somebody hired a torch to set the fires. It could be that somebody let him in, or he found a way to bypass your security. But he didn't finish the job here, so it's likely he'll hit you again."

She forced back a shudder. "That's comforting. That's very comforting."

"I don't want you to be comforted. I want you to be alert. How many people work for you?"

"At Lady's Choice?" Frazzled, she pushed at her hair. "Around six hundred, I think, in Urbana."

"You got a personnel list?"

"I can get one."

"I want it. Look, I'm going to run the data through the computer. See how many known pros we have in the area who use this technique. It's a start."

"You'll keep me up-to-date? I'll be in the office most of the day. My assistant will know how to reach me if I'm out."

He straightened, walked to her and cupped her face. "Why don't you take the day off? Go shopping, go see a movie."

"Are you joking?"

He dropped his hands, shoved them in his pockets. "Listen, Natalie, you've got one more person worried about you. Okay?"

"I think it's okay," she said slowly. "I'll stay available, Ry. But I have a lot of work to do." She smiled in an attempt to lighten the mood. "Starting with getting a cleaning crew and decorators in here."

"Not until I tell you."

"How did I know you'd say that?" Resigned, she glanced toward the wooden cabinets against the left wall. "Is it all right if I get some files out? I only moved them out of the main office a few days ago so I could work on them here." She lifted a shoulder. "Or I'd hoped to work on them here. More delays," she said under her breath.

"Yeah, go ahead. Watch your step."

He watched it, as well, and shook his head. He didn't see how she could walk so smoothly on those skyscraper heels she seemed addicted to. But he had to admit, they did fascinating things to her legs.

"How are your hands?" she asked as she flipped through the files.

"What?"

"Your hands." She glanced back, saw where his gaze was focused, and laughed. "God, Piasecki, you're obsessed."

"I bet they go all the way up to your shoulders." He skimmed his eyes up to hers. "The hands aren't too bad, thanks. When's your doctor's appointment?"

She turned away to give unmerited attention to the files. "I don't need a doctor. I don't like doctors."

"Chicken."

"Maybe. My throat's a little sore, that's all. I can deal with that without a doctor poking at me. And if you're going to lecture me on that, I'll lecture you on deliberately sucking smoke into your lungs."

With a wince, he tucked away the cigarette he'd just pulled out. "I didn't say anything. Are you about done? I want to get this evidence to the lab."

"Yes. The fact that the files didn't go up saves me a lot of time and trouble. I need Deirdre to run an audit after we've dealt with this other mess. I'm hoping things look solid enough for me to scout around and open a branch in Denver."

The little flutter under his heart wasn't easily ignored. "Denver? Are you going to be moving back to Colorado?"

"Hmmm…" Satisfied, she tucked the paperwork in her briefcase. "It depends. I'm not thinking that far ahead yet. First we have to get the stores we have off the ground. That isn't going to happen overnight." She swung the strap of her briefcase over her shoulder. "That should do it."

"I want to see you." It cost him to say it. Even more to admit it to himself. "I need to see you, Natalie. Away from all this."

Her suddenly nervous fingers tugged at the strap of her briefcase. "We're both pretty swamped at the moment, Ry. It might be smarter for us to concentrate on what needs to be done and keep a little personal distance."

"It would be smarter."

"Well, then." She took one step toward the door before he blocked her path.

"I want to see you," he repeated. "And I want to touch you. And I want to take you to bed."

Heat curled inside her, threatening to flash. It didn't seem to matter that his words were rough, blunt, and without finesse. Poetry and rose petals would have left her much less vulnerable.

"I know what you want. I need to be sure what *I* want. What I can handle. I've always been a logical person. You've got a way of clouding that."

"Tonight."

"I have to work late." She felt herself weakening, yearning. "A dinner meeting."

"I'll wait."

"I don't know when I'll be finished. Probably not much before midnight."

He backed her toward the wall. "Midnight, then."

She began to wonder why she was resisting. Her eyes started to cloud and close. "Midnight," she repeated, waiting for his mouth to cover hers. Wanting to taste it, to surge under it.

Her eyes sprang open. She jerked back. "Oh, God. Midnight."

Her cheeks had gone white again. Ry lifted his hands to support her. "What is it?"

"Midnight," she repeated, pressing a hand to her brow. "I didn't put it together. Never thought of it. It was just past twelve when we got here last night."

He nodded, watching her. "So?"

"I got a call when I was dressing for dinner. I never seem to be able to ignore the ring and let the machine pick up, so I answered. He said midnight."

Eyes narrowed, Ry braced her against the wall. "Who?"

"I don't know. I didn't recognize the voice. He said— Let me think." She pushed away to pace out into the hall. "Midnight. He said midnight. The witching hour. Watch for it, or wait for it—something like that." She gestured toward the charred and ruined carpet. "This must be what he meant."

"Why the hell didn't you tell me this before?"

"Because I just remembered." Every bit as angry as he, she whirled on Ry. "I thought it was a crank call, so I ignored it, forgot it. Then, when this happened, I had a little more on my mind than a nuisance call. How was I supposed to know it was a warning? Or a threat?"

He ignored that and took his notebook out of his pocket to write down the words she'd related. "What time did you get the call?"

"It must have been around seven-thirty. I was looking for earrings, and rushing because I'd gotten held up and was running late."

"Did you hear any background noises on the line?"

Unsure, she fought to remember. She hadn't been paying attention. She'd been thinking of Ry. "I didn't notice any. His voice was high-pitched. It was a man, I'm sure of that, but it was a girlish kind of voice. He giggled," she remembered.

Ry's gaze shot to her face, then back to his book. "Did it sound mechanical, or genuine?"

She went blank for a moment. "Oh, you mean like a tape. No, it didn't sound like a tape."

"Is your number listed?"

"No." Then she understood the significance of the question. "No," she repeated slowly. "It's not."

"I want a list of everyone who has your home number. Everyone."

She straightened, forcing herself to keep calm. "I can give you a list of everyone I know who has it. I can't tell you who might have gotten it by other means." She cleared her aching throat. "Ry, do professionals usually call their victims before a fire?"

He tucked his notebook away and looked into her eyes. "Even pros can be crazy. I'll drive you to your office."

"It's not necessary."

Patience. He reminded himself he'd worked overtime so that he could be patient with her. Then he thought, the hell with it. "You listen to this, real careful." He curled his fingers around the lapel of her jacket. "I'm driving you to your office. Got that?"

"I don't see—"

He tugged. "Got it?"

She bit back an oath. It would be petty to argue. "Fine. I'm going to need my car later today, so you'll have to get yourself wherever you're going after you drop me off."

"Keep listening," he said evenly. "Until I get back to you, you're not to go anywhere alone."

"That's ridiculous. I've got a business to run."

"Nowhere alone," he repeated. "Otherwise, I'm going to call some of my pals in Urbana P.D. and have them sit on you." When she opened her mouth to protest, he overrode her. "And I can sure as hell keep your little shop here off-limits to everyone but official fire- and police-department personnel until further notice."

"That sounds like a threat," she said stiffly.

"You're a real sharp lady. You get one of your minions to drive you today, Natalie, or I'll slap a fire-department restriction on the front door of this place for the next couple of weeks."

He could, she realized, reading the determination on his face. And he would. From experience, she knew it was smarter, and more practical, to give up a small point in a negotiation in order to salvage the bottom line.

"All right. I'll assign a driver for any out-of-the-office meetings today. But I'd like to point out that this man is burning my buildings, Ry, not threatening me personally."

"He called you personally. That's enough."

She hated the fact that he'd frightened her. Stringent control kept her dealing with office details coolly, efficiently. By noon, she had a cleanup crew on standby, waiting for Ry's okay. She'd ordered her assistant to contact the decorator about new carpet, wallpaper, draperies and paint. She'd dealt with a frantic call from her Atlanta branch and an irate one from Chicago, and managed to play down the problem with her family back in Colorado.

Impatient, she buzzed her assistant. "Maureen, I needed those printouts thirty minutes ago."

"Yes, Ms. Fletcher. The system's down in Accounting. They're working on it."

"Tell them—" She bit back the searing words, and forced her voice to level. "Tell them it's a priority. Thank you, Maureen."

Deliberately she leaned back in her chair and closed her eyes. Having an edge was an advantage in business, she reminded herself. Being edgy was a liability. If she was going to handle the meetings set for the rest of the day, she had to pull herself together. Slowly she unfisted her hands and ordered her muscles to relax.

She'd nearly accomplished it when a quick knock came at her door. She straightened in her chair as Melvin poked his head in.

"Safe?"

"Nearly," she told him. "Come in."

"I come bearing gifts." He carried a tray into the room.

"If that's coffee, I may find the energy to get up and kiss your whole face."

He flushed brightly and chuckled. "Not only is it coffee, but there's chicken salad to go with it. Even *you* have to eat, Natalie."

"Tell me about it." She pressed a hand to her stomach as

she rose to join him at the sofa. "I'm empty. This is very sweet of you, Melvin."

"And self-serving. You've been burning up the interoffice lines, so I had my secretary put this together. You take a break—" he fiddled with his bright red bow tie "—we take a break."

"I guess I have been playing Simon Legree today." With a little sigh, Natalie inhaled the scent of coffee as she poured.

"You're entitled." He sat beside her. "Have you got time over lunch to tell me how bad things are over at the flagship?"

"Not as bad as they could have been." She indulged herself by slipping out of her shoes and tucking her legs up as she ate. "Minor, really. From what I could tell, it looked like mostly cosmetic damage to the manager's office. It didn't get to the stock."

"Thank God," he said heartily. "I don't know how much my charm would have worked a second time in persuading the branches to part with inventory."

"Unnecessary," she said between bites. "We got lucky this time, Melvin, but—"

"But?"

"There's a pattern here that concerns me. Someone doesn't want Lady's Choice to fly."

Frowning, he picked up the roll on her plate, broke it in half. "Unforgettable Woman's our top competitor. Or we'll be theirs."

"I've thought of that. It just doesn't fit. That company's been around nearly fifty years. It's solid. Respectable." She sighed, hating what she needed to say. "But I am worried about corporate espionage, Melvin. Within Lady's Choice."

"One of our people?" He'd lost his taste for the roll.

"It isn't a possibility I like—or one I can overlook." Thoughtful, she switched from food to coffee. "I could call a meeting of department heads, get input and opinions about their people." And she would, she thought. She would have to. "But that doesn't deal with the department heads themselves."

"A lot of your top people have been with Fletcher for years, Natalie."

"I'm aware of that." Restless, she rose, drinking coffee as she paced. "I can't think of any reason why someone in the organization would want to delay the opening. But I have to look for that reason."

"That puts us all under the gun."

She turned back. "I'm sorry, Melvin. It does."

"No need to be sorry. It's business." He waved it aside, but his smile was a little strained as he rose. "What's the next step?"

"I'm going to meet the adjuster at the shop at one." She glanced at her watch and swore. "I'd better get started."

"Let me do it." Anticipating her, Melvin held up a hand. "You have more than you can handle right here. Delegate, Natalie, remember? I'll meet the agent, give you a full report when I get back."

"All right. It would save me a very frenzied hour." Frowning, she stepped back into her shoes. "If the arson inspector is on-site, you might ask him to contact me with any progress."

"Will do. There's a shipment due in to the shop late this afternoon. Do you want to put a hold on it?"

"No." She'd already thought it through. "Business as usual. I've put a security guard on the building. It won't be easy for anyone to get in again."

"We'll stay on schedule," Melvin assured her.

"Damn right we will."

Chapter 6

Ry preferred good solid human reasoning to computer analysis, but he'd learned to use all available tools. The Arson Pattern Recognition System was one of the best. Over the past few years, he'd become adept enough at the keyboard. Now, with his secretary long gone for the day and the men downstairs settled into sleep, he worked alone.

The APRS, used intelligently, was an effective tool for identifying and classifying trends in data. It was possible, with a series of fires suspected to be related, to use the tool to predict where and when future arsons in the series were most likely to occur.

The computer told him what he'd already deduced. Natalie's production plant was a prime target. He'd already assigned a team to patrol and survey the area.

But he was more concerned about Natalie herself. The

phone call she'd received made it personal. And it had given him a very specific clue.

Reaching for coffee with one hand, Ry tapped on keys and linked up with the National Fire Data System. He plugged in his pattern—incident information, geographical locations and fire data. The process would not only help him, but serve to aid future investigators.

Then he worked on suspects. Again he input the fire data, the method. To these he was able to add the phone call, Natalie's impression of the voice and the wording.

He sat back and watched the computer reinforce his own conclusions.

Clarence Robert Jacoby, a.k.a. Jacoby, a.k.a. Clarence Roberts. Last known address 23 South Street, Urbana. White male. D.O.B. 6/25/52.

It went on to list half a dozen arrests for arson and incendiary fires, all urban. One conviction had put him away for five years. Another arrest, two years ago was still pending, as he'd skipped out on bail.

And the pattern was there.

Jacoby was a part-time pro who liked to burn things. He habitually preferred gasoline as an accelerant, used streamers of convenient, on-site flammables, along with matchbooks from his own collection. He often called his victims. His psychiatric evaluation classified him as a neurotic with sociopathic tendencies.

"You like fire, don't you, you little bastard?" Ry muttered, tapping his finger against the keyboard. "You don't even mind when it burns you. Isn't that what you told me? It's like a kiss."

Ry flipped a switch and had the data printing out. Wearily

he rubbed the heels of his hands over his eyes as the machine clattered. He'd caught about two hours' sleep on the sofa in the outer office that evening. Fatigue was catching up with him.

But he had his quarry now. He was sure of it. And, he thought, he had a trail.

More out of habit than desire, Ry lit a cigarette before punching in numbers on the phone. "Piasecki. I'm swinging by the Fletcher plant on my way home. You can reach me…" He trailed off, checking his watch. Midnight, he noted. On the dot. Maybe he should take that as a sign. "You can reach me at this number until I check in again." He recited Natalie's home number from memory, then hung up.

He shut down the computer, grabbed the printout and his jacket, then hit the lights.

Natalie pulled on a robe, one of her favorites from the Lady's Choice line, and debated whether to crawl into bed or sink into a hot bath. She decided to soothe her nerves with a glass of wine before she did either. She'd tried to reach Ry three times that afternoon, only to be told he was unavailable.

She was supposed to be available, she thought nastily. But he could come and go as he pleased. Not a word all day. Well, he was going to get a surprise first thing in the morning when she walked right into his office and demanded a progress report.

As if she didn't have enough to worry about, with department meetings, production meetings, meeting meetings. And she was tracking the early catalog orders by region. At least that looked promising, she thought, and walked over to enjoy her view of the city.

She wasn't going to let anything stand in her way. Not fires, and certainly not a fire inspector. If there was someone on her staff—in any position—who was responsible for the arson, she would find out who it was. And she would deal with it.

Within a year, she would have pushed Lady's Choice over the top. Within five, she would double the number of branches.

Fletcher Industries would have a new success, one she would have nurtured from inception. She could be proud, and satisfied.

So why was she suddenly so lonely?

His fault, she decided, sipping her wine, for making her restless with her life. For making her question her priorities at a time when she needed all her concentration and effort focused.

Physical attraction, even with this kind of intensity, wasn't enough, shouldn't be enough, to distract her from her goals. She'd been attracted before, and certainly knew how to play the game safely. After all, she was thirty-two, hardly a novice in the relationship arena. Skilled and cautious, she'd always come through unscathed. No man had ever involved her heart quite enough to cause scarring.

Why did that suddenly seem so sad?

Annoyed with the thought, she shook it off.

She was wasting her time brooding about Ryan Piasecki. God knew, he wasn't even her type. He was rough and rude and undeniably abrasive. She preferred a smoother sort. A safer sort.

Why did that suddenly seem so shallow?

She set her half-full glass aside and shook back her hair. What she needed was sleep, not self-analysis. The phone rang just as she reached out to switch off the lights.

"Oh, I hate you," she muttered, and picked up the receiver. "Hello."

"Ms. Fletcher, this is Mark, at the desk downstairs?"

"Yes, Mark, what is it?"

"There's an Inspector Piasecki here to see you."

"Oh, really?" She checked her watch, toying with the idea of sending him away. "Mark, would you ask him if it's official business?"

"Yes, ma'am. Is this official business, Inspector?"

She heard Ry's voice clearly through the earpiece, asking Mark whether he would like him to get a team down there in the next twenty minutes to look for code violations.

When Mark sputtered, Natalie took pity on him. "Just send him up, Mark."

"Yes, Ms. Fletcher. Thank you."

She disconnected, then paced to the door and back. She certainly wasn't going to check her appearance in the mirror.

Of course, she did.

By the time Ry pounded on her door, she'd managed to dash into the bedroom, brush her hair and dab on some perfume.

"Don't you think it's unfair to threaten people in order to get your way?" she demanded when she yanked open the door.

"Not when it works." He took his time looking at her. The floor-length robe was unadorned, the color of heavy cream. The silk crossed over her breasts, nipped in at the belted waist, then fell, thin and close, down her hips.

"Don't you think it's a waste to wear something like that when you're alone?"

"No, I don't."

"Are we going to talk in the hall?"

"I suppose not." She closed the door behind him. "I won't bother to point out that it's late."

He said nothing, only wandered around the living area of the apartment. Soft colors, offset by those vibrant abstract paintings she apparently liked. Lots of trinkets, he noted, but tidy. There were fresh flowers, a fireplace piped for gas, and a wide window through which the lights of the city gleamed.

"Nice place."

"I like it."

"You like heights." He moved to the window and looked down. She was a good twenty floors above any possible ladder rescue. "Maybe I will have this place checked to see if it's up to code." He glanced back at her. "Got a beer?"

"No." Then she sighed. Manners would always rise above annoyance. "I was having a glass of wine. Would you like one?"

He shrugged. He wasn't much of a wine drinker, but his system couldn't handle any more coffee.

Taking that as an indication of assent, Natalie went into the kitchen to pour another glass.

"Got anything to go with it?" he asked from the doorway. "Like food?"

She started to snap at him about mistaking her apartment for an all-night diner, but then she got a good look at his face in the strong kitchen light. If she'd ever seen exhaustion, she was seeing it now.

"I don't do a lot of cooking, but I have some Brie, crackers, some fruit."

Nearly amused, he rubbed his hands over his face. "Brie." He gave a short laugh as he dropped his hands. "Great. Fine."

"Go sit down." She handed him the wine. "I'll bring it out."

"Thanks."

A few minutes later, she found him on her sofa, his legs stretched out, his eyes half-closed. "Why aren't you home in bed?"

"I had some stuff to do." With one hand, he reached for the tray she'd set on the table. With the other, he reached for her. Content with her beside him, he piled soft cheese on a cracker. "It's not half-bad," he said with his mouth full. "I missed dinner."

"I suppose I could send out for something."

"This is fine. I figured you'd want an update."

"I do, but I thought I'd hear from you several hours ago." He mumbled something over a new cracker. "What?"

"Court," he said, and swallowed. "I had to be in court most of the afternoon."

"I see."

"Got your messages, though." The refueling helped, and he grinned. "Did you miss me?"

"The update," she said dryly. "It's the least you can do while you're cleaning out my pantry."

He helped himself to a handful of glossy green grapes. "I've ordered surveillance for your plant on Winesap."

Her fingers tightened on the stem of her glass. "Do you think it's a target?"

"Fits the pattern. Have you noticed a man around any of your properties? White guy, about five-four, a hundred and thirty. Thinning sandy hair. Fifty-something, but with this round, moony face that makes him look like a kid." He broke off to wash crackers down with wine. "Pale, mousy-looking eyes, lots of teeth."

"No, I can't think of anyone like that. Why?"

"He's a torch. Nasty little guy, about half-crazy." The wine wasn't half-bad, either, Ry was discovering, and sipped again. "All-the-way crazy would be easier. He likes to make things burn, and he doesn't mind getting paid for it."

"You think he's the one," Natalie said quietly. "And you know him, personally, don't you?"

"We've met, Clarence and me. Last time I saw him was, oh, about ten years ago. He'd hung around too long on one of his jobs. He was on fire when I got to him. We were both smoking by the time I got him out."

Natalie struggled for calm. "Why do you think it's him?"

Briefly Ry gave her a rundown on his work that evening. "So, it's his kind of job," he added. "Plus, the phone call. He likes the phone, too. And the voice you described—that's pure Clarence."

"You could have told me that this morning."

"Could've." He shrugged. "Didn't see the point."

"The point," she said between her teeth, "is that we're talking about my building, my property."

He studied her a moment. It wasn't such a bad idea, he supposed, to use anger to cover fear. He couldn't blame her for it. "Tell me, Ms. Fletcher, in your position as CEO, or whatever it is you are, do you make reports before, during, or after you've checked your data?"

It irritated, as he'd meant it to. And it deflated. As he'd meant it to. "All right." She expelled a rush of air. "Tell me the rest."

Ry set his glass aside. "He moves around, city to city. I'm betting he's back in Urbana. And I'll find him. Is there an ashtray around here?"

In silence, Natalie rose and took a small mosaic dish from another table. She was being unfair, she realized, and it wasn't like her. Obviously he was dead tired because he'd put in dozens of extra hours—for her.

"You've been working on this all night."

He struck a match. "That's the job."

"Is it?" she asked quietly.

"Yeah." His eyes met hers. "And it's you."

Her pulse began to drum. She couldn't stop it. "You're making it very hard for me, Ry."

"That's the idea." Lazily he skimmed a finger along the lapel of her robe, barely brushing the skin. Her scent rose up from it, subtly, tantalizingly. "You want me to ask you how your day went?"

"No." With a tired laugh, she shook her head. "No."

"I guess you don't want to talk about the weather, politics, sports?"

Natalie paused before she spoke again. She didn't want her voice to sound breathy. "Not particularly."

He grunted, leaned over to crush out his cigarette. "I should go, let you get some sleep."

Her emotions tangled, she rose as he did. "That's probably best. Sensible." It wasn't what she wanted, just what was best. And it wasn't, she'd begun to realize, what she needed. Just what was sensible.

"But I'm not going to." His eyes locked on hers. "Unless you tell me."

Her heartbeat thickened. She could feel the shudder start all the way down in the soles of her feet and work its way up. "Tell you what?"

He smiled, moved closer, stopping just before their bodies brushed. The first answer, whether she wanted him to go or stay, was already easily read in her eyes.

"Where's the bedroom, Natalie?"

A little dazed, she looked over his shoulder, gesturing vaguely. "There. Back there."

With that quick, surprising grace of his, he scooped her up. "I think I can make it that far."

"This is a mistake." She was already raining kisses over his face, his throat. "I know it's a mistake."

"Everybody makes one now and again."

"I'm smart." While her breath hitched, her fingers hurried to unbutton his shirt. "And I'm levelheaded. I have to be, because…" She let out a groan as her fingers found flesh. "God, I love your body."

"Yeah?" He nearly staggered as she tugged his shirt out of his jeans. "Consider it all yours. I should have known."

"Mmm…" She was busy biting at his shoulder. "What?"

"That you'd have a first-class bed." He tumbled with her onto the satin covers.

Already half-mad for him, she dragged at his shirt. "Hurry," she demanded. "I've wanted you to hurry since the first time you touched me."

"Let me catch up." Equally frantic, he crushed his mouth to hers, sinking in.

Breathless, she yanked at the snap of his jeans. "This is insane." She struggled to find him, drinking hungrily from his mouth as they rolled across the bed.

He couldn't catch his breath, or even a slippery hold on control. "It's about to be," he muttered. Tugging her robe open, he found the thin swatch of matching silk beneath. A moan ripped through him as he closed his mouth over her cream-covered breast.

Silk and heat and fragrant flesh. Everything she was filled

him, taunted him, tormented him. Woman, all woman. Beauty and grace and passion. Temptation and torment and triumph. All of it, all of her, obsessed him.

They thrashed over the slick satin spread, groping for more.

Here was fire, the bright, dangerous flash of it. It seared through him, burned, scarred, while her hands and mouth raced over him, igniting hundreds of new flames. He didn't fight it back. For once he wanted to be consumed. With an oath, he tore at the silk and dined greedily on her flesh.

His hands were rough and hard. And wonderful. She'd never felt more alive, or more desperate. She craved him, knew that she had, on some deep level, right from the beginning.

But now she had him, could feel the press of that hard, muscled body against her, could taste the violent urgency of his need whenever their mouths met, could hear his response to her touch, to her taste, in every hurried breath.

If it was elemental, so be it. She felt lusty and wanton and absolutely free. Her teeth dug into his shoulder as he whipped her ruthlessly over the first crest. She cried out his name, all but screamed it, arching upward, taut as a bow.

He arrowed into her, hard, deep.

She was blind and deaf from the pleasure of it, oblivious of her own sobbing breaths as they mated in a frenzied rhythm. Her body plunged against his, tireless, driven by a need that seemed insatiable.

Then body and need erupted.

The light was on. Funny he hadn't even noticed that, when normally he was accustomed to picking up every small detail. The lamp's glow was soft, picking up the cool sherbet tones of her bedroom.

Ryan lay still, his head on her breast, and waited for his system to level. Beneath his ear, her heart continued to thunder. Her flesh was damp, her body limp. Every few moments a tremor shook her.

He didn't smile in triumph, as he might have done, but simply stared in wonder.

He'd wanted to conquer her. He couldn't—wouldn't—deny it. He'd craved the sensation of having her body buck and shudder under his from the first moment he saw her.

But he hadn't expected the tornado of need that had swept through them both, that had them clawing at each other like animals.

He knew he'd been rough. He wasn't a particularly gentle man, so that didn't bother him. But he'd never lost control so completely with any woman. Nor had he ever wanted one so intensely only moments after he'd had her.

"That should have done it," he muttered.

"Hmmm?" She felt weak as water. Achy and sweet.

"It should have gotten it out of my system. Gotten *you* out. At least started getting you out."

"Oh." She found the energy to open her eyes. The light, dim as it was, had her wincing. Slowly, her mind began to clear; quickly, her skin began to heat. She remembered the way she'd torn at his clothes, wrestled him into bed without a single coherent thought except having him.

She let out a breath, drew another in.

"You're right," she decided. "It should have. What's wrong with us?"

With a laugh, he lifted his head, looking at her flushed face, her tousled hair. "Damned if I know. Are you okay?"

Now she smiled. The hell with logic. "Damned if I

know. What just happened here's a bit out of the usual realm for me."

"Good." He lowered his head, skimmed his tongue lightly over her breast. "I want you again, Natalie."

She quivered once. "Good."

When the alarm went off, Natalie groaned, rolled over to shut it off, and bumped solidly into Ry. He grunted, slapped at the buzzer with one hand and brought her to rest on top of him with the other.

"What's the noise for?" he asked, and ran an interested hand down her spine to the hip.

"To wake me up."

He opened one eye. Yeah, he thought, he should have known it. She looked just as good in the morning as she did every other time of the day. "Why?"

"It goes like this." Still groggy, she pushed her hair out of her face. "The alarm goes off, I get up, shower, dress, drink copious cups of coffee, and go to work."

"I've had some experience with the process. Anybody tell you today's Saturday?"

"I know what day it is," she said. At least she did now. "I have work."

"No, you don't, you just think you do." He cradled her head against his shoulder, casting one bleary eye at the clock. It was 7:00 a.m. He calculated they'd had three hours' sleep, at the outside. "Go back to sleep."

"I can't."

He let out a long-suffering sigh. "All right, all right. But you should have warned me you were insatiable." More than willing to oblige, he rolled her over again and began to nibble on her shoulder.

"I didn't mean that." She laughed, trying to wiggle free. "I have paperwork, calls to make." His hand was sneaking up to stroke her breast. Fire kindled instantly in the pit of her stomach. "Cut it out."

"Uh-uh. You woke me up, now you pay."

She couldn't help it, simply couldn't, and she began to stretch under his hands. "We're lucky we didn't kill each other last night. Are you sure you want to take another chance?"

"Men like me face danger every day." He covered her grinning mouth with his.

She was more than three hours behind schedule when she stepped out of the shower. So, she'd work late, Natalie decided, and after wrapping a towel around her hair she began to cream her legs. A good executive understood the merits of flextime.

Yawning, she wiped steam from the bathroom mirror and took a good look at her face. She should be exhausted, she realized. She certainly should look exhausted after the wild night she and Ry had shared.

But she wasn't. And she didn't. She looked...soft, she thought. Satisfied.

And why not? she thought, dragging the towel from her hair. When a woman took thirty-two years to experience just what a bout of hot, sweaty sex could do for the mind and body, she ought to look satisfied.

Nothing, absolutely nothing, she'd ever experienced, came close to what she'd felt, what she'd done, what she'd discovered, during the night with Ry.

So if she smiled like a fool while she combed out her wet

hair, why not? If she felt like singing as she wrapped her ti
gling body in her robe, it was understandable.

And if she had to rearrange her schedule for the day be
cause she'd spent most of the night and all of the mornin
wrestling in bed with a man who made her blood bubbl
more power to her.

She stepped back into the bedroom and grinned at the ta
gled sheets. Lips pursed, she picked up the remains of her che
mise. The strap was torn, and a froth of lace hung lim
Apparently, she decided, her merchandise didn't quite live u
to Ry Piasecki's idea of wear and tear.

And wasn't it fabulous?

Laughing out loud, she tossed the chemise aside and fo
lowed her nose into the kitchen.

"I smell coffee," she began, then paused in the doorway

He was breaking eggs into a bowl with those big, ha
hands of his. His hair was damp, as hers was, because he'
beaten her to the shower. He was barefoot, jeans snug at h
hips, flannel shirt rolled up to the elbows.

Incredibly, she wanted him all over again.

"You have next to nothing in this place to eat."

"I eat out a lot." With an order to control herself, she move
to the coffeepot. "What are you making?"

"Omelets. You had four eggs, some cheddar and son
very limp broccoli."

"I was going to steam it." She cocked her head as she san
pled the coffee. "So you cook."

"Every self-respecting firefighter cooks. You take shifts
the station." He located a whisk, then turned to her. Wet ha
glowing face, sleepy eyes. "Hello, Legs. You look good."

"Thanks." She smiled over the rim of her cup. If he co

tinued to look at her in just that way, she realized, she would drag him right down onto the floor. It might be wise, she decided, to tend to some practical matters. "Am I supposed to help?"

"Can you handle toast?"

"Barely." She set her cup aside and opened the cupboard. They worked in silence for a moment, he beating eggs, she popping bread in the toaster. "I…" She wasn't sure how to put it, delicately. "I suppose when you were fighting fires, you faced a lot of dangerous situations."

"Yeah. So?"

"The scars on your shoulder, your back." She'd discovered them in her explorations in the night, the raised welts and scarred ridges over that taut, really beautiful body. "Line of duty?"

"That's right." He glanced up. In truth, he didn't think about them. But it occurred to him in the harsh light of day that a woman like her might find them offensive. "Do they bother you?"

"No. I just wondered how you got burned."

He set the bowl aside and placed a pan on the stove to heat. Maybe they bothered her, he thought, maybe they didn't. But it seemed best to get the matter out of the way.

"Our friend Clarence. While I was pulling him out of the fire he started, the ceiling collapsed." Ry could remember it still, the rain of flame, the animal roar of it, the staggering nightmare of pain. "It fell down on us like judgment. He was screaming, laughing. I got him outside. I don't remember much after that, until I woke up in the burn ward."

"I'm sorry."

"It could have been a lot worse. My gear went a long way

toward protecting me. I got off lucky." Deliberately focused, he poured the beaten eggs into the pan. "My father went down like that. Fire went into the walls. When they ventilated the ceiling, it went. It all went."

He cursed under his breath. Where the hell had that come from? he wondered. He hadn't meant to say it. The death of his father certainly wasn't typical morning-after conversation.

"You should butter that toast before it gets cold."

She said nothing, could think of nothing, only went to him, wrapping her arms around his waist, pressing her cheek to his back.

"I didn't know you'd lost your father." There was so much, she thought, that she didn't know.

"Twelve years ago. It was in a high school. Some kid who wasn't happy with his chemistry grade torched the lab. It got away from him. Pop knew the risks," he muttered, uncomfortable with the sensation her quiet sympathy was stirring. "We all know them."

She held on. "I didn't mean to open old wounds, Ry."

"It's all right. He was a hell of a smoke eater."

Natalie stayed where she was another moment, baffled by what she was feeling. This need to comfort, to share, this terrible urge to be part of what he was. Cautious, she stepped back. It wouldn't do, she reminded herself. It wouldn't do at all to look for more between them than what there was.

"And this Clarence—how will you find him?"

"I could get lucky and track him down through contacts." With a quick, competent touch, Ry folded the egg mixture. "Or we'll pick him up when he scouts out his next target."

"My plant."

"Probably." More relaxed now that there was a little distance between them, he shot her a look over his shoulder. "Cheer up, Natalie. You've got the best in the city working to protect your nighties."

"You know very well it's not just—" She broke off when her doorbell rang. "Never mind."

"Hold on. Doesn't your doorman call up when someone's coming to see you?"

"Not if it's a neighbor."

"Use the judas hole," he ordered, and reached for plates.

"Yes, Daddy." Amused by him, Natalie went to the door. One look through the peephole had her stifling a shout and dragging back the locks. "Boyd, for heaven's sake!" She threw her arms around her brother. "Cilla!"

"The whole crew," Cilla warned her, laughing as they hugged. "The cop wouldn't let me call ahead and alert you to the invasion."

"I'm just so glad to see you." She bent down to hug her niece and nephews. "But what are you doing here?"

"Checking up on you." Boyd shifted the bag of take-out he carried to his other hip.

"You know the captain," Cilla said. "Bryant, touch nothing under penalty of death." She aimed a cautious look at her oldest son. At eight, he couldn't be trusted. "The minute Deborah called us about the second fire, he herded us up and moved us out. Allison, this isn't a basketball court. Why don't you put that down now?"

Territorial, Allison hugged the basketball to her chest. "I'm not going to throw it or anything."

"She's fine," Natalie assured Cilla, stroking a distracted

hand down Allison's golden hair. "Boyd, I can't believe you'd drag everyone across the country for something like this."

"The kids have Monday off at school." Boyd crouched down to pick up the jacket their youngest had already tossed on the floor. "So we're taking a quick weekend, that's all."

"We're staying with Deborah and Gage," Cilla added. "So don't panic."

"It's not that…"

"And we brought supplies." Boyd held out the bag filled with take-out burgers and fries. "How about lunch?"

"Well, I…" She cleared her throat and looked toward the kitchen. How, she wondered, was she going to explain Ry?

Keenan, with the curiosity of an active five-year-old, had already discovered him. From the kitchen doorway, he grinned up at Ry. "Hi."

"Hi yourself." Curious to see just how Natalie handled things, Ry strolled out of the kitchen.

"Want to see what I can do?" Keenan asked him before anyone else could speak.

"Sure."

Always ready to show off a new skill, Keenan shimmied up Ry's leg, scooting up and around until he was riding piggyback.

"Not bad." Ry gave the boy a little boost to settle him in place.

"That's Keenan," Cilla explained, running her tongue over her teeth as she considered. "Our youngest monkey."

"I'm sorry. Ah…" Natalie dragged a hand through her damp hair. She didn't have to look at Boyd to know he'd have that speculative big-brother look in his eyes. "Boyd and Cilla

Fletcher, Ry Piasecki." She cleared her throat. "And this is Allison, and Bryant." Now she sighed. "You've already met Keenan."

"Piasecki," Boyd repeated. "Arson?" Just the man he wanted to see, Boyd thought. But he hadn't expected to find him barefoot in his sister's kitchen.

"That's right." Brother and sister shared strong good looks, Ry mused. And, he thought, an innate suspicion of strangers. "You're the cop from Denver."

Bryant piped up. "He's a police captain. He wears a gun to work. Can I have a drink, Aunt Nat?"

"Sure. I—" But Bryant was already darting into the kitchen. "Well, this is…" Awkward, she thought. "Maybe I should get some plates before the food gets cold."

"Good idea. All she has is eggs." Ry eyed the bag Boyd still carried, recognizing the package. "Maybe we can work a deal for some of your french fries."

"You're the one investigating the fires, right?" Boyd began.

"Slick," Cilla said, glaring at her husband. "No interrogations on an empty stomach. You can grill him after we eat. We've been on a plane for hours," she explained when Bryant came back in and tried to wrestle the ball away from Allison. "We're a little edgy."

"No problem." An instant before Boyd, Ry snatched the ball that squirted out of flailing hands. "Like to shoot hoop?" he asked Allison.

"Uh-huh." She gave him a quick, winning smile. "I made the team. Bryant didn't."

"Basketball's stupid." Sulking, Bryant slouched in a chair. "I'd rather play Nintendo."

Ry juggled Keenan on his back as he turned the ball in his

hands. "It so happens I've got a game in a couple of hours. Maybe you'd like to come."

"Really?" Allison's eyes lit as she turned to Cilla. "Mom?"

"It sounds like fun." Intrigued, Cilla strolled toward the kitchen. "I'll just give Natalie a hand."

And, she thought, pump her sister-in-law for details.

Chapter 7

The last place Natalie expected to spend her Saturday afternoon was courtside, watching cops and firefighters play round ball. She sulked through most of the first quarter, her elbow on her knee, her chin on her fist.

After all, Ry hadn't mentioned the game to her, hadn't directly invited her. She was there to witness what was obviously an important annual rivalry only because of her niece.

Not that it mattered to her, she assured herself. Ry was certainly under no obligation to include her in his personal entertainment.

The pig.

Beside her, Allison was in basketball heaven, cheering on the red jerseys with a rabid fan's passionate enthusiasm. Her brandy-colored eyes glinted as she followed the action up and down the court of the old west-side gym.

"It's not such a bad way to spend the afternoon," Cilla commented over the shrill sound of the ref's whistle. "Watching a bunch of half-naked guys sweat." Her eyes, the same warm shade as her daughter's, danced. "By the way, your guy's very cute."

"I told you, he's not my guy. We're just…"

"Yeah, you told me." Chuckling, Cilla wrapped an arm around Natalie's shoulders. "Cheer up, Nat. If you'd gone along with Boyd and the boys to unload at Deborah's, your big bro would be grilling you right now."

"You've got a point." She let out a sigh. Despite herself, she was following the action. The cops were double-teaming Ry consistently, she noted. Not a bad strategy, as he played like a steamroller, and had already scored seven points in the first quarter.

Not that she was counting.

"He didn't mention this game to me," she muttered.

"Oh?" Fighting back a grin, Cilla ran her tongue over her teeth. "He must have had something else on his mind. Hey!" She surged to her feet, along with most of the crowd, as one of the blue jerseys rammed an elbow sharply in Ry's ribs. "Foul!" Cilla shouted between her cupped hands.

"He can take it," Natalie mumbled, and tried not to care as Ry approached the foul line. "He's got an iron stomach." She struggled between pride and resentment when he sank his shot.

"Ry's the best." Allison beamed, well into a deep case of hero worship. "Did you see how he moves up-court? And he's got a terrific vertical leap. He's already blocked three shots under the hoop."

So, maybe he looked good, Natalie conceded. Those long,

muscled legs pumping, those broad shoulders slick with sweat, all that wonderful hair flying as he pivoted or leapt. Then there was that look that came into his eyes, wolfish and arrogant.

So, maybe she wanted him to win. That didn't mean she was going to stand up and cheer.

By the third quarter, she was on her feet, like the rest of the crowd, when Ry sank a three-pointer that put the Smoke Eaters over the Bloodhounds by two.

"Nothing but net," she shouted, jostling Cilla. "Did you see that?"

"He's got some great moves," Cilla agreed. "Fast hands."

"Yeah." Natalie felt the foolish grin spread over her face. "Tell me about it."

Heart thumping, she dropped back on the bench. She was leaning forward now, her gaze glued to the ball. The sound of running feet echoed as the men pounded up-court. The cops took a shot, the Smoke Eaters blocked it. The ensuing scuffle left two men on the ground, others snarling in each other's faces as the ref blew his whistle.

Now, Natalie thought grimly, they were playing dirty. With a grunt, she dipped her hand into the bag of salted nuts Cilla offered.

Fast break. Flying elbows, a tangle of bodies under the net as the ball shot up, careened, was pursued.

"Going to put out your fire, Piasecki," one of the cops taunted.

Natalie saw Ry flick the sweaty hair out of his eyes and grin. "Not with that equipment."

Trash talk. Natalie sneered at the cop as she chomped a peanut. No round ball game was complete without it. She

hooted down the referee as he stepped between two over-
enthusiastic competitors, barely preventing an informal box-
ing match.

"Boys, boys," Cilla said with a sigh. "They always take
their games so seriously."

"Games are serious," Natalie muttered.

It was too close to call. Natalie continued to munch on peanuts as a sensible alternative to her fingernails. When a time-
out was called, she glanced at the clock. There was less than
six minutes to go, and the Bloodhounds were up, 108 to 105.

On the sidelines, the Smoke Eaters' coach was surrounded
by his team. The lanky, silver-haired man was punching his
fist into his palm to accentuate whatever instructions he was
giving his men. Most were bent at the waist, hands on knees,
as they caught their breath for the final battle. As they headed
back onto the court, Ry turned. His gaze shot unerringly to
Natalie. And he grinned. Quick, cocky, arrogant.

"Wow," Cilla murmured. "Now *that's* serious. Very powerful stuff."

"You're telling me." Natalie blew out a breath. When that
did nothing to level her system, she used the excess energy
to cheer on her team.

It was a fight to the finish, the lead tipping back to the Smoke
Eaters, then sliding away. As time dripped away, second by second, the crowd stayed on its feet, building a wall of sound.

With seconds to go, the Smoke Eaters a point behind, Natalie was chewing on her knuckles. Then she saw Ry make his
move. "Oh, yes…" She whispered it first, almost like a prayer.
Then she began to shout it as he burst through the line of defense, controlling the ball as if it were attached to the palm
of his hand by an invisible string.

They blocked, he pivoted. He had one chance, and he was surrounded. Natalie's heart tripped as he feinted, faked, then sprang off the floor with a turnaround jump shot that found the sweet spot.

The crowd went wild. Natalie knew *she* did, spinning around to hug Allison, then Cilla. What was left of the peanuts flew through the air like rain. The instant the clock ran out, the stands emptied in a surge of bodies onto the court.

She caught a glimpse of Ry a moment before he was swallowed up. She sank back onto the bench with a hand over her heart.

"I'm exhausted." She laughed and rubbed her damp hands on the knees of her jeans. "I've got to sit."

"What a game!" Allison was bouncing up and down in her sneakers. "Wasn't he great? Did you see, Mom? He scored thirty-three points! Wasn't he great?"

"You bet."

"Can we tell him? Can we go down and tell him?"

Cilla studied the jostling crowd, then looked into her daughter's, shining eyes. "Sure. Coming, Natalie?"

"I'll stay here. If you manage to get to him, tell him I'll hang around and wait."

"Okay. You'll bring him to dinner at Deb's tonight?"

Cautious, Natalie drummed her fingers on her knee. "I'll run it by him."

"Bring him," Cilla ordered, then leaned over and kissed Natalie's cheek. "See you later."

Gradually the gym emptied, the fans swarming out to celebrate, the players heading off to shower. Content, Natalie sat in the quiet. It had been her first full day off in six months, and she'd decided it wasn't such a bad way to spend it after all.

And since Ry hadn't actually asked her to come, he was under no real obligation. Neither of them was. Sensibly, neither of them was looking for restrictions, for commitments, for romance. It was simply a primal urge on both parts, fiercely intense now, and very likely to fade.

It was fortunate that they both understood that, right from the beginning. There was some affection between them, naturally. And respect. But this wasn't a relationship, in the true sense of the word. Neither of them wanted that. It was simply an affair—enjoyable while it lasted, no harm done when it ended.

Then he walked out on court, his hair dark and damp from his shower. His gaze swept up and locked on hers.

Oh, boy, was all she could think while her heart turned a long, slow somersault. She was in trouble.

"Good game," she managed, and forced herself to stand and walk down to him.

"It had its moments." He cocked his head. "You know, it's the first time I've seen you dressed in anything but one of those high-class suits."

To cover the sudden rash of nerves, Natalie reached down and picked up one of the game balls. "Jeans and sweaters aren't usually office attire."

"They look good on you, Legs."

"Thanks." She turned the ball in her hand, studying it rather than him. "Allison had the time of her life. It was nice of you to invite her."

"She's a cute kid. They all are. She's got your mouth, you know. And the jawline. She's going to be a real heartbreaker."

"Right now she's more interested in scoring points on court than scoring them with boys." More relaxed, Natalie looked up again, smiling at him. "You scored a few yourself today, Inspector."

"Thirty-three," he said. "But who's counting?"

"Allison." And she had been, too. Carrying the ball, she wandered out on the court. "I take it this was your annual battle against the Bloodhounds."

"Yeah, we take them on once a year. The proceeds go to charity and all that. But mostly we come to beat the hell out of each other."

Head down, she bounced the ball once, caught it. "You never mentioned it. I mean, not until Allison showed up."

"No." He was watching her, intrigued. If he wasn't mistaken, there was a touch of annoyance in her voice. "I guess I didn't."

She turned her head. "Why didn't you?"

Definitely annoyed, he decided, and scratched his cheek. "I didn't figure it would be your kind of thing."

Now her chin angled. "Oh, really?"

"Hey, it's not the opera, or the ballet." He shrugged and tucked his thumbs in his front pockets. "Or a fancy French restaurant."

She let out a slow breath, drew another in. "Are you calling me a snob again?"

Careful, Piasecki, he warned himself. There was definitely a trapdoor here somewhere. "Not exactly. Let's just say I couldn't see someone like you getting worked up over a basketball game."

"Someone like me," she repeated. Stung, she pivoted, planted her feet, and sent the ball sailing toward the hoop. It swished through, bounced on the court. When she looked back at Ry, she had the satisfaction of seeing his mouth hanging open. "Someone like me," she said again, and went to retrieve the ball. "Just what does that mean, Piasecki?"

He got his hands out of his pockets just in time to catch the ball she heaved at him before it thudded into his chest. He passed it back to her, hard, lifting a brow when she caught it.

"Do that again," he demanded.

"All right." Deliberately she stepped behind the three-point line, gauged her shot and let it rip. The whisper of the ball dropping through the hoop made her smile.

"Well, well, well…" This time Ry retrieved the ball himself. He was rapidly reassessing his opponent. "I'm impressed, Legs. Definitely impressed. How about a little one-on-one?"

"Fine." She crouched, circling him as he dribbled.

"You know, I can't—"

Quick as a snake, she darted in, snatched the ball. She executed a perfect lay-up, tapping the ball on the backboard and into the hoop. "I believe that's my point," she said, and passed the ball back to him.

"You're good."

"Oh, I'm better than good." Flicking her hair back, she moved in to block him. "I was all-state in college, pal. Team captain my junior and senior years. Where do you think Allison gets it?"

"Okay, Aunt Nat, let's play ball."

He pivoted away. She was on him like glue. Good moves, he noted. Smooth, aggressive. Maybe he held back. After all, he wasn't about to send a woman to the boards, no matter how much male ego was on the line.

She didn't have the same sensitivity, and turned into his block hard enough to take his breath away.

Frowning, he rubbed the point under his heart where her shoulder had rammed. Her eyes were glittering now, bold as the Emerald City.

"That's a foul."

She stole the ball, made the point with an impressive over-the-shoulder hook. "I don't see a ref."

She had the advantage, and they both knew it. Not only had he played full-out for an entire game, but she'd had that time to assess his technique, study his moves.

And she was better, he had to admit, a hell of a lot better, than half the cops who had gone up against him that afternoon.

And, worse, she knew it.

He scored off her, but it was no easy thing. She was sneaky, he discovered, using speed and grace and old-fashioned guts to make up for the difference in height.

They juggled the lead. She'd shoved the sleeves of her sweater up. She leapt with him, blocking his shot by a fingertip. And, having no compunctions about using whatever talent she had, let her body bump, linger, then slide against his.

His blood heated, as she'd meant it to. Panting, he picked up the ball and stared at her. Her lips were curved smugly, her face was flushed, her hair was tumbled. He realized he could eat her alive.

He moved in quickly, startling her. She let out a squeal when he snatched her around the waist and hauled her over his shoulder. She was laughing when he sent the ball home with his free hand.

"Now that's definitely a foul."

"I don't see any ref." He shifted her, letting gravity take her down until they were face-to-face, her legs clamped at his waist. He reached out, gathered her hair in one hand and pulled her mouth to his.

Whatever breath she had left clogged. Opening to him, she dived into the greedy kiss and demanded more.

The blood drained so quickly, so completely, out of his head, he nearly staggered. With a sudden, voracious appetite, he tore his mouth from hers and devoured the flesh of her throat.

Smooth, salty, with the lingering undertone of that haunting scent she used. His mouth watered.

"There's a storeroom in the back that locks."

Her hands were already tugging at his shirt. Her breathing was ragged. "Then why are we out here?"

"Good question."

With her locked around him, her teeth doing incredible things to his ear, he pushed through the swinging doors and turned into a narrow corridor. Desperate for her, he fumbled at the knob of the storeroom door, swore, then shoved it open. When he slammed it and locked it at their backs, they were closed in a tiny room crammed with sports equipment and smelling of sweat.

Impatient, Natalie tugged at his hair, dragging his mouth back to hers. He nearly tripped over a medicine ball as he looked around frantically for something, anything, that could double as a bed.

He settled on a weight bench with Natalie on his lap.

"I feel like a damn teenager," he muttered, pulling at the snap of her jeans. Beneath the denim, her skin was hot, damp, trembling.

"Me too." Her heart was beating against her ribs like a hammer. "Oh God, I want you. Hurry."

Frantic hands tore at clothes, scattered them. There was no time, no need, for finesse. Only for heat. It was building inside her so fast, so hot, she felt she might implode and there would be nothing left of her but a shell.

His hands were at her throat, her breasts, her hips, thrilling her. Tormenting her. Nothing and no one mattered but him and this wild, incendiary fire they set together.

She wanted it hotter, higher, faster.

With a low, feline sound that shuddered through his blood, she straddled him. His heart seemed to stop in the instant she imprisoned him, as her body arched back, her eyes closing. She filled his vision, his mind, left him helpless. Then her eyes opened again and locked on his.

She began to move, fast and agile. Already it was flash point. He let the power take him, and her.

"I've never done anything like this before." Staggered and spent, Natalie struggled back into her clothes. "I mean *never.*"

"It wasn't exactly the way I'd planned it." Baffled, Ry dragged a hand through his hair.

"We're worse than a couple of kids." Natalie smoothed down her sweater, sighing lavishly. "It was fabulous."

His lips twitched. "Yeah." Then he sobered. "So are you."

She smiled and tried finger-combing her hair into place. "We'd better stop pushing our luck and get out of here. And I've got to get home and change." She discovered that one of her earrings had fallen out, and located it on the floor. "There's dinner at the Guthries' tonight."

He watched her fasten the earring, foolishly charmed by the simple female act. "I'll give you a lift home."

"I'd appreciate it." Feeling awkward, she turned to unlock the door. "You're welcome to come to dinner. I know Boyd wants a chance to talk with you. About the fires."

He closed a hand over hers on the knob. "How's the food?"

She smiled again, looking back at him. "Fabulous."

She was right about the food, Ry discovered. Rack of lamb, fresh asparagus, glossy candied yams, all accompanied by some golden French wine.

He knew, of course, that Gage Guthrie was dripping with money. But nothing had prepared him for the Gothic mansion of a house, with its towers and turrets and terraces. The next thing to a castle, Ry had thought when he viewed it from the outside.

Inside, it was home, rich and elaborate, certainly, but warm. Deborah had given him a partial tour down winding corridors, up curving steps, before they all settled into the enormous dining room with its ox-roasting stone fireplace and winking crystal chandeliers.

It might, Ry thought, have had the flavor of a museum, if not for the people in it.

He'd clicked with Deborah instantly. He'd heard she was a tough and tenacious prosecutor. She had a softer, more vulnerable look than her sister, but she had a reputation for being formidable in court.

It was obvious her husband adored her. There were little signs—the quick, shared looks, the touch of a hand.

It was very much the same between Boyd and Cilla. Ry calculated that they'd been together for a decade or so, but the spark was still very much in evidence.

And the kids were great. He'd always had a soft spot for children. He recognized and was touched by Allison's preadolescent crush, and obliged her by going over the highlights of the game.

Since Cilla had wisely seen to it that her oldest son was across the table and two chairs down from his sister, Bryant was free to badger Deborah about how many bad guys she'd locked up since last he'd seen her.

And dinner was a relatively peaceful affair.

"Do you ride in a fire truck?" Keenan wanted to know.

"I used to," Ry told him.

"How come you stopped?"

"I told you," Bryant said, rolling his eyes with the disdain only a sibling knows and understands. "He goes after bad guys now, like Dad. Only just bad guys who burn things down. Don't you?"

"That's right."

"I'd rather ride in a fire truck." In a canny move to avoid the asparagus on his plate, Keenan slipped out of his chair and into Ry's lap.

"Keenan," Cilla said. "Ry's trying to eat."

"He's okay." Enjoying himself, Ry shifted the boy onto his knee. "Did you ever ride in one?"

"Nuh-uh." He smiled winningly, using his big, soft eyes. "Can I?"

"If your mom and dad say it's okay, you could come down to the station tomorrow. Take a look around."

"Cool." Bryant had immediately picked up on the invitation. "Can we, Dad?"

"I don't see why not."

"Aunt Nat knows where it is," Ry added as Keenan

bounced gleefully on his knee. "Make it around ten, and I'll give you a tour."

"Pretty exciting stuff." Cilla rose. "And if we're going to pull it off, I'd say you three better get washed up and bedded down." The knee-jerk protest might have been stronger if not for the long day the children had put in. Cilla merely shook her head, looking at Boyd. "Slick?"

"Okay." He rose and tossed Bryant up and over his shoulder, turning whines into giggles. "Let's move out."

"I'll give you a hand." Natalie plucked Keenan from Ry's lap. "Say good-night, pal."

"Good night, pal," he echoed, and nuzzled into her neck. "You smell as good as Thea, Aunt Nat."

"Thanks, honey."

"Am I going to get a story?"

"Swindler," she laughed and carried him out.

"Nice family," Ry commented.

"We like them." Deborah smiled at him. "You've certainly given them something to look forward to tomorrow."

"No big deal. The guys love to show off for kids. Great meal."

"Frank's one in a million," she agreed. "A former pickpocket." She closed her hand over Gage's. "Who now uses those nimble fingers to create gastronomic miracles. Why don't we have coffee in the small salon? I'll go help Frank with it."

"This is some house," Ry said as he and Gage left the dining room and wound their way toward the salon. "Ever get lost?"

"I've got a good sense of direction."

There was a fire burning in the salon, and the lights were

low and welcoming. Again Ry got the impression of home, settled, content.

"You used to be a cop, didn't you?"

Gage stretched out in a chair. "That's right. My partner and I were working on a sting that went wrong. All the way wrong." It still hurt, but the wounds were scarred over now. "He ended up dead, and I was the next thing to it. When I came out of it, I didn't want to pick up a badge again."

"Rough." Ry knew it was a great deal more than that. If he had the story right in his head, Gage had lingered in a coma for months before facing life again. "So you picked up the family business instead."

"So to speak. We have something in common there. You're running the family business, too."

Ry gave Gage a level look. "So to speak."

"I checked you out. Natalie's important to Deborah, and to me. I can tell you in advance, Boyd's going to ask if she's important to you." He glanced up as Boyd walked in. "That was fast."

"I saw my chance and went over the wall." He dropped into a chair, crossed his feet at the ankles. "So, Piasecki, what's going on between you and my sister?"

Ry decided he'd been polite long enough, and took out a cigarette. He lit it, flipped the match into a spotless crystal ashtray. "I'd say anybody who makes captain on the force should be able to figure that out for himself."

Gage smothered a laugh with a cough as Boyd's eyes narrowed. "Natalie's not a tossaway," Boyd said carefully.

"I know what she is," Ry returned. "And I know what she isn't. If you want to grill someone on what's going on between us, Captain, you'd better start with her."

Boyd considered, nodded. "Fair enough. Give me a run-down on the arson investigation."

That he could, and would, do. Ry related the sequence, the facts, his own steps and conclusions, answering Boyd's terse questions with equal brevity.

"I'm betting on Clarence," he finished. "I know his pattern, and how his warped mind works. And I'll get him," he said, and blew out a last stream of smoke. "That's a promise."

"In the meantime, Natalie needs to beef up security." Boyd's mouth thinned. "I'll see to that."

Ry tapped out his cigarette. "I already have."

"I was talking about personal security, not business."

"So was I. I'm not going to let anything happen to her," he continued as Boyd studied him. "That's another promise."

Boyd let out a snort. "Do you really think she'll listen to you?"

"Yeah. She's not going to get a choice."

Boyd paused, reevaluated. "Maybe I'm going to like you after all, Inspector."

"Okay, break it up," Deborah ordered as she wheeled in a cart laden with a huge silver coffee urn and Meissen china. "I know you're talking shop."

Gage rose to take the cart from her and kiss her. "You're just mad because you might have missed something."

"Exactly."

"Jacoby," Boyd tossed at her. "Clarence Robert. Ring any bells?"

Her brow furrowed as she poured coffee. "Jacoby. Also known as Jack Jacoby?" She served Boyd, took another cup to Ry. "Skipped bail a couple of years ago on an arson charge."

"I like your wife," Ry said to Gage. "There's nothing quite like a sharp mind in a first-class package."

"Thanks." Gage poured a cup for himself. "I often think the same."

"Jacoby," Deborah repeated, focusing on Ry. "You think he's the one?"

"That's right."

"We'd have a file on him." She glanced at her husband. The computers in Gage's hidden room could access everything about Jacoby, right down to his shoe size. "I'm not sure who had the case, but I can find out on Monday, see that you get whatever we have."

"I'd appreciate it."

"How'd he manage bail?" Boyd wanted to know.

"I can't tell you until I see the file," Deborah began.

"I can tell you about him." Ry drank his coffee, keeping one ear out for Natalie's return. He wasn't sure she'd appreciate having her business discussed while she was out of the room. "His pattern's empty buildings, warehouses, condemned apartments. Sometimes the owners hire him for the insurance, sometimes he does it for kicks. We only tried him twice, convicted him once. There wasn't any loss of life either time. Clarence doesn't burn people, just things."

"So now he's loose," Boyd said in disgust.

"For the time being," Ry returned. "We're ready for him." He picked up his cup again when he heard Natalie and Cilla laughing in the hallway.

"You're a softie, Nat."

"It's my duty, and my privilege, to spoil them."

They entered together. Cilla immediately headed for Boyd and dropped into his lap. "They had her jumping through hoops."

"They did not." Natalie poured her coffee, then laughed again. "Not exactly." She smiled at Ry before settling beside him. "So," she began, "have you finished discussing my personal and business life?"

"A sharp mind," Ry commented. "In a first-class package."

Later, as they drove away from the Guthrie mansion, Natalie studied Ry's profile. "Should I apologize for Boyd?"

"He didn't pull out the rubber hoses." Ry shrugged. "He's okay. I've got a couple of sisters, I know how it is."

"Oh." Frowning, she looked out the window. "I didn't realize you had siblings."

"I'm Polish and Irish, and you figured me for an only child?" He grinned at her. "Two older sisters, one in Columbus, the other down in Baltimore. And a brother, a year younger than me, living in Phoenix."

"Four of you," she murmured.

"Until you count the nieces and nephews. There were eight of them, last time I checked, and my brother has another on the way."

Which probably explained why he was so easy around children. "You're the only one who stayed in Urbana."

"Yeah, they all wanted out. I didn't." He turned down her street, slowed. "Am I staying tonight, Natalie?"

She looked at him again. How could he be so much of a stranger, she wondered, and so much of a need? "I want you to," she said. "I want you."

Chapter 8

"Can I slide down the pole, Mr. Pisessy? Please, can I slide down it?"

Ry grinned at the way Keenan massacred his name and flipped the brim of the boy's baseball cap to the back of his curly head. "Ry."

"'Cause," Keenan said, big eyes sober and hopeful. "I never, ever did it before."

"No, not why, Ry. You call me Ry. And sure you can slide down it. Hold it." Laughing, he caught Keenan at the waist before the boy could make the leap from floor to pole. "No flies on you, huh?"

Keenan looked around, grinned. "Nuh-uh."

"Let's do it this way." With Keenan firmly at his hip, Ry reached out to grip the pole. "Ready?"

"Let's go!"

In a smooth, practiced move, Ry stepped into air. Keenan laughed all the way down.

"Again!" Keenan squealed. "Let's do it again!"

"Your brother wants a turn." Ry looked up, saw Bryant's anxious, eager face in the opening. "Come on, Bryant, go for it."

"Definitely daddy material," Cilla murmured, watching her son zip down the pole.

"Shut up, Cilla." Natalie slipped her hands into the pockets of her blazer. She was itching to try the ride herself.

"Just an observation. Attagirl, Allison," she added, cheering her daughter on when Allison dropped lightly to the floor. "He's giving the kids the time of their lives here."

"I know. It's very sweet of him." She smiled as Ry obliged Keenan with another trip down the pole. "I didn't know he could be sweet."

"Ah, hidden qualities." Cilla glanced over to where Boyd was holding a conversation with two uniformed firefighters. "Often the most attractive kind in a man. Especially when he's crazy about you."

"He's not." It amazed Natalie to feel heat rising to her cheeks. "We're just…enjoying each other."

"Yeah, sure." With a mother's honed reflexes, Cilla crouched and caught her youngest as he flew at her.

"Look, Mom. It's a real, actual fireman's hat." The helmet Ry had given Keenan to wear slipped down over the boy's face. Inside, it smelled mysteriously, fascinatingly, of smoke. "And Ry says we can go sit in the fire engine now." After wriggling down and dancing in place, he shouted at his brother and sister. "Let's go!"

Accompanied by two firefighters, the children dashed off

to check out the engine. With a signal to Cilla to wait, Boyd disappeared up the steps with Ry.

"Well." Cilla sniffed and shrugged. "The womenfolk have been dismissed. They'll go upstairs to grunt significantly over official business."

"I wish Boyd wouldn't worry so much. There's really nothing he can do."

"Older siblings are programmed to worry." Cilla slung an arm around Natalie's shoulder. "But, if it helps, he's feeling a lot less worried since he's met Ry."

"That's something, I suppose." Relaxed again, she walked with Cilla toward the back of the engine. "So, how's Althea doing?" Around the front, the children were barraging the firefighters with questions. "The last time I talked to her, she claimed she was as big as two houses and miserably bored with desk duty."

"She's the sexiest expectant mother I've ever seen. Since Colt and Boyd ganged up on her, she's at home on full maternity leave. I dropped over to see her one day a couple of weeks ago and caught her knitting."

"Knitting?" Natalie let out a full-throated laugh. "Althea?"

"Funny what marriage and family can do to you."

"Yeah." Natalie's smile faded a bit. "I suppose that's true."

Upstairs, Boyd was frowning over Ry's reports. "Why upstairs, in the office?" he asked. "Why didn't he start the fire in the showroom? It seems to me there would have been more damage more quickly."

"The showroom window could have put him off. I figure the storeroom would have made more sense if he was just looking to burn the place down. It's private, full of stock and boxes." Ry set aside his coffee. He really had to start cutting down. "I figure he was following instructions. Clarence is real good at following instructions."

"Whose?"

"That's the ticket." Ry kicked back in his chair and propped his feet on his desk. "I've got two incendiary fires that are obviously related. The target in both cases is a single business, and both, I believe, were started by a single perpetrator."

"So he's on somebody's payroll." Boyd set the reports aside. "A competitor?"

"We're checking it out."

"But it's unlikely a competitor would be able to give your pal Clarence access to either building. You didn't find any sign of forced entry."

"That's right." Ry lit a cigarette. A man couldn't cut down on two vices at once. "Which leads us to Natalie's organization."

Boyd got up to pace. "I can't claim to know her staff, certainly not in this new project of hers. I don't deal with the business end of Fletcher unless I'm backed into a corner." He regretted that now, only because he would have been more help if he'd been familiar with her procedures and personnel. "But I can get a lot of information from my parents, particularly on her top people."

"It couldn't hurt. The fact that there was only cosmetic damage at the last fire leads to the conclusion that there'll be another. If Clarence follows his pattern, he'll hit her again within the next ten days." He tossed papers aside. "We'll be waiting for him."

Boyd looked back and measured the man. Tough, smart. But, as he knew from personal experience, the job could get sticky when a man found himself involved with a target.

"And while you're waiting for him, you'll keep Natalie out of it."

"That's the idea."

"And while you're doing that, you're going to be able to separate the woman you're involved with from the case you're trying to close."

Ry lifted a brow. That was going to be a challenge, and the difficulty of meeting that challenge had crossed his mind more than once. The trouble was, he wasn't willing to give up either the woman or the case.

"I know what needs to be done, Captain."

With a nod, Boyd placed his palms on the desk and leaned forward. "I'm trusting you with her, Piasecki, on every level. If she gets hurt—on any level—I'm coming after you."

"Fair enough."

An hour later, Natalie stood on the curb outside the station, waving goodbye. "You were a big hit, Inspector."

"Hey, a shiny red fire truck, a long brass pole—how could I miss?"

Laughing, she turned to link her arms around his neck. "Thanks." She kissed him lightly.

"For?"

"For being so nice to my family."

"It wasn't a hardship. I like kids."

"It shows. And—" she kissed him again "—that's for putting Boyd's mind at ease."

"I don't know if I'd go quite that far. He's still thinking about punching me out if I make the wrong move with his baby sister."

"Well, then…" Her eyes danced up at his. "You'd better be careful, because my big brother is plenty tough."

"You don't have to draw me a picture." He swung her toward the doors. "Come on back up with me. I need to get a couple of things."

"All right." They'd barely started up the stairs when the bell sounded. "Oh." The sound of clattering feet echoed below them. "I'm sorry the kids missed this." Then she stopped, wincing. "That's terrible, acting like a fire's a form of entertainment."

"It's a natural reaction. Bells, whistles, men in funny uniforms. It's a hell of a show."

They crossed over to his office. She waited while he sorted through papers. "Do you ever get cats out of trees?"

"Yep. And kid's heads out of the pickets on railings. I got someone's pet iguana out of a sewer pipe once."

"You're joking."

"Hey, we don't joke about rescue."

He looked up and grinned. She looked so tidy, he thought, in her navy blazer and slacks, with the cashmere sweater, red as one of his engines, softly draped at the neck. Her hair was loose, honey gold. When she tucked it behind her ear in that fluid, unconscious movement, he could see the wink of rich blue stones. Sapphires, he assumed. Only the genuine article would suit Natalie Fletcher.

"What is it?" A little self-conscious under his stare, she shifted. "Did Keenan leave something edible smeared on my face?"

"No. You look good, Legs. Want to go somewhere?"

"Go somewhere?" The idea put her off balance. Apart from the challenge of that first meal, they hadn't actually *gone* anywhere.

"Like a movie. Or…" He supposed he could handle it. "A museum or something."

"I… Yes, that'd be nice." It shouldn't be so awkward, she thought, to plan a simple date with someone you'd been sleeping with.

"Which?"

"Either."

"Okay." He stuffed some papers in a battered briefcase. "The guys should have a newspaper downstairs. We'll check it out."

"Fine." When they started out, Natalie glanced first toward the stairs and then back toward the poles. She took a deep breath and gave up. "Ry?"

"Yeah."

"Can I slide down the pole?"

He stopped dead and stared down at her. "You want to slide down the pole?"

Amused at herself, Natalie shrugged her shoulders. "Ry, I've *got* to slide down the pole. It's driving me crazy."

"No kidding?" His grin broke out as he put a hand on her shoulder and turned her around. "Okay, Aunt Nat. I'll go down first, in case you lose your nerve."

"I'm not going to lose my nerve," she said huffily. "I'll have you know I've been rock-climbing dozens of times."

"There's that height thing again. You get a good grip," he continued, demonstrating. "Swing yourself forward. You can wrap your legs around it as you go down."

He flowed down, smooth and fast. Frowning, she leaned over, peering at him through the opening.

"You didn't wrap your legs around it."

"I don't have to," he said dryly. "I'm a professional. Come on, and don't worry—I'll catch you."

"I don't need you to catch me." Insulted, she tossed bac
her hair. She reached out, took a good grip on the brass pole
then swung agilely into space.

It took a matter of seconds. Her heart had barely had tim
to settle before her feet hit the floor. Laughing, she looke
longingly up again. "See? I didn't need—" Her boast ende
on a squeal of surprise as he scooped her up into his arms
"What?"

"You're a natural." He was grinning as he lowered hi
mouth to hers. And a constant surprise to him, he thought.

She angled her head, settling her arms comfortably aroun
his neck. "I could do it again."

"If you'd do it in red suspenders, a pair of those really lit
tle shorts and let me take a picture, the guys would be ver
grateful."

She lifted a brow. "I think I'll just make a cash donatio
to the department."

"It's not the same."

"Inspector?" The dispatcher poked his head out of a door
way. His smile spread slowly at the sight of the woman bun
dled in Ry's arms. "Suspicious fire over at 12 East Newberry
They want you."

"Tell them I'm on my way." He set Natalie back on he
feet. "Sorry."

"It's all right. I know how it is." Her disappointment wa
completely out of proportion, she lectured herself. "I've go
some work I should be catching up on, anyway. I'll grab
cab."

"I'll take you home," Ry told her. "On my way." He steere
her toward the bench where she'd left her coat. "Are you jus
going to be hanging around at the apartment?"

"Yes. There are some spreadsheets I should have looked at yesterday."

"So I'll call you."

As Ry helped her on with her coat, she glanced over her shoulder. "All right."

He turned her completely around and indulged himself with one long, hard kiss. "Tell you what, I'll just come by when I'm done."

Natalie worked on getting her breath back. "Better," she managed. "That's even better."

By the middle of the week, Natalie had discovered that for the first time in memory she was behind on her own personal schedule. Not only had she blown the previous weekend, but she hadn't put in a decent night's work all week.

How could she, when she and Ry were spending every free moment together? Every evening they settled into her apartment, ordered dinner—which more often than not had to be reheated after they'd feasted on each other.

She didn't think of work from the time he arrived on her doorstep until she rushed into her office the next morning.

She didn't think of anything but him.

Besotted was what she was, Natalie admitted as she stared out her office window. Fascinated by the man, and by what happened every time they got within arm's reach of each other.

It was crazy, of course. She knew it. But it was so wonderful at the moment, it didn't seem to matter.

And she could justify it, since she hadn't yet missed any meetings or business deadlines. Now that Ry had given her the go-ahead, she'd authorized the cleanup and redecorating at the flagship store. The stock there was nearly all in place, and the window-dressing was complete.

It was only a matter of days before the grand opening, nationwide, and there'd been no more incidents. That was how she liked to think of the fires now. As incidents.

She should, of course, be making plans to visit all the branches within the next ten days. But the thought of traveling just then seemed so annoying, so depressing. So lonely.

She could delegate Melvin or Donald to make the tour. It wouldn't even be outside of proper business procedure to do so. But it wasn't her style to delegate what should be done by her.

Maybe, if things got settled somehow, Ry could get a few days off, go with her. It would be wonderful to have company—his company—on a quick business trip. She could put it off until after the grand opening, instead of before, and then—

Turning away from the window, she answered the buzzer on her desk. "Yes, Maureen."

"Ms. Marks to see you, Ms. Fletcher."

"Thanks. Send her in." With an effort, Natalie shifted her personal thoughts to the back of her mind and welcomed her accounting executive. "Deirdre, have a seat."

"I'm sorry I'm so behind." Deirdre blew her choppy bangs out of her eyes before she dropped a thick stack of files on Natalie's desk. "Every time we turn around, the system's down."

Natalie frowned as she picked up the first file. "Have you called in the engineer?"

"He's practically living in my lap." Deirdre plopped into

a chair and set one practical flat-heeled shoe on her knee. "He fixes it, we forge ahead, and it goes down again. Believe me, running figures has become a challenge."

"We've still got some time before the end of the quarter. I'll call the computer people myself this afternoon. If their equipment's unstable, they'll have to replace it. Immediately."

"Good luck," Deirdre said dryly. "The good news is, I was able to run a chart on the early catalog sales. I think you'll be pleased with the results."

"Mmm, hmm…" Natalie was already flipping through the files. "Fortunately, the fires didn't destroy records. You'd have a real accounting nightmare on your hands if it had gotten to the files at the flagship."

"You're telling me." Deirdre rubbed her fingers over her eyes. "The way the system's been hiccuping, I'd sweat bullets without those hard copies."

"Well, relax. I've got copies of the copies, as well as the backup disks, tucked away. I was hoping to run a full audit by the middle of March." She saw the wince before Deirdre could mask it. "But," she added, leaning back, "if we keep running into these glitches, we'll have to put it off until after the tax-season rush."

"My life for you." Solemnly, Deirdre thumped a fist on her breast. "Now to the nitty-gritty. Your outlay is still within the projected parameters. Barely. With the insurance payments, we'll offset some of that."

Natalie nodded, and made herself focus on budgets and percentages.

A few hours later, in a seedy downtown motel, Clarence Jacoby sat on his sagging bed, lighting matches. His hands were pudgy, smooth as a girl's. Each time he would strike the match and watch the magic flare, waiting, waiting until the heat just kissed the tips of his fingers, before blowing it out.

The ashtray beside him was overflowing with the matches that had already flared and burned. Clarence could entertain himself for hours with nothing more.

He thought nearly every night about burning down the hotel. It would be exciting to start the blaze right in his own room, watch it grow and spread. But he wouldn't be alone, and that stopped him.

Clarence didn't care overmuch about people, or the risk to their lives. He simply preferred to be alone with his fires.

He'd learned not to stay overlong after he'd ignited them. The rippling scars over his neck and chest were daily reminders of how quickly, how fiercely, the dragon could turn, even on one who loved it.

So he contented himself with merely conceiving the fire, basking for a regrettably short time in its heat, before fleeing.

Six months before, in Detroit, he'd torched an abandoned warehouse that the owner had no longer needed or wanted. It was the kind of favor, a profitable one on all sides, that Clarence enjoyed. He had stayed to watch that fire burn. Oh, he'd been out of the building and deep in the shadows. But they'd nearly caught him. Those cops and arson people scanned the crowds at the scene just for a face like his.

A worshipful face. A happy face.

With a giggle, Clarence struck another match. But he'd gotten away. And he'd learned another lesson. It wasn't smart to stay and watch. He didn't need to stay and watch. There were so many fires, so many fierce and beautiful blazes living in his mind and heart, he didn't need to stay.

He had only to close his eyes and see them. Feel them. Smell them.

He was humming to himself when the phone rang. His round, childlike face beamed happily when he heard the sound. Only one person had his number here. And that person would have only one reason to call.

It was time, he knew, to free the dragon again.

At his desk, Ry pored over lab reports. It was nearly seven, and already dark outside. He'd given up on cutting down on coffee, and drank it hot and black from a chipped mug.

He needed to quit for the day. He recognized the slow process of shutting down in his mind and body. Somehow or other, in the past couple of weeks, he'd gotten into a routine he was now beginning to depend on.

No, not somehow or other, Ry reminded himself, scrubbing his hands over his face. Someone.

He was getting much too used to knocking off for the day and heading for her apartment. He even had a key to her front door in his pocket now. Something that had been given and taken without ceremony. As if neither of them wanted to acknowledge what that simple piece of metal stood for.

They'd have a meal, he thought. They'd talk, maybe watch one of the old movies on television—something they'd discovered by accident they both loved.

Most of what they'd discovered about each other, he mused, had been by accident. Or by observation.

He knew she liked long bubble baths in the evening, with

the water too hot and a glass of chilled wine sitting on the rim of the tub. She stepped out of those ankle-breakers she wore the minute she walked in the door. And she put everything away in its place.

She slept in silk and hogged the blankets. Her alarm went off at seven on the dot every morning, and if he wasn't quick enough to delay her, she was out of the bed seconds later.

She had a weakness for strawberry ice cream and big-band music.

She was loyal and smart and strong.

And he was in love with her.

Sitting back, Ry rested his eyes. A problem, he thought. His problem. They'd had an unspoken agreement going in, and he knew it. No ties, no tangles.

He didn't want them.

God knew he couldn't afford them with her.

They were opposites on every level but one. The physical needs that had brought them together, no matter how intense, couldn't override everything else. Not in the long term.

So there couldn't be a long term.

He would do what was smart, what was right, and see her through the arson investigation. And that would be that. Would have to be that.

And to save them both an unpleasant scene, he'd start backing away a little. Starting now.

He rose and grabbed his jacket. He wouldn't go to her place tonight. He looked guiltily at the phone, thinking of calling her, making some excuse.

With an oath, he turned out the lights. He wasn't her damn husband, he reminded himself.

He never would be.

* * *

Compelled by a nagging sense of unrest, like an itch between his shoulder blades, Ry drove out to Natalie's plant. He'd done a great deal of driving around since he left the station.

It was after ten o'clock now, moonless, windless.

He sat in his car, slumped behind the wheel, and tried not to think of her.

Of course, he thought of her.

She was probably wondering where he was, he figured. She'd assume he'd gotten a call. She'd wait up. Guilt worked at him again. It was his least favorite emotion. It wasn't right to be inconsiderate, to worry her just because he'd had a scare.

And maybe he wasn't in love with her. Maybe he was just hung up. A man could get hung up on a woman without wanting to slit his throat when she walked away. Couldn't he?

Disgusted, Ry reached for his car phone. The least he could do was call and tell her he was busy. It wasn't like checking in, he assured himself. It was just being polite.

And since when had he worried about manners?

Cursing, he began to dial.

But the itch came back. Slowly, his eyes scanning the dark, he replaced the phone. Had he heard something? A check of his watch told him the patrol he'd assigned would make their run by in another ten minutes.

No harm, he decided, in taking a look around himself on foot in the meantime.

He eased his door open and slipped out. He could hear nothing now but the faint swish of traffic two blocks away. Cautious, he reached back in the car for his flashlight, but he didn't turn it on.

Not yet, he thought. His eyes were accustomed enough to the dark for him to see where he was going.

Instinct had him heading silently around the back.

He'd already cased the plant himself, noting where the exits were located, the security, the fire doors. He'd make a circle, check each door and window on the main level himself.

He heard it again, the scrape of a foot over gravel. Ry shifted the flashlight in his hand, holding it like a weapon now as he moved closer. Tensed, ready, he slipped through the shadows. If it was the security guard, Ry knew, he was about to give the man the fright of his life. Otherwise…

A giggle. Faint and delighted. The slow, moaning whine of a metal door moving on its hinges.

Ry flashed on his light, and spotlighted Clarence Jacoby.

"How's it going, Clarence?" Ry grinned as the man blinked against the glare. "I've been waiting for you."

"Who's that?" Clarence's voice raced up a register. "Who's that?"

"Hey, I'm hurt." Ry lowered the light out of Clarence's eyes and stepped closer. "Don't you recognize your old pal?"

Squinting, Clarence separated the man from the shadows. In a moment, his baffled face exploded in a wide grin. "Piasecki. Hey, Ry Piasecki. How's it going? You're Inspector now, right? I hear you're an inspector now."

"That's right. I've been looking for you, Clarence."

"Oh, yeah?" Shyly Clarence dipped his head. "How come?"

"I put out that little campfire you started the other night. You must be losing your touch, Clarence."

"Oh, hey…" Still grinning, Clarence spread his arms out.

"I don't know nothing about that. You remember when we got burned, Piasecki? Hell of a night, wasn't it? That dragon was really big. Almost ate us up."

"I remember."

Clarence moistened his lips. "Scared you bad, too. I heard the nurses talking in the burn ward about the nightmares."

"I had a few of them."

"And you don't fight fire no more, do you? Don't want to slay the dragon now, do you?"

"I like squashing little bugs like you better." Ry swung his light down, shone it on the gas cans at Clarence's feet. "What do you know, Clarence? You still use premium grade, too."

"I didn't do nothing." Clarence whirled to make a dash into the dark. Even as Ry leapt forward, the man jerked back, as if on a string.

Staggered, Ry stared at the dark-clad arms that seemed to shoot straight out from the building's wall and wrap around Clarence's neck.

Then it was a shadow flowing out of nothing. Then it was a man flowing out of the shadow.

"I don't believe the inspector was finished talking to you, Clarence." Nemesis kept one arm hooked around Clarence's neck as he faced Ry. "Were you, Inspector?"

"No, I wasn't." Ry let out a long breath. "Thanks."

"My pleasure."

"It's a ghost. A ghost's got me." Clarence's eyes turned up, white, and he fainted dead away.

"I imagine you could have handled him on your own." Nemesis passed the limp body to Ry, waiting until Ry had hefted Clarence over his shoulder.

"I appreciate it, anyway."

There was a quick flash of teeth as Nemesis smiled. "I like your style, Inspector."

"Same goes. You want to explain that little trick when you came out of the wall?" Ry began, but he was talking to air before the sentence was finished. "Not bad," he muttered, and was shaking his head as he carted Clarence to the car. "Not bad at all."

The phone awakened Natalie from where she'd dozed off on the couch. Groggy, she stumbled toward it, trying to read the time on her watch.

"Yes, hello?"

"It's Ry."

"Oh." She rubbed the sleep from her eyes. "It's after one. I was—"

"Sorry to wake you."

"No, it's not that. I just—"

"We've got him."

"What?" Her irritation that he had yet to let her finish a sentence sharpened the word.

"Clarence. I picked him up tonight. I thought you'd want to know."

Now her head was reeling. "Yes, of course. That's wonderful. But when—?"

"I'm tied up here, Natalie. I'll get back to you when I can."

"All right, but—" She took the receiver away from her ear and glared at the dial tone. "Congratulations, Inspector," she muttered, and hung up.

With her hands on her hips, she took several deep breaths to calm herself, and to clear her head.

She'd been worried sick. Her own fault, she admitted. Ry was certainly under no obligation to come to her after work, or to call. Even if he had been doing just that for days. And even if she had waited by the phone for hours until simple fatigue spared her the continued humiliation.

Put that aside, she ordered herself. The important matter here was that Clarence Jacoby was in custody. There would be no more fires—no more incidents.

And in the morning, she promised herself as she stomped bad-temperedly off to the bedroom, she'd track Ry down and get the whole story.

In the meantime, she thought as she slipped out of her robe, all she had to do was teach herself to sleep alone again.

Even as she settled onto the pillow, she knew it was going to be a very long night.

Chapter 9

Since there seemed little point in going home after he'd finished at the police station, Ry dropped down on the sagging sofa in his office and caught three hours' sleep before the sirens awakened him.

Following old habit, his feet hit the floor before he remembered he didn't have to answer the bell any longer. Years of training would have allowed him to simply roll over and go back to sleep. Instead, he staggered, bleary-eyed, toward the coffeepot, measuring, flipping switches. His only goal at the moment was to take a giant mug of coffee to the showers with him, and to stay there for an hour.

He lit a cigarette, scowling at the pot as it filled, drop by stingy drop.

The brisk knock on his door only made his scowl deepen. Turning, he aimed his bad temper at Natalie.

"Your secretary isn't in."

"Too early," he mumbled, and rubbed a hand over his face. Why in hell did she always have to look so perfect? "Go away, Natalie. I'm not awake yet."

"I won't go away." Struggling not to be hurt, she set her briefcase down, put her hands on her hips. Obviously, she told herself, he'd had little or no sleep. She'd be patient. "Ry, I need to know what happened last night, so I can plan what steps need to be taken."

"I told you what happened."

"You weren't very generous with details."

Muttering, he snatched up a mug and poured the miserly half cup that had brewed. "We got your torch. He's in custody. He won't be lighting any fires for a while."

Patience, Natalie reminded herself and took a seat. "Clarence Jacoby?"

"Yeah." He looked at her. What choice did he have? She was there, stunning and polished and perfect. "Why don't you go to work, let me pull it together here? I'll have a report for you."

Nerves jittered up her spine, and down again. "Is something wrong?"

"I'm tired," he snapped. "I can't get a decent cup of coffee, and I need a shower. And I want you to stop breathing down my neck."

Surprise registered first, then retreated behind hurt. "I'm sorry," she said, voice cool and stiff, as she rose. "I was concerned about what happened last night. And I wanted to make sure you were all right. Since I can see that you are fine…" She picked up her briefcase. "And since you haven't had time to put your report together, I'll get out of your way."

He swore, dragging a hand through his hair. "Natalie, sit down. Please," he added, when she just stood aloofly in the doorway. "I'm sorry. I'm feeling a little raw this morning, and you made the mistake of being the first person in the line of fire."

"I was worried about you." She said it quietly, but didn't step back into the room.

"I'm fine." Turning away, he topped off his coffee. "Want some of this?"

"No. I should have waited for you to contact me. I realize that." It was, she thought, like suddenly walking on eggshells. One night apart shouldn't make them so awkward with each other.

"If you had, I'd have been worried about you." He managed a smile. It was low, he decided, real low, to lash out at her because all at once he was deathly afraid of where they were heading. "Sit down. I'll give you the highlights."

"All right."

While she did, he walked around his desk and kicked back in his chair. "I had an itch, a hunch. Whatever. I decided to take a run by your plant—take a look around, check the security myself." He blew out a stream of smoke, smiled through it. "Somebody else had the same idea."

"Clarence."

"Yeah, he was there. It was a real party. He'd knocked out the alarm. Had himself a full set of keys to the rear door."

"Keys." Eyes sharpening, Natalie leaned forward.

"That's right. Shiny new copies. The cops have them now. There wouldn't have been any sign of break-in. He also had a couple of gallons of high-test gas, a few dozen matchbooks. So we started to have a little conversation. I guess Clarence didn't like the way it was going, and he made a break for it."

Ry paused, drawing in smoke, shaking his head. "I've never seen anything like it," he murmured. "I'm still not sure I *did* see it."

"What?" Impatient, Natalie rapped a hand on his desk. "Did you chase him?"

"Didn't have to. Your pal took care of it."

"My pal?" Baffled she sat back again. "What pal?"

"Nemesis."

Her eyes went wide and stunned. "You saw him? He was there?"

"Yes and no. Or no and yes. I'm not sure which. He came out of the wall," Ry said, half to himself. "He came out of the damn wall, like smoke. He wasn't there, then he was. Then he wasn't."

Natalie cocked a brow. "Ry, I really think you need some sleep."

"No question about that." Rubbing the back of his stiff neck, he blew out a breath. "But that's how it went. He came out of the wall. First his arms. I was standing a foot away, and I saw arms come out of the wall and grab Clarence. Then he was just there—Nemesis. Clarence took one look at him and fainted." Enjoying the memory, Ry grinned. "Folded up like a deck chair. So Nemesis hands him over to me and I haul him over my shoulder. Then he's gone."

"Clarence?"

"Nemesis. Keep up."

She blinked, trying to. "He—Nemesis—just left?"

"He just went. Back into the wall, into the air." He flicked his fingers to demonstrate. "I don't know. I probably stood there for five minutes with my mouth hanging open before I carried Clarence to the truck."

Brow knit, Natalie spoke slowly, carefully. "You're telling me the man disappeared. In front of your eyes. Just vanished?"

"That's exactly what I'm telling you."

"Ry," she said, still patient. "That's not possible."

"I was there," he reminded her. "You weren't. Clarence came to and started babbling about ghosts. He was so spooked he tried to jump out of the car while I was driving." Ry sipped at his coffee. "I had to knock him out."

"You…you knocked him out."

It was another memory he couldn't help but relish. One short punch to that moon-shaped jaw. "He was better off. Anyway, he's in custody now. He's not talking, but I'm going to interview him in a couple hours and see if we can change that."

She sat silently for a moment, trying to absorb it all, and sort it out. The business with Nemesis was fascinating, and not so difficult to explain. It had been dark. Ry was a trained observer, but even he could make a mistake in the dark. People didn't just vanish.

Rather than argue with him about it, she focused on Clarence Jacoby. "He hasn't said why, then? If he was hired, or by whom?"

"Right now he's claiming he was just out for a walk."

"With several gallons of gasoline?"

"Oh, he says I must have brought the gas with me. I'm framing him because I got burned saving his worthless life."

Insulted, Natalie lunged to her feet. "No one believes that."

Her instant defense amused and touched him. "No, Legs, nobody's buying it. We've got him cold on this one, and it shouldn't take long for the cops to tie him in with the other fires. Once Clarence realizes he's looking at a long stretch, he's likely to sing a different tune. Nobody likes to go down alone."

Natalie nodded. She didn't believe in honor among thieves. "If and when he does name someone, I'll need to know right away. I'm limited as to the steps I can take in the meantime."

Ry rapped his fingers on the desk. He didn't like the possibility that someone in her organization, someone who might be close to her, could be behind the fires. "If Clarence points the finger at one of your people, the cops take the steps. And they're going to be a lot tougher on them than just firing them or taking away their dental plan."

"I'm aware of that. I'm also aware that even though the man who held the match has been caught and my property is safe, it's not over." But the tension that had knotted her shoulders was smoothing away. "I appreciate you looking out for what's mine, Inspector."

"That's what your tax dollars are for." He studied her over the rim of his cup. "I missed being with you last night," he said, before he could stop himself.

Her lips curved slowly. "Good. Because I missed being with you. We could make up for it tonight. Celebrate seeing my tax dollars at work."

"Yeah." If he was sinking, Ry thought, he just didn't have the energy to fight going under for the third time. "Why don't we do that?"

"I'll let you get that shower." She bent down for her briefcase. "Will you let me know what happens when you talk to Clarence?"

"Sure. I'll be in touch."

"I'm going to plan on getting home early," she said as she headed for the door.

"Good plan," he murmured when the door shut behind her. Third time, hell, he thought. He'd drowned days ago, and hadn't even noticed.

Natalie arrived at work with a spring in her step, and called a staff meeting. By ten she was seated at the head of the table in the boardroom, her department heads lining both sides of the polished mahogany.

"I'm pleased to announce that the national grand opening of Lady's Choice will remain, as scheduled, for this coming Saturday."

As expected, there were polite applause and congratulatory murmurs.

"I'd like to take this opportunity," she continued, "to thank you all for your hard work and dedication. Launching a new company of this size takes teamwork, long hours, and constant innovation. I'm grateful to all of you for giving me your best. I particularly appreciate all of your help in the past couple of weeks, when the company faced such unexpected difficulties."

She waited until the murmurs about the fires had died down.

"I'm aware that our budget is stretched, but I'm also aware that we wouldn't be on schedule without the extra effort each one of you, and your staff, have given. Therefore, Lady's Choice is pleased to present bonuses to each and every employee on the first of next month."

This announcement was greeted with a great deal of enthusiasm. Only Deirdre winced and rolled her eyes. Natalie flashed a grin at her that held more pleasure than apology.

"We still have a great deal of work ahead of us," Natalie went on. "I'm sure Deirdre will tell you that I've given her an enormous headache, rather than a bonus." Natalie waited for the laughter to subside. "I have faith in her, and in Lady's Choice warranting it. In addition…" She paused, the smile still in place, her gaze sweeping from face to face. "I want to ease everyone's mind. Last night the arsonist was apprehended. He's now in police custody."

There was applause, a barrage of questions. Natalie sat with her hands folded on the table, watching for, waiting for, some sign that would tell her if one of the people sitting with her had begun to sweat.

"I don't have all the details," she said, holding up a hand for quiet. "Only that Inspector Piasecki apprehended the man outside our plant. I expect a full report within forty-eight hours. In the meantime, we can all thank the diligence of the fire and police departments, and get on with our jobs."

"Was there a fire at the plant?" Donald wanted to know. "Was anything damaged?"

"No. I do know that the suspect was caught before he entered the building."

"Are they sure it's the same one who started the fires at the warehouse and the flagship?" Brow furrowed, Melvin tugged at his bow tie.

Natalie smiled. "As a sister of a police captain, I'm certain the authorities won't make a statement like that until they have absolute proof. But that's the way it looks."

"Who is he?" Donald demanded. "Why did he do it?"

"Again, I don't have all the details. He's a known arsonist. A professional, I believe. I'm sure the motive will come to light before too long."

* * *

Ry wasn't nearly as certain. By noon, he'd been with Jacoby for an hour, covering the same ground. The interrogation room was typically dull. Beige walls, beige linoleum, the wide mirror that everyone knew was two-way glass. He sat on a rock-hard chair, leaning against the single table, smoking lazily, while Clarence grinned and toyed with his own fingers.

"You know they're going to lock the door on you, Clarence," Ry said. "By the time you get out this round, you'll be so old, you won't be able to light a match by yourself."

Clarence grinned and shrugged his shoulders. "I didn't hurt nobody. I never hurt nobody." He looked up then, his small, pale eyes friendly. "You know, some people like to burn other people. You know that, don't you, Ry?"

"Yeah, Clarence, I know that."

"Not me, Ry. I never burned nobody." The eyes lit up happily. "Just you. But that was an accident. You got scars?"

"Yeah, I got scars."

"Me too." Clarence giggled, pleased that they shared something. "Wanna see?"

"Maybe later. I remember when we got burned, Clarence."

"Sure. Sure you do. Like a dragon's kiss, right?"

Like being in the bowels of hell, Ry thought. "The landlord paid you to light the dragon that time, remember?"

"I remember. Nobody lived there. It was just an old building. I like old, empty buildings. The fire just eats along, sniffs up the walls, hides in the ceiling. It talks to you. You've heard it talk, haven't you?"

"Yeah, I've heard it. Who paid you this time, Clarence?"

Playfully Clarence put the tips of his fingers together, making a bridge. "I never said anybody paid me. I never said I did anything. You could've brought the gas, Ry. You're mad at me for burning you." Suddenly his smile was crafty. "You had nightmares in the burn ward. I heard about them. Nightmares about the dragon. And now you don't slay the dragon anymore."

The throb behind his eyes had Ry reaching for another cigarette. Clarence was fascinated by the nightmares, had probed time and again during the interview for details. Even if he'd wanted to, Ry couldn't have given many. It was all a blur of fire and smoke, blessedly misted with time.

"I had nightmares for a while. I got over it. I got over being mad at you, too, Clarence. We were both just doing our job, right?"

Ry caught the glint in Clarence's eyes when the match was lit. Experimentally, Ry held the small flame between them. "It's powerful, isn't it?" he murmured. "Just a little flame. But you and me, we know what it can do—to wood, paper. Flesh. It's powerful. And when you feed it, it gets stronger and stronger."

He touched the match to the tip of his cigarette. Still watching Clarence, Ry licked his forefinger and snuffed out the flame. "Douse it with water, cut off its air, and *poof*." He tossed the broken match into the overburdened ashtray. "We both like to control it, right?"

"Yeah." Clarence licked his lips, hoping Ry would light another match.

"You get paid for starting them. I get paid for putting them out. Who paid you, Clarence?"

"They're going to send me up anyway."

"Yeah. So what have you got to lose?"

"Nothing." Sly again, Clarence looked up at Ry through thin, pale lashes. "I'm not saying I started any fire. But if we was to suppose *maybe* I did, I couldn't say who asked me to."

"Why not?"

"Because if we was to suppose I did, I never saw who asked me to."

"Did you talk to him?"

Clarence began to play with his fingers again, his face so cheerful Ry had to grit his teeth to keep himself from reaching out and squeezing the pudgy neck. "Maybe I talked to somebody. Maybe I didn't. But maybe if I did, the voice on the phone was all screwed up, like a machine."

"Man or woman?"

"Like a machine," Clarence repeated, gesturing toward Ry's tape recorder. "Maybe it could have been either. Maybe they just sent me money to a post-office box before, and after."

"How'd they find you?"

Clarence moved his right shoulder, then his left. "Maybe I didn't ask. People find me when they want me." His grin lit his face. "Somebody always wants me."

"Why that warehouse?"

"I didn't say nothing about a warehouse," Clarence said, pokering up.

"Why that warehouse?" Ry repeated. "Maybe."

Pleased that Ry was playing the game, Clarence scooted forward in his chair. "Maybe for the insurance. Maybe because somebody didn't like who owned the place. Maybe for fun. There's lots of reasons for fire."

Ry pressed him. "And the store. The same person owned the store."

"There were pretty things in the store. Pretty girl things." Forgetting himself, Clarence smiled in reminiscence. "It smelled pretty, too. Even prettier after I poured the gas."

"Who told you to pour the gas, Clarence?"

"I didn't say I did."

"You just did."

Clarence pouted like a child. "Did not. I said maybe."

The tape would prove different, but Ry kept his probing steady. "You liked the girl things in the store."

Clarence's eyes twinkled. "What store?"

Biting back an oath, Ry leaned back. "Maybe I should call my friend back and let him talk to you."

"What friend?"

"From last night. You remember last night."

All color drained from Clarence's face. "He was a ghost. He wasn't really there."

"Sure he was there. You saw him. You felt him."

"A ghost." Clarence began to gnaw on his fingernails. "I didn't like him."

"Then you'd better talk to me, or I'm going to have to go get him."

Panicked, Clarence darted his eyes around the room. "He's not here."

"Maybe he is," Ry said, enjoying himself. "Maybe he isn't. Who paid you, Clarence?"

"I don't know." His lips began to tremble. "Just a voice. That's all. Take the money and burn. I like money, I like to burn. Started on the nice shiny desk in the store with the girl things, just like the voice said to. Coulda done better in the storeroom, but the voice said do the desk." Uneasy, he looked around. "Is he in here?"

"What about the envelopes? Where are the envelopes the money came in?"

"Burned them." Clarence grinned again. "I like to burn things."

Natalie very nearly burned the chicken.

It wasn't that she was incompetent in the kitchen. It was simply, she told herself, that she rarely found the opportunity to use the culinary skills she possessed—meager though they might be.

With a great deal of cursing and trepidation, she removed the browned chicken from the skillet and set it aside, as per Frank's meticulous directions. By the time she had the sauce simmering, she was feeling smug. Cooking wasn't really such a big deal, she decided, if you just concentrated and went step-by-step. Read the recipe as if it were a contract, she thought, carefully sliding the chicken into the sauce. Overlook no clause, study the small print. And… Humming to herself, she set the cover on the skillet, then looked around at the wreck of her kitchen.

And, she decided, blowing the hair out of her eyes, clean up after yourself—because no deal should ever look as though you'd sweat over it.

It took her longer to set the kitchen, and herself, to rights than it had to prepare the meal. After one quick glance at the time, she dashed to light the candles and create the mood.

With a long sigh, she dropped onto the arm of the sofa and scanned the room. Soft lights, quiet music, the scent of flowers and good food, the golden glow of sedate flames in the hearth. Pleased, Natalie smoothed a hand down her long silk skirt. Everything was perfect, she decided.

Now where was Ry?

He was pacing the hallway outside her door.

Making too big a deal out of it, Piasecki, he warned himself. You're just two people enjoying each other. No strings, no promises. Now that Clarence was in custody, they would start to drift apart. Naturally. No sweat, no strain.

So why in the hell was he standing outside her door, nervous as a teenager on a first date? Why was he holding a bunch of stupid daffodils in his hand?

He should never have brought her flowers in the first place, he decided. But if he'd had the urge, he should have gone for roses, at least, or orchids. Something with class. Just because the yellow blooms had caught his eye and the street vendor had been pushing them, that was no reason to dump a bunch of backyard flowers on a woman like Natalie.

He thought seriously about dropping them in front of her neighbor's door. The idea made him feel even more foolish. Muttering under his breath, he pulled out his key and unlocked the door.

Coming home. It was a ridiculous sensation, walking into an apartment that wasn't his. But it was there, as bold as a ten-foot sign, as subtle as a peck on the cheek.

She rose from her perch on the couch and smiled at him. "Hi."

"Hi."

He had the flowers behind his back, hardly realizing the move was defensive. She looked incredible, the thin-strapped, flowing dress—the color of ripe peaches—skimming down, candle and firelight flickering over her. When she moved, he swallowed. The dress sliced open from the ankle to the trio of gold buttons running down her left hip.

"Long day," she asked, and kissed him lightly on the mouth.

"Yeah. I guess." His tongue had tied itself into knots. "You?"

"Not too bad. The good news has everybody pumped up. I have some wine chilling." She tilted her head, smiling at him. "Unless you'd rather have a beer."

"Whatever," he murmured as she strolled toward the table by the window, which she had set for two. "It looks nice in here. You look nice."

"Well, I thought, since we were celebrating…" She poured two glasses. "I had planned on doing this after the grand opening on Saturday, but it seems appropriate now." With the glasses on the table behind her, she held out a hand. "I have a lot to thank you for."

"No, you don't. I did what I was paid to do…." He trailed off, seeing that her gaze had shifted, softened. With some discomfort, he realized it was riveted on the flowers he'd used to gesture her thanks away.

"You brought me flowers." The simple shock in her voice didn't help his nerves.

"This guy on the corner was selling them, and I just—"

"Daffodils," she said with a sigh. "I love daffodils."

"Yeah?" Miserably awkward, he thrust them at her. "Well, here you go."

Natalie buried her face in the bright trumpets and, for reasons she couldn't fathom, wanted to weep. "They're so pretty, so happy." She lifted her head again, eyes glowing. "So perfect. Thank you."

"It's no big—" But the rest of his words were cut off when her mouth closed over his.

Instant desire. Like a switch flicked on inside him. One touch, he thought as his arms came hard around her, and he wanted her. Her body molded to his, her arms circled. He fought back a desperate need to drag her to the floor and release the helpless passion she stirred up inside him.

"You're tense," she murmured, stroking a hand over his shoulders. "Did something happen with Clarence during the interview that you didn't tell me?"

"No." Clarence Jacoby and his moon-pie face were the last things on Ry's mind. "I'm just wired, I guess." And in need of some basic control. "Something smells good," he said as he eased back. "Besides you."

"Frank's fricassee."

"Frank's?" Taking another step back, Ry reached for his wine. "Guthrie's cook made us dinner?"

"No, it's his recipe." She tucked her hair behind her ear. "I made us dinner."

Ry snorted into his wine. "Yeah. Right. Where'd you get it? The Italian place?"

Torn between amusement and insult, Natalie took her wine. "*I* made it, Piasecki. I know how to turn on a stove."

"You know how to pick up the phone and order." More relaxed now, Ry took her hand and pulled her toward the kitchen. He walked directly to the skillet and lifted the lid. It certainly looked homemade. Frowning, he sniffed at the thick, bubbling sauce covering the golden pieces of chicken. "You cooked this? Yourself?"

Exasperated, Natalie tugged her hand away and sipped her wine. "I don't see why that should be such a shock. It's just a matter of following directions."

"You cooked this," he said again, shaking his head. "How come?"

"Well, because… I don't know." With a little snap of metal on metal, she covered the skillet again. "I felt like it."

"I just can't picture you puttering around the kitchen."

"There wasn't a lot of puttering." Then she laughed. "And it wasn't a very pretty sight. So, no matter what it tastes like, you're required to praise, lavishly. I need to put the flowers in water."

He waited while she got a vase and arranged the daffodils on the kitchen counter.

She looked softer tonight, he thought. All feminine and cozy. And she handled each individual bloom as though he'd brought her rubies. Unable to resist, he lifted his hand to stroke it gently down her hair. She looked up, with surprise, her uncertainty at the show of tenderness evident.

"Is something wrong?"

"No." Cursing himself, he dropped his hand to his side. "I like to touch you."

Her eyes cleared, danced. "I know." She turned into his arms, inviting. "The chicken needs to simmer for a while." She nipped lightly, teasingly, at his lip. "An hour, anyway. Why don't we—"

"Sit down," he finished, to keep from exploding. He was not, he absolutely was not, going to drag her down and take her on the kitchen floor.

"Okay." Left uneasy by his withdrawal, she nodded and picked up her wine again. "We should enjoy the fire."

In the living room, she curled up next to him and rested her head on his shoulder. Obviously, he had something on his mind. She could wait for him to share it with her. It was lovely just sitting here, she thought with a sigh, watching the fire together as dinner cooked and an old Cole Porter tune drifted through the speakers.

It was as if they sat like this every night. Comfortable with each other, knowing there was time, all the time in the world simply to be. After a long, busy day, what better end could there be than to sit beside someone you loved and—

Oh, God. Her thoughts had her jerking straight upright. *Loved.* She loved him.

"What's wrong?"

"Nothing." She swallowed hard, fought to keep her voice even. "Just something I…forgot. I can deal with it later."

"No shoptalk, okay?"

"No." She took a hasty sip of wine. "Fine."

She couldn't get a decent night's sleep when he wasn't beside her. She'd had an irresistible urge to cook him a meal. Her heart turned over every time he smiled at her. She'd even been rerouting a business trip with him in mind.

Oh, why hadn't she seen it before? It had been staring her in the face every time she looked in the mirror.

What was she going to do?

Closing her eyes, she ordered her body to relax. Her emotions were her problem, she reminded herself. She was a grown woman who had gone into an affair with the rules plain on both sides. She couldn't—wouldn't—change the terms in midstream.

What was needed was some clear and careful thought. Some time, she added, concentrating on breathing evenly. Then a plan. She was an excellent planner, after all.

His fingertips brushed lightly over her shoulder. Her pulse scrambled.

"I'd better check on dinner."

"It hasn't been an hour." He liked the way she was curled against him, and wanted to keep her there. Stupid to be worried about where they were heading, he decided, letting himself get drunk on the smell of her hair. Where they were now was exactly the right place to be.

"I was...going to make a salad," she said uncertainly.

"Later."

He slid his fingers under her chin and turned her face toward his. Odd, he thought, it seemed as though his nerves had drained out of him and into her. Experimentally he dipped his head, letting his lips cruise over hers.

She trembled against him.

Intrigued, he drew her lower lip into his mouth, bathing it with his tongue while his eyes watched emotions come and go in hers.

She shuddered.

"Why are we always in a hurry?" he murmured, addressing the question as much to himself as to her.

"I don't know." She had to get away, clear her head, before she made some foolish mistake. "We need more wine."

"I don't think so." Slowly he brushed the hair back from her face so that he could frame it with his hands. He held her there, his eyes on hers. "Do you know what I think, Natalie?"

"No." She moistened her lips, struggling to find her balance.

"I think we've missed a step here."

"I don't know what you mean."

He pressed his lips to her brow, drew back, and watched her eyes cloud. "Seduction," he whispered.

Chapter 10

Seduction? She didn't need to be seduced. She wanted him, always wanted him. Before she realized she loved him, she had equated her response to him as a kind of volatile chemical reaction. But now, couldn't he see…

Her thoughts trailed off into smoke as his lips roamed lazily down her temple.

"Ry." She put her hand to his chest, told herself she would keep her voice light, joking…disentangle herself long enough to clear her mind and regain her balance. But his fingers were stroking along her collarbone, and his mouth was nipping closer, closer to hers. She only said, "Ry," again.

"We're good at moving straight ahead, you and me, aren't we, Natalie?" But now there was something smooth and easy riding through him. Fascinated by his own reaction, he traced his tongue over her lips. "Fast, with no detours, that's us. I think it's time we took a little side trip."

"I think…" But she couldn't think. Not after his mouth fit itself to hers. He'd never kissed her like this before, never like this, so slow, so deep, with a lazy kind of possession that shot simmering heat straight to the marrow of her bones.

Her body went lax, as fluid as the wax pooling the wicks of the candles around them. Beneath her palm, his heart beat hard, and not quite steady, and the low, helpless sound that vibrated in her throat quickened it. Yet he continued that slow, deep exploration of her mouth, as if he would be content with that, only that, for hours.

Her head fell back. He cupped it, shifting her slightly to change the angle of the kiss, toying with her lips, her tongue. Her breath caught and released, caught and released, shuddering once when his fingers brushed up over her breast.

Now, she knew, now would come the speed and the power she understood. There would be control again, in the sheer lack of control as they rushed to take each other. But his fingers simply skimmed up her throat and lay with devastating tenderness on her cheek.

In defense, she reached for him, pulling him tight against her.

"Not this time." He drew back just enough to study her face. Confusion, need, and arousal made a beautiful combination. However much his own blood was pounding, he intended to confuse her more, intended to see to each and every need, and arouse her until her body was limp.

"I want you." She tore hurriedly at the buttons of his shirt. "Now, Ry. I want you now."

He pulled her down on the floor in front of the fire. Th

ght from the flames flickered over her skin, danced in her air. She was golden. Like some exotic treasure a man might pend his life in search of. And for now, for tonight, Ry ought, she was only his.

He stretched her arms out to the sides, linked his fingers ith hers. "You'll have to wait," he told her. "Until I'm fin-hed seducing you."

"I don't need to be seduced." She arched up to him, offer-g her mouth, her body, herself.

"Let's see."

He covered her mouth with his, softly, dipping in when her ps trembled open. Under his hands, hers flexed, and gripped ard. How often had he loved her? It hadn't been long since ey'd met, but he couldn't count the number of times he'd t his body take control, go wild with hers.

This time, he'd make love to her with his mind.

"I love your shoulders," he murmured, taking his mouth om hers for a slow exploration of the curve. "Soft, strong, mooth."

With his teeth, he caught the thin strap of her dress, tugged down until there was nothing between him and flesh. Varmth, her taste, her scent, were all warmth. Absorbing em, he trailed his tongue over her shoulder, along the ele-ant line of throat, down again until the other strap gave way.

"And this spot here." He rubbed his lips just above the silk aat curved over her breast. Teasingly, devastatingly, he damp-ned the skin under the silk with his tongue until her body oved restlessly beneath his. "You should relax and enjoy, Iatalie. I'm going to be a while."

"I can't." The gentle brush of lips, the solid weight of him, ere tormenting her. "Kiss me again."

"My pleasure."

There was a flicker of heat this time, bright and hot, before he banked the fires again. She moaned, straining agains
him, wanting release, craving the torture. He made the choic
for her, kissing her with a focused intensity until her finger
went limp and her rushed breathing slowed and thickened.

Smoke. She could all but smell it. She was rising up on cloud
of it, weightless, helpless, unable to do more than float and sig
when his mouth left hers to trail down again. A gentle nip at th
jaw, and then light, slow kisses down her throat, her shoulder

His body shifted downward, his hands still covering her
Inch by inch, he tasted her, nudging the silk down. She fe
his hair brush her breast, then his mouth traveling around th
curve, nuzzling at the sensitive underside. His tongue slid ove
her nipple, shooting an ache down to her center. Then h
caught the peak between his teeth, making her moan hi
name, and her body began to throb to a low, primitive beat

He wanted her to absorb him, and all the pleasure he coul
give her. Her eyes were closed, her lips just parted. And muc
too tempting. He needed to taste them again, and when he di
he let himself sink into the texture, the flavor.

Time spun out.

There was power here, in tenderness. He'd never felt it before, not in himself, and certainly not for anyone else. But fo
her he had a bottomless well of tenderness, of soft, sumptu
ous kisses, of endless sighs.

He took his hands from hers to shrug out of his shirt, t
feel the thrill of his flesh against her flesh. Sliding smooth
building heat. With a murmur of approval, he slipped h
hand through the slit of her skirt, lightly caressing, teasing th
edge of some frilly something she wore beneath.

He flicked open a button, then two, then the third, fascinated by the way the material slid and parted under his hands. Nuzzling along her bared hip, he fought back a sudden, vicious urge to take when her hands brushed, then pressed, at his shoulders.

More, he promised himself. There was more.

For his own pleasure, he slipped the silk aside. And found more.

Beneath she wore a fancy of silk and lace, the same color as the dress that pooled beside them. Strapless, it hugged her breasts, rode high up her hips. Letting out a long breath, he sat back on his heels and toyed with one lacy garter.

"Natalie."

Weak…she was so gloriously weak she could barely open her eyes. When she did, she saw only him, the firelight teasing the red out of his dark hair, his eyes nearly black. She reached out, her arm heavy, nearly boneless. He merely took her hand, and kissed it.

"I wanted to tell you how happy I am you're in the lingerie business."

Her lips curved. She nearly managed a laugh before, with one quick flick, he detached the first garter. She could only utter a helpless moan.

"And how beautiful you look." Flick went the second garter. "Modeling your own products." With his eyes on hers, he rolled the stocking down thigh and knee and calf.

Her vision hazed. She could feel him. Oh, God, she could feel him—every brush of fingertip and mouth. Surrender had come gliding through her like a shadow, and had left her completely vulnerable. Whatever he wanted. Anything he wanted, she would give, as long as he never stopped touching her.

There was the low, steady heat from the fire. It was nothing, nothing, compared to the slow burn he had kindled inside her. As if down a long, velvet-lined tunnel, she could hear the music still. A quiet backdrop to her own trembling breathing. The scent of flowers and candle wax, the taste of him and the wine that lingered on her tongue, all melded together into one stunning intoxication.

Then he slipped a finger under the lace-edged hem, sliding it slowly toward, and then into, the heat.

She erupted. Her body quaked and reared. His name burst from her lips, even as the staggering pleasure careened through her system. She was wrapped around him as the power of the climax built in force, then echoed away and left her drained.

She wanted to tell him she was empty, had to be empty. But he was peeling away the silk and lace, exposing her with those clever fingers, swallowing whatever words she might have spoken with that relentlessly patient mouth.

"I want to fill you, Natalie." His hands weren't as steady as they had been, but he laid her gently back on the carpet so that he could tug off his clothes. "All of you. With all of me."

While the blood pounded in his ears, he began a slow journey up her legs, stoking the fires again, waiting, watching, for that moment before she would flash again.

He felt her body tense, saw the power of what was to come flicker over her face. Even as she cried out, he was inside her.

It was almost painful to hold himself back. And it was very sweet. Seeing her heavy eyes open, seeing the glaze of pleasure cloud them as he fought to keep from racing for the finish.

Swamped by a swirl of sensations, all but suffocating i

the layers of them, she groped for his hands. When their fingers locked again, her heart was ready to burst. Her eyes stayed open and looked on his as each thrust rocked them, pushed them closer.

Then she was cartwheeling off the edge, reeling, tumbling free. His mouth came to hers, his lips forming her name as he leapt with her.

Twice on the elevator ride to her office the next morning, Natalie caught herself singing. Both times, she cleared her throat, shifted her briefcase from hand to hand and pretended not to notice the speculative looks of her fellow passengers.

So what? she thought as the elevator climbed. She felt like singing. She felt like dancing. So what? She was in love.

And what was wrong with that? she asked herself as the elevator stopped to let off passengers on the thirty-first floor. Everyone was entitled to be in love, to feel as though their feet would never touch the ground again, to know the air had never smelled sweeter, the sun had never shone brighter.

It was wonderful to be in love. So wonderful, she wondered why she'd never tried it before.

Because there'd never been Ry before, she thought, and grinned.

How foolish she'd been to panic when she realized what she felt for Ry. How cowardly and ridiculous to be afraid, even for a moment, of loving.

If it made a woman vulnerable, comical, if it dazed and baffled her, what was wrong with that? Love should make you feel giddy and strong and soft-headed. She'd just never realized it before.

Humming to herself, she stepped out of the elevator on her floor and all but waltzed toward her office.

"Good morning, Ms. Fletcher." Maureen glanced surreptitiously at her clock. It wasn't up to her to point out that the boss was late. Even three minutes late was a precedent for Natalie Fletcher.

"Good morning, Maureen." She all but sang it, and thrust out a clutch of daffodils.

"Oh, thank you. They're lovely."

"Everyone should have daffodils this morning. Absolutely everyone." Natalie shook back her hair, scattering raindrops. "It's a gorgeous day, isn't it?"

Drizzling and chilly was what it was, but Maureen found herself grinning back. "Absolutely a classic spring morning. You've got a conference call scheduled for ten o'clock. Atlanta, Chicago."

"I know."

"And Ms. Marks was hoping you could fit her in afterward."

"Fine."

"Oh, and you're due at the flagship at 11:15, right after your 10:30 with Mr. Hawthorne."

"No problem."

"You have a lunch with—"

"I'll be there," Natalie called out, and swung into her office.

For the first time in recent memory, Natalie bypassed the coffeepot. She didn't need caffeine to pump through her blood. It was already swimming. She hung up her coat, set her briefcase aside, then moved to the office safe behind her favorite abstract print.

Taking out a pair of disks, she went to her desk to draft a brief memo to Deirdre.

An hour later, she was elbow-deep in work, making hasty notes as she juggled information and requests from three of her branches on the conference call.

"I'll fax authorization for that within the hour," she promised Atlanta. "Donald, see if you can squeeze out the time to go to the flagship with me—11:15. We can have our meeting on the way."

"I've got an ll:30 with Marketing," he told her. "Let me see if I can push it to after lunch."

"I'd appreciate it. I'd like tear sheets of all the ads and newspaper articles in Chicago. You can fax copies, but I'd like you to overnight the originals. I'll be checking in with L.A. and Dallas this afternoon, and we'll have a full report for all branches by end of day tomorrow."

She sat back, let out a long breath. "Gentlemen, synchronize your watches and alert the troops. 10:00 a.m., Saturday. Coast to coast."

After she closed the conference, Natalie pressed her buzzer. "Maureen, let Deirdre know I'm free for about twenty minutes. Oh, and buzz Melvin for me."

"He's in the field, Ms. Fletcher."

"Oh, right." Annoyed with her lapse, Natalie glanced at her watch, calculated time. "I'll see if I can catch him at the plant later this afternoon. Leave a memo on his voice mail that I should be by around three."

"Yes, ma'am."

"After you buzz Deirdre, get me the head of shipping at the new warehouse."

"Right away."

By the time Deirdre knocked on the door and stepped in, Natalie was tapping at the keys on her desk computer. "Yes,

I see that." Phone tucked at her ear, she gestured Deirdre to a seat. "Put a trace on that shipment. I want it in Atlanta no later than 9:00 a.m. tomorrow." She nodded, tapped. "Let me know as soon as it's located. Thanks."

She hung up, brushed a stray hair from her cheek. "There's always a glitch near zero hour."

Deirdre's brow wrinkled. "Bad?"

"No, just a slight delay on a shipment. Even without it, Atlanta's well stocked for the opening. But I don't want them to run low. Coffee?"

"No, I've already burned a hole in my stomach lining, thanks. Or you have." She aimed a steely look at her boss. "Bonuses."

"Bonuses," Natalie agreed. "I have the percentages I want you to work with right here. Salary ratios, and so forth." She smiled a little. "I figured you wouldn't be wondering about how best to murder me if I did the preliminaries."

"Wrong."

Now Natalie laughed. "Deirdre, do you know why I value you so highly?"

"Nope."

"You have a mind like a calculator. The bonuses were earned, and I also consider them a good investment. Incentive to keep up the pace during the weeks ahead. There's usually a dip after the initial sales in a new business, both in profit and in labor. I think this will keep that dip from becoming a dive."

"That's all very well in theory," Deirdre began.

"Let's make it reality. And since it's basically a standard ratio across the board, I'd like you to hand the problem over to your assistant. That way you can concentrate on running the audit."

Still smiling, she handed over the disks, and her memo. "A great deal of what you'll need to run will be parallel with tax preparation. Take whatever time, and however many bodies in Accounting, you feel you'll need."

With a grimace, Deirdre accepted the disk. "You know why I value you so highly, Natalie?"

"Nope."

"Because there's no budging you, and you give impossible orders with such reasonableness."

"It's a gift," Natalie agreed. "You might want these hard copies."

Deirdre rose, hefting the file. "Thanks a lot."

"Anytime." She glanced up with a smile as Donald poked his head in the door.

"I'm clear until 12:30," he told her.

"Great. We'll head out now. Take your time," Natalie repeated to Deirdre as she crossed to the closet for her coat. "As long as I have the first figures on this quarter's profit and loss, and the totals from each department, by the end of next week."

Deirdre rolled her eyes at Donald. "Reasonably impossible." She set the disks on top of the file. "You're next," she warned him.

"Don't let her scare you, Donald. She's just gearing up to pit black ink against red." Natalie sailed through the door. "Just make sure the black wins."

"Quite a mood she's in," Donald murmured to Deirdre.

"She's flying, all right." Deirdre stared down at the files. "Let's hope we can keep it that way."

"Perfect, isn't it?" Content after their visit to the store, Natalie stretched out her legs in the back of the car, while her driver threaded through the lunch-hour traffic. "You'd never know there was a fire."

"A hell of a job," Donald agreed. "And the window treatment's spectacular. The salesclerks are going to be run ragged come Saturday."

"I'm counting on it." She touched a hand to his arm. "A lot of it's your doing, Donald. We never would have gotten off the ground like this without you, especially after the warehouse."

"Damage control." He brushed off her thanks with a shrug. "In six months we'll barely remember we had damage to control. And the profits will bring a smile even to Deirdre's face." He was counting on it.

"That would be a real coup."

"Just drop me off at the next corner," he told the driver. "The restaurant's only a couple of doors down."

"I appreciate you making time to go with me."

"No problem. Seeing the flagship back in shape made my day. It wasn't pleasant visualizing the office torn up like that. That wonderful antique desk ruined. The replacement's stunning, by the way."

"I had it shipped out from Colorado," Natalie said absently, as something niggled at her brain. "I had it in storage."

"Well, it's perfect." He patted her hand as the car swung to the curb.

She waved him off, then settled back, dissatisfied, when the car merged back into traffic. Then, with a shrug, she gauged the traffic, the distance to her lunch meeting, and decided she had time for one quick phone call.

Ry answered himself on the third ring. "Arson. Piasecki."

"Hi." The pleasure of hearing his voice wiped out everything else. "Your secretary's out?"

"Lunch."

"And you're having yours at your desk."

He glanced down at the sandwich he had yet to touch. "Yeah. More or less." He shifted, making his chair squeak. "Where are you?"

"Looks like Twelfth and Hyatt, heading east, toward the Menagerie."

"Ah." The Menagerie, he thought. High-class. No tuna on wheat for lunch there. He could see her, ordering designer water and a salad with every leaf called a different name. "Look, Legs, about tonight—"

"I was thinking about that. Maybe you could meet me at the Goose Neck." She rolled her shoulders. "I have a feeling I'm going to want to unwind."

He rubbed a hand over his chin. "I, ah… Come by my place instead. Okay?"

"Your place?" This was new. She'd stopped wondering why he'd never taken her there.

"Yeah. About seven, seven-thirty."

"All right. Do you want me to pick up something for dinner?"

"No, I'll take care of it. See you." He hung up and sat back in his chair. He was going to have to take care of a lot of things.

He picked up Chinese. It was nearly seven when Ry carried the little white cartons up the two flights to his apartment. He took a good look around while he did.

It wasn't a dump. Unless, of course, you compared it with Natalie's glossy building. There was no graffiti on the walls, but the walls were thin. As he climbed the steps, Ry could hear the muted sounds of televisions playing, children squabbling. The steps themselves were worn down in the centers from the passage of countless feet.

As he turned onto the second floor, he heard a door slam beneath him.

"All right, all right. I'll go get the damn beer myself."

Lip curled, Ry unlocked his door. Yeah, he thought. It was a real class joint. There was a definite scent of garlic in the hall. Courtesy of his neighbor, he assumed. The woman was always cooking up pots of pasta.

He let himself in, flicked on the lights and studied the room.

It was clean. A little dusty, maybe. He barely spent enough time in it to mess it up. It had been nearly three weeks since he'd spent a night there. The sofa that folded out into a bed needed recovering. It wasn't something he'd noticed before, or would have bothered with. But now the faded blue uphol-stery annoyed him.

He walked past it, taking about half a dozen steps into the alcove that served as his kitchen. He got out a beer and popped the top. The walls needed painting, too, he decided, chugging the beer as he looked around. And the bare floors could have used a carpet.

But it served him well enough, didn't it? he thought grimly He didn't need fancy digs. Just a couple of rooms a short hop from the office. He'd been content here for nearly a decade That was enough for anyone.

But it wasn't enough, couldn't be enough, for Natalie.

She didn't belong here. He knew it. And he'd asked her to come to prove it to both of them.

The night before had been a revelation to him. That she could make him feel the way she'd made him feel. That she could make him forget, as he'd forgotten, that there was any thing or anyone on the planet except the two of them.

It wasn't fair to either of them to go on this way. The longer he let it drift, the more he needed her. And the more he needed, the more difficult it would be to let her walk away.

His divorce hadn't hurt him. Oh, a couple of twinges, he thought now. Plenty of regrets. But no real pain. Not the deep-rooted, searing kind of pain he was already feeling at the thought of living without Natalie.

He could keep her. There was a good chance he could keep her. The physical thing between them was outrageously intense. Even if it faded by half, it would still be stronger than anything he'd ever experienced before.

And he was well aware of his effect on her.

He could hold her with sex alone. It might be enough for her. But he'd understood when he awakened beside her this morning that it wasn't enough for him.

No, it wasn't enough, not when he'd started to imagine white picket fences, kids in the yard—the kind of things that went with marriage, permanence, a lifetime.

That hadn't been the deal, he reminded himself. And he had no right to change the rules, to expect her to settle. He'd already proven he wasn't any good at marriage, and that had been with someone from his own neighborhood, his own lifestyle. No way was he going to fit in with Natalie, and the fact that he wanted to, needed to, scared the hell out of him.

Worse than that, even worse, was the idea that she would turn him down cold if he asked her to try.

He wanted all of her. Or nothing. So it made sense, didn't it, to push her out before he got in any deeper? And he would do it here, right here, where the differences between them would slap her between the eyes.

At the knock on his door, he carried his beer over to answer it.

It was just as he'd thought. She stood in the hallway, slim, golden, an exotic fish completely out of water. She smiled at him, leaning up to kiss him.

"Hi."

"Hi. Come on in. No trouble finding the place?"

"No." She skimmed her sweep of hair back, looking around. "I took a cab."

"Good thinking. If you left that fancy car on the street around here, there'd be nothing left but the door handles when you went back out. Want a beer?"

"No." Interested, she wandered over to the window.

"Not much of a view," he said, knowing she was looking out at the face of the next building.

"Not much," she agreed. "It's still raining," she added and slipped out of her coat. She smiled when she spotted another of his basketball trophies. "MVP," she murmured, reading the plaque. "Impressive. I say I can outscore you nine times out of ten."

"I wasn't fresh." He turned into the kitchen. "I don't have any wine."

"That's okay. Mmm...Chinese." She opened one of the cartons he'd set on the counter, and sniffed. "I'm starved. All I had was a stingy salad for lunch. I've been all over the city today, nailing down details for Saturday. Where are the plates?" Very much at home, she opened a cabinet herself. "I'm really going to have to make a sweep of the branches next week. I was thinking—" She broke off when she turned back and found him staring at her. "What?"

"Nothing," he muttered, and took the plates out of her hands.

She wasn't supposed to stride right in and start chattering, he thought, and dumped food on a plate. She was supposed to see how wrong it was, right from the start. She was supposed to make it easy on him.

"Damn it, do you see where you are?" He whirled on her, taking her back a step.

She blinked. "Ah…in the kitchen?"

"Look around you." Incensed, he took her by the arm and dragged her into the next room. "Look around. This is it. This is the way I live. This is the way I am."

"All right." She pushed his hand away, because his fingers hurt. Trying to oblige, she took another survey of the room. It was spartan, masculine in its very simplicity. Small, she noted, but not crowded. A table across the room held framed snapshots of a family she hoped to get a closer look at.

"It could use some color," she decided after a moment.

"I'm not asking for decorating advice," he snapped out.

There was something under the anger in his tone, something final, that had her heart stuttering. Very slowly, she turned back to him. "What are you asking for?"

Cursing, he spun into the kitchen for his beer. If she was going to look at him with that confused, wounded look in her eyes, he was a dead man. So, he would have to be cruel, and he would have to be quick. He sat on the arm of the couch, and tipped back his beer.

"Let's get real here, Natalie. You and I started this thing because we were hot for each other."

She could feel the warmth drain out of her cheeks, leaving them cold and stiff. But she kept her eyes level, and her voice steady. "Yes, that's right."

"Things happened fast. The sex, the investigation. Things got tangled up."

"Did they?"

His mouth was dry, and the beer wasn't helping. "You're a beautiful woman. I wanted you. You had a problem. It was my job to fix it for you."

"Which you did," she said carefully.

"For the most part. The cops'll track down whoever was paying Clarence. Until they do, you've got to be careful. But things are pretty much under control. On that level."

"And on the personal level?"

He frowned down into the bottle. "I figure it's time to step back, take a clearer look."

Natalie's legs were trembling. She locked her knees to stop it. "Are you dumping me, Ry?"

"I'm saying we've got to look behind the way things are in bed. The way you are." He lifted his gaze. "The way I'm not. We've got plenty of heat, Natalie. The problem with that is, you get blinded by the smoke. Time to clear the air, that's all."

"I see." She wouldn't beg. Nor would she cry, not in front of him. Not when he was looking at her so coolly, his voice so casual as he cut out her heart. She wondered if he'd been so gentle, so loving and sweet, the night before because he'd already decided to break things off.

"Well, I suppose you've cleared it." Despite her resolve, her vision blurred, the lamplight refracting in the tears that trembled much too close to the surface.

The minute her eyes filled, he was on his feet. "Don't."

"I won't. Believe me, I won't." But the first tear spilled over as she turned toward the door. "I appreciate you no doing this in a public place." She clamped a hand over the doorknob. Her fingers were numb, she realized. She couldn't even feel them.

"Natalie."

"I'm all right." To prove it to both of them, she turned to face him, her head up. "I'm not a child, and this isn't the first relationship I've had that hasn't worked. It is the first time for something, though, and you're entitled to know it. You jerk." She sniffed, and wiped a tear away. "I've never been in love with anyone before, but I fell in love with you. I hate you for it."

She yanked open the door and dashed out without her coat.

Chapter 11

For ten minutes, Ry paced the room, convincing himself he'd done the right thing for both of them. Sure, she'd be a little hurt. Her pride was bruised. He hadn't exactly been a diplomat.

For the next ten, he worked on convincing himself that she hadn't meant what she'd said. That parting shot had been just that. A weapon hurled to hurt as she'd been hurt.

She wasn't in love with him. She couldn't be. Because if she was, then he was the world's biggest idiot.

Oh, God. He was the world's biggest idiot.

He snatched up her coat, forgot his own, and raced downstairs and out into the rain.

He'd left his car at the station, and cursed himself for it. Praying for a cab, he loped to the corner, then to the next, working his way across town.

His impatience cost him more time than a simple wait

would have. By the time he hailed an empty cab, he was twelve blocks from his home and soaking wet.

The cab fought its way through rain and traffic, creeping along, then sprinting, creeping, then sprinting, until Ry tossed a fistful of money at the driver and leapt out.

He'd have made better time on foot.

Nearly an hour had passed by the time he arrived at Natalie's door. He didn't bother to knock, but used the key she hadn't thought to demand back from him.

There was no welcome this time, no cozy sense of coming home. He knew the minute he stepped inside that she wasn't there. Denying it, he called out for her and began a dripping search through the apartment.

So he'd wait, he told himself. She'd come home sooner or later, and he'd be there. Make things right again somehow. He'd grovel if he had to, he decided, pacing from the living room to the bedroom.

She'd probably gone to her office. Maybe he should go there. He could call. He could send a telegram. He could do something.

Good God, the woman was in love with him, and he'd used both hands to shove her out the door.

He dropped to the side of the bed and snatched up the phone. It was then that he saw the note, hastily scrawled, on the nightstand.

Atlanta—National—8:25

National, he thought. National Airlines. The airport.

Ry was out of the apartment and harassing the doorman for a cab in three minutes flat.

He missed her plane by less than five.

* * *

"No, Inspector Piasecki, I don't know precisely when Ms. Fletcher expects to return." Cautiously, Maureen smiled. The man looked wild, as though he'd spent a very rough night in his clothes. Things were upended enough, with the boss's sudden trip, without her having to face down a madman at 9:00 a.m.

"Where is she?" Ry demanded. He'd very nearly caught the next flight out to Atlanta the night before, but then it had occurred to him that he didn't have a clue where to find her.

"I'm sorry, Inspector. I'm not allowed to give you that information. I will be happy to relay any message you might have when Ms. Fletcher calls in."

"I want to know where she is," Ry said between his teeth.

Maureen gave serious thought to calling Security. "It's company policy—"

He gave a one-word assessment of company policy and pulled out his ID. "Do you see this? I'm in charge of the arson investigation. I've got information Ms. Fletcher requires immediately. Now, if you don't let me know where to reach her, I'll have to go to my superiors."

He let that hang, and hoped.

Torn, Maureen bit her lip. It was true Ms. Fletcher had ordered her specifically not to divulge her itinerary. It was also true that during the harried phone call the night before, nothing had been mentioned specifically about information from Inspector Piasecki. And if it was something to do with the fires…

"She's staying at the Ritz-Carlton, Atlanta."

Before she'd finished the sentence, Ry was out the door. It was best, he decided, if a man was going to whimper, to do it in private.

Fifteen minutes later, he burst into his office, startling his secretary, and slammed the door behind him. "Ritz-Carlton, Atlanta. Get them on the phone."

"Yes, sir."

He paced his office, muttering to himself, until she signaled him. "Natalie Fletcher," he barked into the phone. "Connect me."

"Yes, sir. One moment, please."

One endless moment, while the line whispered, then began to ring. Ry let out a long, relieved breath when he heard Natalie's voice at the other end.

"Natalie—what the hell are you doing in Atlanta? I need to—" Then he could only swear as the phone clicked loudly in his ear. "Damn it all to hell and back, get that number for me again."

Wide-eyed, his secretary hurriedly placed the call.

Calm, Ry ordered himself. He knew how to be calm in the face of fire and death and misery. Surely he could be calm now. But when the phone continued to ring and he pictured her coolly looking out the window of her hotel room and ignoring it, he nearly ripped the receiver out of the wall.

"Call the airport," Ry ordered while his secretary goggled at him. "Book me on the next available flight to Atlanta."

She was gone when he got there.

He couldn't believe it. More than ten hours after his rushed departure, Ry was back in Urbana. Alone. He hadn't even managed to see her. He'd spent hours on planes, more time chasing her around Atlanta, from her hotel to the downtown branch of Lady's Choice, back to her hotel, to the airport. Each time he'd missed her by inches.

It was, he thought as he trudged up the stairs to his apartment, as if she'd known he was behind her. He dropped down on the couch, rubbing his hands over his face.

He had no choice but to wait.

"I'm so glad to see you." Althea Grayson Nightshade smiled as she rubbed a hand over her mountain of a belly.

"That goes double." Natalie laughed. "Literally. How are you feeling?"

"Oh, like a cross between the Goodyear blimp and Moby Dick."

"Neither of them ever looked so good." It was true, Natalie mused. Pregnancy had only enhanced Althea's considerable beauty. Her eyes were gold, her skin was dewy, her hair was a fiery cascade to her shoulders.

"I'm fat, but I'm healthy." Althea's lips twitched. "Colt's been a demon about seeing that I eat right, sleep enough, exercise, rest. He even typed up a daily schedule. Mr. Play-It-By-Ear went into a tailspin when he found out we were expecting."

"The nursery's wonderful." Natalie wandered the sunny mint-and-white room, running her fingers over the antique crib, the fussy dotted-swiss curtains.

"I'll be glad when it's filled. Any time now," Althea said with a sigh. "I feel great, really, but I swear, this has been the longest pregnancy in recorded history. I want to see my baby, damn it." She stopped and laughed at herself. "Listen to me. I never thought I'd want children, much less be itching to change the first diaper."

Intrigued, Natalie looked over her shoulder. Althea sat in a rocking chair, a small, poorly knit blanket in her hands. "No? You never wanted to be a mom?"

"Not with the job and my background." She shrugged. "Didn't figure I was cut out for it. Then along comes Night-shade, and then this." She patted her belly. "Maybe gestating isn't my natural milieu, but I've loved every minute of it. Now I'm antsy to get on to the nurturing. Can you see me," she said with a laugh, "sitting here, rocking a baby?"

"Yes, I can." Natalie came back, crouched, and took Althea's hands. "I envy you, Thea. So much. To have some-one who loves you, to make a baby between you. Nothing else is as important." Defenses crumbled. Her eyes filled.

"Oh, honey, what is it?"

"What else?" Disgusted with herself, Natalie straightened. "A man."

"A jerk." She fought back the tears and stuffed her hands in her pockets.

"Would this jerk be an arson investigator?" Althea smiled a little when Natalie scowled at her. "News travels, even to Denver. The fact is, your family and Colt and I have been bit-ing our tongues, trying not to ask what you're doing out here."

"I explained. I'm siting. I want to open another branch here. I was traveling, anyway."

"Instead of being in Urbana for your opening."

She resented that, laid the blame for it right at Ry's door-step. "I was in Dallas for the opening there. Each of my branches is of equal importance to me."

"Yeah, and word is it was a smash."

"The tallies for the first week's sales look promising."

"So why aren't you back home, basking in it?" Althea in-clined her head. "The jerk?"

"I'm entitled to a little time before I… Well, yes," she ad-mitted. "The jerk. He dumped me."

"Oh, come on. Cilla said the guy was crazy about you."

"We were good in bed," Natalie said flatly, then pressed her lips together. "I made the mistake of falling in love with him. A real first for me. And he broke my heart."

"I'm sorry." Concerned, Althea pushed herself out of the chair.

"I'll get over it." Natalie squeezed Althea's offered hands. "It's just that I've never felt this way about anyone. I didn't know I could. I've managed to get through my whole life without being hurt like this. Then, *pow.* It's like being cut into very small pieces," she murmured. "I just haven't been able to put them all back together yet."

"Well, he's not worth it," Althea said loyally.

"I wish that were true. It'd be easier. He's a wonderful man, tough, sweet, dedicated." She moved her shoulders restlessly. "He didn't mean to hurt me. He's called several times while I've been on the road."

"He must want to apologize, to make things up with you."

"Do you think I'd give him the chance?" Natalie's chin angled. "I'm not taking his calls. I'm not taking anything from him. He can send me flowers all over the country, for all the difference it would make."

"He sends you flowers." A smile was beginning to lurk around the corners of Althea's mouth.

"Daffodils. Every time I turn around, I'm getting a bunch of idiotic daffodils." She set her teeth. "Does he think I'm going to fall for that again?"

"Probably."

"Well, I'm not. One broken heart's enough for me. More than enough."

"Maybe you should go back, let him beg. Then kick him

in the teeth." Althea winced at the twinge. The third one, she noted with a glance at her watch, in the past half hour.

"I'm thinking about it. But until I'm ready, I'm not—" Natalie broke off. "What is it? Are you all right?"

"Yeah." Althea let out a long breath. This twinge was lasting longer. "You know, I think I could be going into labor."

"What?" The blood drained out of Natalie's face. "Now? Sit. Sit down, for God's sake. I'll get Colt."

"Maybe I will." Gingerly Althea lowered herself back into the chair. "Maybe you'd better."

Deirdre was glad she'd decided to take the work home with her. The miserable cold she'd picked up from somewhere was hanging on like a leech. At least she could take her mind off her stuffy head and scratchy throat with work.

She sniffed disinterestedly at the cup of instant chicken soup she'd zapped in the microwave and indulged herself with the hot toddy instead. Nothing like a good shot of whiskey to make a cup of tea sit up and sing.

If she was lucky, very lucky, she'd have the cold on the run and the preliminary figures in before Natalie got back from Denver.

She took another hefty slug of the spiked tea and tapped keys. She stopped, frowned, and adjusted her glasses.

That couldn't be right, she thought, and tapped more keys. No way in hell could that be right. Her mouth became drier, and a thin line of sweat rolled down her back that had nothing to do with the slight fever she was fighting.

She sat back and took a couple of easy breaths. It was simply a mistake, she assured herself. She'd find the discrepancy and fix it. That was all.

But it didn't take much longer for her to realize it wasn't a mistake. Or an accident.

It was a quarter of a million dollars. And it was gone.

She snatched up the phone, and rapidly dialed. "Maureen. Deirdre Marks."

"Ms. Marks, you sound dreadful."

"I know. Listen, I need to talk to Natalie, right away."

"Who doesn't?"

"It's urgent, Maureen. She's with her brother, right? Let me have the number."

"I can't do that, Ms. Marks."

"It's urgent, I tell you."

"I understand, but she's not there. Her plane left Denver an hour ago. She's on her way home."

A son. Althea and Colt had a son, a tiny and beautiful boy. It had taken Althea twelve hard hours to push him into the world, and he'd come out howling.

Natalie remembered it now as her plane traveled east. It had been a thrill to be allowed in the birthing room, to support Colt when he was ready to climb the walls, to watch him and Althea work together to welcome that new life.

She hadn't wept until it was over, until she'd left Colt and Althea nuzzling their new son. Boyd had left the hospital with her. He'd either been too deep in the memories of his own children's births or had sensed her mood. Either way, he hadn't badgered her.

Now she was going home, because there was work to do. And because it was cowardly to keep jumping from city to city because she was hurt.

It had been a good trip. Professionally successful. Personally soothing. She was going to give some thought to moving back to Colorado. She'd found an excellent site. And a new branch in Denver would benefit from her personal touch.

If the move would have the added benefit of escape, whose business was it but hers?

She would have to wait, of course, until they had unearthed whoever had paid Clarence Jacoby. If it was indeed one of her people in Urbana, that person had to be weeded out. Once that was done, Donald could take over that office.

It would be a simple matter. Donald had the talent. From a business standpoint, the change would be little more than having him move from his office to hers, his desk to hers.

Desk, she thought, frowning. There was something odd about the desk. Not her desk, she realized all at once. The desk that had been damaged at the flagship.

He'd known about that. Her heart began to thud uncomfortably. How had Donald known the desk in the manager's office was an antique? How had he known specifically that it had been damaged?

Cautiously she began to think over the details, recalling her movements from the time of the second fire to the day she and Donald had visited the flagship. He hadn't been in the office there since it had been decorated. At least not to her knowledge. So how could he have known the desks had been switched?

Because he'd been there. That was all, she tried to assure herself. He'd swung by at some point and hadn't mentioned it. It made sense, more sense than believing he had had something to do with the fires.

Yet he'd been at the warehouse the morning after it had

burned. Early, she remembered. Had she called him? She couldn't be sure, didn't recall. He could have heard about it on the news. Had there been reports that early? Detailed reports? She wasn't sure about that, either, and it worried her.

Why should he do something so drastic to harm a business he was an integral part of? she wondered. What possible motive could there be for him to want to see stock and equipment destroyed?

Stock, equipment, and, she thought on a jolt of alarm, records. There'd been records at the warehouse, and at the flagship—at the point of the fire's origin.

Determined to keep calm, she thought of the files she'd given Deirdre, of the copies still in the safe at her office. She'd check them herself the minute she landed, just to ease her mind.

She was wrong about Donald, of course. She had to be wrong.

She was late. It was a hell of a thing, Ry thought as he paced the gate area at the airport, for a woman who was so fixated on being on time. Now, when he was all but jumping out of his skin, she had to be late.

It didn't matter that the plane was late, and she just happened to be on it. He took it as a personal affront.

If Maureen hadn't taken pity on him, he wouldn't have known she was coming back tonight. It grated a bit, to know that Natalie's secretary felt sorry for him. That she must have seen that he looked like a lovesick mongrel.

Even the men at the station were starting to talk about him behind his back.

Oh, he knew it, all right. The mutters, the snickers, the pity.

ing looks. Anybody with eyes in his head could see that the past ten days had been torment for him.

He'd made a mistake, damn it. One little mistake, and she'd paid him back. Big-time.

They were just going to have to put that behind them.

He clutched the daffodils, paced, and felt like a fool. His heart took one frantic leap when her flight was announced.

He saw her, and his palms began to sweat.

She saw him, turned sharply left, and kept walking.

"Natalie." He caught up with her in two strides. "Welcome home."

"Go to hell."

"I've been there for the past ten days. I don't like it." It wasn't hard to keep up with her, since she was wearing heels. "Here."

She glanced down at the daffodils, cutting a scathing look up to his face. "You don't want me to tell you what you can do with those stupid flowers, do you?"

"You could have talked to me when I called."

"I didn't want to talk to you." Deliberately she swung into the closest ladies' room.

Ry gritted his teeth and waited.

She told herself she wasn't pleased that he was still there when she came out. Saying nothing, she quickened her pace toward the baggage-claim area.

"How was your trip?"

She snarled at him.

"Look, I'm trying to apologize here."

"Is that what you're doing?" With a toss of her head, she stepped onto the escalator heading down. "Save it."

"I screwed up. I'm sorry. I've been trying to tell you for days, but you won't take my calls."

"That should indicate something, Piasecki, even to someone of your limited intelligence."

"So," he continued, biting back hot words, "I'm here to pick you up, so we can talk."

"I've ordered a car."

"We canceled it. That is…" He had to choose his words carefully, with that icy look in her eyes freezing him. "I canceled it, when I found out you were coming in." No need to make Maureen fry with him, he decided. "So I'll give you a lift."

"I'll take a cab."

"Don't be so damn stubborn. I'll get tough if I have to," he muttered as they joined the throng at Baggage Claim. "I can have you up in a fireman's carry in two seconds. Embarrass the hell out of you. Either way, I'm driving you home."

She debated. He would embarrass her. There was no point in giving him the satisfaction. Nor was she going to tell him of her suspicions, not until she had something solid. Not until she had no choice but to deal with him on a professional level.

"I'm not going home. I need to go to the office."

"The office is closed. It's almost nine o'clock."

"I'm going to the office," she said flatly, and turned away from him.

"Fine. We'll talk at the office."

"That one." She pointed to a gray tweed Pullman. "And that one." A matching garment bag. "And that." Another Pullman.

"You didn't have time to pack all this before I got to your apartment that night."

Interested despite herself, she watched him heft cases. picked up luggage and clothes along the way."

"Enough for a damn modeling troupe," he muttered.

"I beg your pardon?" Her tone lowered the temperature in the terminal by ten degrees.

"Nothing. Your opening made a real splash," he continued as they walked out of the terminal.

"It met our expectations."

"You're getting write-ups in *Newsday* and *Business Week*." He shrugged when she looked at him. "I heard."

"And *Women's Wear Daily*," she added. "But who's counting?"

"I've been. It's great, Natalie, really. I'm happy for you. Proud of you." He set her luggage beside his car, and his limbs went weak. "God, I've missed you."

She stepped back, evading him, when he reached for her. He was not going to hurt her again, she promised herself. She would not allow it.

"Okay." Slowly, stunned by the ache that one quick rejection caused, he lifted his hands, palms out. "I had that coming. I've got plenty coming. I'll give you the chance to take all the shots you want."

"I'm not interested in fighting with you," she said wearily. "I've had a long trip. I'm too tired to fight with you."

"Let me take you home, Natalie."

"I'm going to the office." She stepped back and waited for him to unlock the car. Once inside, she sat back and shut her eyes. She just sighed when Ry laid the bright yellow flowers in her lap.

"They, ah, haven't gotten any more out of Clarence," he said, hoping to chip at the wall she'd erected between them.

"I know." She couldn't think about her suspicions yet. "I've kept in touch."

"You moved around fast."

"I had a lot of ground to cover."

"Yeah." He dug out money for the parking attendant. "I got the picture, after I chased you around Atlanta."

She opened her eyes then. "Excuse me?"

"I couldn't get a damn cab," he muttered. "You must have hooked one the minute you walked out of my apartment."

"Yes, I did."

"Figures. I'm running the marathon to your apartment then you're gone when I get there. I see the note, figure the airport, and get there in time to see your plane take off."

She felt herself softening, and stiffened. "Is that supposed to be my fault, Piasecki?"

"No, it's not your fault, damn it. It's my fault. But if you could have sat still in Atlanta for five minutes, we'd have settled this."

"We *have* settled it."

"Not by a long shot." Turning his head, he aimed a deadl look at her. "I hate it when people hang up on me."

"It was," she said with relish, "my pleasure."

"I might have strangled you for it when I got down there If I could have caught you. 'No, Ms. Fletcher's at her shop Then I get to the shop, and it's 'Sorry, Ms. Fletcher's gon back to her hotel.' I get back to the hotel, and you've checke out. I get to the airport and you're in the sky. I spent hou chasing my tail, trying to catch up with you."

She shrugged. She didn't want to be pleased, but sh couldn't prevent a little frisson of pleasure at the frustratio in his voice. "Don't expect an apology." Still, she gather up the flowers to keep them from sliding from her lap wh he braked.

"I'm trying to give *you* one."

"There's no need. I've had time to think about it, and I've decided you were absolutely right. I don't like the style you used, but the bottom line rings true. We had some interesting chemistry. That's all."

"We had a lot more than that. We've got more than that. Natalie—"

"This is my stop." Forgetting her luggage, she bolted out of the car. By the time Ry had parked, illegally, she was waiting for the security guard to open the front door of her building.

"Damn it, Natalie, would you hold still?"

"I have work. Good evening, Ben."

"Ms. Fletcher. Working late?"

"That's right." She breezed past the guard, with Ry at her heels. "There's no need for you to come up with me, Ry."

"You said you loved me."

Ignoring the guard's speculative look, Natalie pressed the elevator button. "I got over it."

Panic spurted through him, freezing him in place. He barely made it into the elevator before the doors shut in his face. "You did not."

"I know what I did, I know what I didn't." She jabbed the button for her floor. "It's all ego with you. You're causing a scene because I didn't come back when you called." She tossed her hair back. Her eyes were bright. Not with tears, he saw with some relief. But with anger. "Because I don't need you."

"It has nothing to do with ego. I was—" He couldn't admit he'd been scared, down-to-the-bone scared. "I was wrong," he said. That was hard enough, but at least it wasn't humiliating. "It was you—there in my place. I asked you to come because it was so obvious."

"What was obvious?"

"That it couldn't be real. I didn't see how it could be real. Who you are, the way you are. And me."

Her eyes sharpened, narrowed. "Am I following you here, Inspector? You dumped me because I didn't fit in with your apartment."

It didn't have to sound that stupid. His voice rose in defense. "With everything. With me. I can't give you…the things. The first time I remembered I should give you flowers once in a while, you looked at me like I'd clipped you on the jaw. I never take you anywhere. I don't think of it. You've got friends who live in mansions. And look, damn it, you've got diamonds in your ears right now." He tossed up his hands, as if that should explain everything. "Diamonds, for God's sake."

Her cheeks were hot now. She was all but radiating heat as she stepped toward him. "Is this about money? Is that it? You broke my heart over money?"

"No, it's about…things." How could he explain what made no sense at all anymore? "Natalie, let me touch you."

"The hell with you." She shoved him back, bounding through the elevator the minute the doors open. "You tossed me aside because you thought I wanted you to get me diamonds, or a mansion, or flowers?" Furious, she tossed the daffodils on the floor. "I can get my own diamonds, or anything else I want. What I wanted was you."

"Don't walk away. Don't." Swearing, he rushed after her. Somewhere down the long corridor, a phone rang. "Natalie." He grabbed her by the shoulders, spun her around. "I didn't think that, exactly."

She rammed her briefcase hard into his gut. "And you had the nerve to call me a snob."

Out of patience, he rammed her back against the wall. "It was wrong. It was stupid. *I* was stupid. What more do you want me to say? I wasn't thinking. I was just feeling."

"You hurt me."

"I know." He rested his brow on hers, tried to get his bearings. He could smell her, feel her, and the thought of losing her made him weak in the knees. "I'm sorry. I didn't know I could hurt you. I thought it was just me. I thought you'd walk."

"So you walked first."

He drew back a little. "Something like that."

"Coward." She jerked away. "Go away, Ry. Leave me alone. I have to think about this."

"You're still in love with me. I'm not going anywhere until you tell me."

"Then you'll have to wait, because I'm not ready to tell you anything." Phones were ringing. Wearily rubbing her temple, Natalie wondered who would be calling so long after hours. "I'm raw, don't you understand? I realized I loved you and had you break it off almost simultaneously. I'm not going to serve you my emotions on a platter."

"Then I'll give you mine," he said quietly. "I love you, Natalie."

Her heart swam into her eyes. "Damn you. *Damn* you! That's not fair."

"I can't be worried about fair." He stepped closer, and reached out to touch her hair. His hand froze when he saw the flicker of light at the end of the hall. It danced through the glass in a pattern he recognized too well. "Take the fire stairs down, now. Call Dispatch."

"What? What are you talking about?"

"Go," he repeated, and dashed down the hall. He could smell smoke now, and cursed it. Cursed himself for being so intent on his own needs that he'd missed it. He saw it, the crafty plume under the door that flowed out, sucked in.

"Oh, God. Ry."

She was right behind him. He had time to see the flames writhing behind the glass, time to judge. Then he turned, leapt and knocked Natalie to the ground as the window exploded. Lethal shards of glass rained over them.

Chapter 12

She felt pain, sharp and shocking, as her head thudded against the floor, and pinpricks of heat from the glass and flame. For a terrifying moment, she thought Ry was unconcious, or dead. His body was fully spread over hers, a shield protecting her from the worst of the blast.

Before she could even sob in the breath to scream his name, he was up and dragging her to her feet.

"Are you burned?"

She shook her head, aware only of the throbbing, and the smoke that was beginning to sting her eyes, her throat. She could barely see his face through it, but she saw the blood.

"Your face, your arm—you're bleeding."

But he wasn't listening. He had her hand vised in his, and was dragging her away from the flame. Even as they dashed down the hall, another window exploded. Fire roared out.

It surrounded them, golden and greedy, unbelievably hot. She screamed once as she saw it race along the floor, eating its way toward them, spitting like a hundred hungry snakes.

Panic gripped her, icy fingers clutching at her stomach, squeezing her throat, in taunting contrast to the heat pulsing around them. They were trapped, fire writhing on either side of them. Terrified, she fought him when he pushed her to the floor.

"Stay low." However grim his thoughts, his voice was calm. He gripped her hair in one hand to keep her face turned to his. He needed her to hold on to control.

"I can't breathe." The smoke was choking her, making her gasp for air and expel what little she had in gritty coughs.

"There's more air down here. We don't have much time." He was aware—too well aware—of how quickly the fire would reach them, how well it blocked their exit to the stairs. He had nothing with which to fight it.

If the fire didn't kill them, the smoke would, long before rescue could reach them.

"Get out of your coat."

"What?"

Her movements were already sluggish. He fought back panic and yanked her coat from her shoulders. "We're going through it."

"We can't." She couldn't even scream at the next explosion of glass, could only huddle, racked by coughing. Her mind was dull, stunned by smoke. She wanted only to lie down and draw in the precious air that still hovered just above the floor. "We'll burn. I don't want to die that way."

"You're not going to die." Tossing the coat over her head, he dragged her to her feet. When she staggered, he lifted her over his shoulder. He stood, fire lapping on both sides, flaming sea around him. In seconds, the tidal wave would reach them, and they'd drown in it.

He gauged the distance and sprinted into the wave.

For an instant, they were in hell. Fire, heat, the roaring of its anger, the quick, ravenous licking of its tongues. For no more than two heartbeats—an eternity—flames engulfed them. He felt the hair on his hands singe, knew from the intense heat on his back and arms that his jacket would catch. He knew exactly what fire did to human flesh. He wouldn't allow it to have Natalie.

Then they were through it, and into a wall of smoke. Blinded, lungs straining, he groped for the fire door.

Instinctively he checked it for heat, thanked God, then shoved it open. Smoke was billowing up the stairwell, rising as if in a chimney that meant fire below, as well, but they didn't have a choice. Moving fast, he ripped the smoldering coat away from her and leaned her against the wall while he stripped off his own jacket.

The leather was burning, sluggishly.

Dazed by the smoke and teetering into shock, Natalie slid bonelessly to the floor.

"You're not giving up," he snapped at her as he hauled her back over his shoulder. "Hang on, damn it. Just hang on."

He streaked down the steps, one flight, then two, then a third. She was dead weight now, her head lolling, her arms limp. His eyes were watering from the smoke, the tears joining the river of sweat rolling down his face. The coughing that seized him felt as if it would shatter his ribs. All he knew was that he had to get her to safety.

He counted each level, keeping his mind focused. The smoke began to thin, and he began to hope.

She never stirred, not even when he tested the door at the lobby level, found it cool, and staggered through.

He heard the shouts, the sirens. His vision grayed as two firefighters rushed toward him.

"God almighty, Inspector."

"She needs oxygen." Still holding her, Ry shoved the offer of assistance aside and carried her outside, into clean air.

Lights were swirling. All the familiar sounds and scents and sights of a fire scene. Like a drunk, he weaved toward the closest engine.

"Oxygen," he ordered. "Now." Another coughing fit battered him as he laid her down.

Her face was black with soot, and her eyes were closed. He couldn't see if she was breathing, couldn't hear. Someone was shouting, raging, but he had no idea it was him. Hands pushed his own fumbling ones aside and fit an oxygen mask over Natalie's face.

"You need attention, Inspector."

"Keep away from me." He bent over her, searching for a pulse. Blood dripped down his arm and onto her throat. "Natalie. Please."

"Is she all right?" With tears streaming down her face, Deirdre dropped down beside him. "Is she going to be all right?"

"She's breathing," was all Ry could say. "She's breathing," he repeated, stroking her hair.

Mercifully, most of the next hour was a blur. He remembered climbing into the ambulance with her, holding her hand. Someone pressed oxygen on him, bound up his arm. They took her away the minute they hit the E.R. His panicked raging came out in hacking coughs.

Then the world turned upside down.

He found himself flat on his back on an examining table. When he tried to push himself upright, he was restrained.

"Just lie still." A small, gray-haired woman was scowling at him. "I like my stitches neat and tidy. You lost a fair amount of blood, Inspector Piasecki."

"Natalie…"

"Ms. Fletcher's being tended to. Now let me do my job, will you?" She stopped what she was doing and eyed him again. "If you keep shoving at me, mister, I'm going to sedate you. My job was a lot easier when you were out cold."

"How long?" he managed to croak.

"Not long enough." She knotted the suture, and snipped. "We picked the glass out of your shoulder. Not much damage there, but this arm's nasty. Fifteen stitches." She granted him a smile. "Some of my best work."

"I want to see Natalie." His voice was raspy, but there was no mistaking the threat underneath. "Now."

"Well, you can't. You're going to stay where I put you until I'm done. Then, if you're a very good boy, I'll have someone check on Ms. Fletcher for you."

Ry used his good arm and grabbed the doctor by the coat. "Now."

She only sighed. In his condition, she was well aware, she could knock him back with a shrug. But agitation wasn't going to help him. "Stay," she ordered, and went to the curtain. Pushing it aside, she called for a nurse. After a few brisk instructions, she turned back to Ry. "Your update's on the way. I'm Dr. Milano, and I'll be saving your life this evening."

"She was breathing," he said, as if daring Milano to disagree.

"Yes." She moved back to take his hand. "You took in a lot of smoke, Inspector. I'm going to treat you, and you're going to cooperate. After we've cleaned you out, I'll arrange for you to see Ms. Fletcher."

The nurse came back to the curtained opening, and Milano moved off again to hold a murmured consultation with her.

"Smoke inhalation," she announced. "And she's in shock. A few minor burns and lacerations. I imagine we'll keep her in our fine establishment for a day or two." Her face softened when she saw Ry's eyes close in relief. "Come on, big guy, let's work together here."

He might be weak as a baby, but he wasn't going to let them shove him into a hospital room. Over Milano's disgusted protests, he walked out into the waiting area. Deirdre sprang up from a chair the moment she saw him.

"Natalie?"

"They're working on her. They told me she's going to be all right."

"Thank God." With a muffled sob, Deirdre covered her face.

"Now, Ms. Marks, why don't you tell me what the hell you were doing outside the office tonight?"

Taking a deep breath, Deirdre levered herself into a chair. "I'd be glad to. I called Natalie's brother," she added. "I suppose he's already on his way out. I told him she was hurt, but I tried to play it down."

Ry merely nodded. Though he hated the weakness, he had to sit. Nausea was threatening again. "That was probably wise."

"I also gave him the bare bones of what I found out earlier today." She took a long breath. "I haven't been in the office the last couple of days—I've been nursing a cold. But I took work home. Including files and a couple of computer disks Natalie gave me before she went on the road. I was running figures, and I found some discrepancies. Some very large discrepancies. The kind that equals embezzlement."

Money, Ry thought. It almost always came around to money. "Who?"

"I can't say for sure—"

He interrupted her, in a tone that made her shiver. "Who?"

"I'm telling you, I can't be sure. I can only narrow it down, considering how and where the money was siphoned off. And I'm not giving you a name so you can go off and beat somebody to a pulp."

Which was exactly what he had in mind, she was certain. Despite the fact that he looked like a survivor of a quick trip to hell, there was murder in his eyes.

"I could be wrong. I need to talk to Natalie," she said, half to herself. "As soon as I was sure of what I'd found, I tried to contact her in Colorado, but she'd already left. I knew she'd go by the office before heading home. It's the way she works. So I decided I'd meet her there. Tell her what I'd found out." She tapped the briefcase at her feet. "Show her. When I parked outside, I glanced up. I saw—"

She shut her eyes, knew she would relive it over and over again. "I saw these crazy lights in some of the windows. At first I didn't know, then I realized what it was. I called 911 on the car phone." Unnerved by the memory, she pressed a hand to her mouth. "I ran inside, told the security guard. And we heard, like, an explosion."

She was crying now, quietly. "I knew she was up there. I just knew it. But I didn't know what to do."

"Yes, you did. And you did it." Ry patted her awkwardly on the shoulder.

"Inspector?" Milano strode out, the usual scowl on her face. "I got you a pass to see your lady, not that you'll bother to thank me for it."

He was on his feet. "She's okay?"

"She's stabilized, and sedated. But you can look at her, since that seems to be your goal in life."

He glanced back at Deirdre. "Are you going to wait?"

"Yes. If you'd just let me know how she is."

"I'll be back." He headed off after the quick-stepping doctor.

Natalie's room was private, and dimly lit. She lay very still, very pale. But her hand, when he took it in his, was warm.

"Are you planning on spending the night here?" Milano asked from the doorway.

"Are you going to give me a hard time about it?" Ry returned without looking around.

"Who, me? I aim to serve. It's not likely she'll wake up but that's not going to stop you. Neither is trying to sleep in that hideously uncomfortable chair.

"I'm a fireman, Doc. I can sleep anywhere."

"Well, fireman, make yourself at home. I'll go tell you friend in the waiting room that all's well."

"Yeah." He never took his eyes from Natalie's face. "That'd be good."

"Oh, you're more than welcome," Milano said sourly, an closed the door behind her.

Ry pulled the chair up to the side of the bed and sat wi Natalie's hand in his.

* * *

He dozed once or twice. Occasionally a nurse came into the room and scooted him out. It was during one of those short, restless breaks that he saw Boyd rushing down the corridor.

"Piasecki."

"Captain. She's sleeping." Ry gestured toward the door. "There."

Without another word, Boyd moved past him and inside.

Ry walked into the waiting lounge, poured a cup of muddy coffee, and stared out the window. He couldn't think. It seemed better that way, just to let the night drift. If he focused, he would see it again, the terror on her face, the fire around her. And he would remember how he'd felt, carrying her down flight after flight, not knowing if she was alive or dead.

The burning on his hand made him look down. He saw he'd crushed the paper cup into a ball and spilled the hot coffee over his bandaged hands.

"Want another?" Boyd said from behind him.

"No." Ry tossed the cup away, and wiped his hand on his jeans. "You want to go outside and pound on me awhile?"

With a short laugh, Boyd poured coffee for himself. "Have you taken a look in a mirror?"

"Why?"

"You look like hell." Experimentally, Boyd sipped. It was even more pathetic than precinct coffee. "Worse than hell. It wouldn't look good for me to start swinging at a guy in your condition."

"I heal quick." When Boyd said nothing, Ry shoved his hands in his pockets. "I told you I wouldn't let her get hurt. I damn near killed her."

"You did?"

"I lost it. I knew it wasn't just Clarence. I knew there was somebody behind it. But I was so…wrapped up in her. I never thought about him getting another torch, or trying something himself. The phones, damn it. I heard the phones ringing."

Intrigued, Boyd sat back. "Which means?"

"A delaying device," Ry shot back, whirling around. "It's a classic. Matchsticks, soaked in accelerant. Tape them to the phone, call the number. The phone rings, the ringer sparks the match."

"Clever. But you know, you can't think of everything all the time."

"It's my job to think of everything."

"And to have a crystal ball."

His voice was raw from the abuse his throat had taken, tight with the emotion he couldn't afford to let loose. "I was supposed to take care of her."

"Yeah." Acknowledging that, Boyd sipped again. "I made a lot of calls on the flight from Denver. One of the perks of Fletcher Industries is having a private plane at your disposal. I talked to the fire marshal, to the doctor who treated Natalie, to Deirdre Marks. You got her out, carried her down every damn step in that building. How many stitches have you got in that arm?"

"That's hardly the point."

"The point is, the fire marshal gave me some idea of what you were facing up there on the forty-second floor, and what kind of shape you were in when you got her outside. Her doctor told me that if she'd been in there another ten minutes, it isn't likely she'd be sleeping right now. So, do I want to punch you? I don't think so. I owe you my sister's life."

Ry remembered how she had looked when he laid her on the ground next to the engine. How she looked now, pale and still, in a hospital bed. "You don't owe me anything."

"Natalie's as important to me as she is to you." Boyd set his coffee aside and rose. "What did you do to tick her off?"

Ry grimaced. "We're working it out."

"Well, good luck." Boyd held out a hand.

After a moment, Ry clasped it with his. "Thanks."

"I figure you're going to be here awhile. I've got a little job to do."

Ry tightened his grip, and narrowed his eyes. "Deirdre told you who's responsible."

"That's right. I also spoke with my counterpart here in Urbana while I was in the air. It's being taken care of." He saw the look in Ry's eyes, understood it. "This part's up to my team, Ry. You and yours just make damn sure you hang him for the arson."

"Who?" Ry said between his teeth.

"Donald Hawthorne. I got it down to four likely suspects two days ago." He smiled a little. "Some background checks, bank and phone records. Sometimes it pays to be a cop."

"And you didn't pass the information along to me."

"I intended to, when I narrowed it down a bit further. Now I have, and I am."

Boyd knew what it was to love, to need to protect, and to live with the terror of seeing your woman fight for her life.

"Listen," he said briskly, "if you kill him—however much it might appeal to both of us right now—I'd have to arrest you. I'd hate to throw my brother-in-law in a cell."

Ry unfisted his hands long enough to stick them in his pockets. "I'm not your brother-in-law."

"Not yet. Go on in with her, get some sleep."

"You'd better put Hawthorne somewhere where I can't find him."

"I intend to," Boyd said as he walked away.

Natalie stirred at dawn. Ry was watching the way the slats of light through the blinds bloomed over her when her lashes fluttered.

He bent over her, talking softly, quickly, so that her first clear thoughts wouldn't be fearful ones. "Natalie, you're okay. We got out okay. You just swallowed some smoke. Everything's all right now. You've been sleeping. I'm right here. I don't want you to talk. Your throat's going to be miserable for a while."

"You're talking," she whispered, her eyes still closed.

"Yeah." And it felt as though he'd swallowed a flaming sword. "That's why I don't recommend it."

She swallowed and winced. "We didn't die."

"Doesn't look like it." Gently he cupped her head and held a cup of water so that she could sip through the straw. "Just take it easy."

There was a fear lurking deep inside her. But she had to know. "Are we burned badly?"

"We're not burned. A couple of singes, maybe."

Relief made her shiver. "I can't feel anything, except—" She reached up to touch the bruise on her forehead.

"Sorry." He pressed his lips to the lump, felt himself begin to tremble, and drew back again. "You got that when I tackled you."

She opened her eyes then. They felt weighted. Her whole body felt weighted. "Hospital?" she asked. Then her breath caught as she focused on him. Scratches on his face, a bandage at his temple, and a larger one that started just below his shoulder and nearly reached the elbow. His hands, his beautiful hands, were wrapped in gauze.

"Oh, God, Ry. You're hurt."

"Cuts and bruises." He smiled at her. "Singed my hair a little."

"You need a doctor."

"I've had one, thanks. I don't think she likes me. Now shut up and rest."

"What happened?"

"You're going to have to move your office." When she started to speak again, he held up a hand. "I'll tell you what I know if you keep quiet. Otherwise, I'll just leave you to stew. Deal?" Satisfied, he sat on the edge of the bed. "Deirdre tried to call you in Colorado," he began.

When he finished, her head was throbbing. Impotent fury ate away at the remnant of the sedative until she was wide awake and aching. Anticipating her, Ry laid his hand over her mouth.

"There's nothing you can do until you're on your feet. Not much you can do then. It's up to the departments—fire and police. And it's being handled. Now I'm going to ring for the nurse so they can take a look at you."

"I don't—" Her protest turned into a spasm of coughing. By the time she'd regained control, a nurse was gesturing Ry out of the room.

She didn't see him again for more than twenty-four hours.

"You could use another day here, Nat." Boyd crossed his feet at the ankles as he watched Natalie pack the small overnight case he'd brought her.

"I hate hospitals."

"You've made that clear. I need your word you're taking a full week off, at home, or I'm calling in the troops. And not just Cilla, but Mom and Dad."

"There's no need for them to fly all the way out here."

"That's up to you, pal."

She pouted. "Three days off."

"A full week. Anything less is a deal-breaker. I can be just as tough a negotiator as you," he said with a grin. "It's in the blood."

"Fine, fine, a week. What difference does it make?" She snatched up the water glass and drank. It seemed she could never get enough to drink these days. "Everything's in shambles. Half my building's destroyed, one of my most trusted executives is responsible. I don't even have an office to go to."

"You'll take care of that. Next week. Hawthorne has a lot to answer for. The fact that he didn't know you and Ry were in the building isn't going to save him."

"All for greed." Too angry to pack the few things Boyd had brought her, she paced. Her body still felt weak, but there was too much energy boiling within to allow her to keep still. "Draining a little here, a little there, losing it on speculative stocks. Then draining more and more, until he was so desperate he risked burning down entire buildings just to destroy records and delay the audit records."

She whirled back. "How frustrated he must have been when I told him I had duplicates of everything that was lost in the warehouse fire."

"And he wasn't sure where you kept them. Fire destroys everything," Boyd pointed out. "So, he'd take one of the buildings, and hope. If he didn't hit, the confusion in the af termath would keep everyone so busy, you wouldn't get around to the audit until, he hoped, he'd managed to replace the siphoned funds."

"So he thought."

"He doesn't know you like I do. You always get things done on time. The office was his last shot, and the most desperate, since he had to do it himself. When we picked him up and he found out you and Ry had been in there and that he was facing attempted murder charges, he gave us everything."

"I trusted him," Natalie murmured. "I can't stand knowing I could be so wrong about anyone I thought I knew." She glanced up as the door opened.

"Good to see you, Ry," Boyd said, and rose. This looked like his cue to make a quick and discreet exit.

Ry nodded at Boyd, then focused on Natalie. "Why aren't you in bed?"

"I've been discharged."

"You're not ready to leave the hospital."

"Excuse me." Boyd slipped toward the door. "I have a sudden urge for a cup of bad coffee."

Neither Natalie nor Ry bothered to say goodbye. They only continued to argue in raspy croaks.

"Do you have a medical degree now, Inspector?"

"I know what shape you were in when you got here."

"Well, if you'd bothered to check in since, you'd have seen that I'm recovered."

"I had a lot of details to tie up," he told her. "And you needed to rest."

"I'd rather have had you."

He held out the flowers. "I'm here now."

She sighed. Should she let him off the hook so easily when

she'd been pining for him for so long? And why shouldn't she make him pay a bit for dumping her for the most ridiculous reason?

"Why don't you go take those daffodils to someone who needs them."

He tossed them on the bed. "I'm going to go talk to the doctor."

"You certainly will not talk to *my* doctor. I don't need your permission to leave the hospital. You didn't ask me for mine. And I did not need rest. I needed to see you. I was worried about you."

"Were you?" Encouraged, he lifted a hand to her face.

"I wanted you here, Ry. Dozens of other people came, but obviously you didn't see the need—"

"I had work," he shot back. "I wanted to get the evidence on that sonofabitch as soon as possible. It's all I can do. I'd kill him if I could get to him."

She started to snap back, then felt an icy chill at the look on his face. "Stop that." Unnerved, she turned her back on him, away from the murder in his eyes, and tossed a robe in her case. "I don't want to hear you talk that way."

"I didn't know if you were alive." He spun her around, his fingers digging into her shoulders. "I didn't know. You weren't moving. I didn't know if you were breathing." Suddenly he dragged her against him and buried his face in her hair. "God, Natalie, I've never been so scared."

"All right." She brought her arms around him, to soothe "Don't think about it."

"I didn't let myself, until you woke up yesterday. Since then I haven't been able to think about anything else." Struggling for composure, he eased away. "I'm sorry."

"Sorry for saving my life? For risking your own to keep me from being hurt? You shielded me from the explosion. You carried me through fire." She shook her head quickly, before he could speak. "Don't tell me you were doing your job. I don't give a damn whether you want to be a hero or not. You're mine."

"I love you, Natalie."

Her heart softened and swelled. Carefully she turned and picked up the daffodils. It was foolish to waste their emotions on anger. They were alive. "You mentioned that, before we were interrupted."

"There's something else I should have mentioned. Why I pushed you away."

Staring down, she flicked a finger over a bright yellow trumpet. "You listed the reasons."

"I listed the excuses. Not the reason. Maybe you could look at me while I grovel?"

She turned back, trying to smile. "It's not necessary, Ry."

"Yeah, it is. You haven't decided whether you're going to give me another chance yet." He reached out, tucked her hair behind her ear. "I could wear you down eventually, because you're crazy about me. But you deserve to know what was going on in my head."

She stiffened automatically. "I don't think arrogance is very appropriate, so why don't you—"

"I was scared," he said quietly, and watched the heat fade from her eyes. "Of you, of me. Of us." He let out a long breath when she said nothing. "I didn't think I could say it. Admit it. Not until I realized what it was to be *really* scared. Down-to-the-bone scared. It makes being afraid of being in love pretty stupid."

"Then it looks like we were both stupid, because I was scared, too." Her mouth curved a little. "You were more stupid, of course."

"My whole life," he said quietly, "I've never felt anything like what I feel for you. Not for anyone."

"I know." Her breath trembled out. "I know. It's the same with me."

"And it just keeps getting bigger, and scarier. Are you going to give me another chance?"

She looked at him—the bony face, the dark eyes, the unruly hair. "I probably owe you that much, seeing as you've saved my life and come clean, groveled and apologized." Her smile spread. "I suppose I could give us both another chance."

"Want to marry me?"

The flowers drifted to the floor as her fingers went numb. "Excuse me?"

"With you feeling generous, it seemed like a good time to push my luck." Feeling foolish, he bent down and gathered up the daffodils. "But it can wait."

She cleared her aching throat, accepting the flowers again. "Would you mind repeating the question?"

His eyes shot back to hers. It took him a moment to find his voice again. It was a risk, he realized. One of the biggest risks he'd ever faced. And he had to leave his fate in her hands.

"Will you marry me?"

"I could do that," she said, and let out the breath she'd been holding, even as Ry let out his own. "Yes, I could do that." Laughing, she launched herself into his arms.

"I've got you." Dazzled, Ry buried his face in her hair. "I've got you, Legs, from now on." And kissed her.

"I want babies," she told him the minute her mouth was free.

"No kidding?" With a grin, he pushed her hair back so that he could read her face. What he saw made his heart leap. "Me, too."

"That makes it handy."

He scooped his arms under her legs and lifted her. "What do you say we get out of here and get started?"

She managed to snag her overnight case before he headed to the door. "That'll make it nine months from today." She kissed his cheek as he carried her from the room. "And I'm always on time."

In this case, she managed to be eight days early.

Ryan and Natalie Piasecki
are pleased to announce the birth of their son,
Fletcher Joseph Piasecki,
who arrived promptly at 4:05 a.m., January 5.
Fletcher weighted 7 pounds 10 ounces and has
ten fingers and ten toes.
Both parents counted.

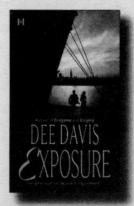

NORA ROBERTS

(limited quantities available)

TOTAL AMOUNT	$	_____
POSTAGE & HANDLING	$	_____
($1.00 FOR 1 BOOK, 50¢ for each additional)		
APPLICABLE TAXES*	$	_____
TOTAL PAYABLE	$	_____

(check or money order—please do not send cash)

To order, complete this form and send it, along with a check or money order for the total above, payable to Harlequin Books, to: **In the U.S.:** 3010 Walden Avenue, P.O. Box 9077, Buffalo, NY 14269-9077; **In Canada:** P.O. Box 636, Fort Erie, Ontario, L2A 5X3.

Name: _____
Address: _____ City: _____
State/Prov.: _____ Zip/Postal Code: _____
Account Number (if applicable): _____
075 CSAS

*New York residents remit applicable sales taxes.
*Canadian residents remit applicable GST and provincial taxes.

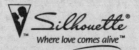

Silhouette®
Where love comes alive™